morning**glories**

volume**one**

for a **better future.**

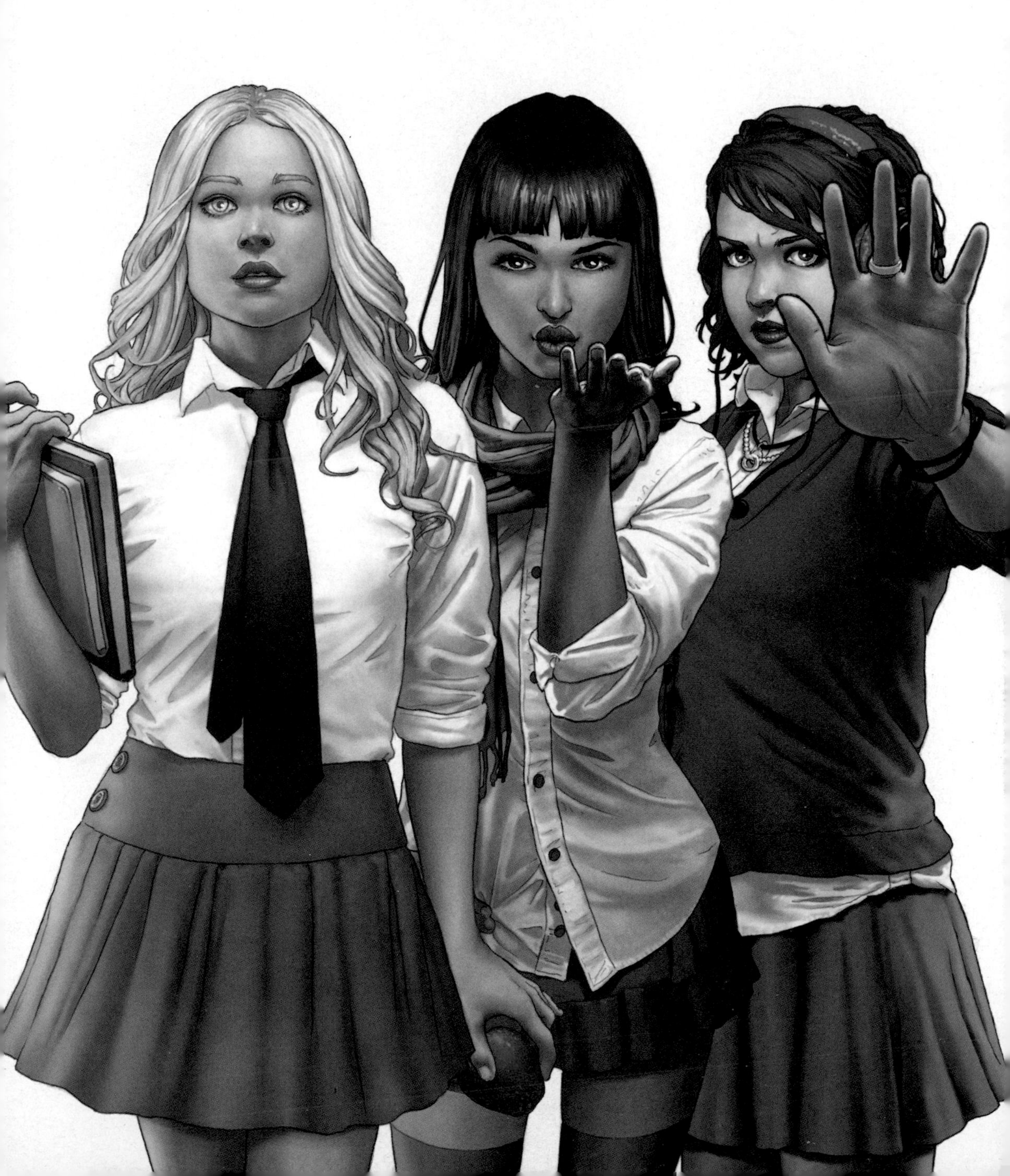

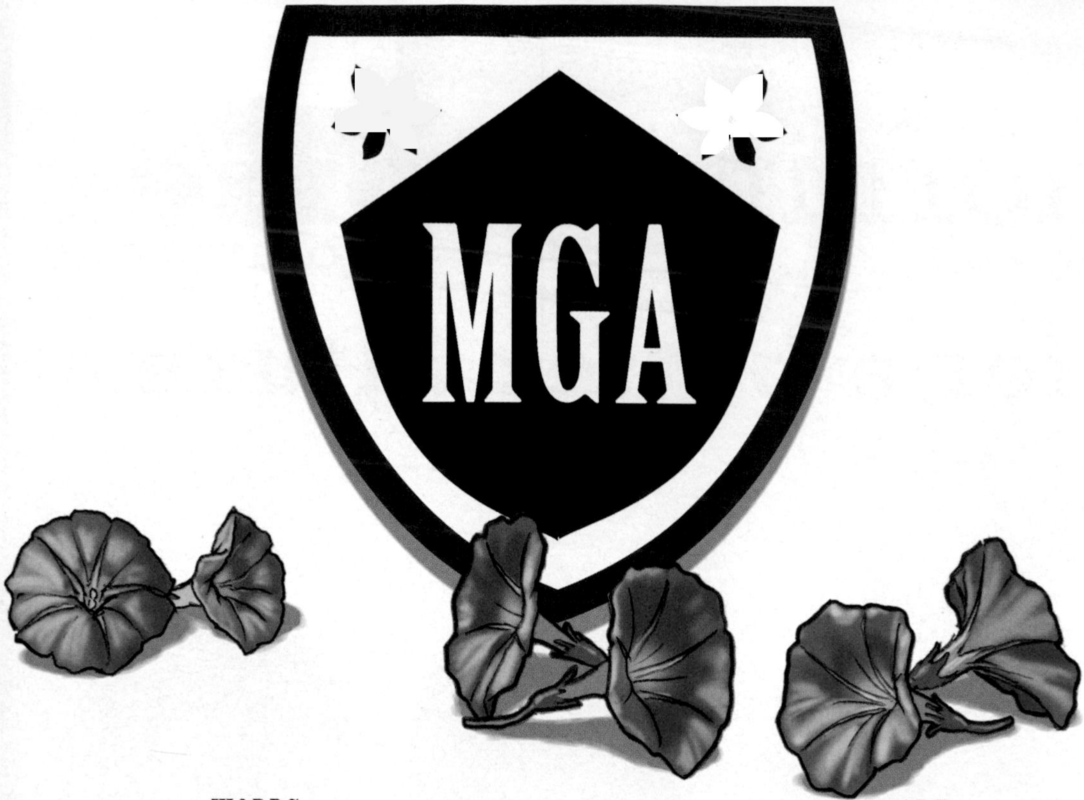
MGA

WORDS
NICK SPENCER

ART
JOE EISMA

RODIN ESQUEJO
COVERS

ALEX SOLLAZZO - **JOHNNY LOWE** - **TIM DANIEL**
COLORS LETTERS DESIGN

JIM VALENTINO
PUBLISHER/REPRINT EDITOR

image

IMAGE COMICS, INC.
Robert Kirkman - chief operating officer Erik Larsen - chief financial officer Todd McFarlane - president
Marc Silvestri - chief executive officer Jim Valentino - vice-president
Eric Stephenson - publisher Todd Martinez - sales & licensing coordinator Betsy Gomez - pr & marketing coordinator
Branwyn Bigglestone - accounts manager Sarah deLaine - administrative assistant Tyler Shainline - production manager
Drew Gill - art director Jonathan Chan - production artist Monica Howard - production artist Vincent Kukua - production artist Kevin Yuen - production artist
www.imagecomics.com

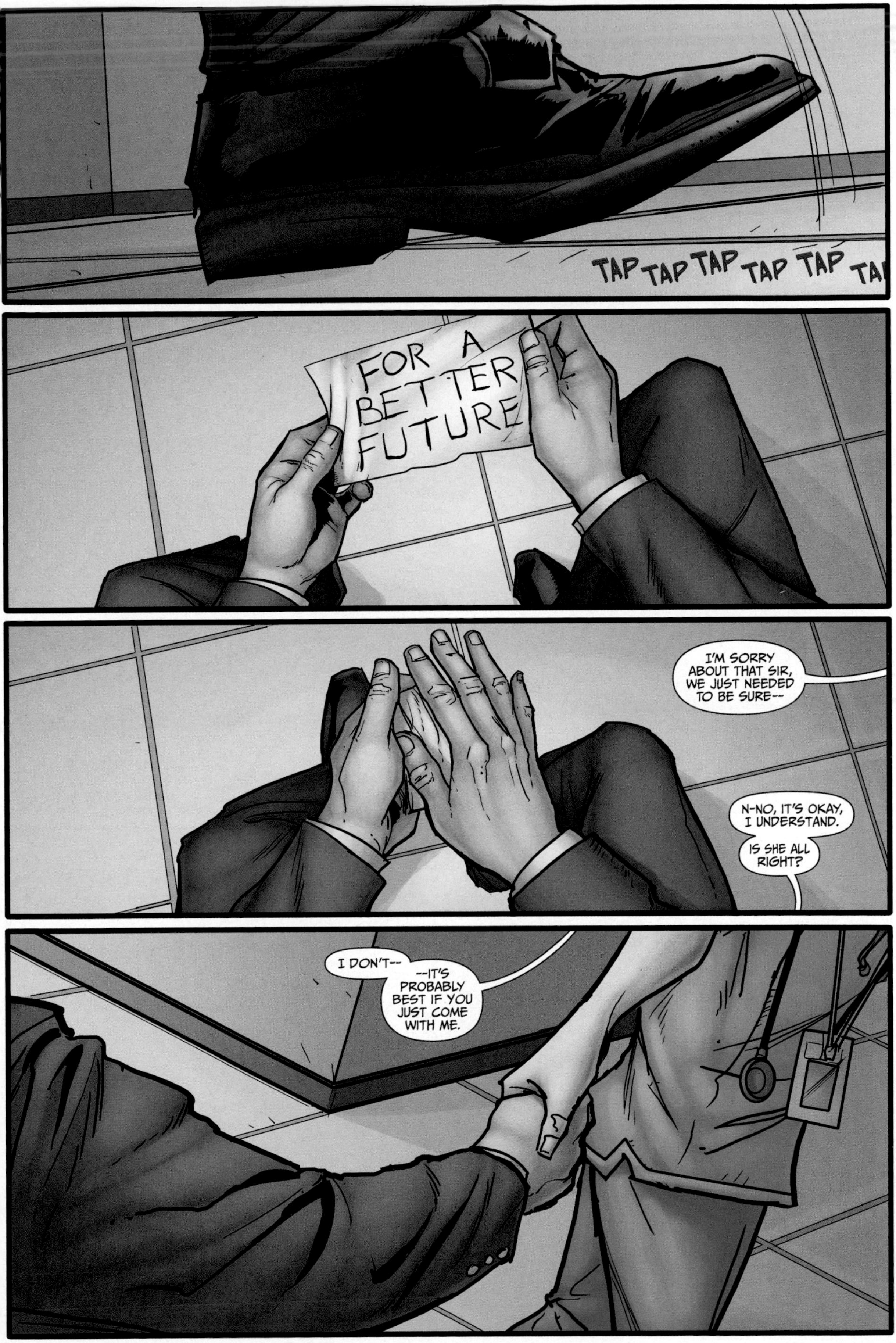
TAP TAP TAP TAP TAP TA
FOR A BETTER FUTURE
I'M SORRY ABOUT THAT SIR, WE JUST NEEDED TO BE SURE--
N-NO, IT'S OKAY, I UNDERSTAND.
IS SHE ALL RIGHT?
I DON'T--
--IT'S PROBABLY BEST IF YOU JUST COME WITH ME.

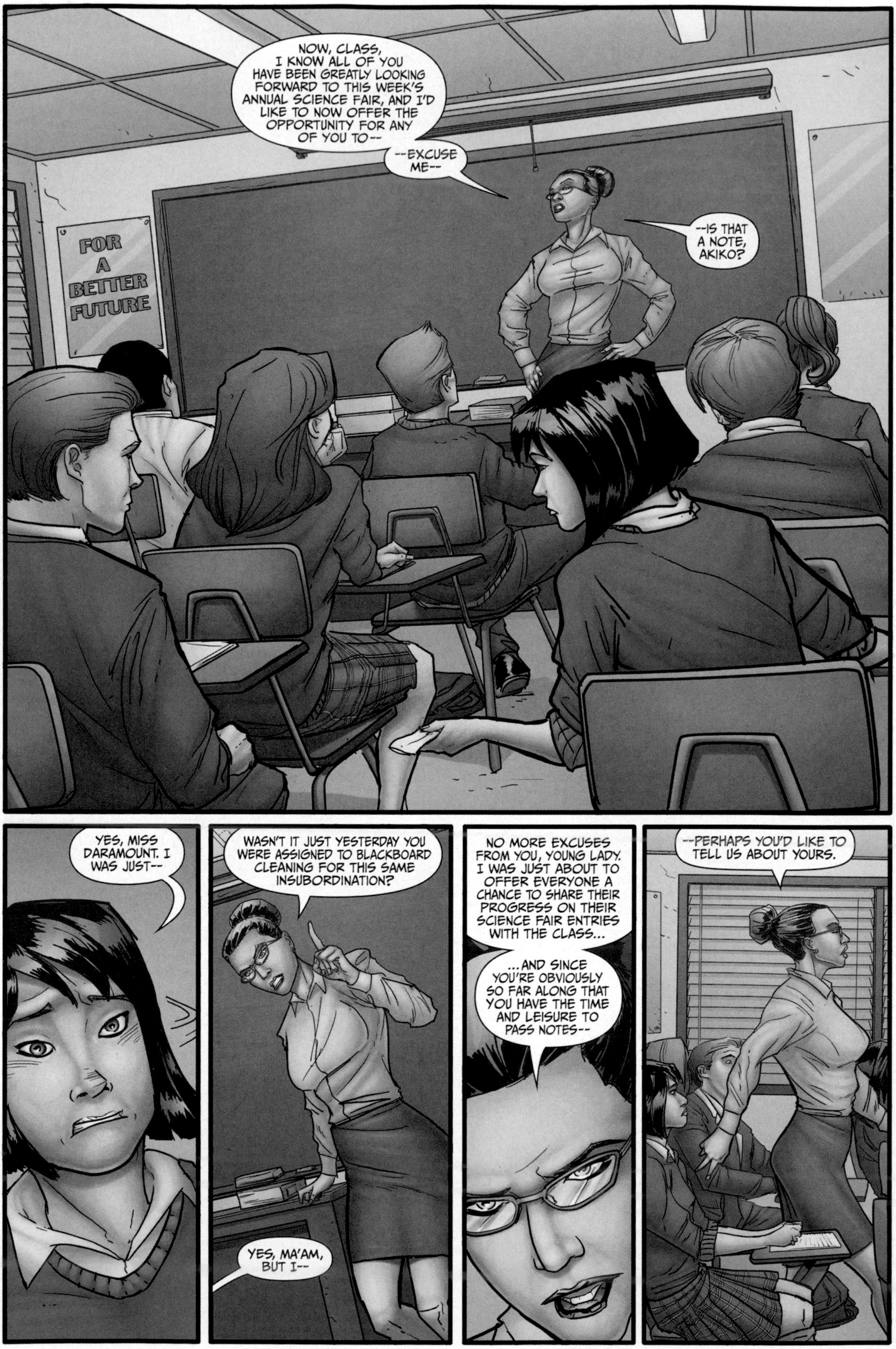
NOW, CLASS, I KNOW ALL OF YOU HAVE BEEN GREATLY LOOKING FORWARD TO THIS WEEK'S ANNUAL SCIENCE FAIR, AND I'D LIKE TO NOW OFFER THE OPPORTUNITY FOR ANY OF YOU TO--
--EXCUSE ME--
--IS THAT A NOTE, AKIKO?
FOR A BETTER FUTURE
YES, MISS DARAMOUNT. I WAS JUST--
WASN'T IT JUST YESTERDAY YOU WERE ASSIGNED TO BLACKBOARD CLEANING FOR THIS SAME INSUBORDINATION?
YES, MA'AM, BUT I--
NO MORE EXCUSES FROM YOU, YOUNG LADY. I WAS JUST ABOUT TO OFFER EVERYONE A CHANCE TO SHARE THEIR PROGRESS ON THEIR SCIENCE FAIR ENTRIES WITH THE CLASS...
...AND SINCE YOU'RE OBVIOUSLY SO FAR ALONG THAT YOU HAVE THE TIME AND LEISURE TO PASS NOTES--
--PERHAPS YOU'D LIKE TO TELL US ABOUT YOURS.

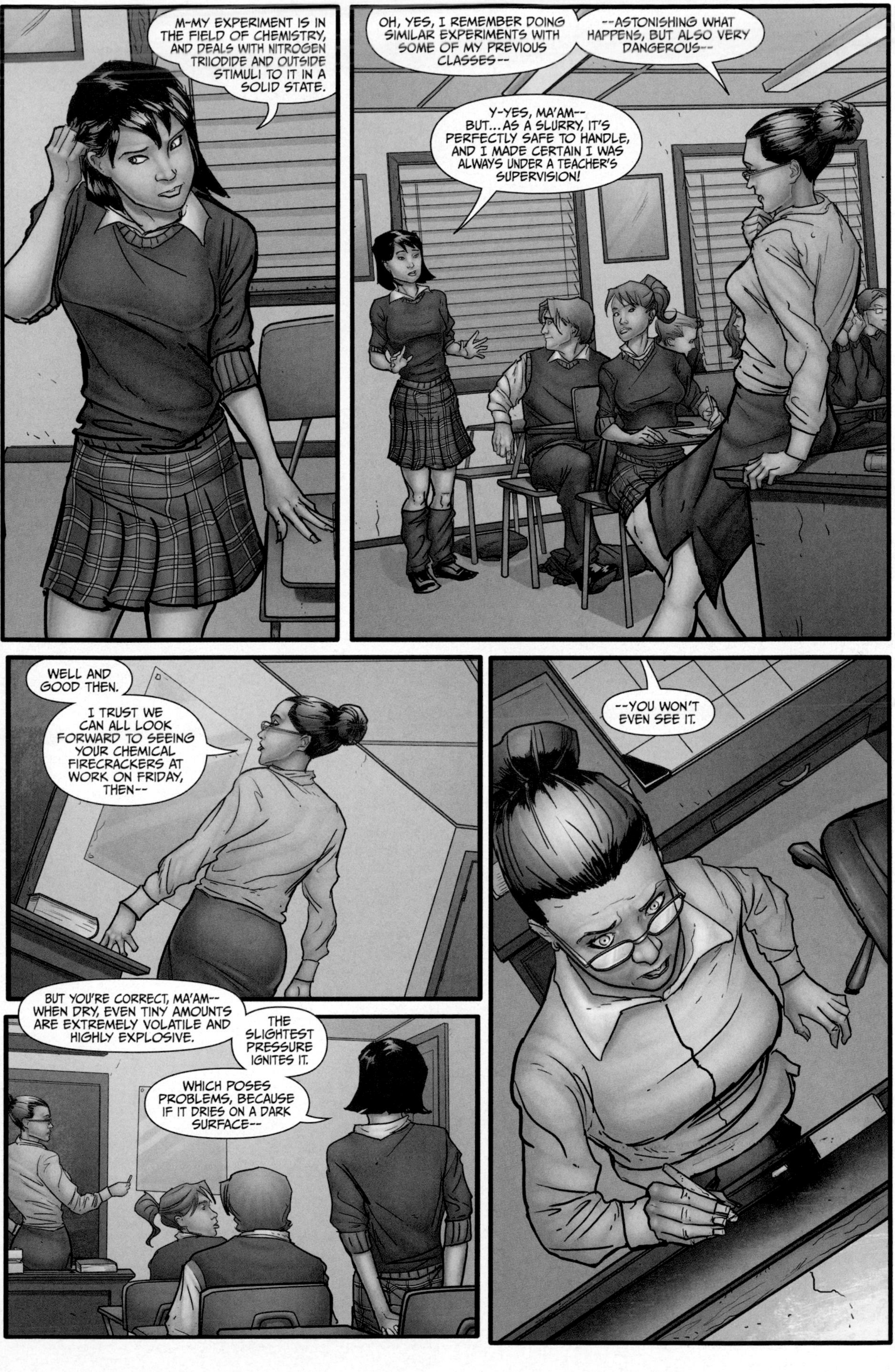
M-MY EXPERIMENT IS IN THE FIELD OF CHEMISTRY, AND DEALS WITH NITROGEN TRIIODIDE AND OUTSIDE STIMULI TO IT IN A SOLID STATE.
OH, YES, I REMEMBER DOING SIMILAR EXPERIMENTS WITH SOME OF MY PREVIOUS CLASSES--
--ASTONISHING WHAT HAPPENS, BUT ALSO VERY DANGEROUS--
Y-YES, MA'AM-- BUT... AS A SLURRY, IT'S PERFECTLY SAFE TO HANDLE, AND I MADE CERTAIN I WAS ALWAYS UNDER A TEACHER'S SUPERVISION!
WELL AND GOOD THEN.
I TRUST WE CAN ALL LOOK FORWARD TO SEEING YOUR CHEMICAL FIRECRACKERS AT WORK ON FRIDAY, THEN--
BUT YOU'RE CORRECT, MA'AM-- WHEN DRY, EVEN TINY AMOUNTS ARE EXTREMELY VOLATILE AND HIGHLY EXPLOSIVE.
THE SLIGHTEST PRESSURE IGNITES IT.
WHICH POSES PROBLEMS, BECAUSE IF IT DRIES ON A DARK SURFACE--
--YOU WON'T EVEN SEE IT.

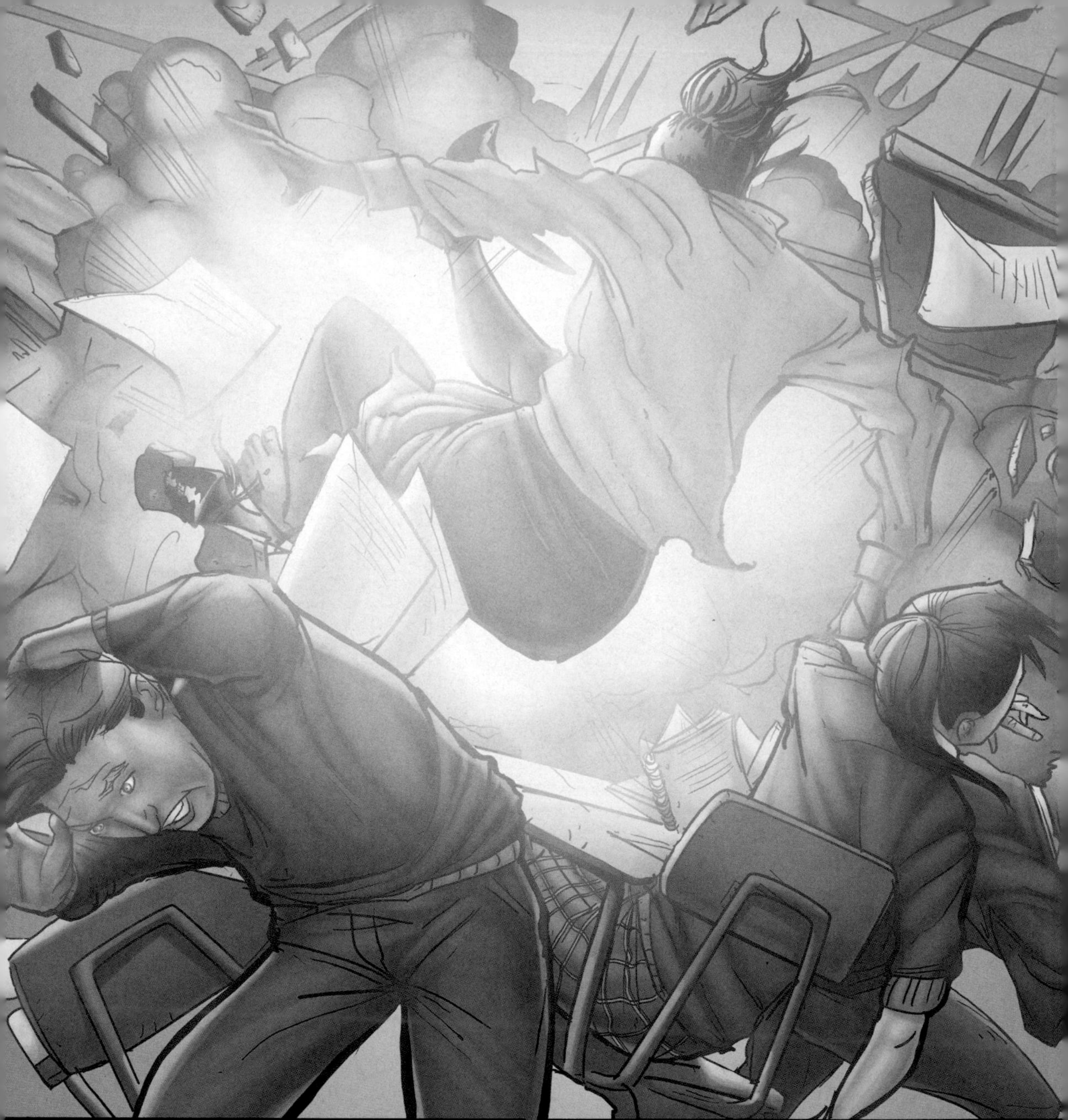

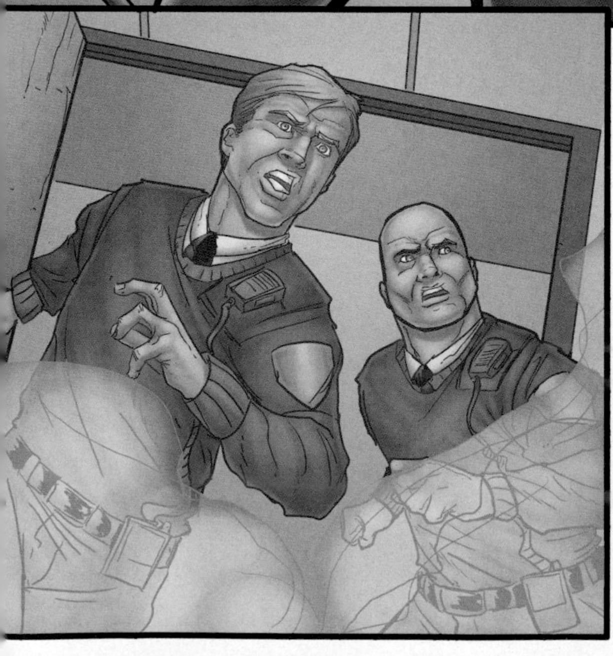

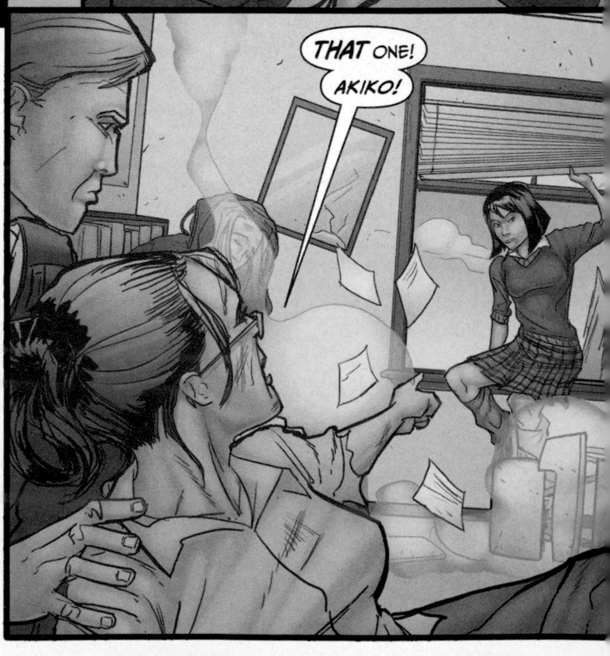
THAT ONE!
AKIKO!

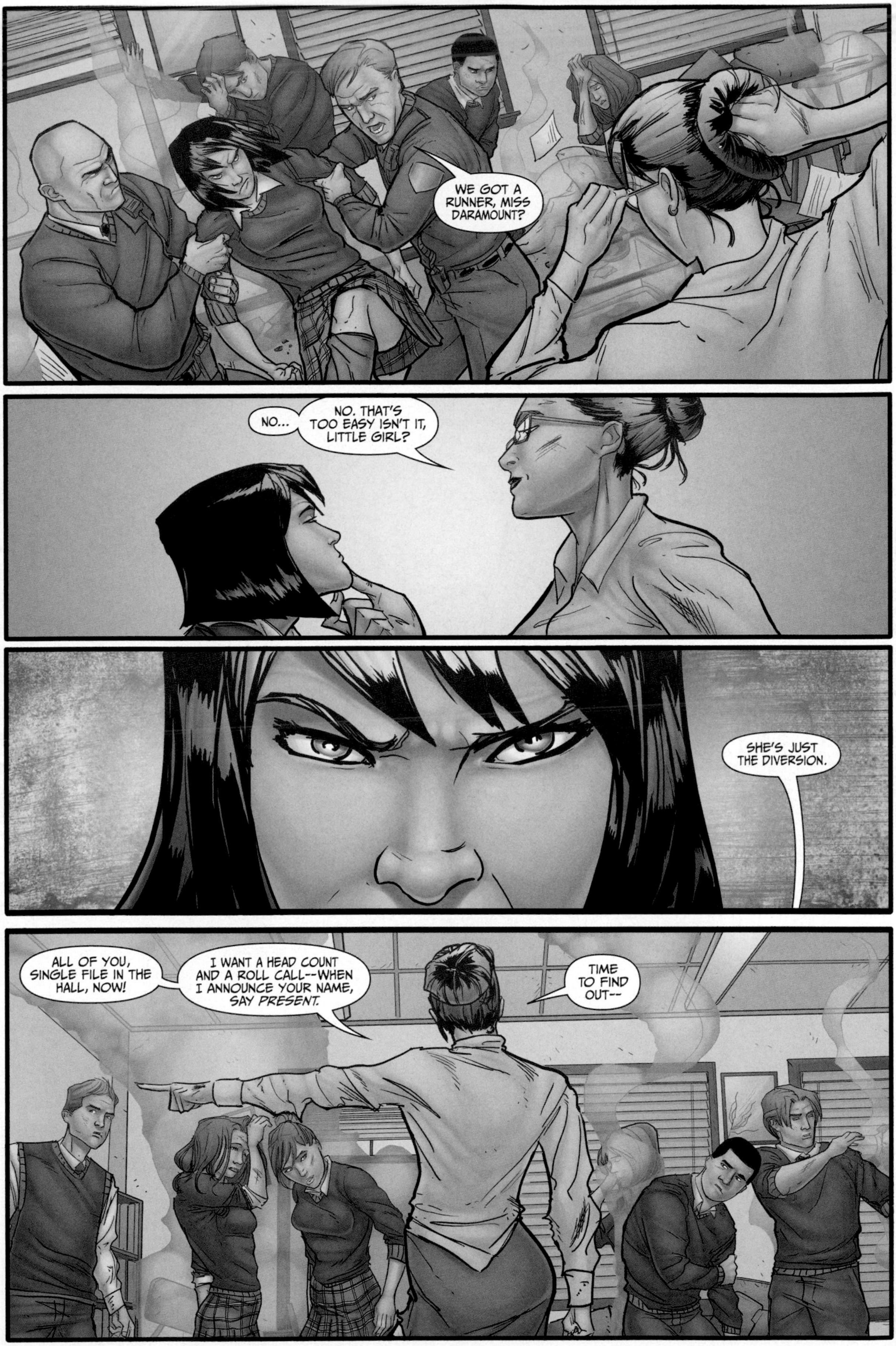
WE GOT A RUNNER, MISS DARAMOUNT?
NO...
NO. THAT'S TOO EASY ISN'T IT, LITTLE GIRL?
SHE'S JUST THE DIVERSION.
ALL OF YOU, SINGLE FILE IN THE HALL, NOW!
I WANT A HEAD COUNT AND A ROLL CALL--WHEN I ANNOUNCE YOUR NAME, SAY *PRESENT.*
TIME TO FIND OUT--

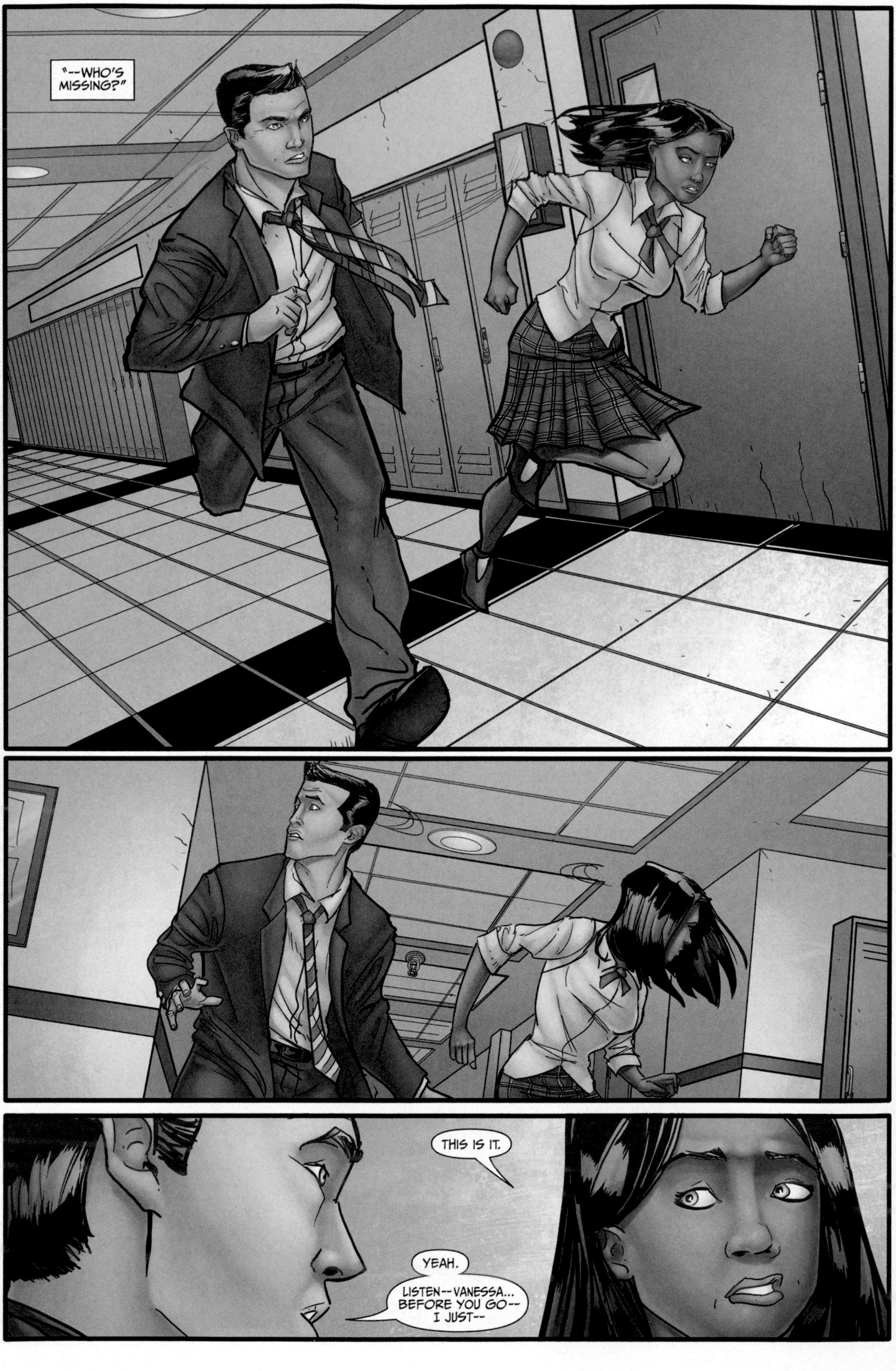
"--WHO'S MISSING?"
THIS IS IT.
YEAH.
LISTEN--VANESSA... BEFORE YOU GO-- I JUST--

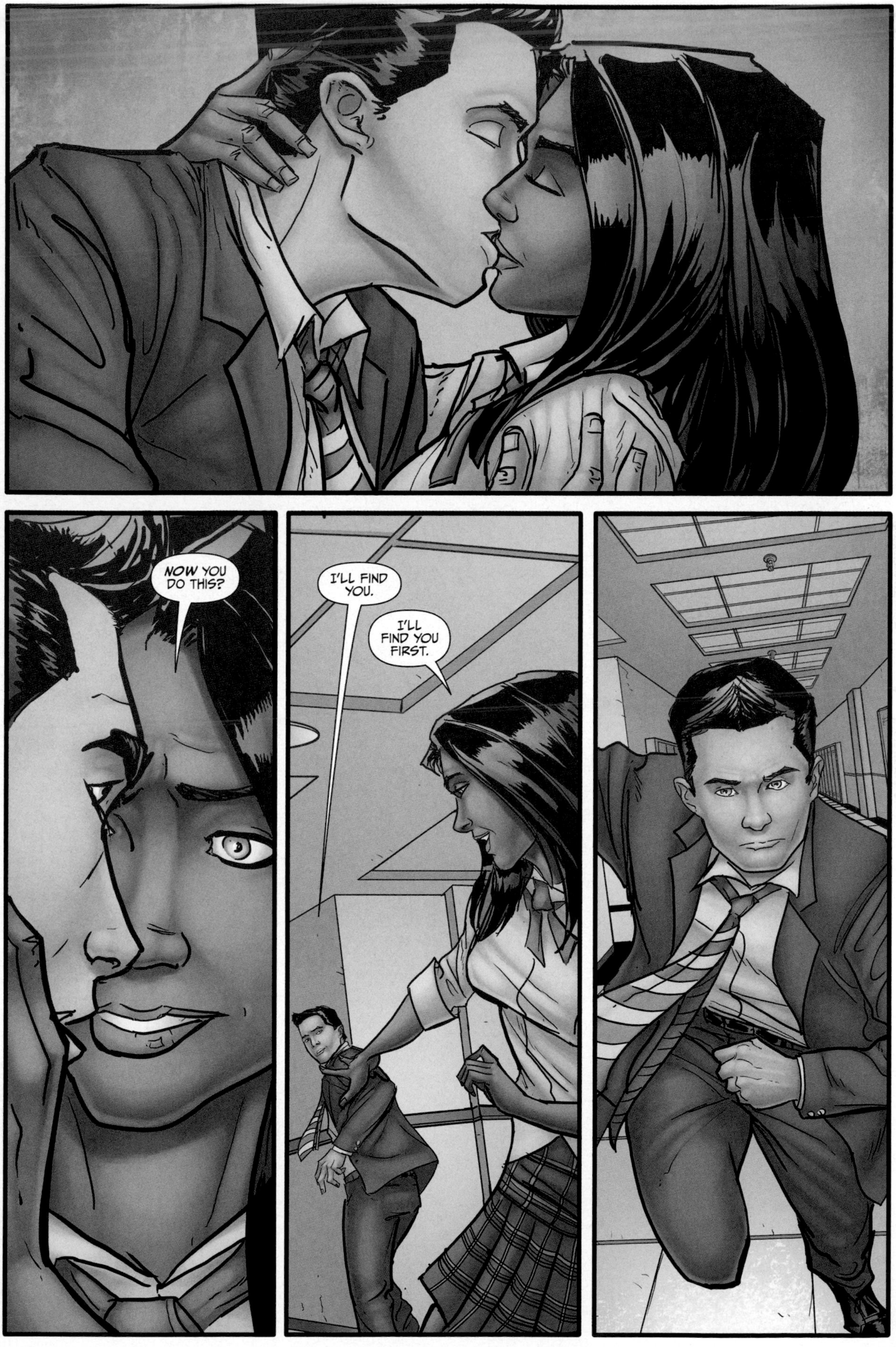
NOW YOU DO THIS?
I'LL FIND YOU.
I'LL FIND YOU FIRST.

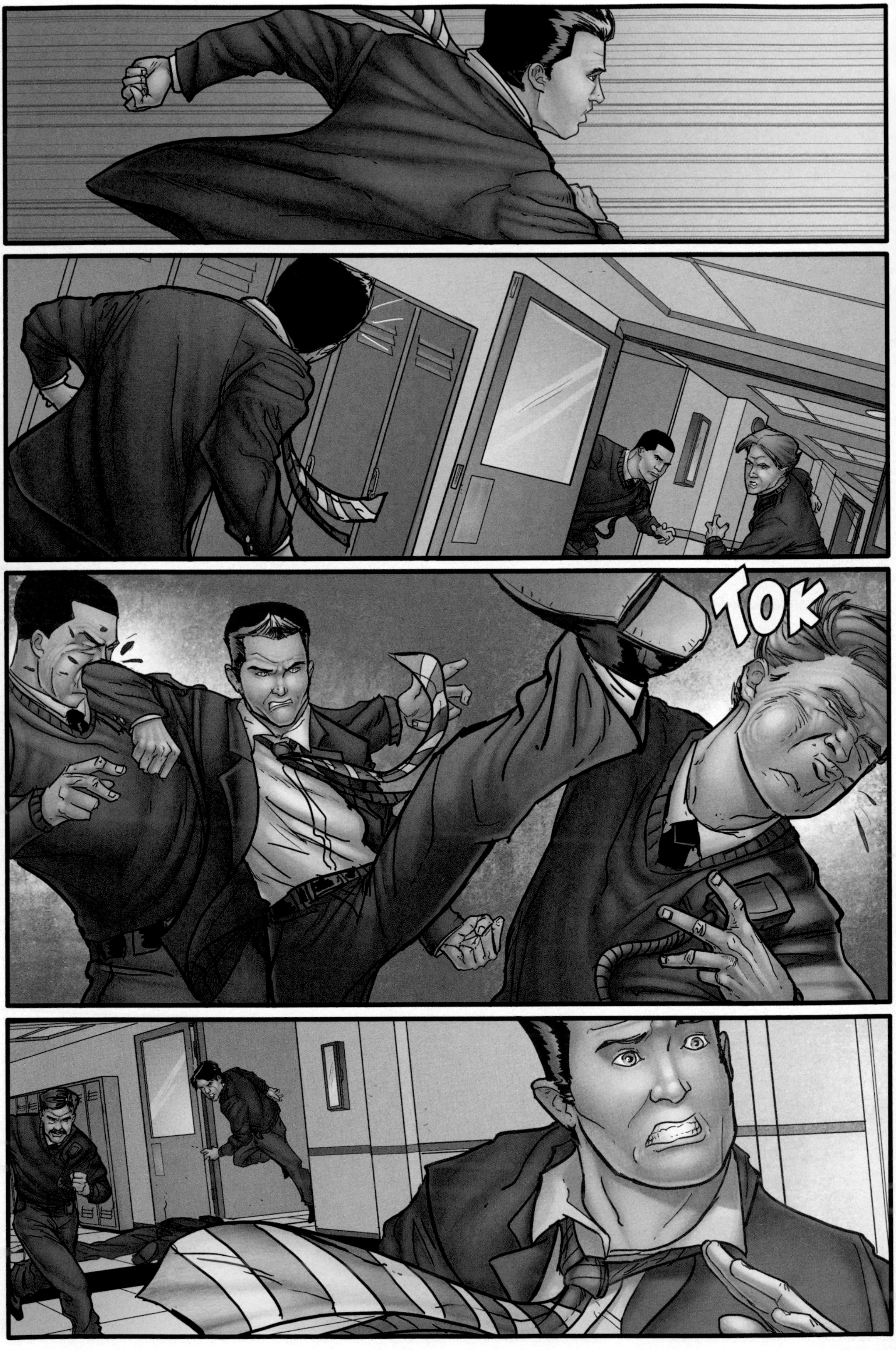
TOK

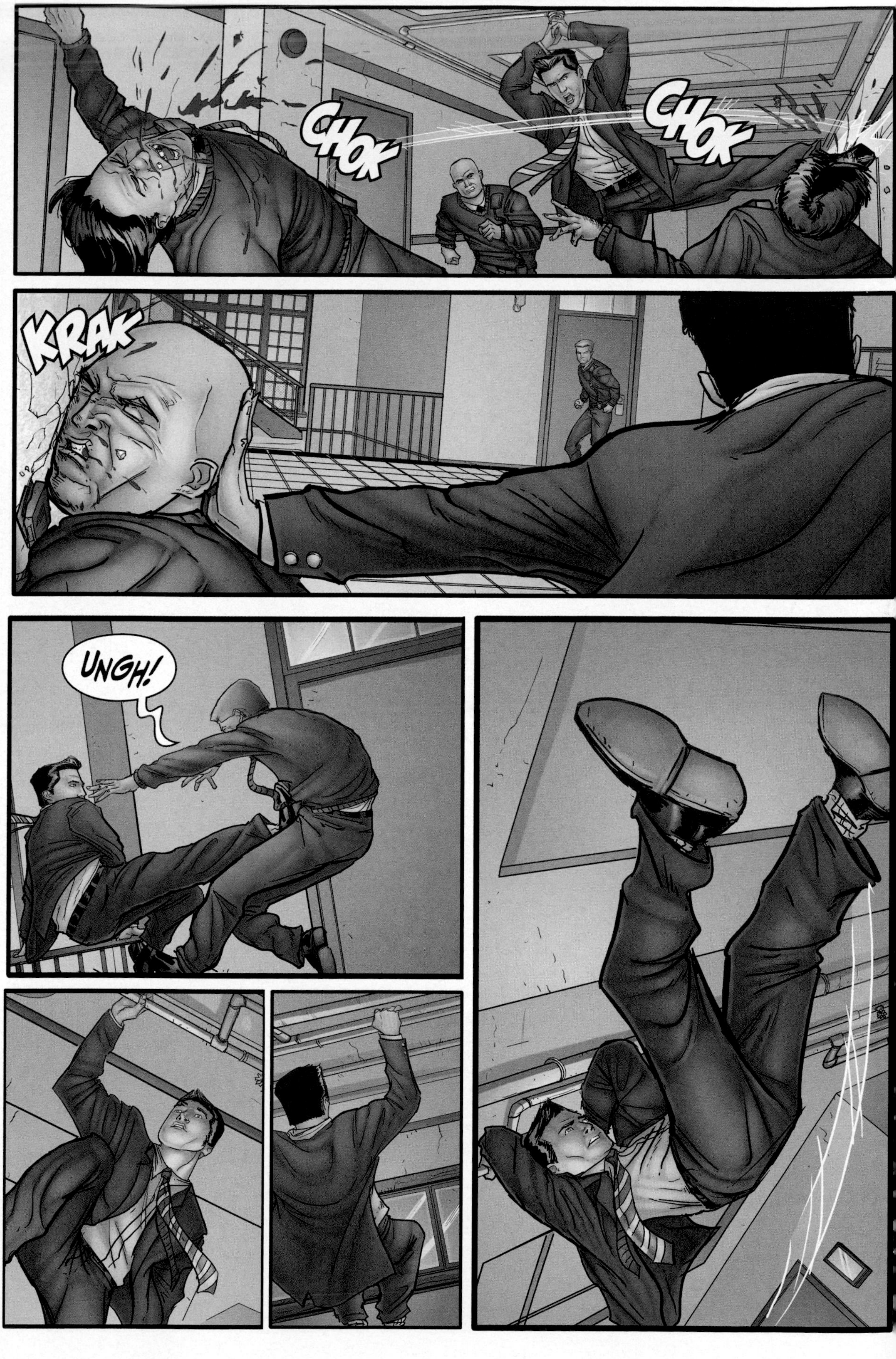
CHOK
CHOK
KRAK
UNGH!

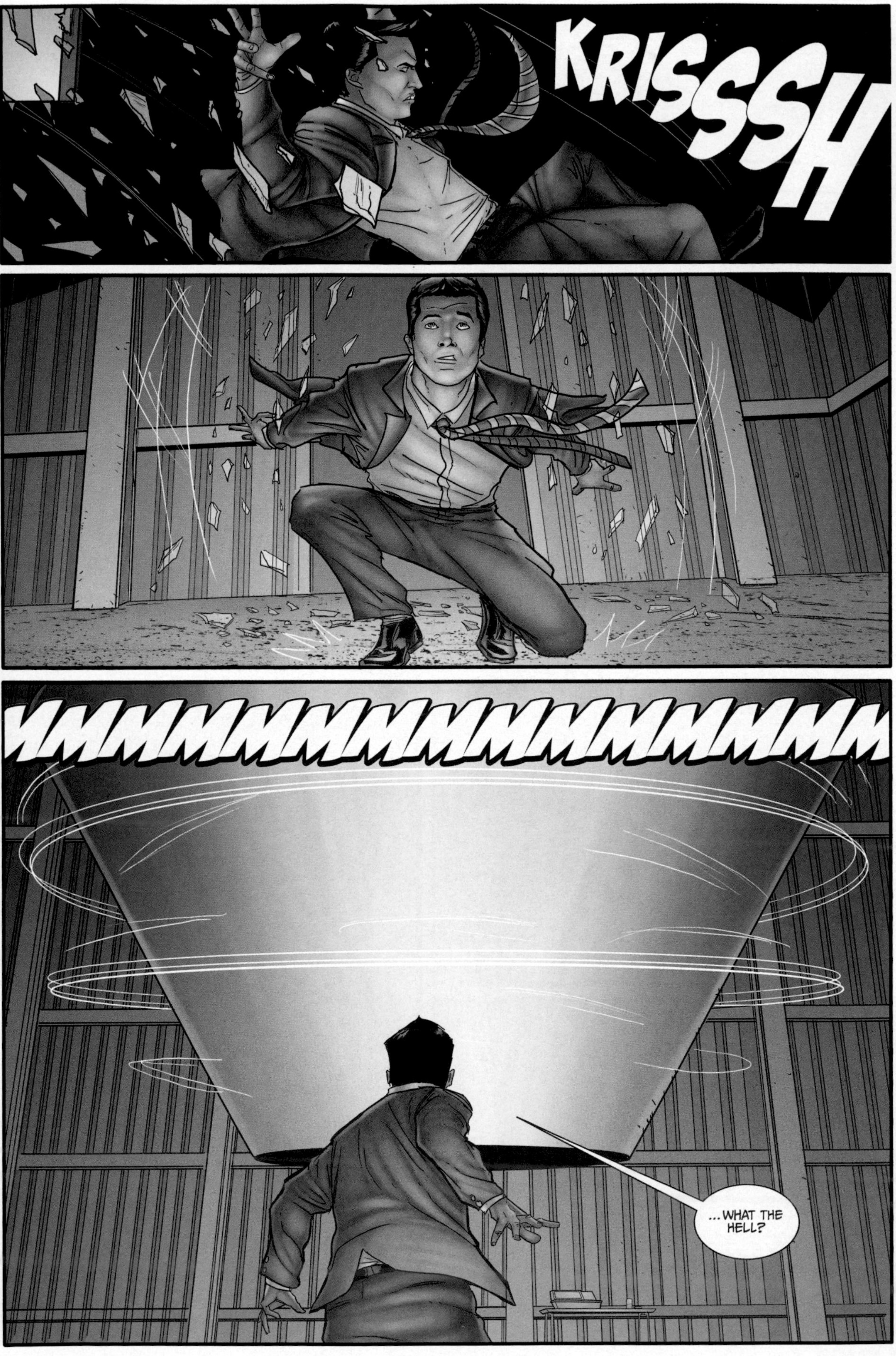
KRISSSH
MMMMMMMMMMMMMMMMMM
...WHAT THE HELL?

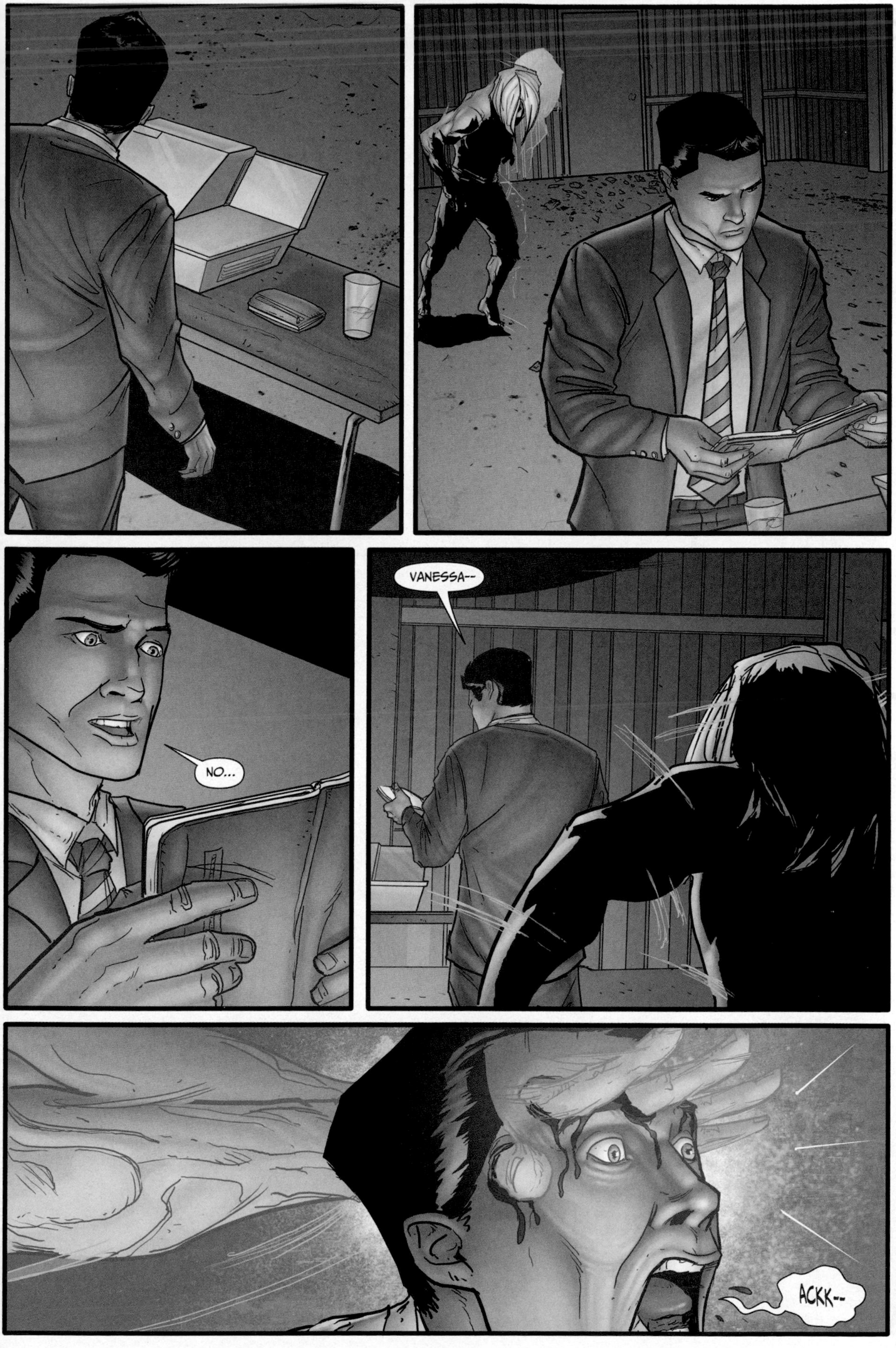
NO...
VANESSA--
ACKK--

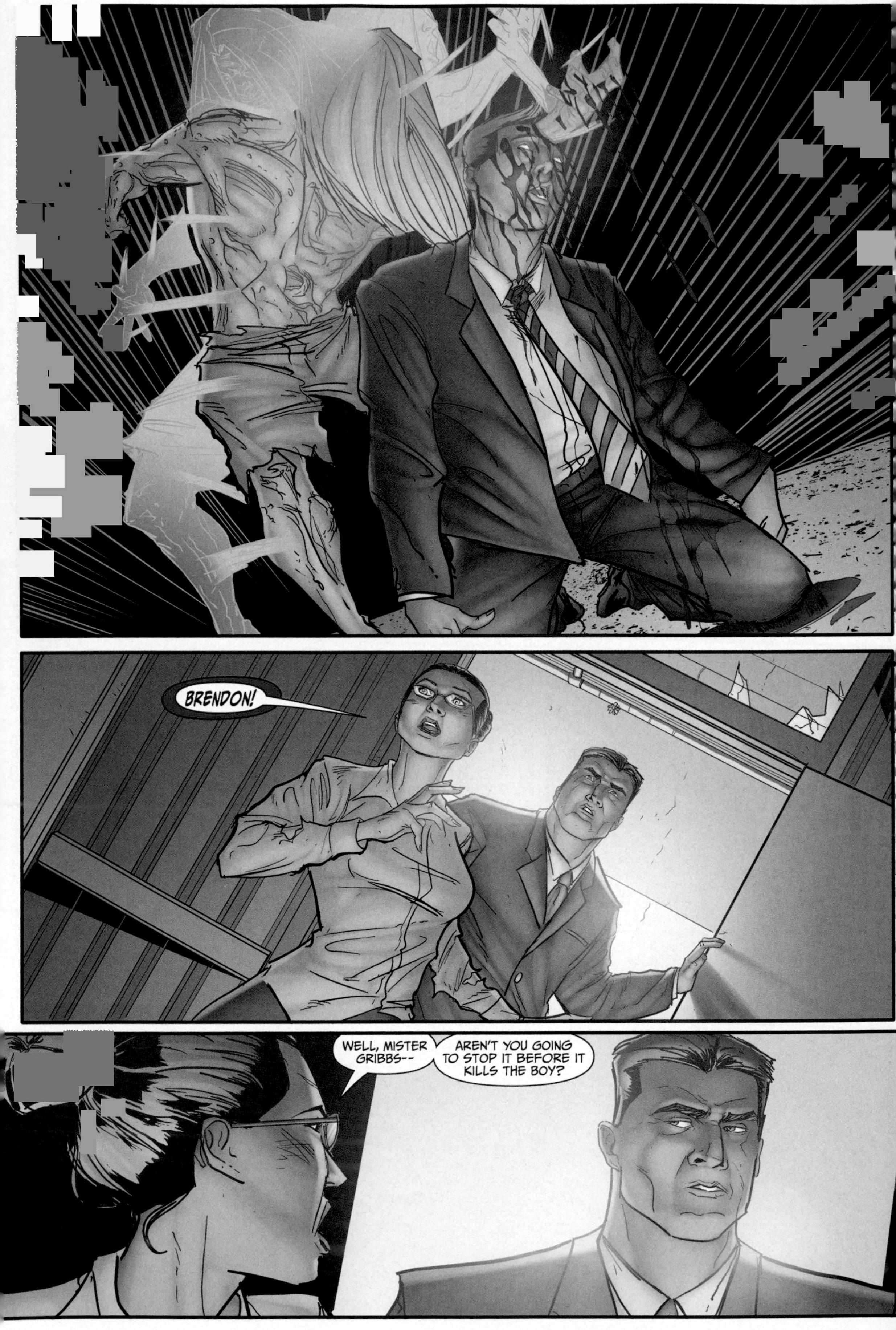
BRENDON!
WELL, MISTER GRIBBS--
AREN'T YOU GOING TO STOP IT BEFORE IT KILLS THE BOY?

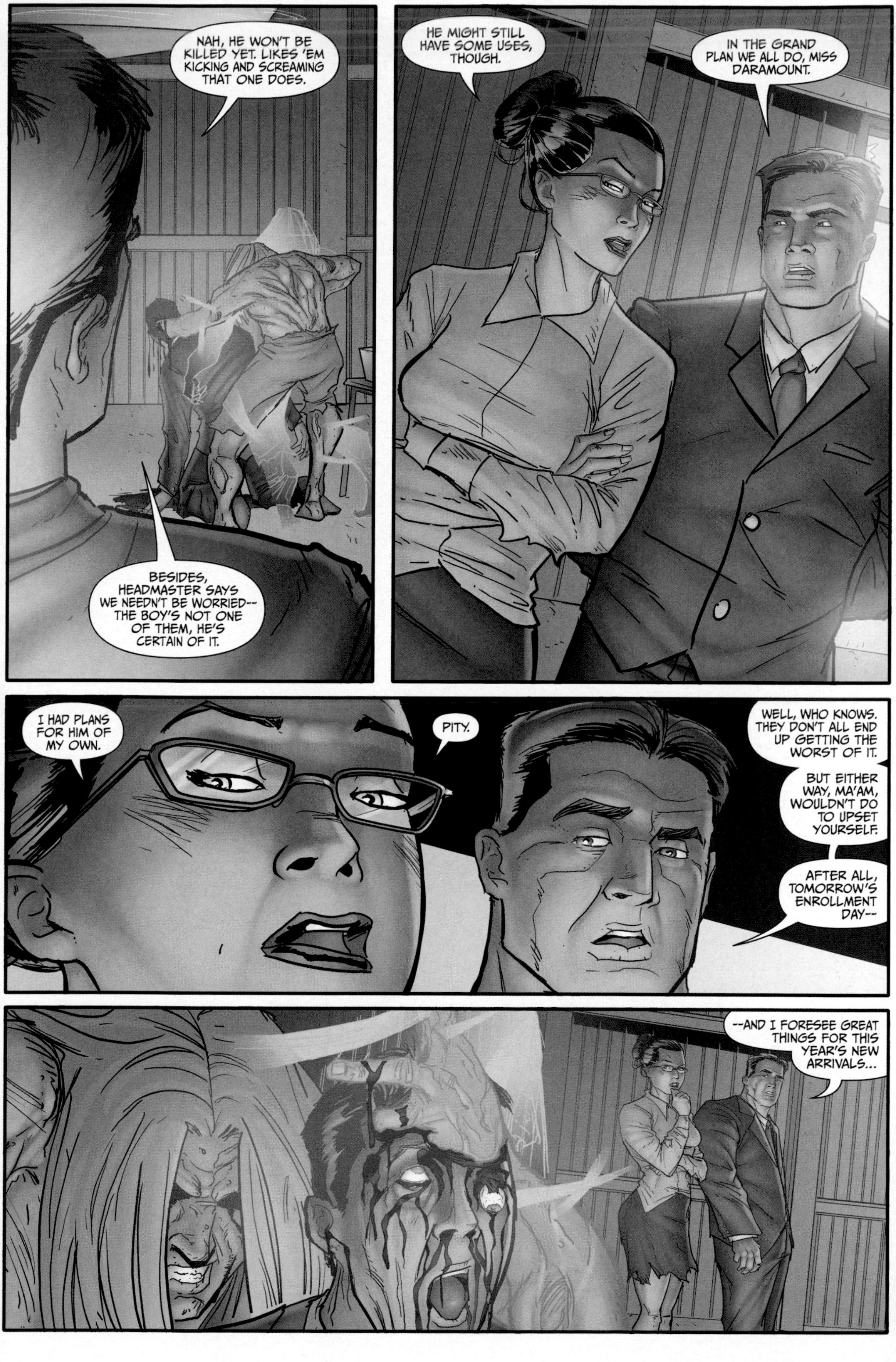
NAH, HE WON'T BE KILLED YET. LIKES 'EM KICKING AND SCREAMING THAT ONE DOES.
BESIDES, HEADMASTER SAYS WE NEEDN'T BE WORRIED-- THE BOY'S NOT ONE OF THEM, HE'S CERTAIN OF IT.
HE MIGHT STILL HAVE SOME USES, THOUGH.
IN THE GRAND PLAN WE ALL DO, MISS DARAMOUNT.
I HAD PLANS FOR HIM OF MY OWN.
PITY.
WELL, WHO KNOWS. THEY DON'T ALL END UP GETTING THE WORST OF IT.
BUT EITHER WAY, MA'AM, WOULDN'T DO TO UPSET YOURSELF.
AFTER ALL, TOMORROW'S ENROLLMENT DAY--
--AND I FORESEE GREAT THINGS FOR THIS YEAR'S NEW ARRIVALS...

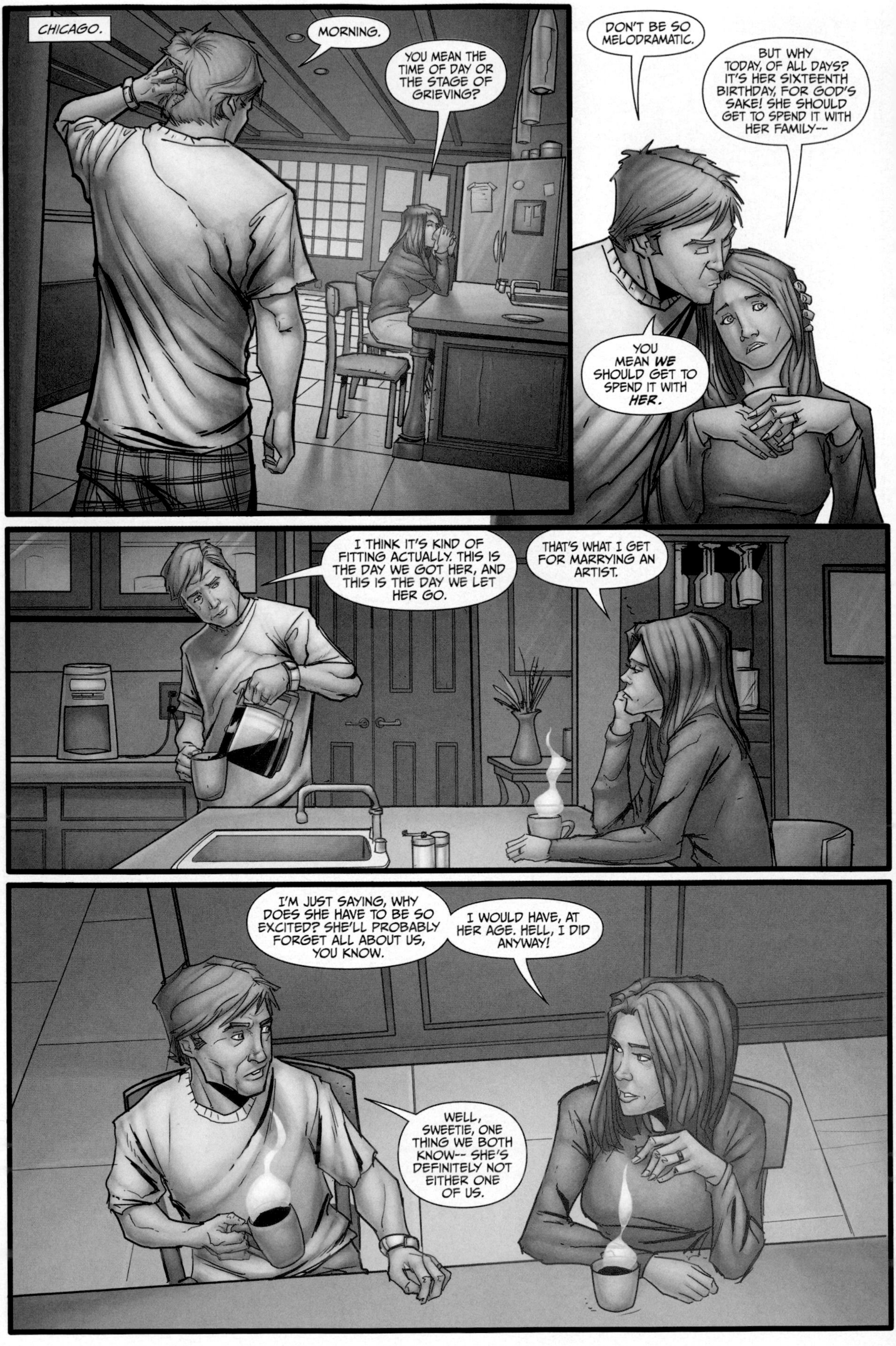
CHICAGO.
MORNING.
YOU MEAN THE TIME OF DAY OR THE STAGE OF GRIEVING?
DON'T BE SO MELODRAMATIC.
BUT WHY TODAY, OF ALL DAYS? IT'S HER SIXTEENTH BIRTHDAY, FOR GOD'S SAKE! SHE SHOULD GET TO SPEND IT WITH HER FAMILY--
YOU MEAN *WE* SHOULD GET TO SPEND IT WITH *HER*.
I THINK IT'S KIND OF FITTING ACTUALLY. THIS IS THE DAY WE GOT HER, AND THIS IS THE DAY WE LET HER GO.
THAT'S WHAT I GET FOR MARRYING AN ARTIST.
I'M JUST SAYING, WHY DOES SHE HAVE TO BE SO EXCITED? SHE'LL PROBABLY FORGET ALL ABOUT US, YOU KNOW.
I WOULD HAVE, AT HER AGE. HELL, I DID ANYWAY!
WELL, SWEETIE, ONE THING WE BOTH KNOW-- SHE'S DEFINITELY NOT EITHER ONE OF US.

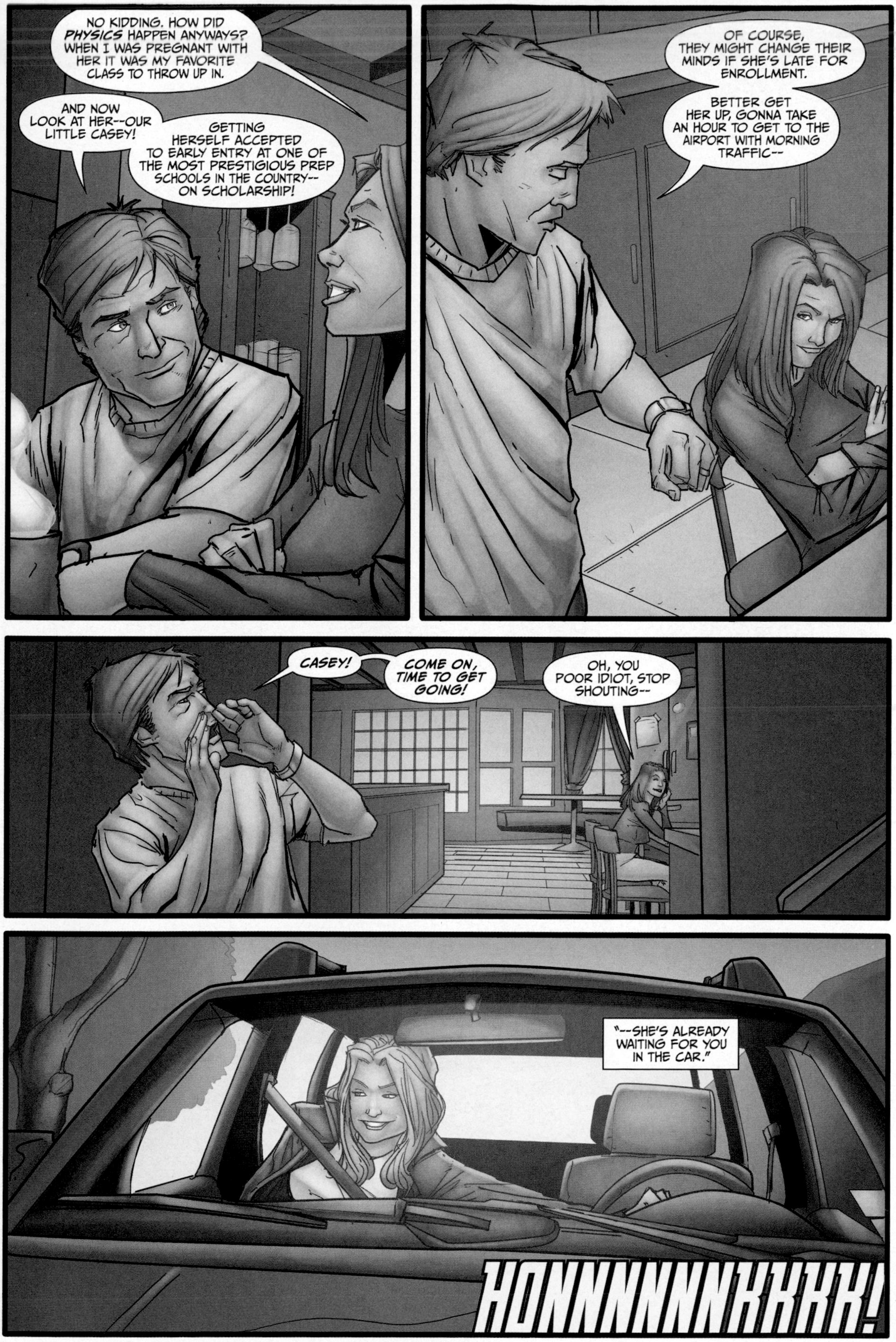
NO KIDDING. HOW DID *PHYSICS* HAPPEN ANYWAYS? WHEN I WAS PREGNANT WITH HER IT WAS MY FAVORITE CLASS TO THROW UP IN.
AND NOW LOOK AT HER--OUR LITTLE CASEY!
GETTING HERSELF ACCEPTED TO EARLY ENTRY AT ONE OF THE MOST PRESTIGIOUS PREP SCHOOLS IN THE COUNTRY--ON SCHOLARSHIP!
OF COURSE, THEY MIGHT CHANGE THEIR MINDS IF SHE'S LATE FOR ENROLLMENT.
BETTER GET HER UP, GONNA TAKE AN HOUR TO GET TO THE AIRPORT WITH MORNING TRAFFIC--
CASEY!
COME ON, TIME TO GET GOING!
OH, YOU POOR IDIOT, STOP SHOUTING--
"--SHE'S ALREADY WAITING FOR YOU IN THE CAR."
HONNNNNNKKKK!

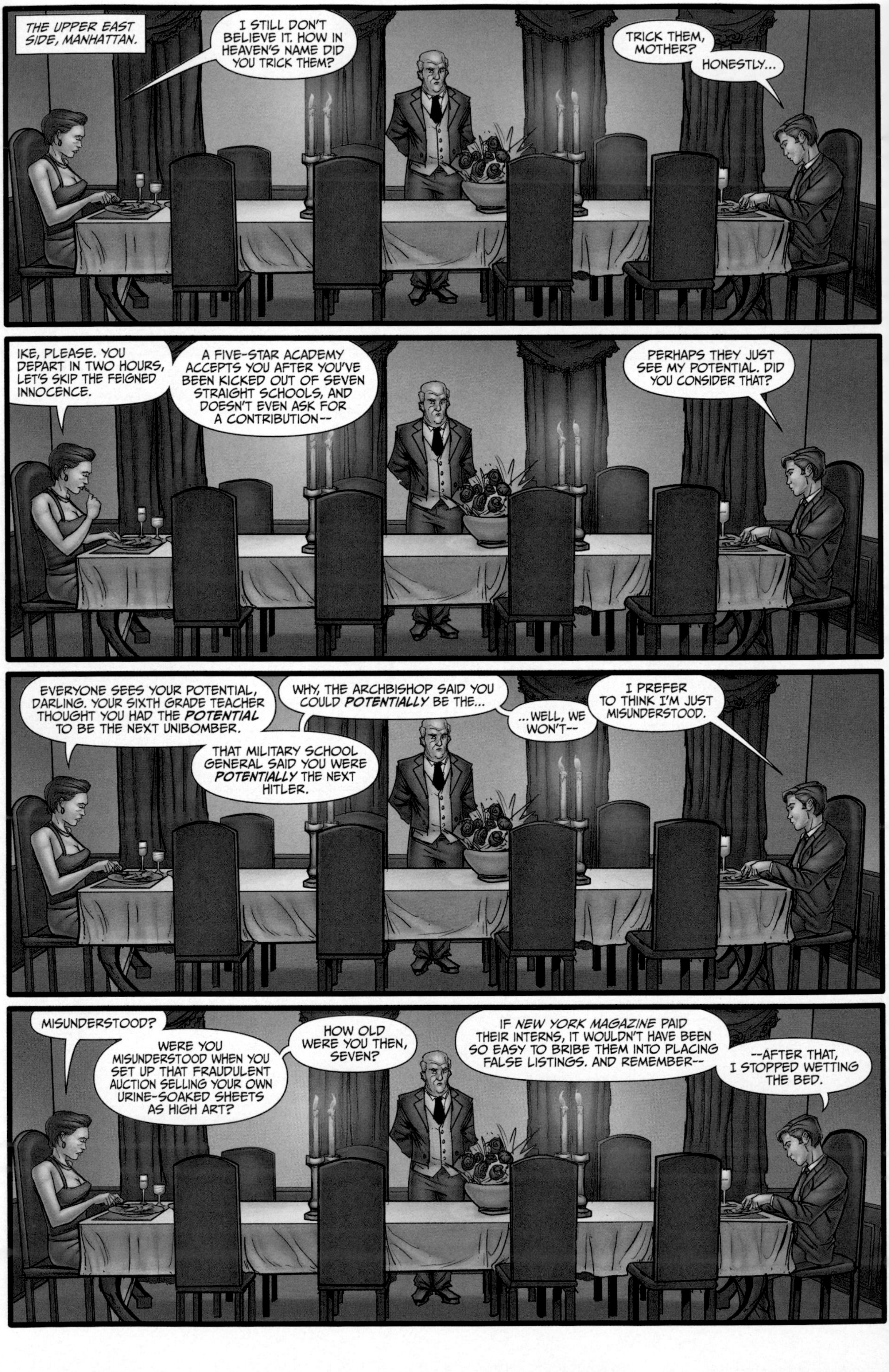
THE UPPER EAST SIDE, MANHATTAN.
I STILL DON'T BELIEVE IT. HOW IN HEAVEN'S NAME DID YOU TRICK THEM?
TRICK THEM, MOTHER?
HONESTLY...
IKE, PLEASE. YOU DEPART IN TWO HOURS, LET'S SKIP THE FEIGNED INNOCENCE.
A FIVE-STAR ACADEMY ACCEPTS YOU AFTER YOU'VE BEEN KICKED OUT OF SEVEN STRAIGHT SCHOOLS, AND DOESN'T EVEN ASK FOR A CONTRIBUTION--
PERHAPS THEY JUST SEE MY POTENTIAL. DID YOU CONSIDER THAT?
EVERYONE SEES YOUR POTENTIAL, DARLING. YOUR SIXTH GRADE TEACHER THOUGHT YOU HAD THE *POTENTIAL* TO BE THE NEXT UNIBOMBER.
THAT MILITARY SCHOOL GENERAL SAID YOU WERE *POTENTIALLY* THE NEXT HITLER.
WHY, THE ARCHBISHOP SAID YOU COULD *POTENTIALLY* BE THE...
...WELL, WE WON'T--
I PREFER TO THINK I'M JUST MISUNDERSTOOD.
MISUNDERSTOOD?
WERE YOU MISUNDERSTOOD WHEN YOU SET UP THAT FRAUDULENT AUCTION SELLING YOUR OWN URINE-SOAKED SHEETS AS HIGH ART?
HOW OLD WERE YOU THEN, SEVEN?
IF *NEW YORK MAGAZINE* PAID THEIR INTERNS, IT WOULDN'T HAVE BEEN SO EASY TO BRIBE THEM INTO PLACING FALSE LISTINGS. AND REMEMBER--
--AFTER THAT, I STOPPED WETTING THE BED.

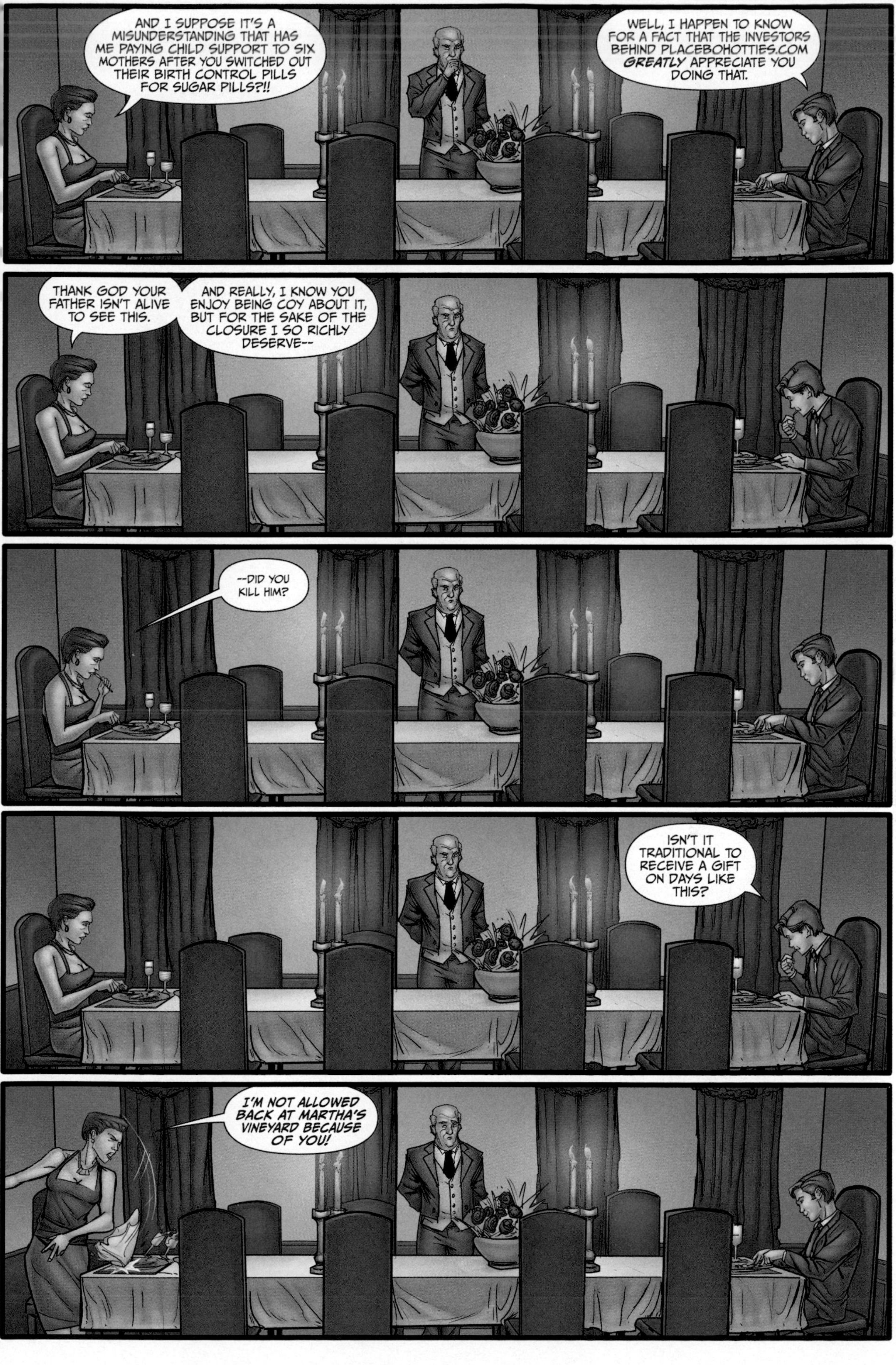

AND I SUPPOSE IT'S A MISUNDERSTANDING THAT HAS ME PAYING CHILD SUPPORT TO SIX MOTHERS AFTER YOU SWITCHED OUT THEIR BIRTH CONTROL PILLS FOR SUGAR PILLS?!!
WELL, I HAPPEN TO KNOW FOR A FACT THAT THE INVESTORS BEHIND PLACEBOHOTTIES.COM *GREATLY* APPRECIATE YOU DOING THAT.
THANK GOD YOUR FATHER ISN'T ALIVE TO SEE THIS.
AND REALLY, I KNOW YOU ENJOY BEING COY ABOUT IT, BUT FOR THE SAKE OF THE CLOSURE I SO RICHLY DESERVE--
--DID YOU KILL HIM?
ISN'T IT TRADITIONAL TO RECEIVE A GIFT ON DAYS LIKE THIS?
I'M NOT ALLOWED BACK AT MARTHA'S VINEYARD BECAUSE OF YOU!

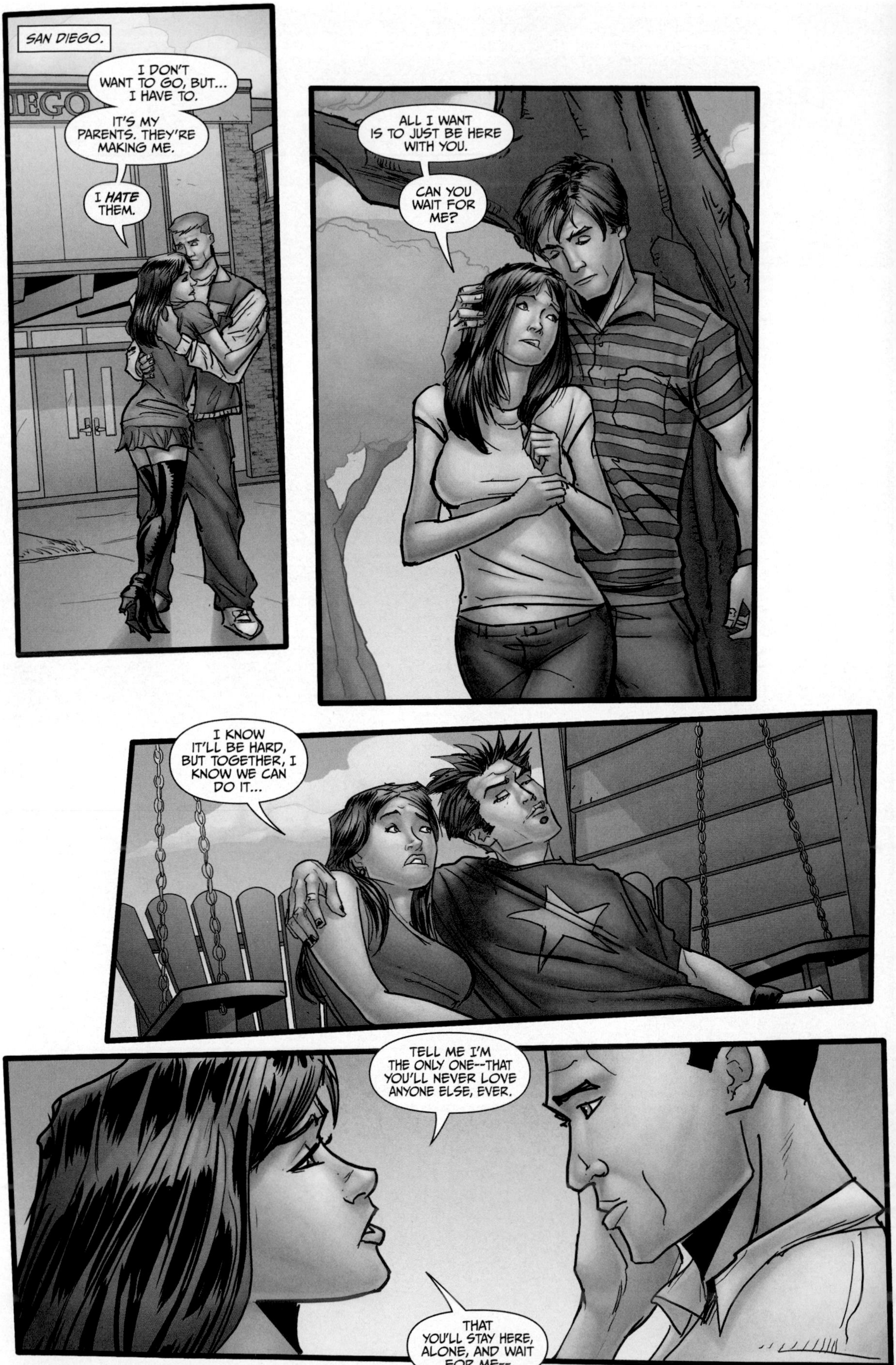
SAN DIEGO.
I DON'T WANT TO GO, BUT... I HAVE TO.
IT'S MY PARENTS. THEY'RE MAKING ME.
I *HATE* THEM.
ALL I WANT IS TO JUST BE HERE WITH YOU.
CAN YOU WAIT FOR ME?
I KNOW IT'LL BE HARD, BUT TOGETHER, I KNOW WE CAN DO IT...
TELL ME I'M THE ONLY ONE--THAT YOU'LL NEVER LOVE ANYONE ELSE, EVER.
THAT YOU'LL STAY HERE, ALONE, AND WAIT FOR ME--

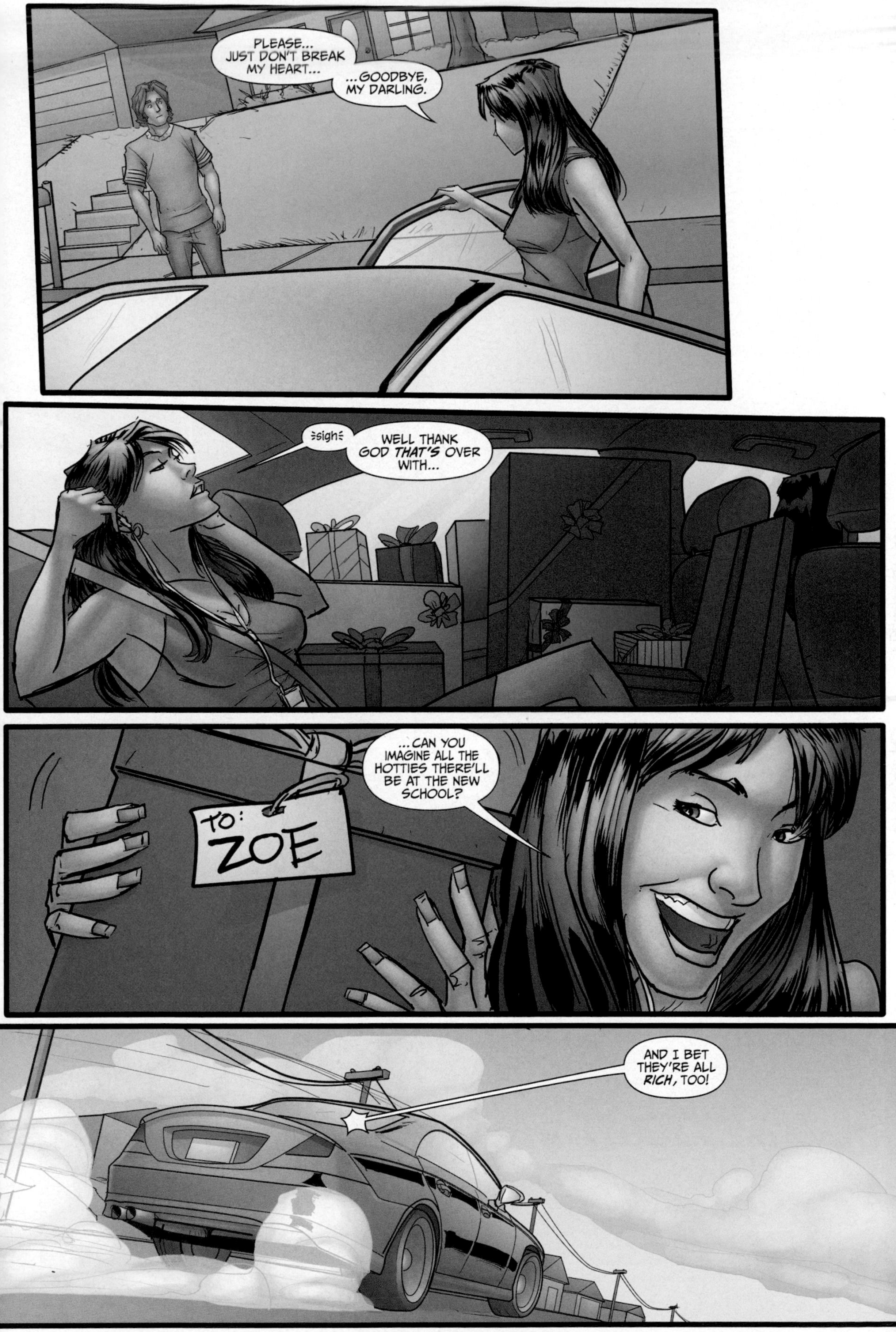
PLEASE... JUST DON'T BREAK MY HEART...
...GOODBYE, MY DARLING.
sigh
WELL THANK GOD THAT'S OVER WITH...
TO: ZOE
...CAN YOU IMAGINE ALL THE HOTTIES THERE'LL BE AT THE NEW SCHOOL?
AND I BET THEY'RE ALL RICH, TOO!

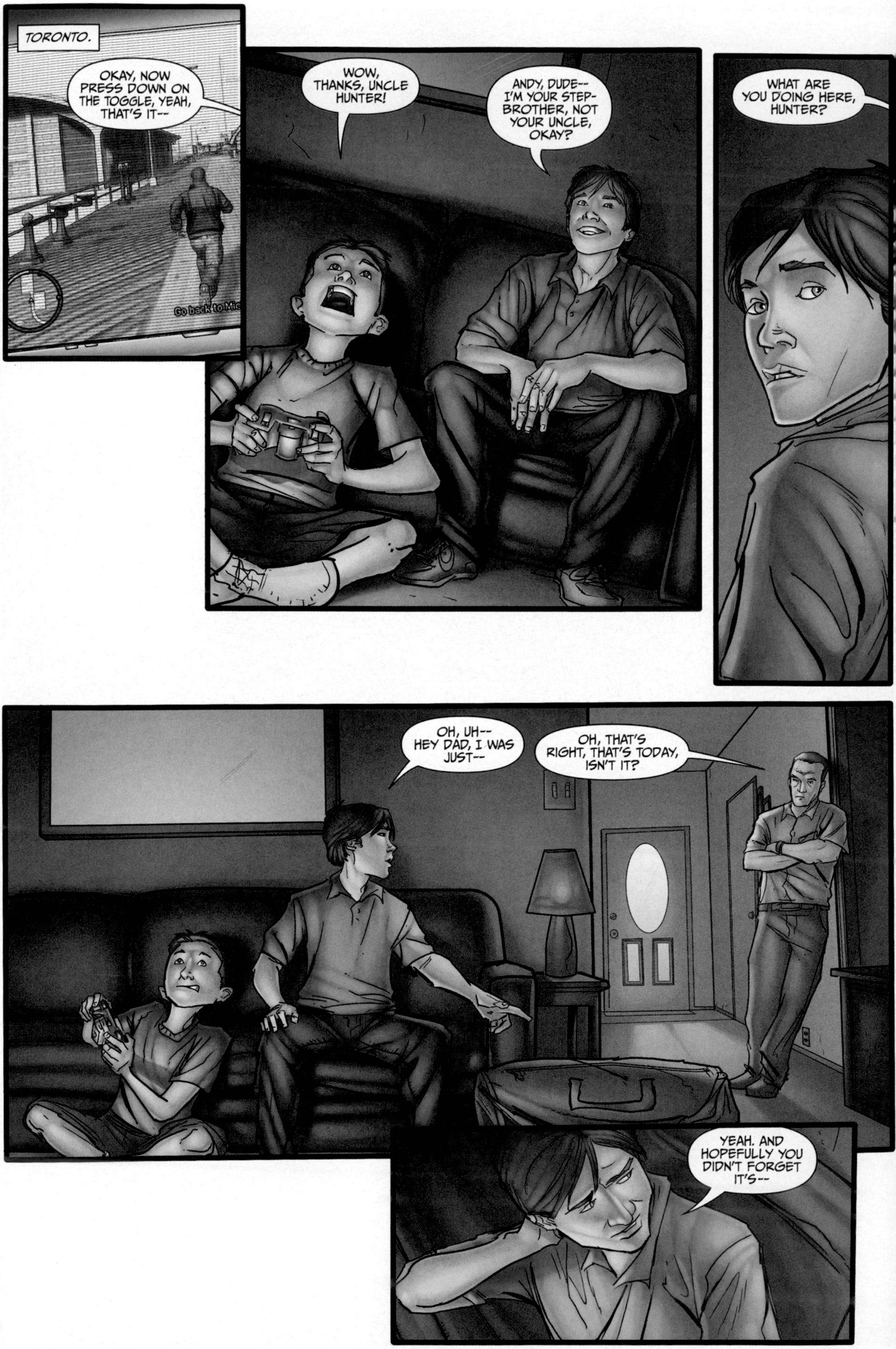
TORONTO.
OKAY, NOW PRESS DOWN ON THE TOGGLE, YEAH, THAT'S IT--
Go back to Mic
WOW, THANKS, UNCLE HUNTER!
ANDY, DUDE-- I'M YOUR STEP-BROTHER, NOT YOUR UNCLE, OKAY?
WHAT ARE YOU DOING HERE, HUNTER?
OH, UH-- HEY DAD, I WAS JUST--
OH, THAT'S RIGHT, THAT'S TODAY, ISN'T IT?
YEAH. AND HOPEFULLY YOU DIDN'T FORGET IT'S--

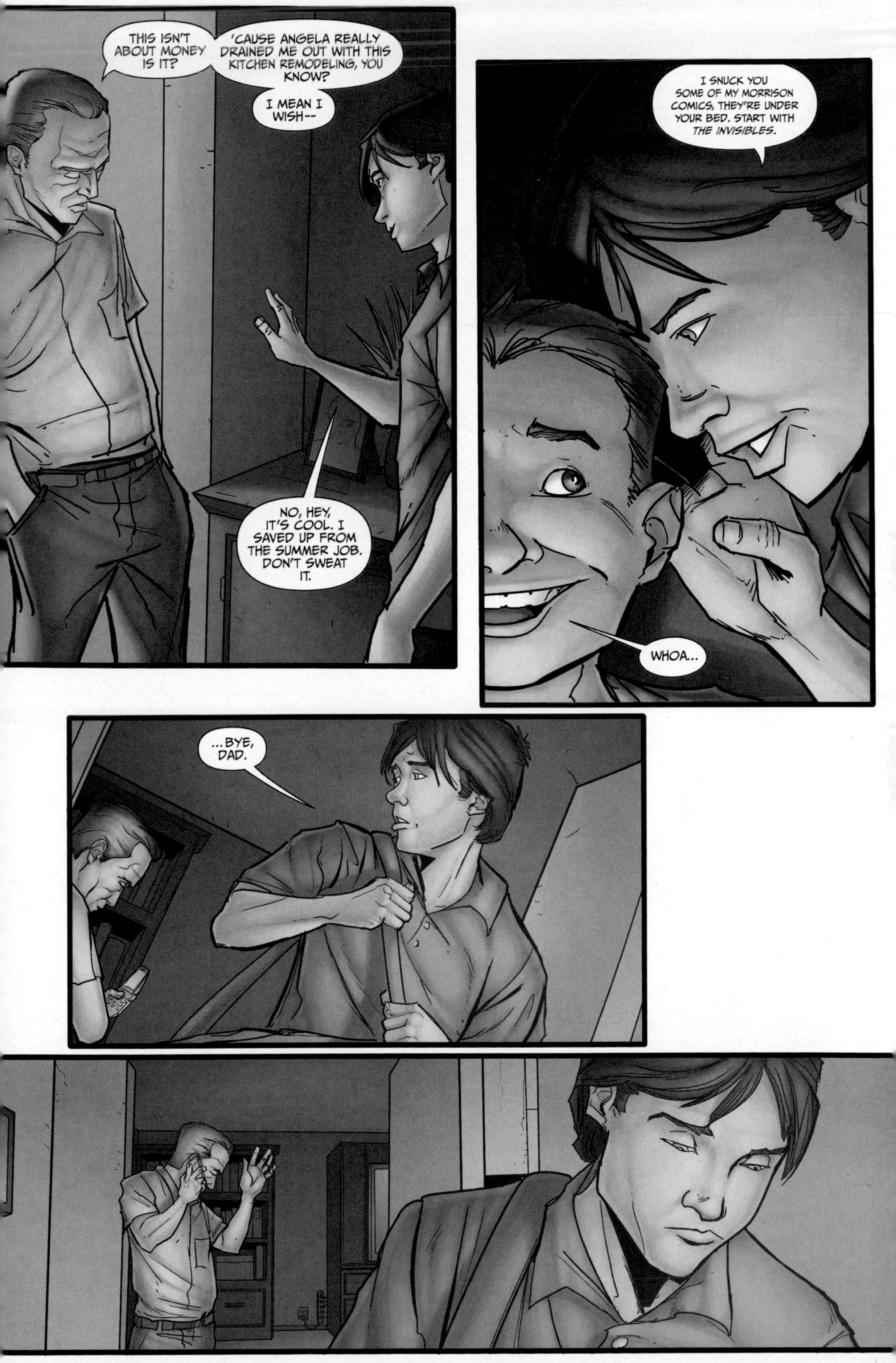
THIS ISN'T ABOUT MONEY IS IT?
'CAUSE ANGELA REALLY DRAINED ME OUT WITH THIS KITCHEN REMODELING, YOU KNOW?
I MEAN I WISH--
NO, HEY, IT'S COOL. I SAVED UP FROM THE SUMMER JOB. DON'T SWEAT IT.
I SNUCK YOU SOME OF MY MORRISON COMICS, THEY'RE UNDER YOUR BED. START WITH *THE INVISIBLES*.
WHOA...
...BYE, DAD.

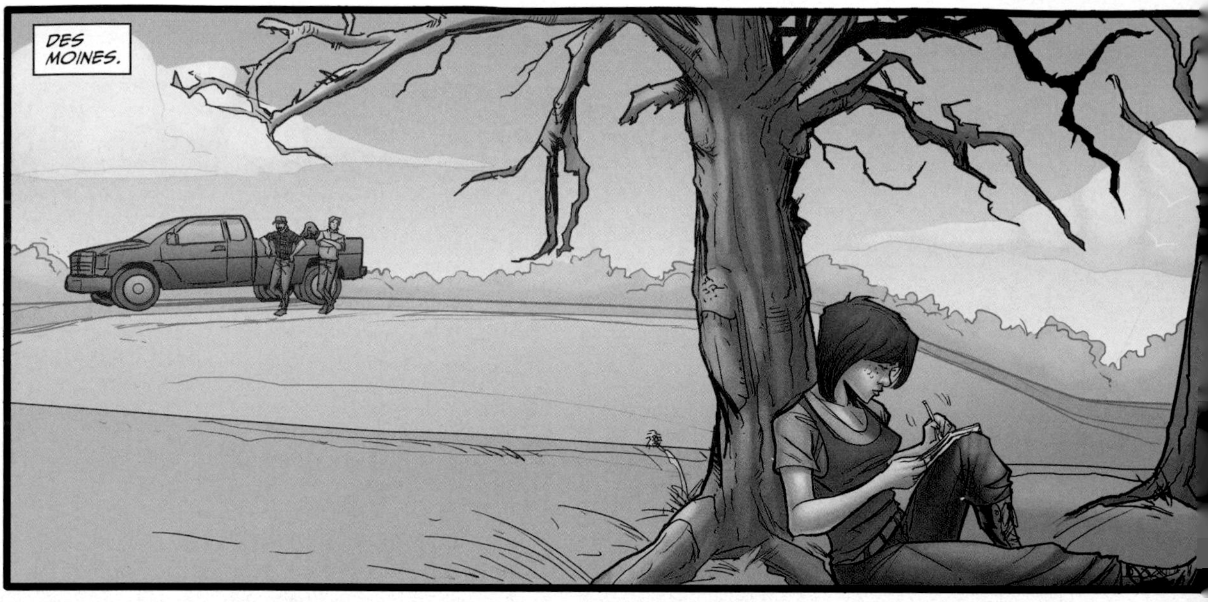
DES MOINES.

The cold breeze leaves me feeling empty. memories of Marcus, and the times I felt his hand touch mine are all I can consider now. That and the pain. the pain that invades my soul like sunlight bursting into a vampire's sleeping tomb. I don't want to feel it, but I always do, and know that I always shall.

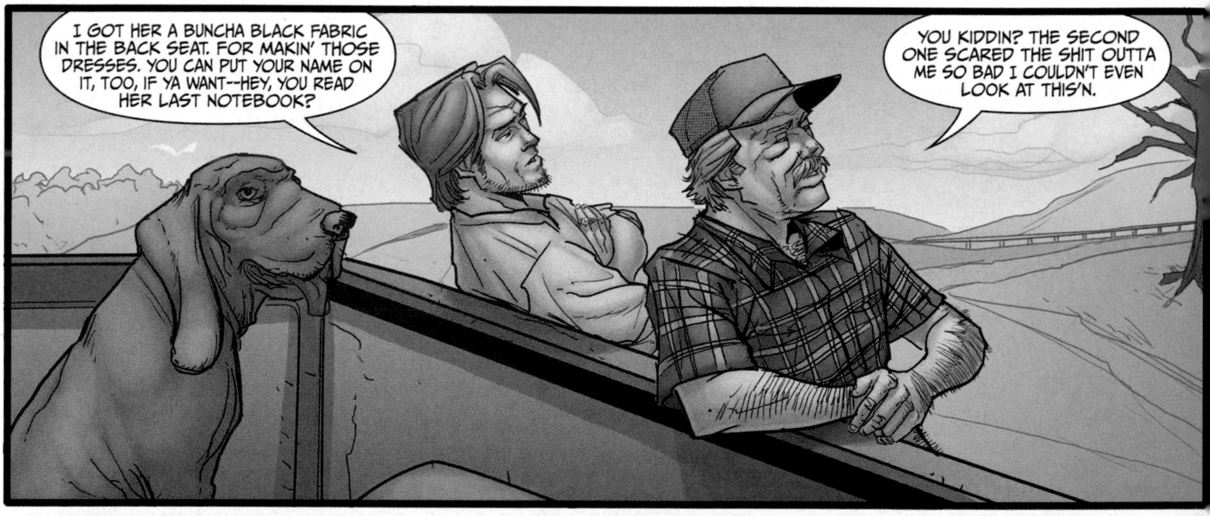
I GOT HER A BUNCHA BLACK FABRIC IN THE BACK SEAT. FOR MAKIN' THOSE DRESSES. YOU CAN PUT YOUR NAME ON IT, TOO, IF YA WANT--HEY, YOU READ HER LAST NOTEBOOK?
YOU KIDDIN? THE SECOND ONE SCARED THE SHIT OUTTA ME SO BAD I COULDN'T EVEN LOOK AT THIS'N.

My father. my brother. They never understand. They're afraid to. They want to live in their small worlds full of nothings. I'm not like them. and now they send me away, to a prison. a prison without marcus. Will I find others like me? Maybe. One step farther in this journey into night.

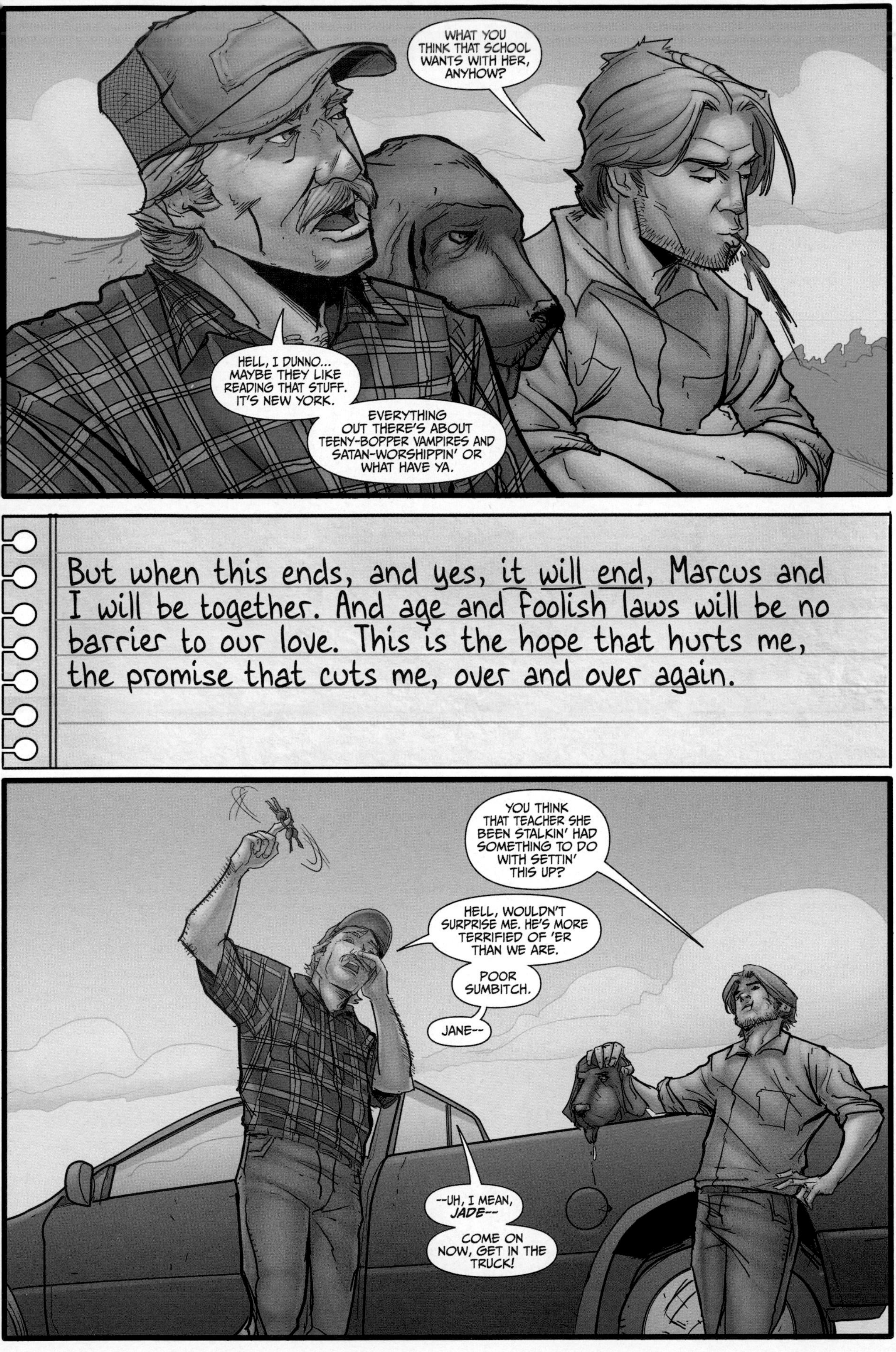
WHAT YOU THINK THAT SCHOOL WANTS WITH HER, ANYHOW?
HELL, I DUNNO... MAYBE THEY LIKE READING THAT STUFF. IT'S NEW YORK.
EVERYTHING OUT THERE'S ABOUT TEENY-BOPPER VAMPIRES AND SATAN-WORSHIPPIN' OR WHAT HAVE YA.
But when this ends, and yes, it will end, Marcus and I will be together. And age and foolish laws will be no barrier to our love. This is the hope that hurts me, the promise that cuts me, over and over again.
YOU THINK THAT TEACHER SHE BEEN STALKIN' HAD SOMETHING TO DO WITH SETTIN' THIS UP?
HELL, WOULDN'T SURPRISE ME. HE'S MORE TERRIFIED OF 'ER THAN WE ARE.
POOR SUMBITCH.
JANE--
--UH, I MEAN, JADE--
COME ON NOW, GET IN THE TRUCK!

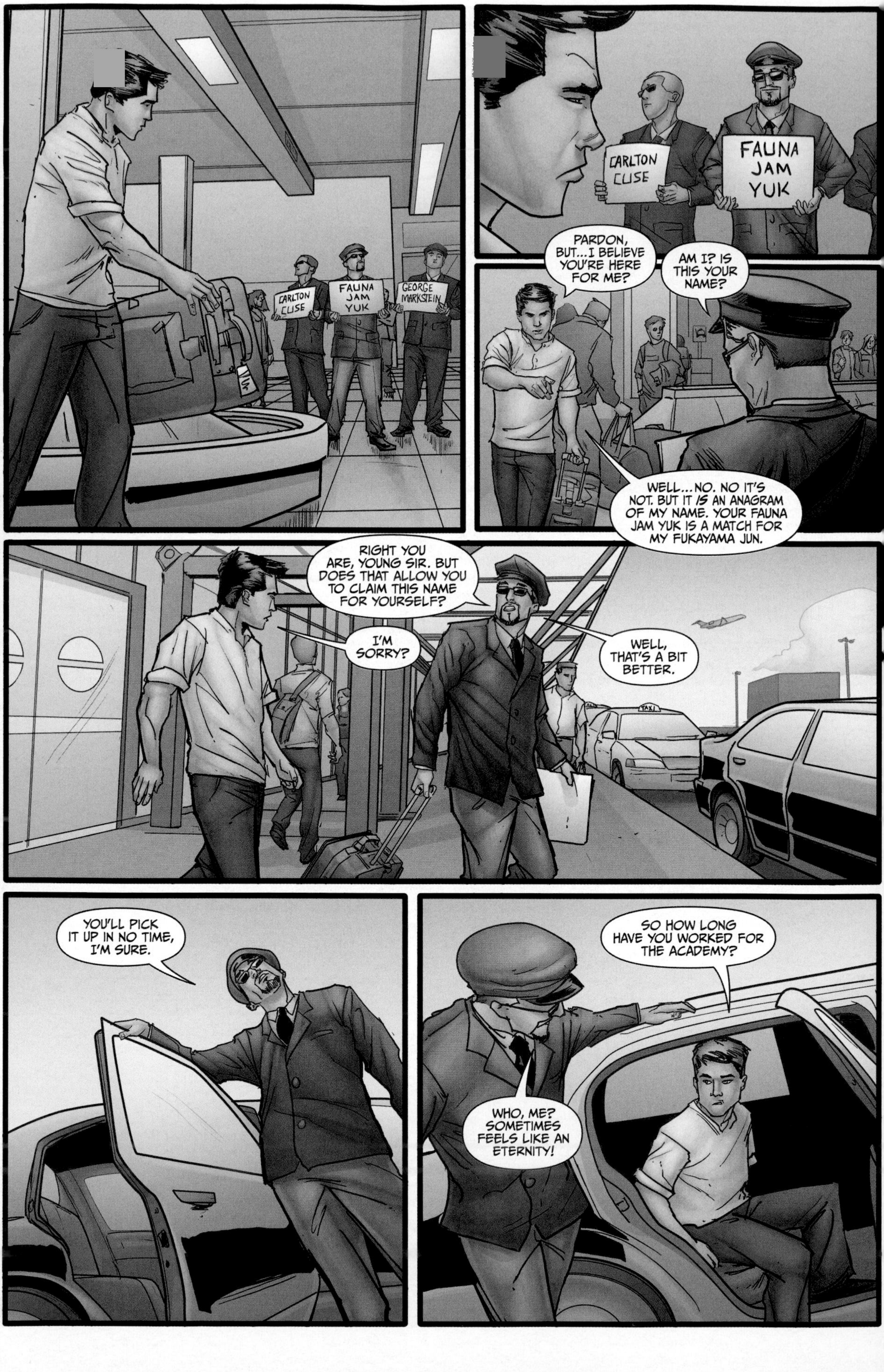
CARLTON CUSE
FAUNA JAM YUK
GEORGE MARKSTEIN
CARLTON CUSE
FAUNA JAM YUK
PARDON, BUT...I BELIEVE YOU'RE HERE FOR ME?
AM I? IS THIS YOUR NAME?
WELL...NO. NO IT'S NOT. BUT IT *IS* AN ANAGRAM OF MY NAME. YOUR FAUNA JAM YUK IS A MATCH FOR MY FUKAYAMA JUN.
RIGHT YOU ARE, YOUNG SIR. BUT DOES THAT ALLOW YOU TO CLAIM THIS NAME FOR YOURSELF?
I'M SORRY?
WELL, THAT'S A BIT BETTER.
TAXI
YOU'LL PICK IT UP IN NO TIME, I'M SURE.
SO HOW LONG HAVE YOU WORKED FOR THE ACADEMY?
WHO, ME? SOMETIMES FEELS LIKE AN ETERNITY!

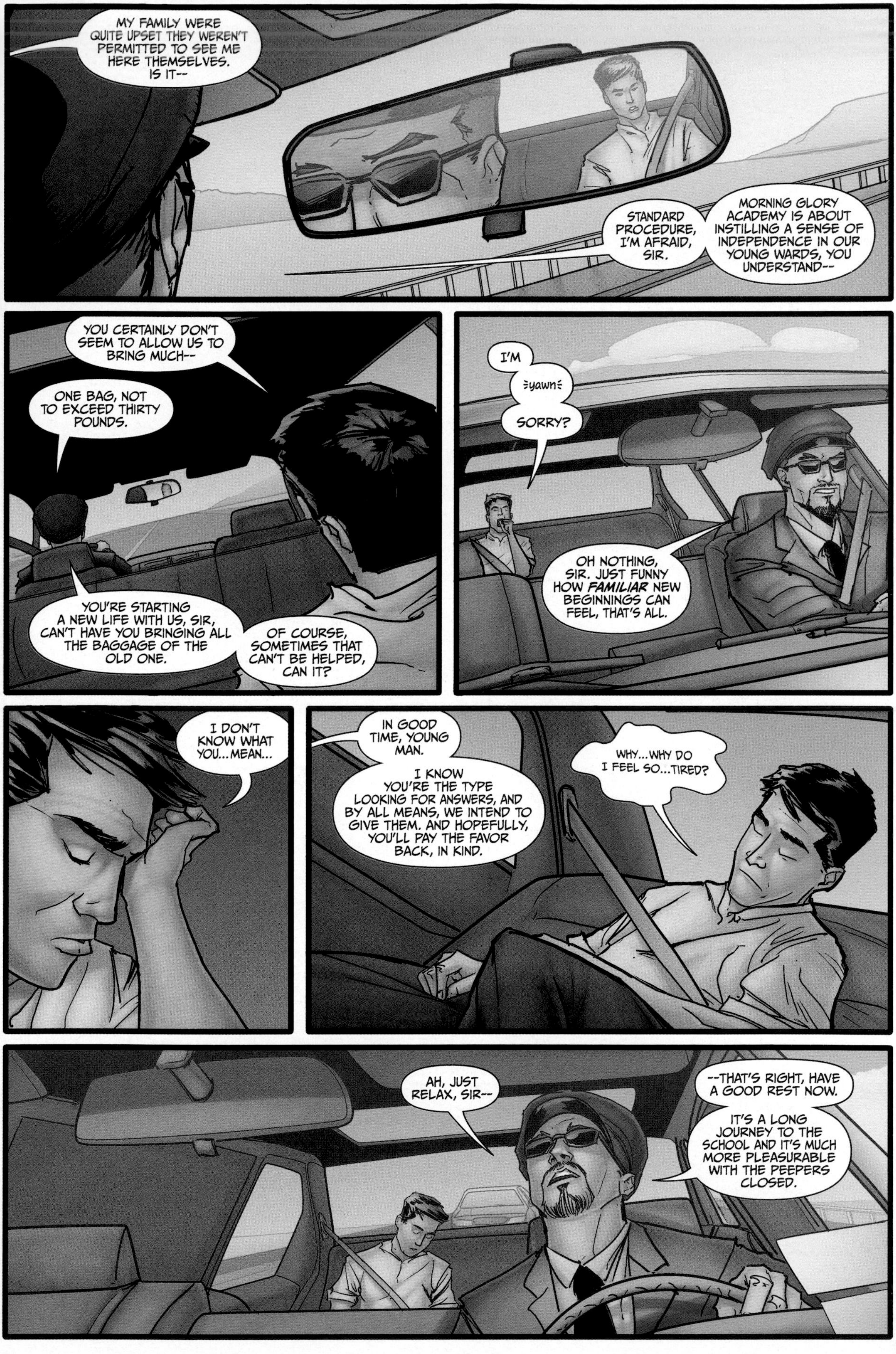
MY FAMILY WERE QUITE UPSET THEY WEREN'T PERMITTED TO SEE ME HERE THEMSELVES. IS IT--
STANDARD PROCEDURE, I'M AFRAID, SIR.
MORNING GLORY ACADEMY IS ABOUT INSTILLING A SENSE OF INDEPENDENCE IN OUR YOUNG WARDS, YOU UNDERSTAND--
YOU CERTAINLY DON'T SEEM TO ALLOW US TO BRING MUCH--
ONE BAG, NOT TO EXCEED THIRTY POUNDS.
YOU'RE STARTING A NEW LIFE WITH US, SIR, CAN'T HAVE YOU BRINGING ALL THE BAGGAGE OF THE OLD ONE.
OF COURSE, SOMETIMES THAT CAN'T BE HELPED, CAN IT?
I'M
yawn
SORRY?
OH NOTHING, SIR. JUST FUNNY HOW *FAMILIAR* NEW BEGINNINGS CAN FEEL, THAT'S ALL.
I DON'T KNOW WHAT YOU...MEAN...
IN GOOD TIME, YOUNG MAN.
I KNOW YOU'RE THE TYPE LOOKING FOR ANSWERS, AND BY ALL MEANS, WE INTEND TO GIVE THEM. AND HOPEFULLY, YOU'LL PAY THE FAVOR BACK, IN KIND.
WHY...WHY DO I FEEL SO...TIRED?
AH, JUST RELAX, SIR--
--THAT'S RIGHT, HAVE A GOOD REST NOW.
IT'S A LONG JOURNEY TO THE SCHOOL AND IT'S MUCH MORE PLEASURABLE WITH THE PEEPERS CLOSED.

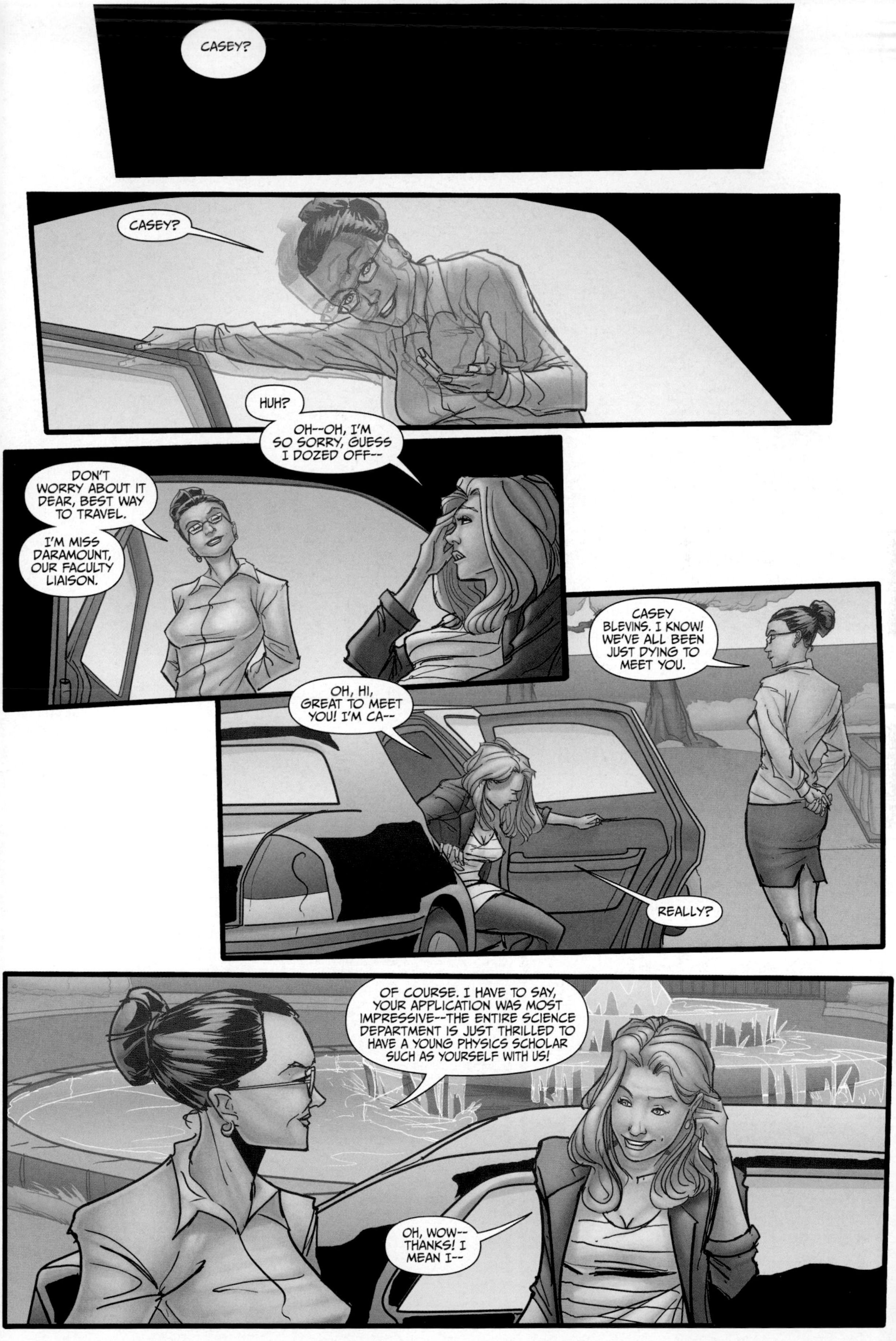

CASEY?
CASEY?
HUH?
OH--OH, I'M SO SORRY, GUESS I DOZED OFF--
DON'T WORRY ABOUT IT DEAR, BEST WAY TO TRAVEL.
I'M MISS DARAMOUNT, OUR FACULTY LIAISON.
OH, HI, GREAT TO MEET YOU! I'M CA--
CASEY BLEVINS. I KNOW! WE'VE ALL BEEN JUST DYING TO MEET YOU.
REALLY?
OF COURSE. I HAVE TO SAY, YOUR APPLICATION WAS MOST IMPRESSIVE--THE ENTIRE SCIENCE DEPARTMENT IS JUST THRILLED TO HAVE A YOUNG PHYSICS SCHOLAR SUCH AS YOURSELF WITH US!
OH, WOW-- THANKS! I MEAN I--

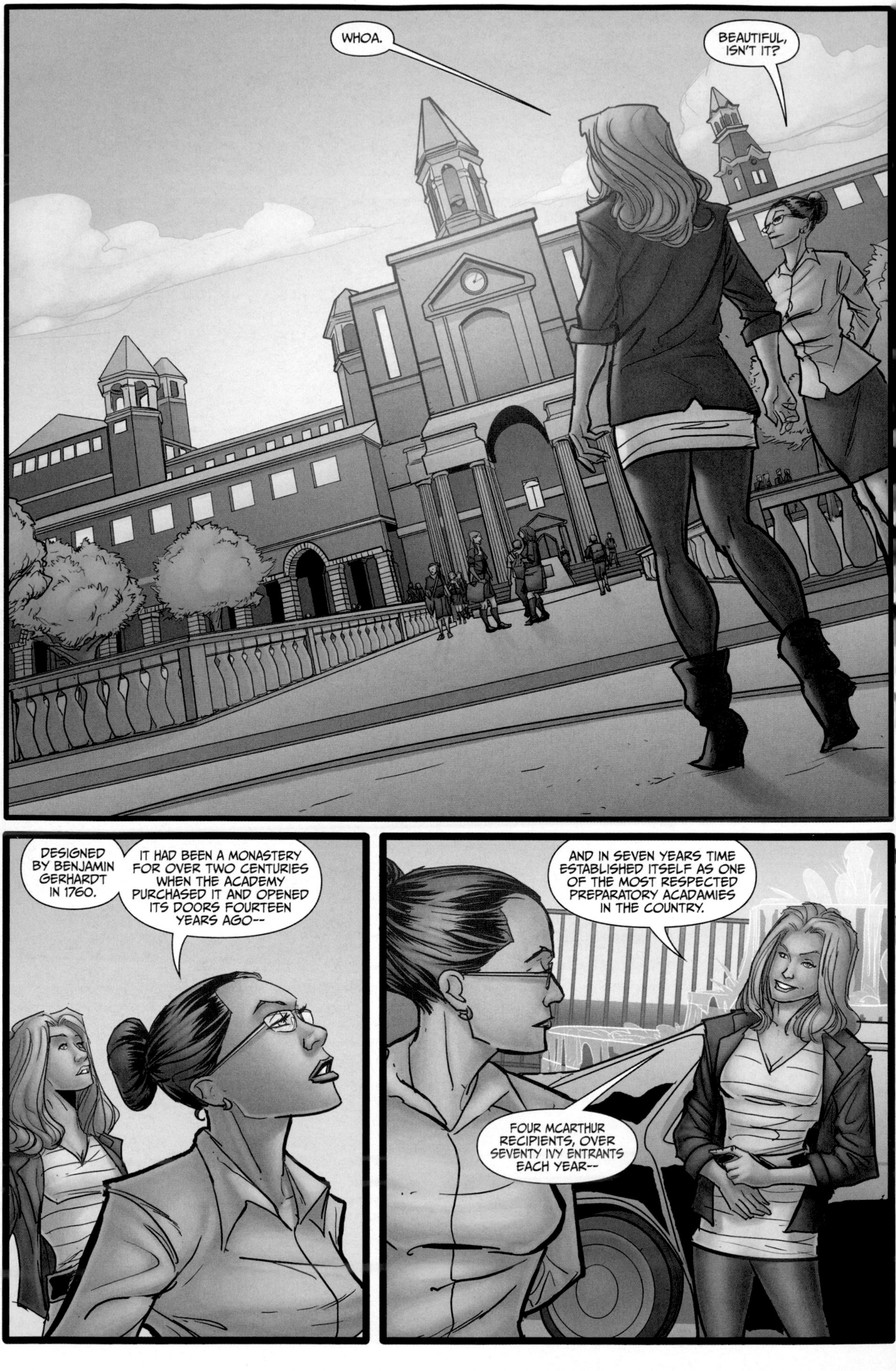
WHOA.
BEAUTIFUL, ISN'T IT?
DESIGNED BY BENJAMIN GERHARDT IN 1760.
IT HAD BEEN A MONASTERY FOR OVER TWO CENTURIES WHEN THE ACADEMY PURCHASED IT AND OPENED ITS DOORS FOURTEEN YEARS AGO--
AND IN SEVEN YEARS TIME ESTABLISHED ITSELF AS ONE OF THE MOST RESPECTED PREPARATORY ACADAMIES IN THE COUNTRY.
FOUR MCARTHUR RECIPIENTS, OVER SEVENTY IVY ENTRANTS EACH YEAR--

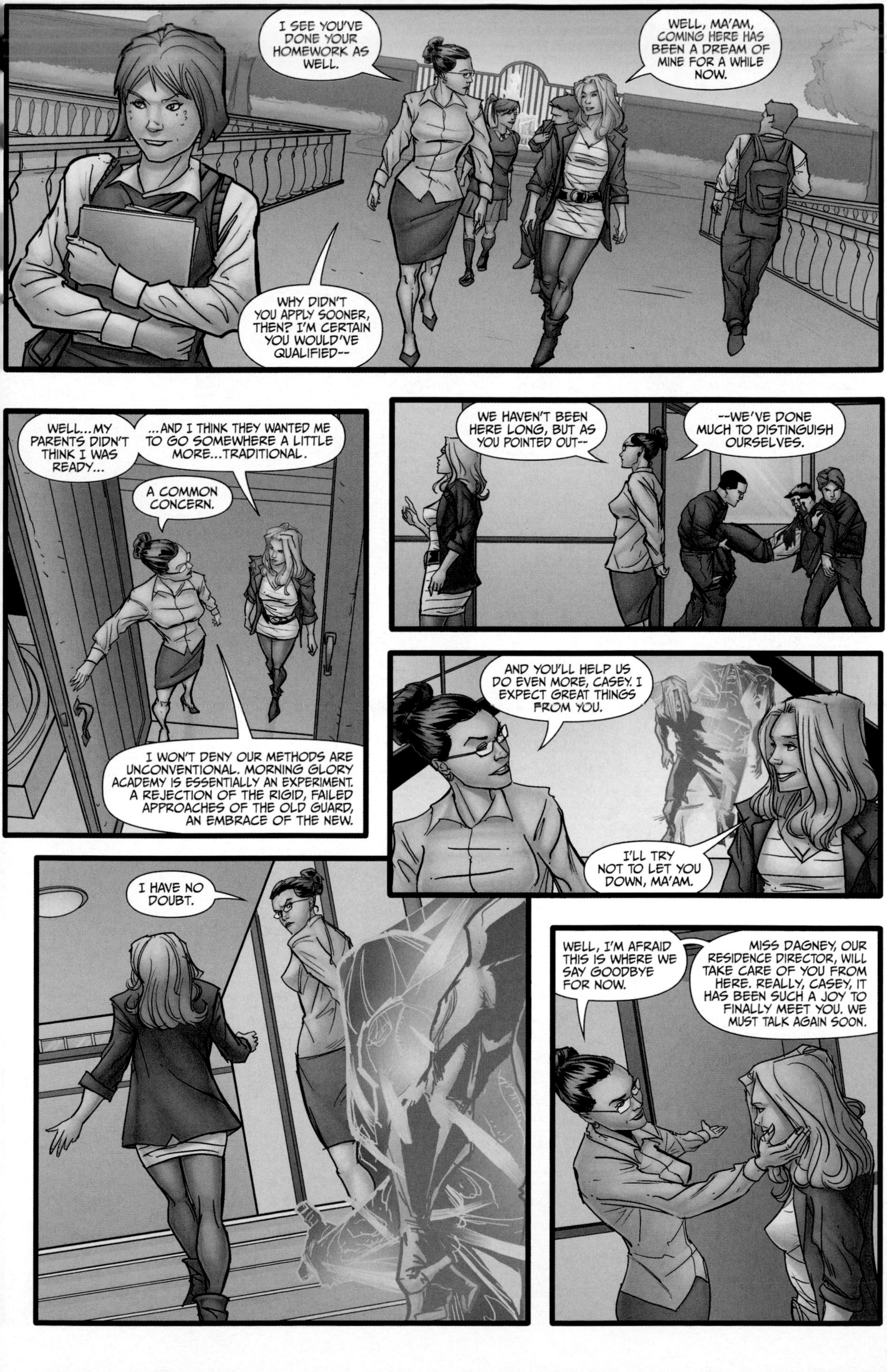
I SEE YOU'VE DONE YOUR HOMEWORK AS WELL.
WELL, MA'AM, COMING HERE HAS BEEN A DREAM OF MINE FOR A WHILE NOW.
WHY DIDN'T YOU APPLY SOONER, THEN? I'M CERTAIN YOU WOULD'VE QUALIFIED--
WELL...MY PARENTS DIDN'T THINK I WAS READY...
...AND I THINK THEY WANTED ME TO GO SOMEWHERE A LITTLE MORE...TRADITIONAL.
A COMMON CONCERN.
I WON'T DENY OUR METHODS ARE UNCONVENTIONAL. MORNING GLORY ACADEMY IS ESSENTIALLY AN EXPERIMENT. A REJECTION OF THE RIGID, FAILED APPROACHES OF THE OLD GUARD, AN EMBRACE OF THE NEW.
WE HAVEN'T BEEN HERE LONG, BUT AS YOU POINTED OUT--
--WE'VE DONE MUCH TO DISTINGUISH OURSELVES.
AND YOU'LL HELP US DO EVEN MORE, CASEY. I EXPECT GREAT THINGS FROM YOU.
I'LL TRY NOT TO LET YOU DOWN, MA'AM.
I HAVE NO DOUBT.
WELL, I'M AFRAID THIS IS WHERE WE SAY GOODBYE FOR NOW.
MISS DAGNEY, OUR RESIDENCE DIRECTOR, WILL TAKE CARE OF YOU FROM HERE. REALLY, CASEY, IT HAS BEEN SUCH A JOY TO FINALLY MEET YOU. WE MUST TALK AGAIN SOON.

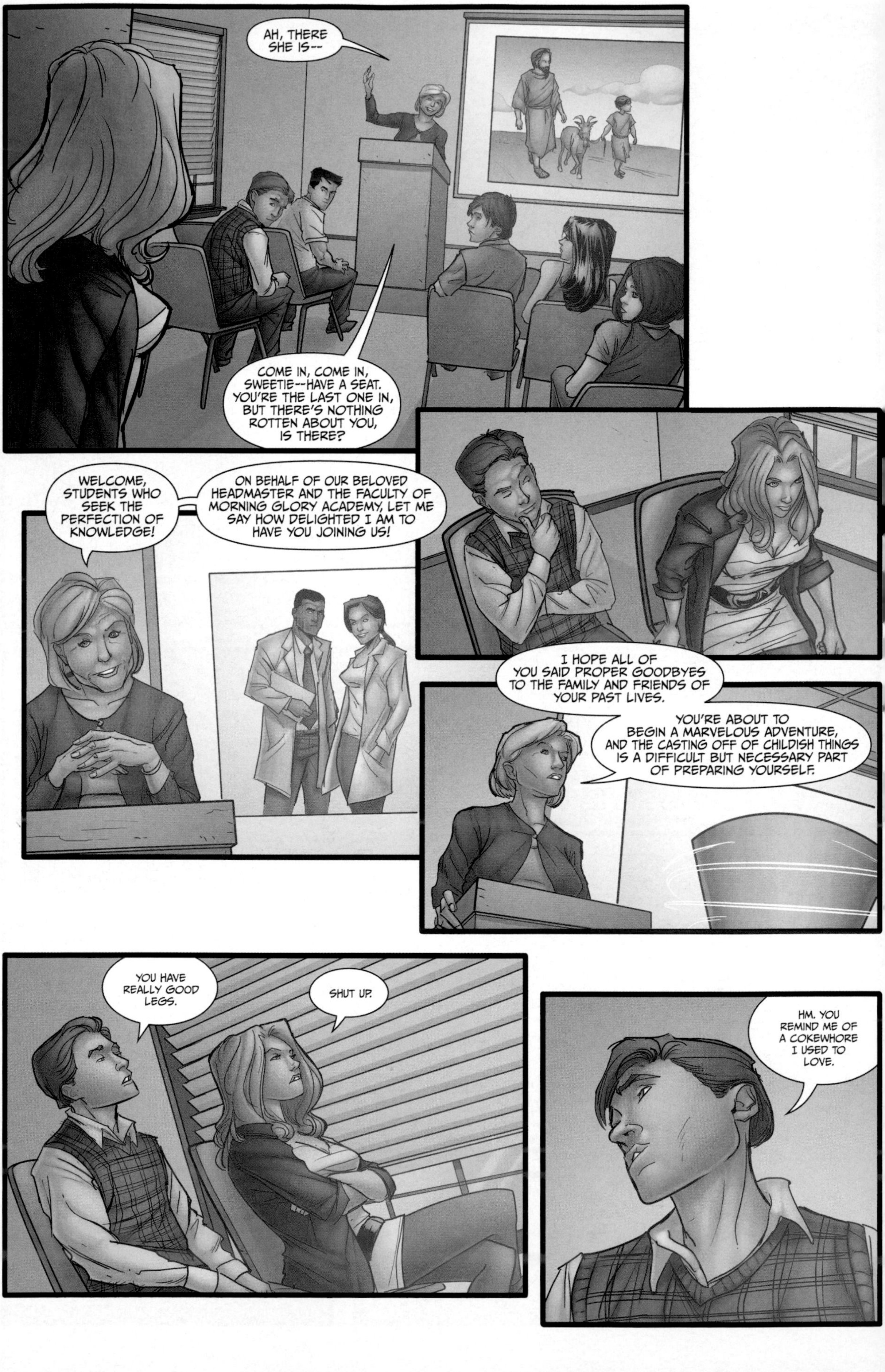
AH, THERE SHE IS--
COME IN, COME IN, SWEETIE--HAVE A SEAT. YOU'RE THE LAST ONE IN, BUT THERE'S NOTHING ROTTEN ABOUT YOU, IS THERE?
WELCOME, STUDENTS WHO SEEK THE PERFECTION OF KNOWLEDGE!
ON BEHALF OF OUR BELOVED HEADMASTER AND THE FACULTY OF MORNING GLORY ACADEMY, LET ME SAY HOW DELIGHTED I AM TO HAVE YOU JOINING US!
I HOPE ALL OF YOU SAID PROPER GOODBYES TO THE FAMILY AND FRIENDS OF YOUR PAST LIVES.
YOU'RE ABOUT TO BEGIN A MARVELOUS ADVENTURE, AND THE CASTING OFF OF CHILDISH THINGS IS A DIFFICULT BUT NECESSARY PART OF PREPARING YOURSELF.
YOU HAVE REALLY GOOD LEGS.
SHUT UP.
HM. YOU REMIND ME OF A COKEWHORE I USED TO LOVE.

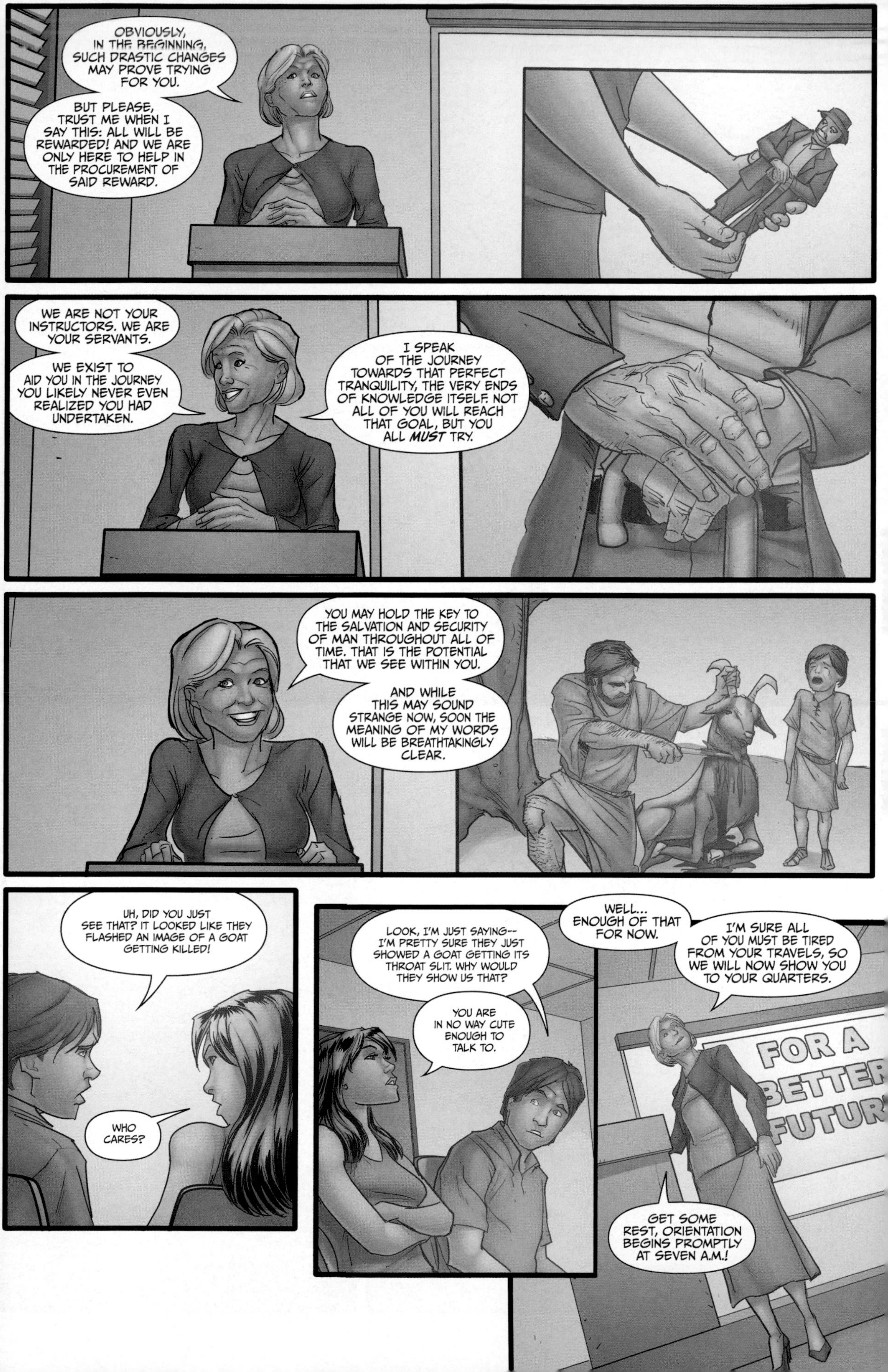
OBVIOUSLY, IN THE BEGINNING, SUCH DRASTIC CHANGES MAY PROVE TRYING FOR YOU.
BUT PLEASE, TRUST ME WHEN I SAY THIS: ALL WILL BE REWARDED! AND WE ARE ONLY HERE TO HELP IN THE PROCUREMENT OF SAID REWARD.
WE ARE NOT YOUR INSTRUCTORS. WE ARE YOUR SERVANTS.
WE EXIST TO AID YOU IN THE JOURNEY YOU LIKELY NEVER EVEN REALIZED YOU HAD UNDERTAKEN.
I SPEAK OF THE JOURNEY TOWARDS THAT PERFECT TRANQUILITY, THE VERY ENDS OF KNOWLEDGE ITSELF. NOT ALL OF YOU WILL REACH THAT GOAL, BUT YOU ALL *MUST* TRY.
YOU MAY HOLD THE KEY TO THE SALVATION AND SECURITY OF MAN THROUGHOUT ALL OF TIME. THAT IS THE POTENTIAL THAT WE SEE WITHIN YOU.
AND WHILE THIS MAY SOUND STRANGE NOW, SOON THE MEANING OF MY WORDS WILL BE BREATHTAKINGLY CLEAR.
UH, DID YOU JUST SEE THAT? IT LOOKED LIKE THEY FLASHED AN IMAGE OF A GOAT GETTING KILLED!
WHO CARES?
LOOK, I'M JUST SAYING-- I'M PRETTY SURE THEY JUST SHOWED A GOAT GETTING ITS THROAT SLIT. WHY WOULD THEY SHOW US THAT?
YOU ARE IN NO WAY CUTE ENOUGH TO TALK TO.
WELL... ENOUGH OF THAT FOR NOW.
I'M SURE ALL OF YOU MUST BE TIRED FROM YOUR TRAVELS, SO WE WILL NOW SHOW YOU TO YOUR QUARTERS.
FOR A BETTER FUTUR
GET SOME REST, ORIENTATION BEGINS PROMPTLY AT SEVEN A.M.!

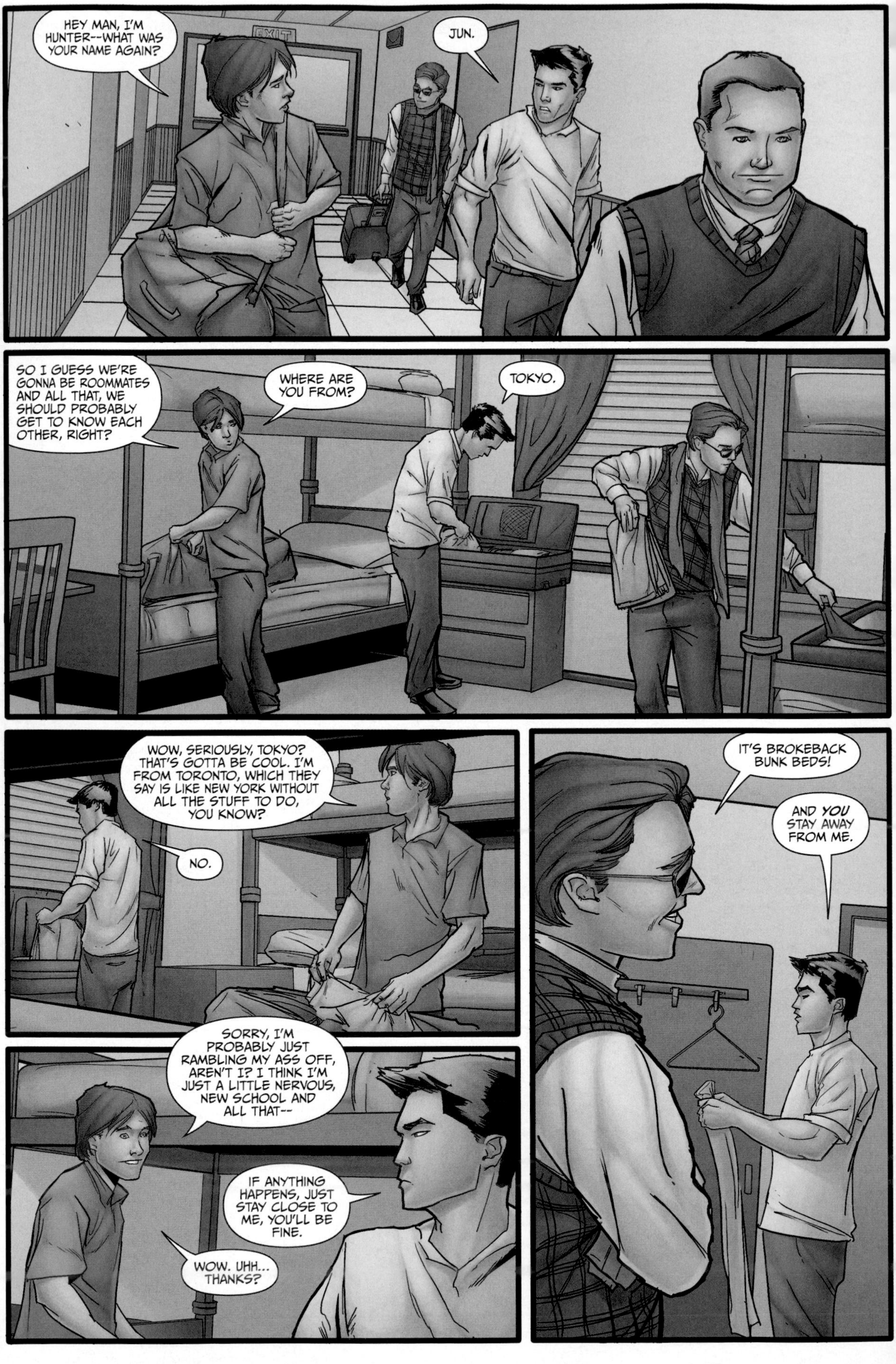
HEY MAN, I'M HUNTER--WHAT WAS YOUR NAME AGAIN?
JUN.
SO I GUESS WE'RE GONNA BE ROOMMATES AND ALL THAT, WE SHOULD PROBABLY GET TO KNOW EACH OTHER, RIGHT?
WHERE ARE YOU FROM?
TOKYO.
WOW, SERIOUSLY, TOKYO? THAT'S GOTTA BE COOL. I'M FROM TORONTO, WHICH THEY SAY IS LIKE NEW YORK WITHOUT ALL THE STUFF TO DO, YOU KNOW?
NO.
SORRY, I'M PROBABLY JUST RAMBLING MY ASS OFF, AREN'T I? I THINK I'M JUST A LITTLE NERVOUS, NEW SCHOOL AND ALL THAT--
IF ANYTHING HAPPENS, JUST STAY CLOSE TO ME, YOU'LL BE FINE.
WOW. UHH... THANKS?
IT'S BROKEBACK BUNK BEDS!
AND *YOU* STAY AWAY FROM ME.

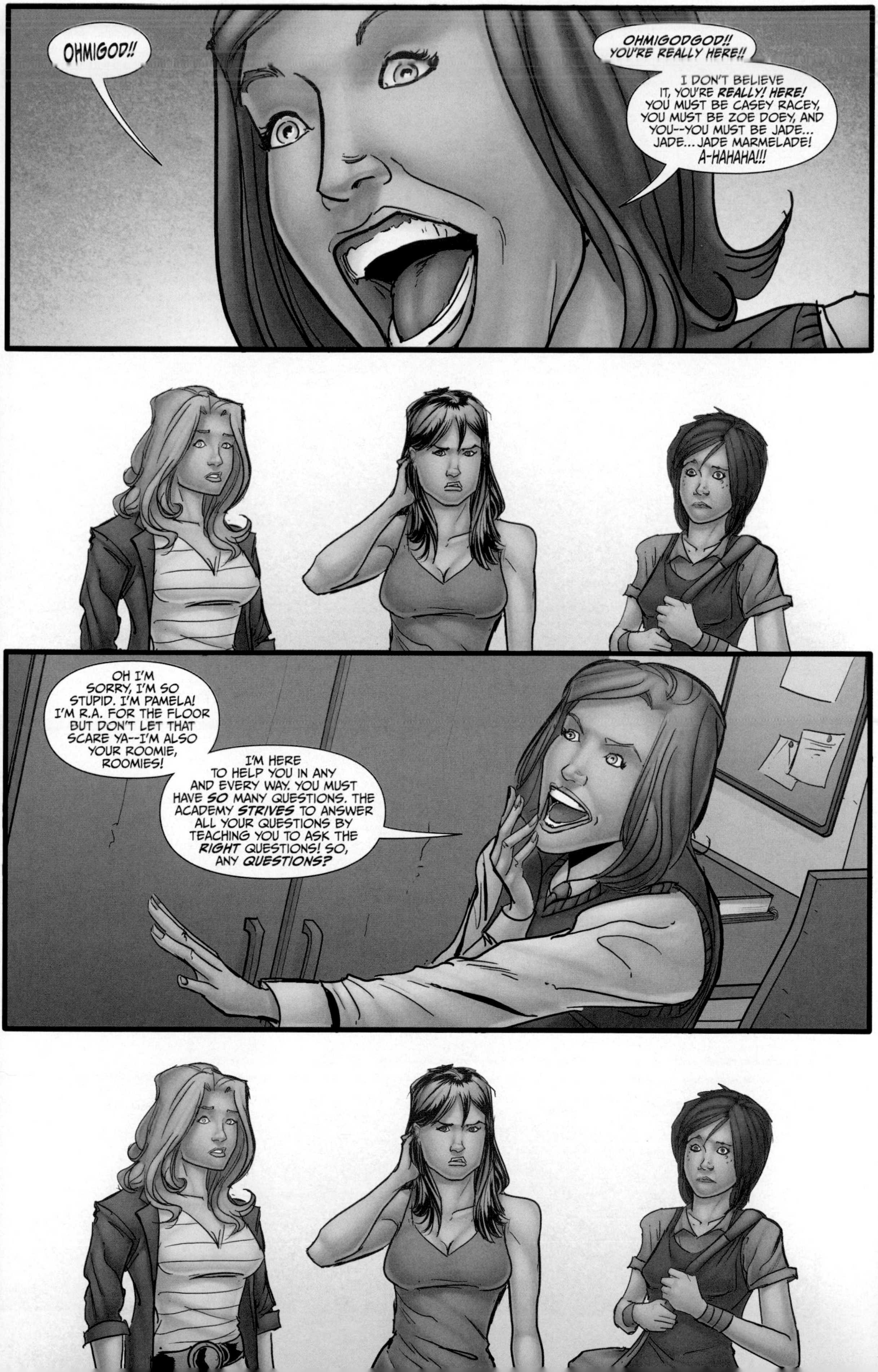
OHMIGOD!!
OHMIGODGOD!! YOU'RE REALLY HERE!!
I DON'T BELIEVE IT, YOU'RE REALLY! HERE! YOU MUST BE CASEY RACEY, YOU MUST BE ZOE DOEY, AND YOU--YOU MUST BE JADE... JADE... JADE MARMELADE! A-HAHAHA!!!
OH I'M SORRY, I'M SO STUPID. I'M PAMELA! I'M R.A. FOR THE FLOOR BUT DON'T LET THAT SCARE YA--I'M ALSO YOUR ROOMIE, ROOMIES!
I'M HERE TO HELP YOU IN ANY AND EVERY WAY. YOU MUST HAVE SO MANY QUESTIONS. THE ACADEMY STRIVES TO ANSWER ALL YOUR QUESTIONS BY TEACHING YOU TO ASK THE RIGHT QUESTIONS! SO, ANY QUESTIONS?

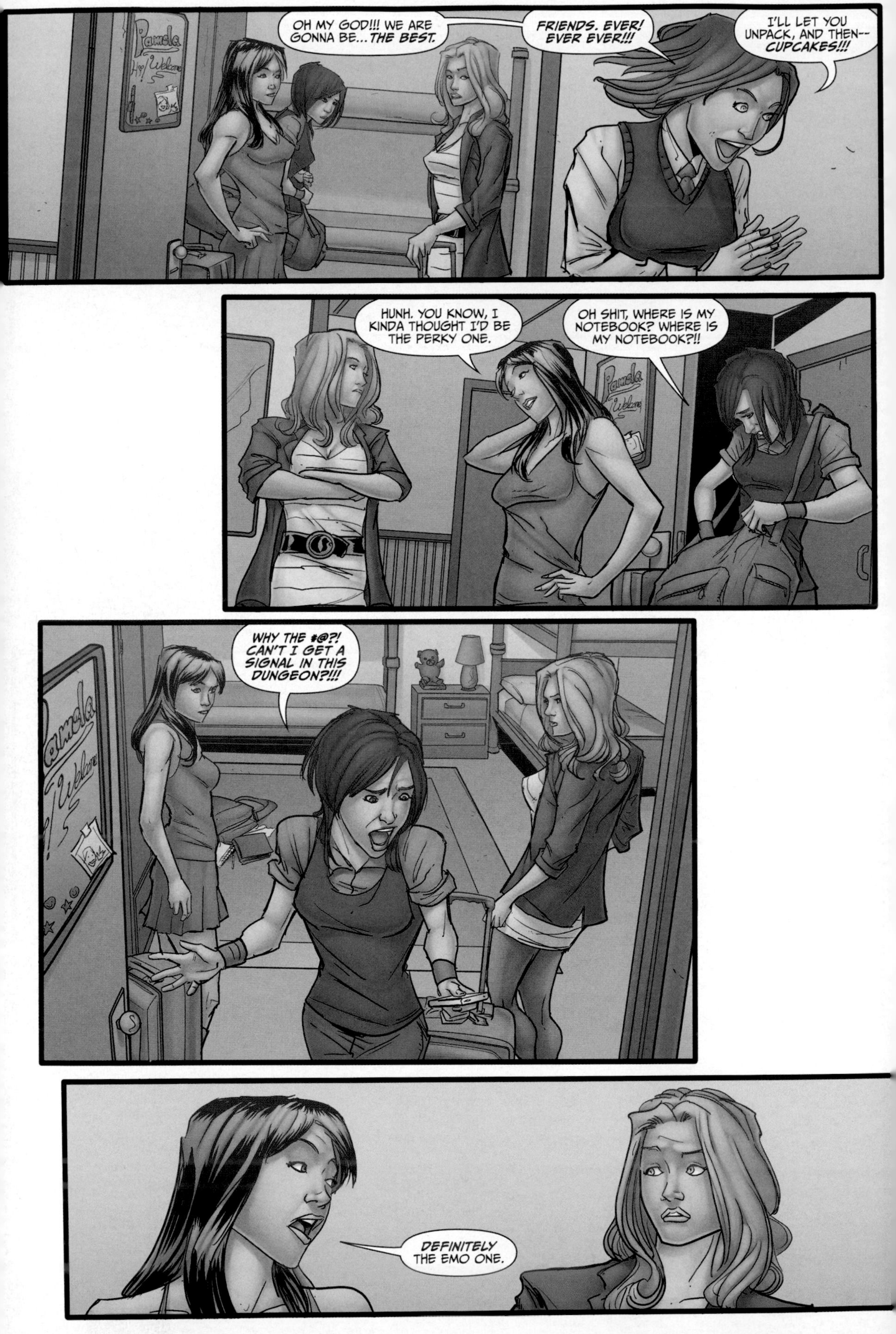
OH MY GOD!!! WE ARE GONNA BE... THE BEST.
FRIENDS. EVER! EVER EVER!!!
I'LL LET YOU UNPACK, AND THEN-- CUPCAKES!!!
HUNH. YOU KNOW, I KINDA THOUGHT I'D BE THE PERKY ONE.
OH SHIT, WHERE IS MY NOTEBOOK? WHERE IS MY NOTEBOOK?!!
WHY THE #@?! CAN'T I GET A SIGNAL IN THIS DUNGEON?!!!
DEFINITELY THE EMO ONE.

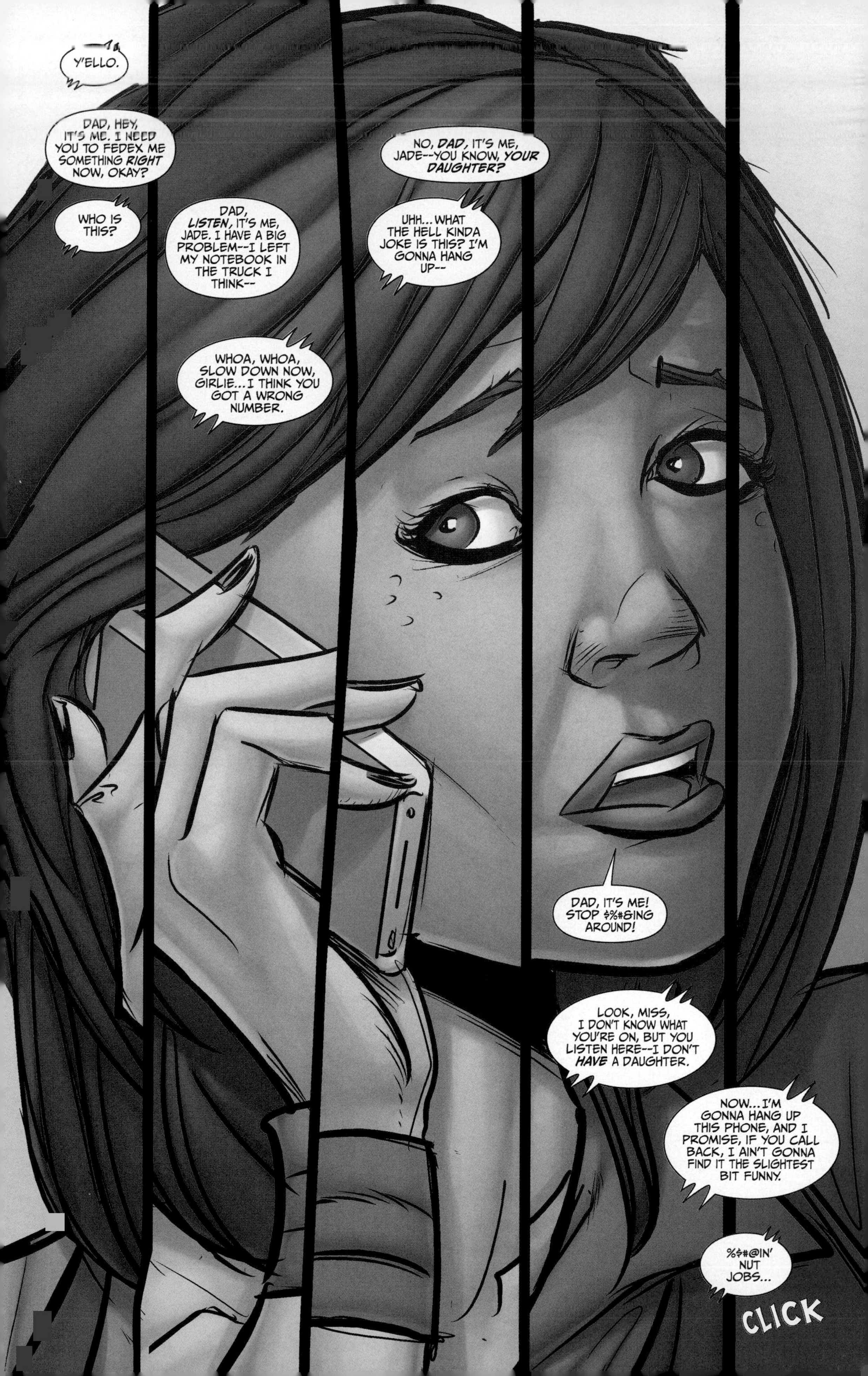
Y'ELLO.
DAD, HEY, IT'S ME. I NEED YOU TO FEDEX ME SOMETHING RIGHT NOW, OKAY?
WHO IS THIS?
DAD, LISTEN, IT'S ME, JADE. I HAVE A BIG PROBLEM--I LEFT MY NOTEBOOK IN THE TRUCK I THINK--
WHOA, WHOA, SLOW DOWN NOW, GIRLIE...I THINK YOU GOT A WRONG NUMBER.
NO, DAD, IT'S ME, JADE--YOU KNOW, YOUR DAUGHTER?
UHH...WHAT THE HELL KINDA JOKE IS THIS? I'M GONNA HANG UP--
DAD, IT'S ME! STOP $%#&ING AROUND!
LOOK, MISS, I DON'T KNOW WHAT YOU'RE ON, BUT YOU LISTEN HERE--I DON'T HAVE A DAUGHTER.
NOW...I'M GONNA HANG UP THIS PHONE, AND I PROMISE, IF YOU CALL BACK, I AIN'T GONNA FIND IT THE SLIGHTEST BIT FUNNY.
%$#@IN' NUT JOBS...
CLICK

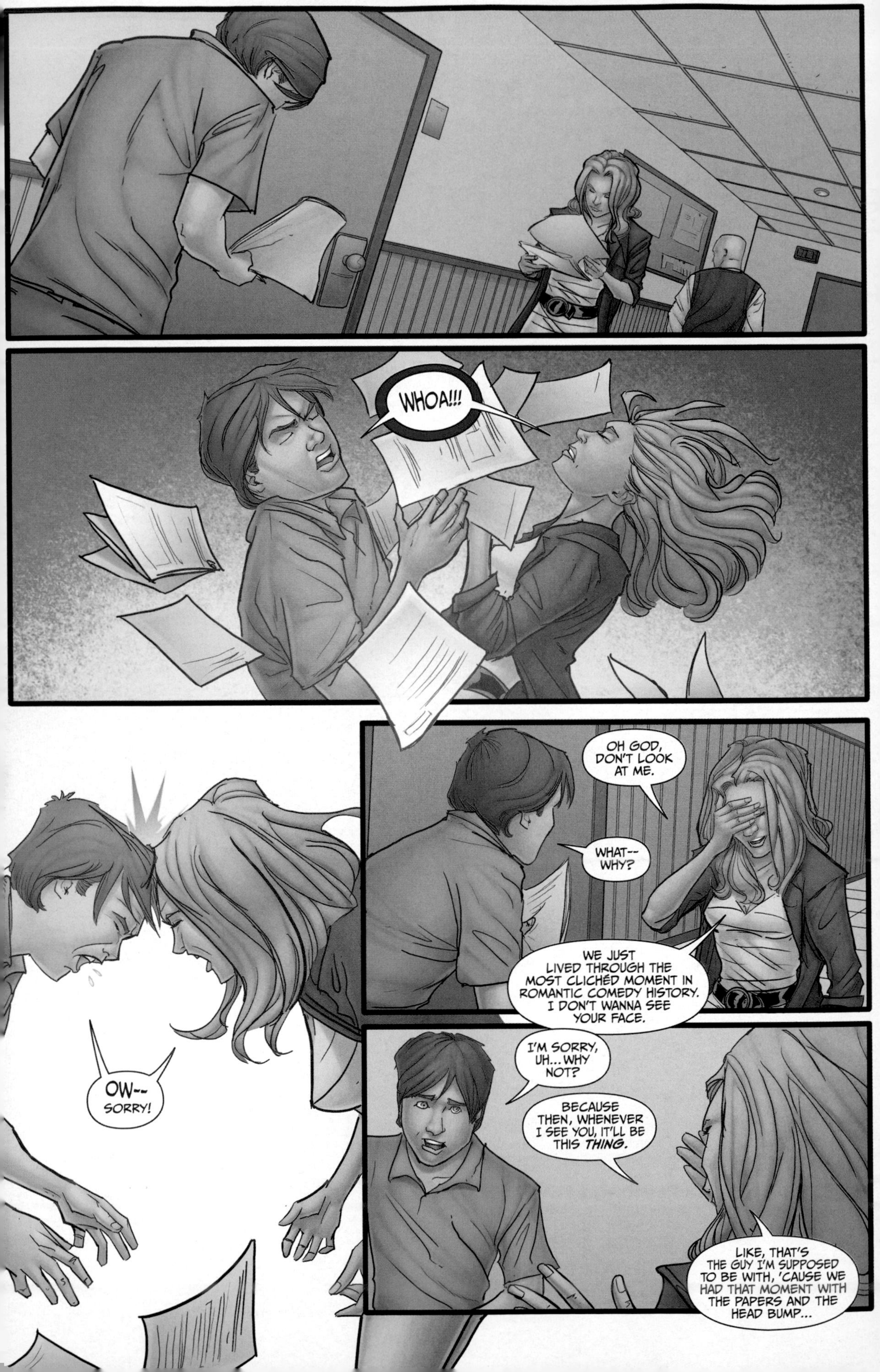
WHOA!!!
OW-- SORRY!
OH GOD, DON'T LOOK AT ME.
WHAT-- WHY?
WE JUST LIVED THROUGH THE MOST CLICHÉD MOMENT IN ROMANTIC COMEDY HISTORY. I DON'T WANNA SEE YOUR FACE.
I'M SORRY, UH... WHY NOT?
BECAUSE THEN, WHENEVER I SEE YOU, IT'LL BE THIS *THING.*
LIKE, THAT'S THE GUY I'M SUPPOSED TO BE WITH, 'CAUSE WE HAD THAT MOMENT WITH THE PAPERS AND THE HEAD BUMP...

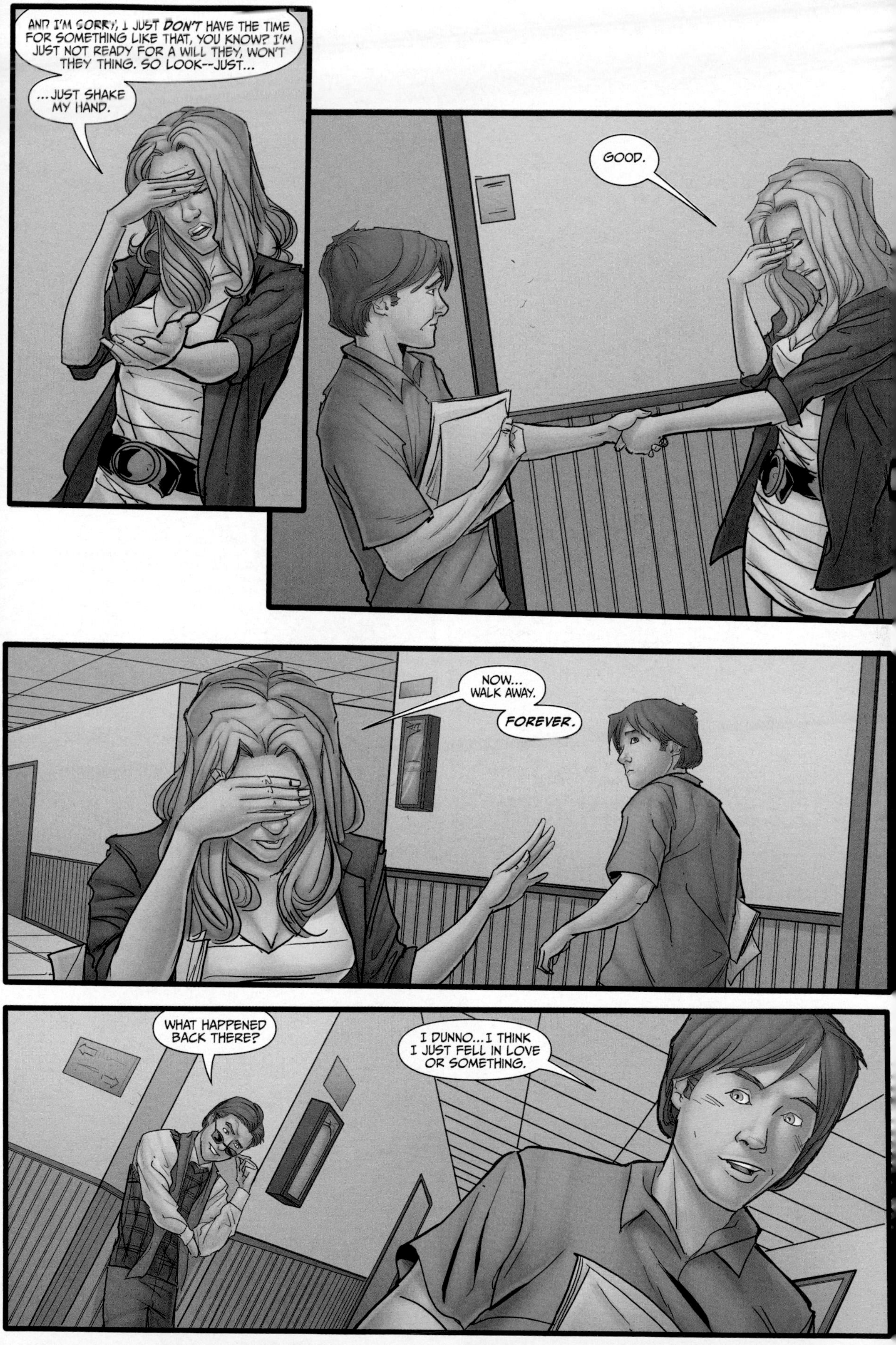
AND I'M SORRY, I JUST DON'T HAVE THE TIME FOR SOMETHING LIKE THAT, YOU KNOW? I'M JUST NOT READY FOR A WILL THEY, WON'T THEY THING. SO LOOK--JUST...
...JUST SHAKE MY HAND.
GOOD.
NOW... WALK AWAY.
FOREVER.
WHAT HAPPENED BACK THERE?
I DUNNO...I THINK I JUST FELL IN LOVE OR SOMETHING.

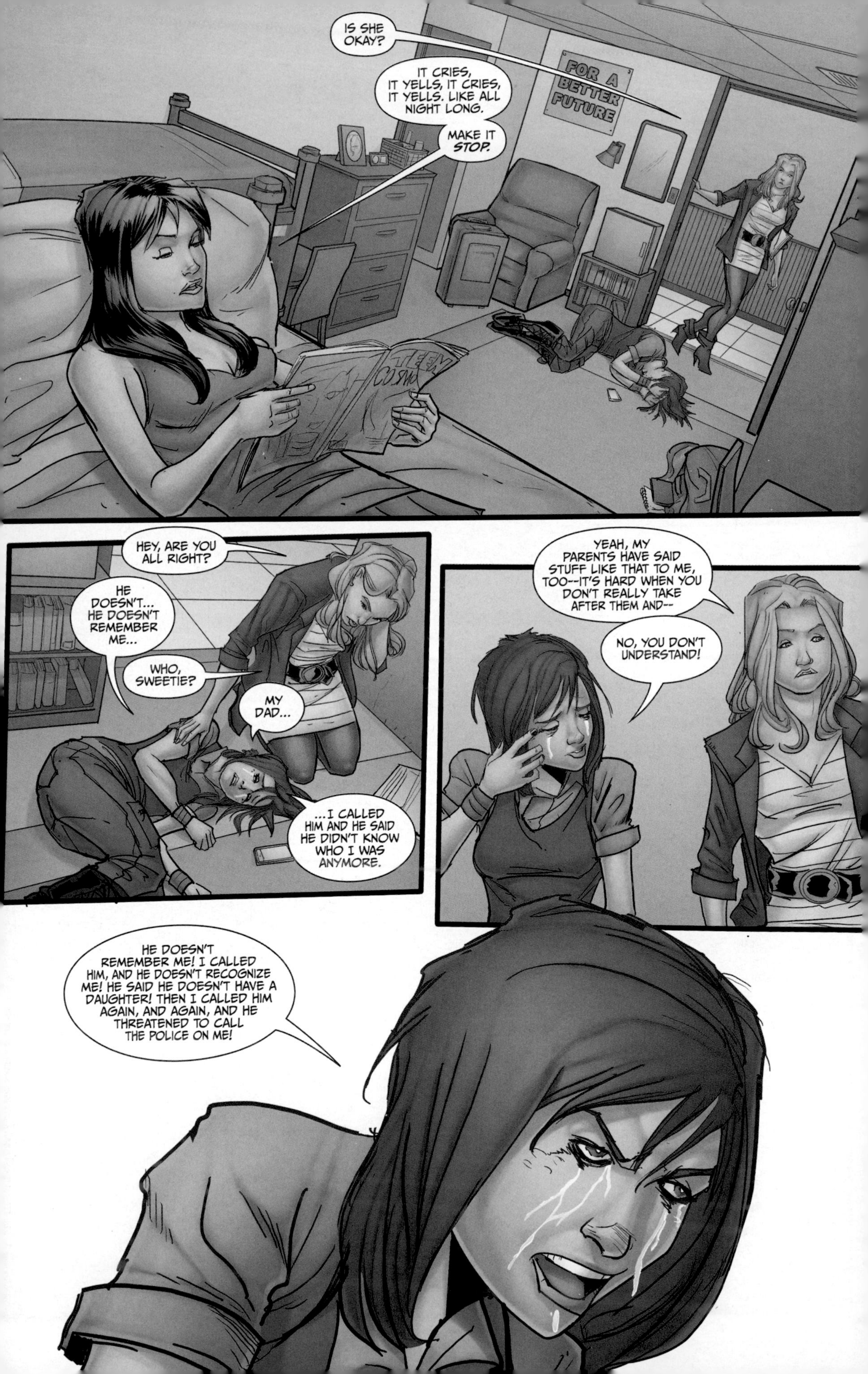
IS SHE OKAY?
IT CRIES, IT YELLS, IT CRIES, IT YELLS. LIKE ALL NIGHT LONG.
MAKE IT STOP.
FOR A BETTER FUTURE
TEEN COSMO
HEY, ARE YOU ALL RIGHT?
HE DOESN'T... HE DOESN'T REMEMBER ME...
WHO, SWEETIE?
MY DAD...
...I CALLED HIM AND HE SAID HE DIDN'T KNOW WHO I WAS ANYMORE.
YEAH, MY PARENTS HAVE SAID STUFF LIKE THAT TO ME, TOO--IT'S HARD WHEN YOU DON'T REALLY TAKE AFTER THEM AND--
NO, YOU DON'T UNDERSTAND!
HE DOESN'T REMEMBER ME! I CALLED HIM, AND HE DOESN'T RECOGNIZE ME! HE SAID HE DOESN'T HAVE A DAUGHTER! THEN I CALLED HIM AGAIN, AND AGAIN, AND HE THREATENED TO CALL THE POLICE ON ME!

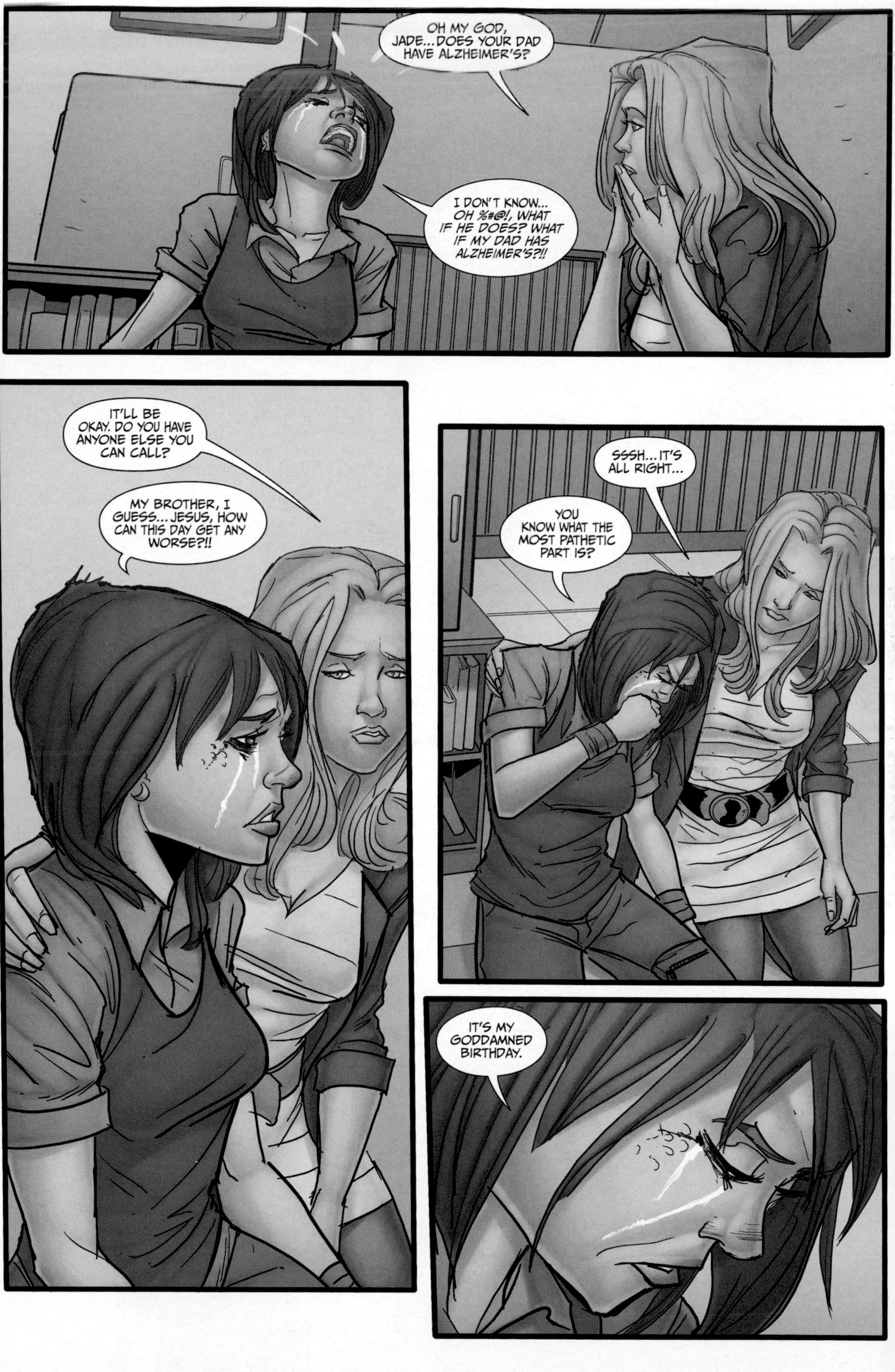
OH MY GOD, JADE... DOES YOUR DAD HAVE ALZHEIMER'S?
I DON'T KNOW... OH %#@!, WHAT IF HE DOES? WHAT IF MY DAD HAS ALZHEIMER'S?!!
IT'LL BE OKAY. DO YOU HAVE ANYONE ELSE YOU CAN CALL?
MY BROTHER, I GUESS... JESUS, HOW CAN THIS DAY GET ANY WORSE?!!
SSSH... IT'S ALL RIGHT...
YOU KNOW WHAT THE MOST PATHETIC PART IS?
IT'S MY GODDAMNED BIRTHDAY.

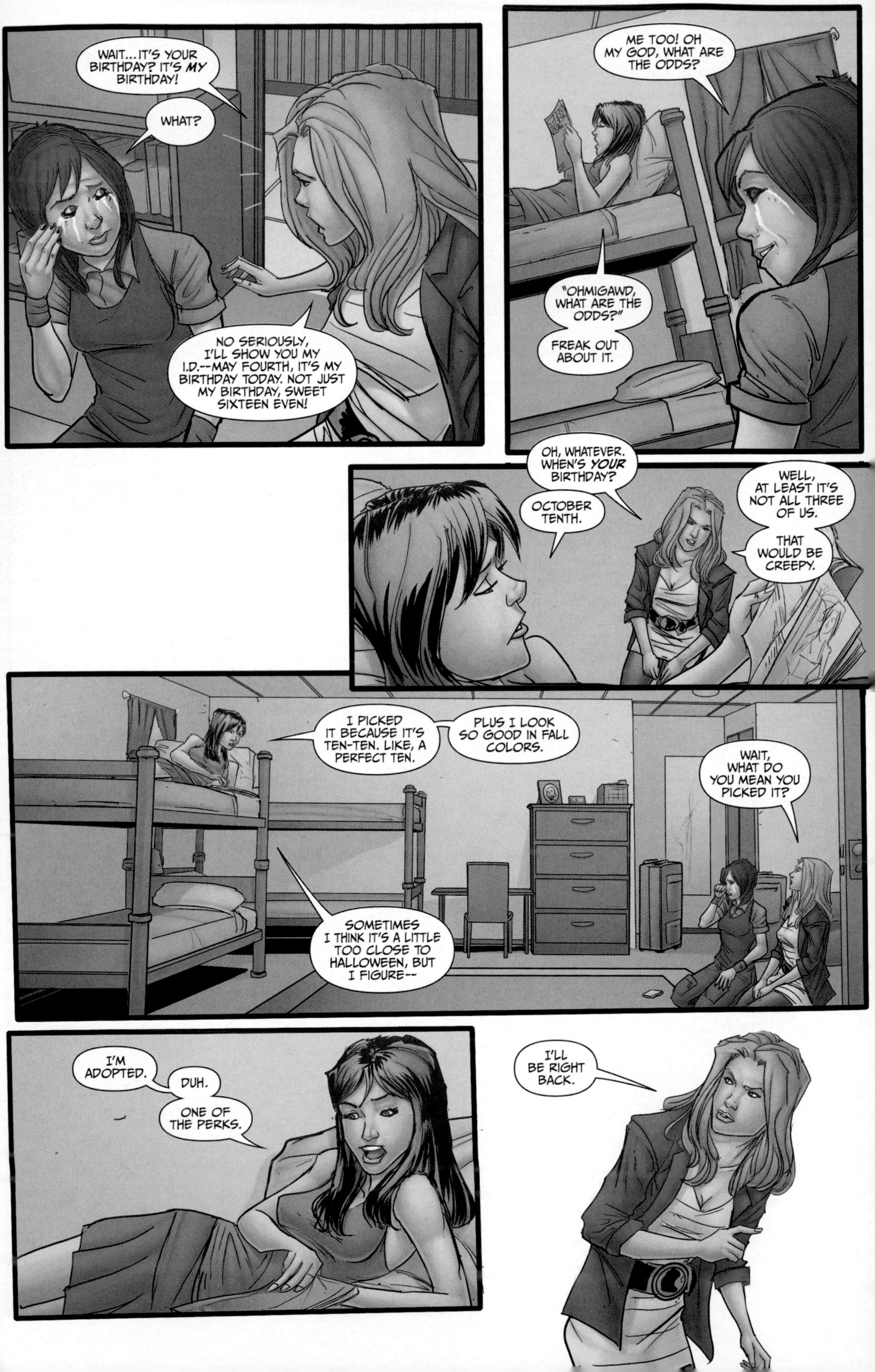
WAIT... IT'S YOUR BIRTHDAY? IT'S *MY* BIRTHDAY!
WHAT?
NO SERIOUSLY, I'LL SHOW YOU MY I.D.--MAY FOURTH, IT'S MY BIRTHDAY TODAY. NOT JUST MY BIRTHDAY, SWEET SIXTEEN EVEN!
ME TOO! OH MY GOD, WHAT ARE THE ODDS?
"OHMIGAWD, WHAT ARE THE ODDS?"
FREAK OUT ABOUT IT.
OH, WHATEVER. WHEN'S *YOUR* BIRTHDAY?
OCTOBER TENTH.
WELL, AT LEAST IT'S NOT ALL THREE OF US.
THAT WOULD BE CREEPY.
I PICKED IT BECAUSE IT'S TEN-TEN. LIKE, A PERFECT TEN.
PLUS I LOOK SO GOOD IN FALL COLORS.
WAIT, WHAT DO YOU MEAN YOU PICKED IT?
SOMETIMES I THINK IT'S A LITTLE TOO CLOSE TO HALLOWEEN, BUT I FIGURE--
I'M ADOPTED.
DUH.
ONE OF THE PERKS.
I'LL BE RIGHT BACK.

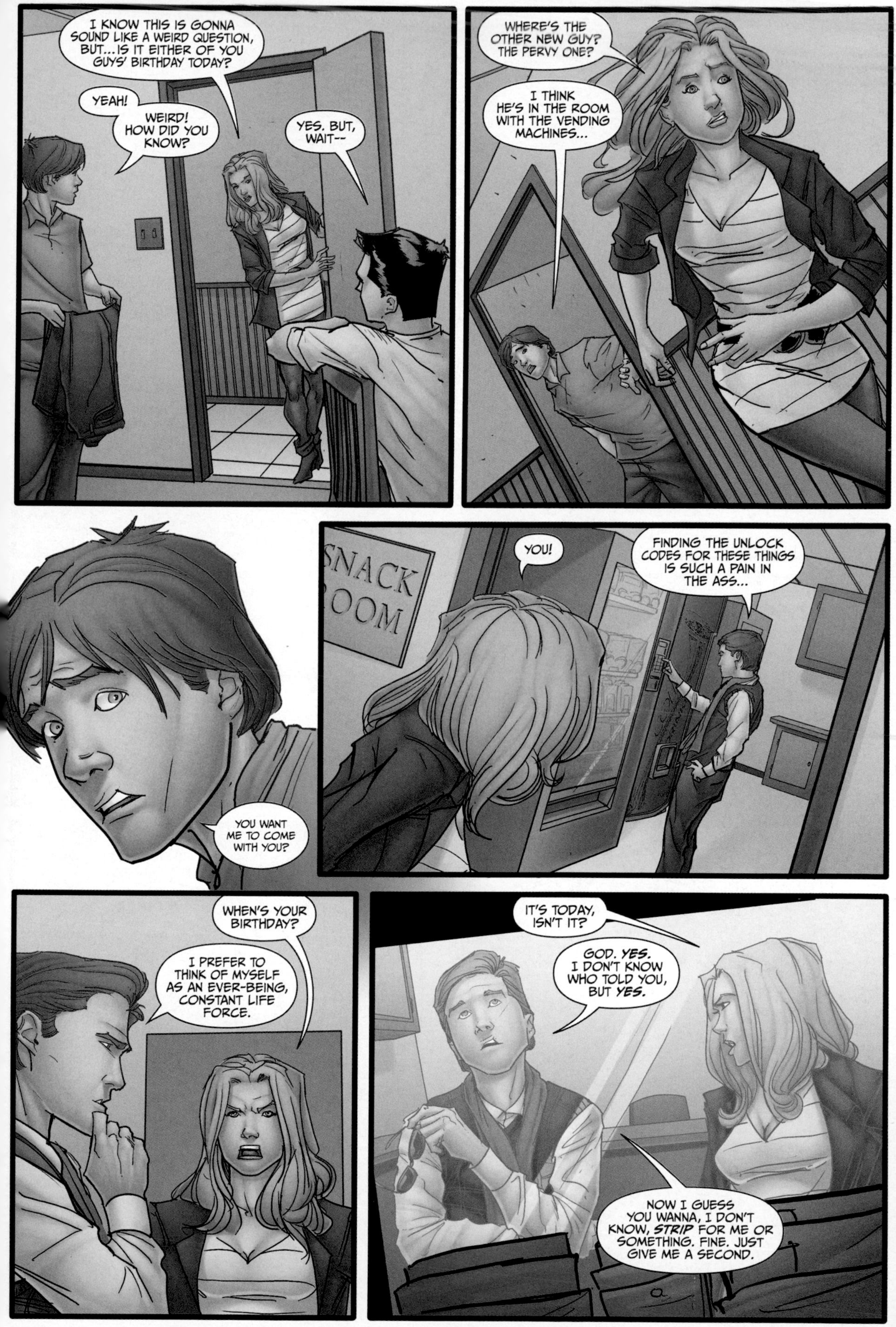
I KNOW THIS IS GONNA SOUND LIKE A WEIRD QUESTION, BUT...IS IT EITHER OF YOU GUYS' BIRTHDAY TODAY?
YEAH!
WEIRD! HOW DID YOU KNOW?
YES. BUT, WAIT--
WHERE'S THE OTHER NEW GUY? THE PERVY ONE?
I THINK HE'S IN THE ROOM WITH THE VENDING MACHINES...
YOU WANT ME TO COME WITH YOU?
SNACK ROOM
YOU!
FINDING THE UNLOCK CODES FOR THESE THINGS IS SUCH A PAIN IN THE ASS...
WHEN'S YOUR BIRTHDAY?
I PREFER TO THINK OF MYSELF AS AN EVER-BEING, CONSTANT LIFE FORCE.
IT'S TODAY, ISN'T IT?
GOD. ***YES.*** I DON'T KNOW WHO TOLD YOU, BUT ***YES.***
NOW I GUESS YOU WANNA, I DON'T KNOW, ***STRIP*** FOR ME OR SOMETHING. FINE. JUST GIVE ME A SECOND.

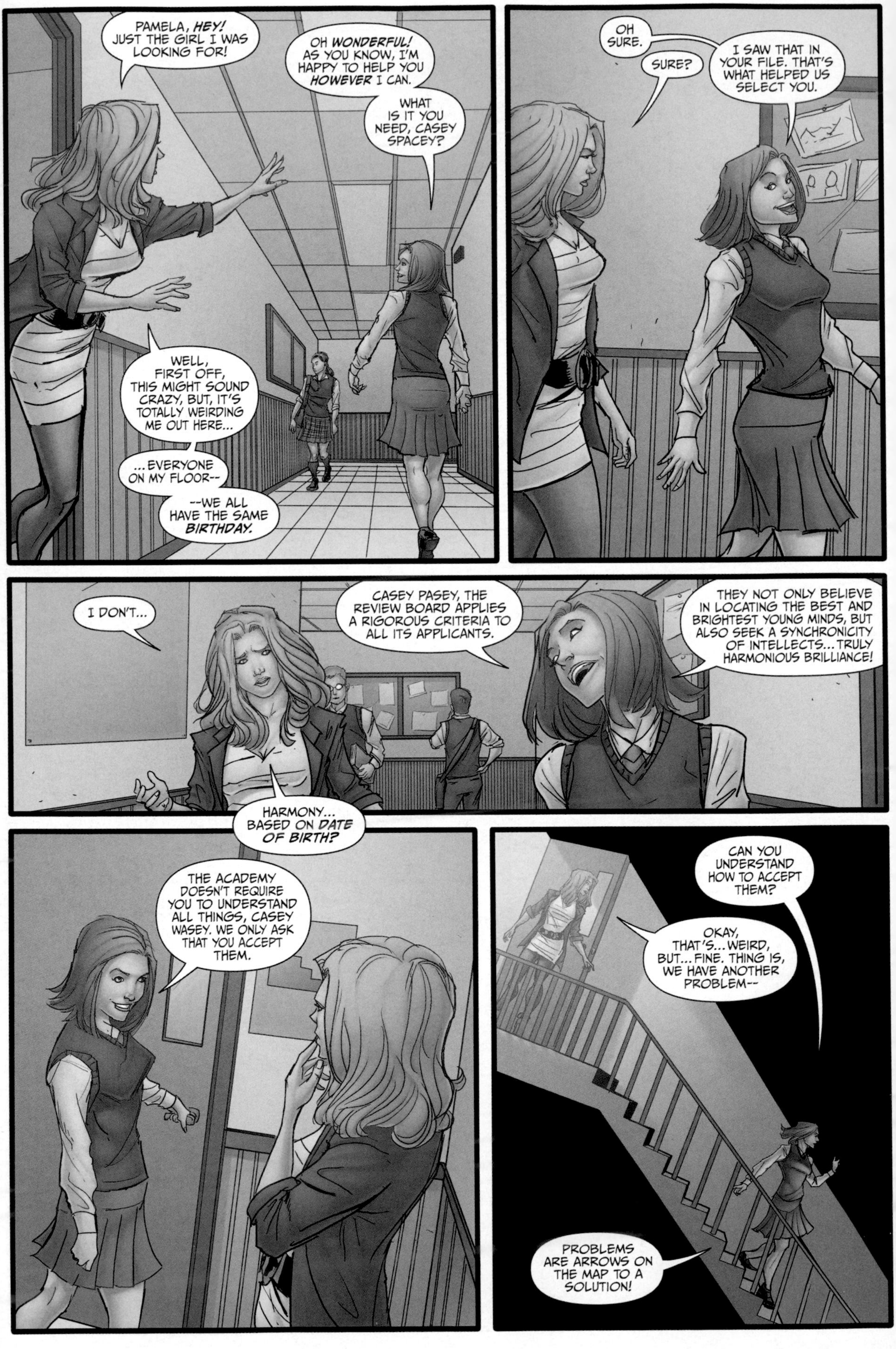
PAMELA, HEY! JUST THE GIRL I WAS LOOKING FOR!
OH WONDERFUL! AS YOU KNOW, I'M HAPPY TO HELP YOU HOWEVER I CAN.
WHAT IS IT YOU NEED, CASEY SPACEY?
WELL, FIRST OFF, THIS MIGHT SOUND CRAZY, BUT, IT'S TOTALLY WEIRDING ME OUT HERE...
...EVERYONE ON MY FLOOR--
--WE ALL HAVE THE SAME BIRTHDAY.
OH SURE.
SURE?
I SAW THAT IN YOUR FILE. THAT'S WHAT HELPED US SELECT YOU.
I DON'T...
CASEY PASEY, THE REVIEW BOARD APPLIES A RIGOROUS CRITERIA TO ALL ITS APPLICANTS.
THEY NOT ONLY BELIEVE IN LOCATING THE BEST AND BRIGHTEST YOUNG MINDS, BUT ALSO SEEK A SYNCHRONICITY OF INTELLECTS...TRULY HARMONIOUS BRILLIANCE!
HARMONY... BASED ON DATE OF BIRTH?
THE ACADEMY DOESN'T REQUIRE YOU TO UNDERSTAND ALL THINGS, CASEY WASEY. WE ONLY ASK THAT YOU ACCEPT THEM.
CAN YOU UNDERSTAND HOW TO ACCEPT THEM?
OKAY, THAT'S...WEIRD, BUT...FINE. THING IS, WE HAVE ANOTHER PROBLEM--
PROBLEMS ARE ARROWS ON THE MAP TO A SOLUTION!

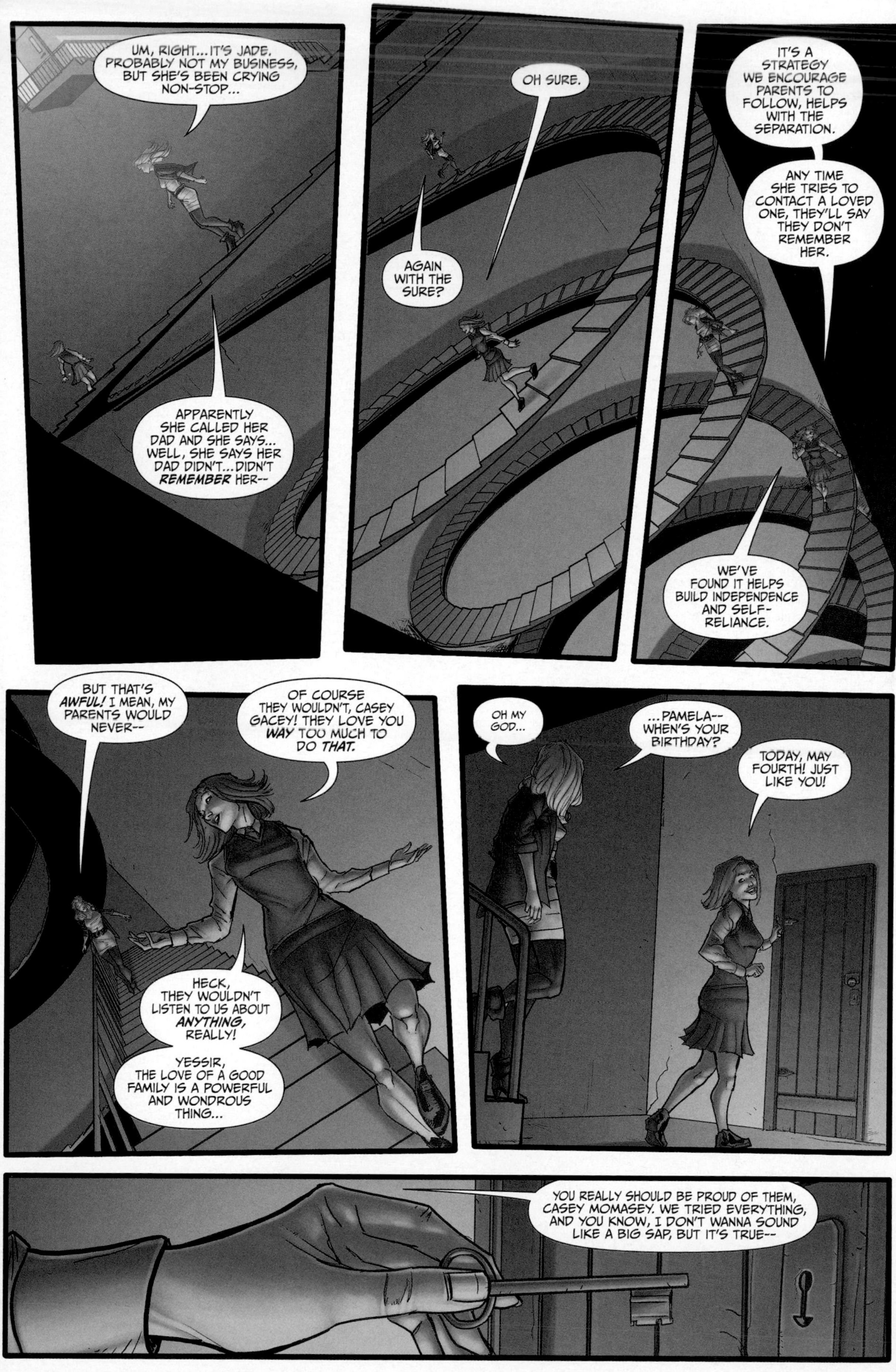
UM, RIGHT... IT'S JADE. PROBABLY NOT MY BUSINESS, BUT SHE'S BEEN CRYING NON-STOP...
APPARENTLY SHE CALLED HER DAD AND SHE SAYS... WELL, SHE SAYS HER DAD DIDN'T...DIDN'T *REMEMBER* HER--
OH SURE.
AGAIN WITH THE SURE?
IT'S A STRATEGY WE ENCOURAGE PARENTS TO FOLLOW, HELPS WITH THE SEPARATION.
ANY TIME SHE TRIES TO CONTACT A LOVED ONE, THEY'LL SAY THEY DON'T REMEMBER HER.
WE'VE FOUND IT HELPS BUILD INDEPENDENCE AND SELF-RELIANCE.
BUT THAT'S *AWFUL!* I MEAN, MY PARENTS WOULD NEVER--
OF COURSE THEY WOULDN'T, CASEY GACEY! THEY LOVE YOU *WAY* TOO MUCH TO DO *THAT.*
HECK, THEY WOULDN'T LISTEN TO US ABOUT *ANYTHING,* REALLY!
YESSIR, THE LOVE OF A GOOD FAMILY IS A POWERFUL AND WONDROUS THING...
OH MY GOD...
...PAMELA-- WHEN'S YOUR BIRTHDAY?
TODAY, MAY FOURTH! JUST LIKE YOU!
YOU REALLY SHOULD BE PROUD OF THEM, CASEY MOMASEY. WE TRIED EVERYTHING, AND YOU KNOW, I DON'T WANNA SOUND LIKE A BIG SAP, BUT IT'S TRUE--

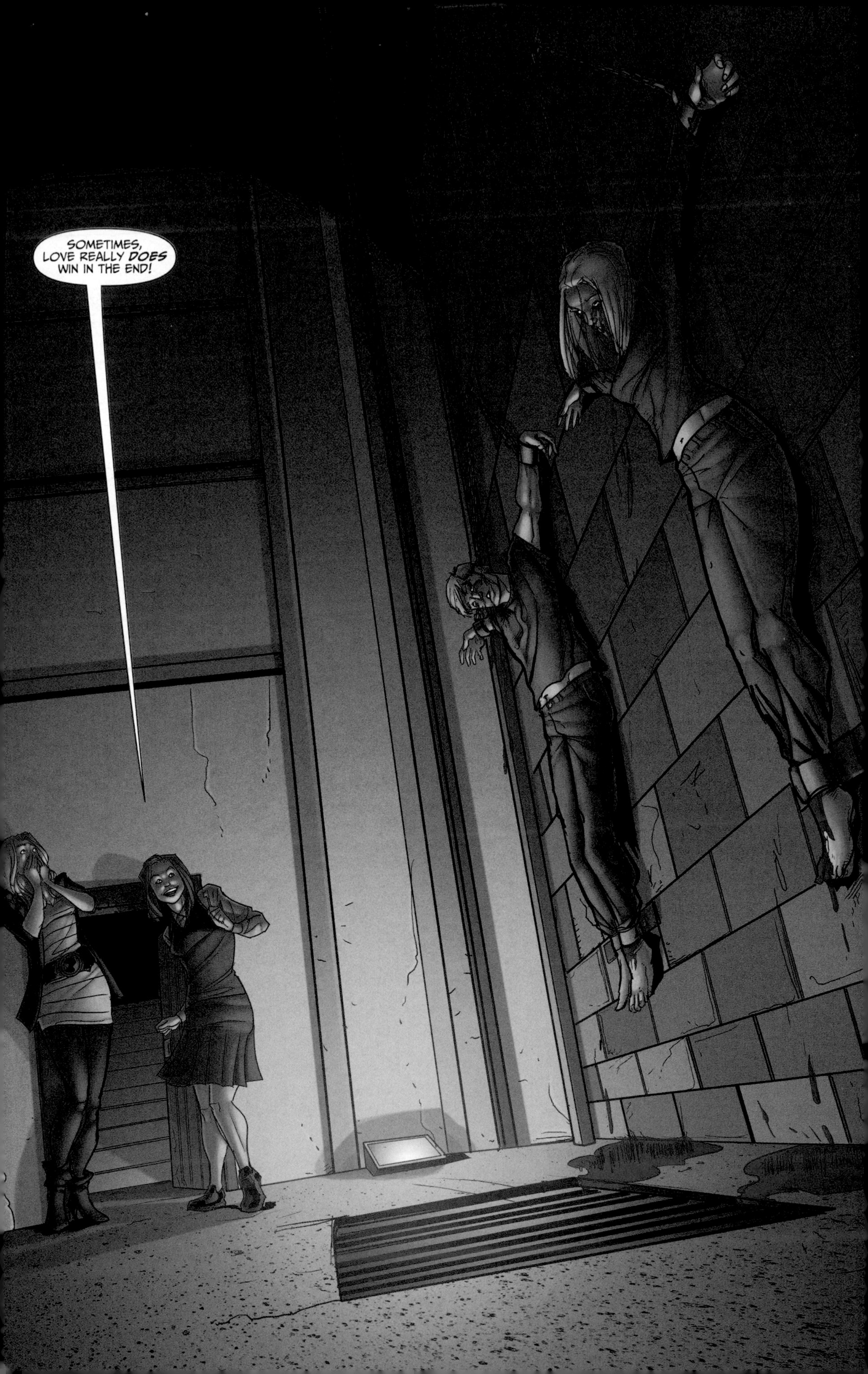
SOMETIMES, LOVE REALLY *DOES* WIN IN THE END!

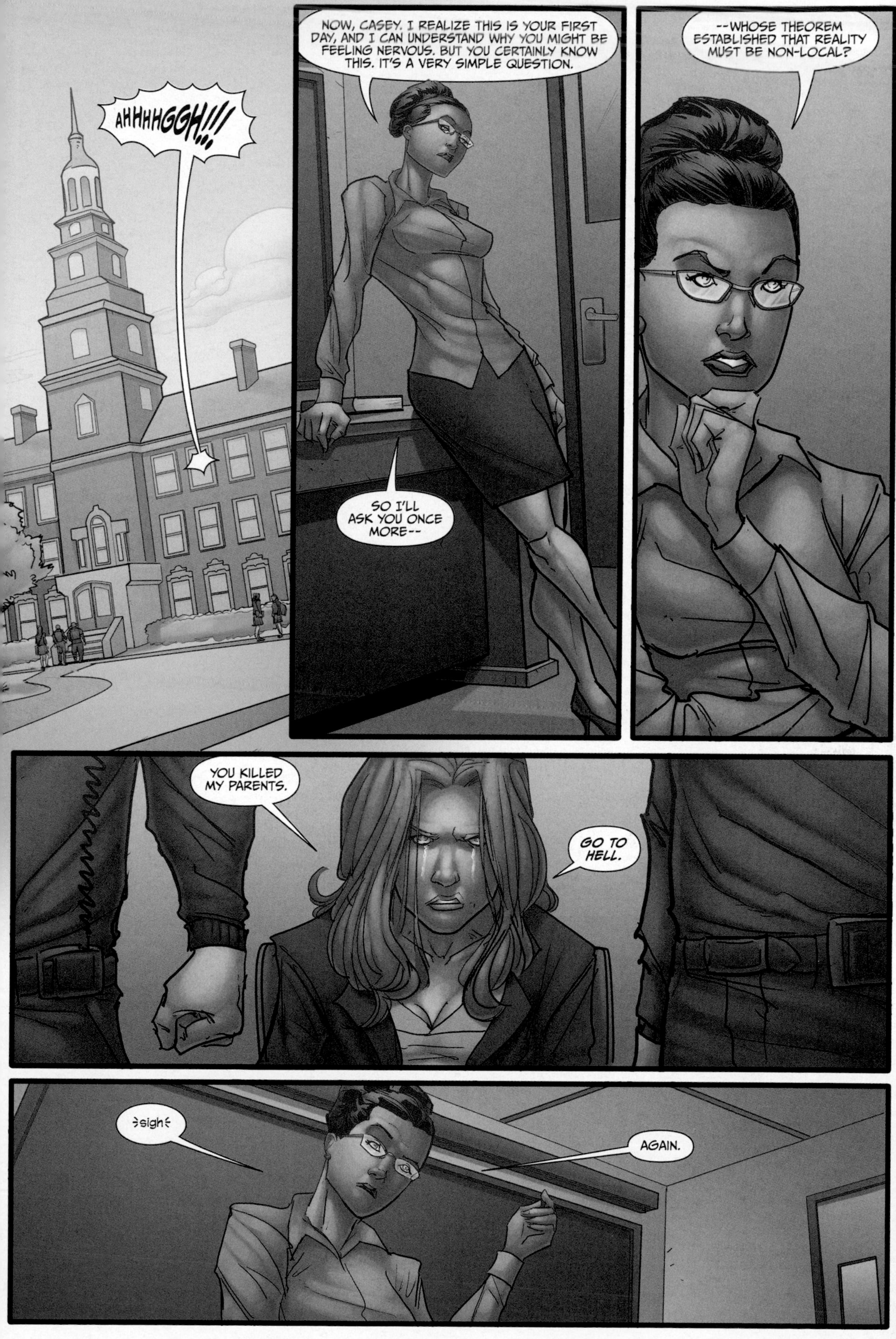
AHHHHGGH!!!
NOW, CASEY. I REALIZE THIS IS YOUR FIRST DAY, AND I CAN UNDERSTAND WHY YOU MIGHT BE FEELING NERVOUS. BUT YOU CERTAINLY KNOW THIS. IT'S A VERY SIMPLE QUESTION.
SO I'LL ASK YOU ONCE MORE--
--WHOSE THEOREM ESTABLISHED THAT REALITY MUST BE NON-LOCAL?
YOU KILLED MY PARENTS.
GO TO HELL.
sigh
AGAIN.

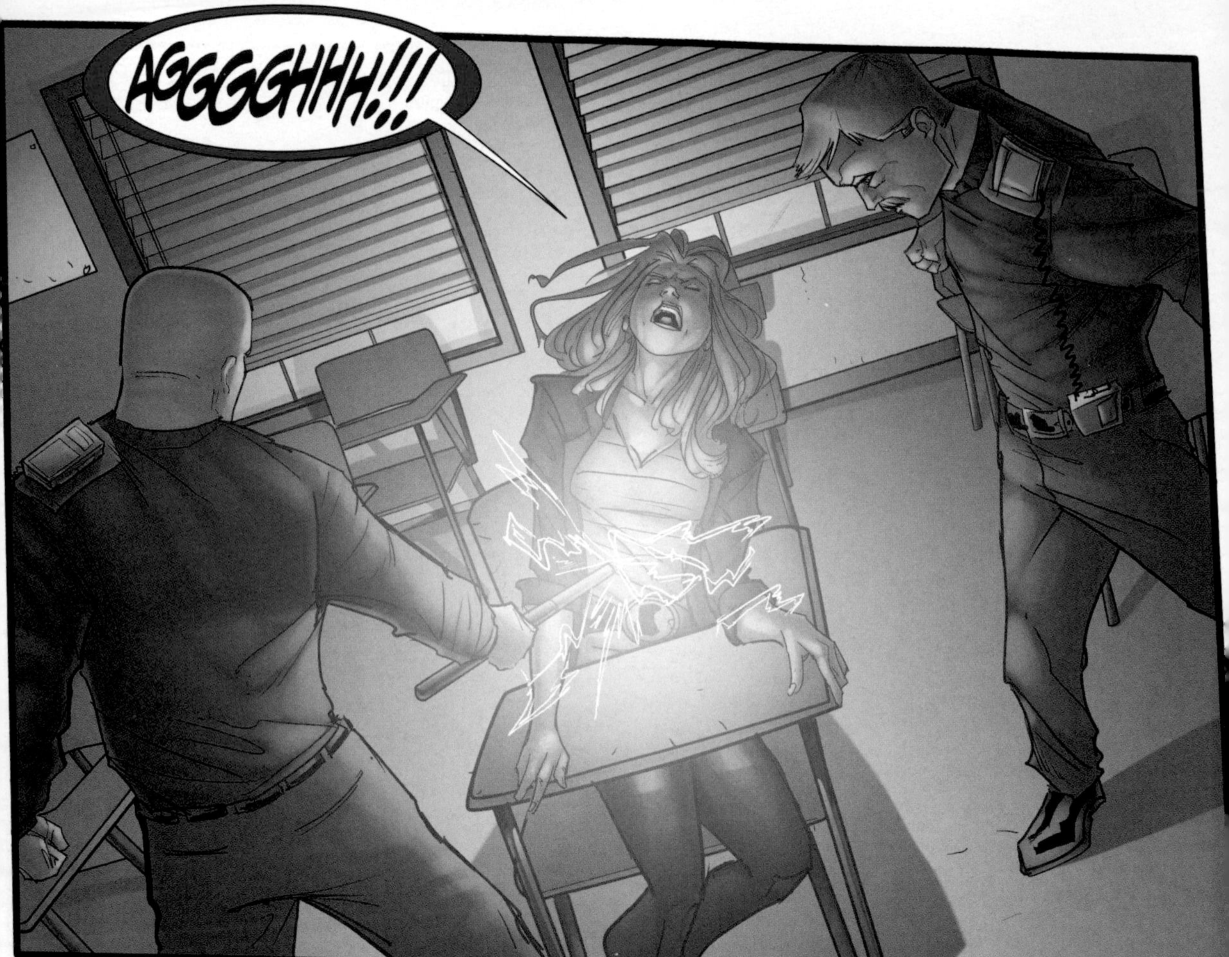
AGGGGHHH!!!

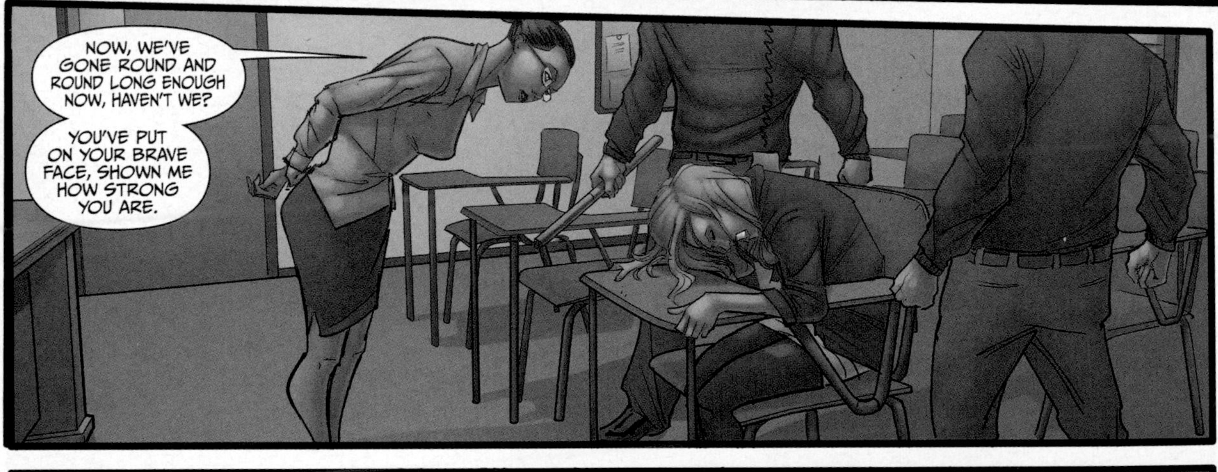
NOW, WE'VE GONE ROUND AND ROUND LONG ENOUGH NOW, HAVEN'T WE?
YOU'VE PUT ON YOUR BRAVE FACE, SHOWN ME HOW STRONG YOU ARE.

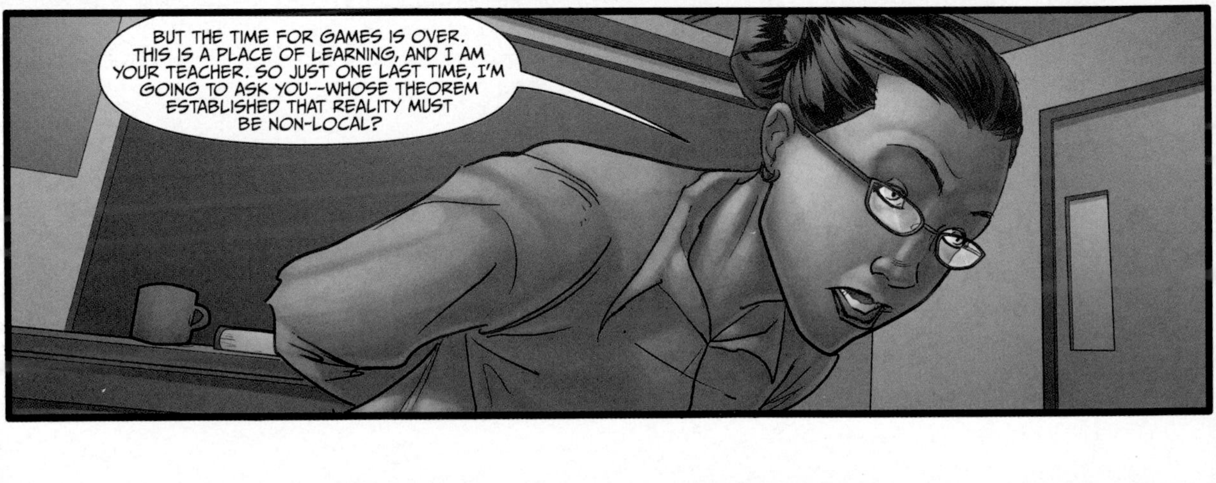
BUT THE TIME FOR GAMES IS OVER. THIS IS A PLACE OF LEARNING, AND I AM YOUR TEACHER. SO JUST ONE LAST TIME, I'M GOING TO ASK YOU--WHOSE THEOREM ESTABLISHED THAT REALITY MUST BE NON-LOCAL?

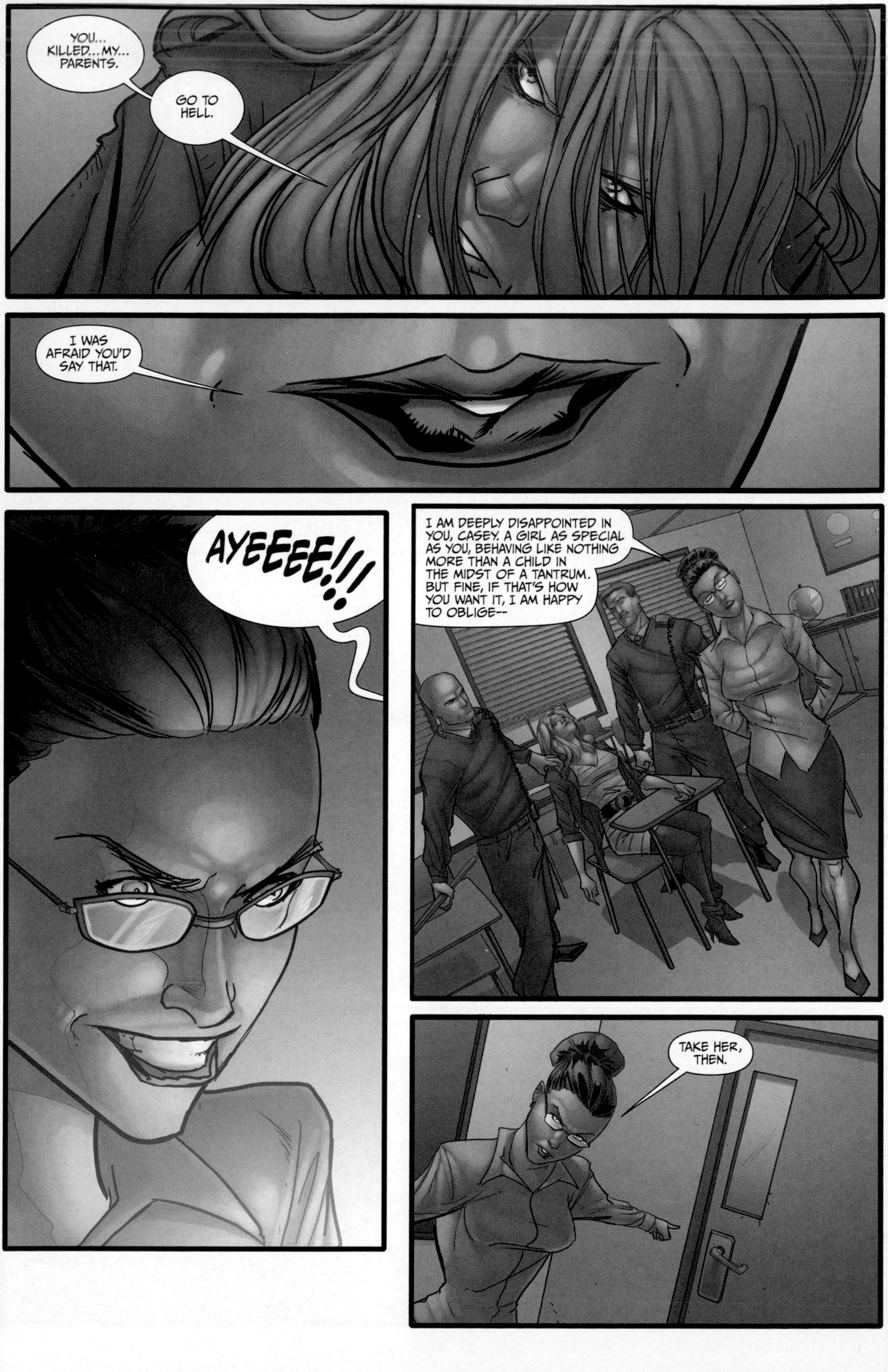
YOU... KILLED... MY... PARENTS.
GO TO HELL.
I WAS AFRAID YOU'D SAY THAT.
AYEEEE!!!
I AM DEEPLY DISAPPOINTED IN YOU, CASEY. A GIRL AS SPECIAL AS YOU, BEHAVING LIKE NOTHING MORE THAN A CHILD IN THE MIDST OF A TANTRUM. BUT FINE, IF THAT'S HOW YOU WANT IT, I AM HAPPY TO OBLIGE--
TAKE HER, THEN.

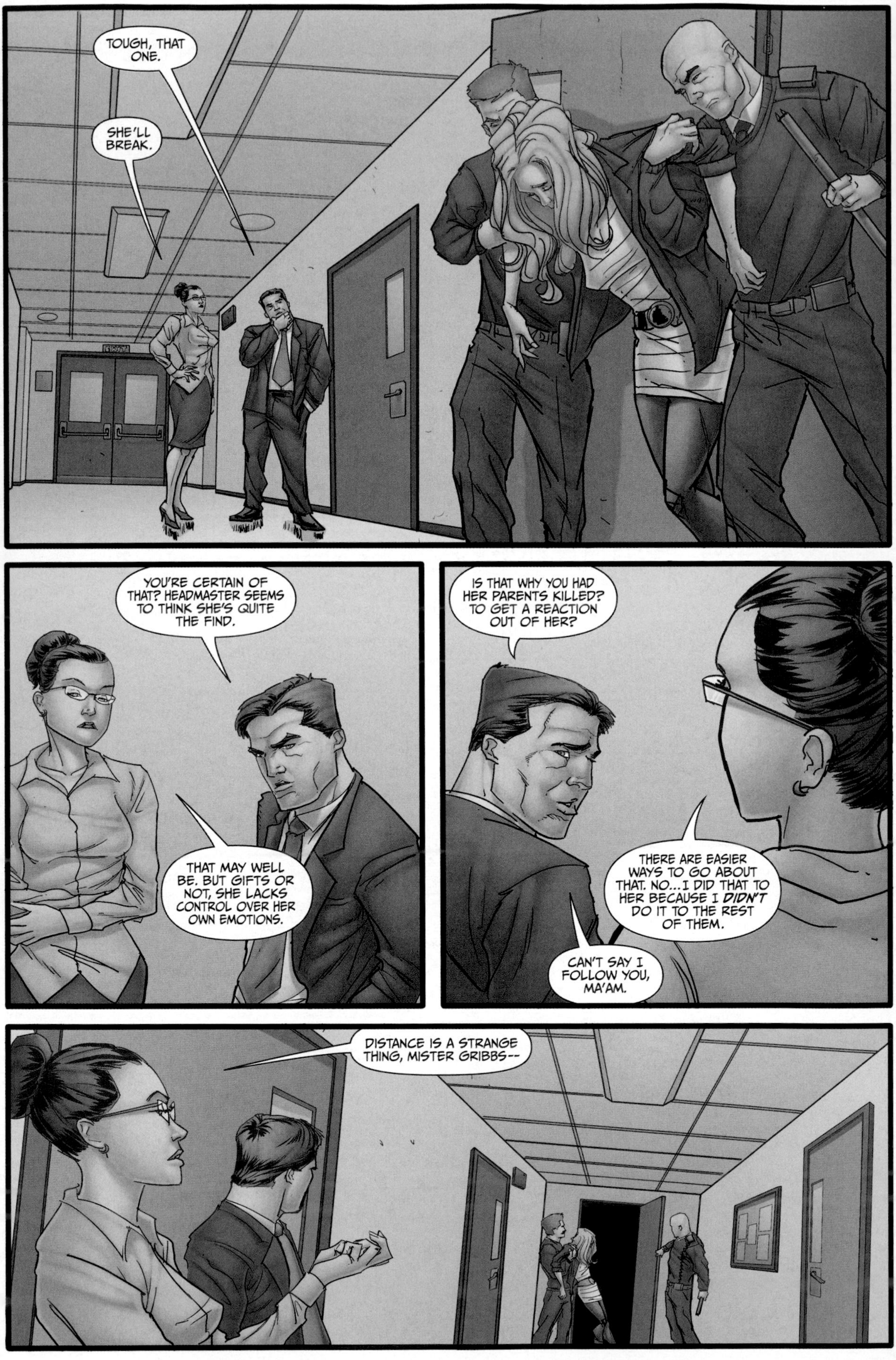
TOUGH, THAT ONE.
SHE'LL BREAK.
YOU'RE CERTAIN OF THAT? HEADMASTER SEEMS TO THINK SHE'S QUITE THE FIND.
THAT MAY WELL BE. BUT GIFTS OR NOT, SHE LACKS CONTROL OVER HER OWN EMOTIONS.
IS THAT WHY YOU HAD HER PARENTS KILLED? TO GET A REACTION OUT OF HER?
THERE ARE EASIER WAYS TO GO ABOUT THAT. NO...I DID THAT TO HER BECAUSE I *DIDN'T* DO IT TO THE REST OF THEM.
CAN'T SAY I FOLLOW YOU, MA'AM.
DISTANCE IS A STRANGE THING, MISTER GRIBBS--

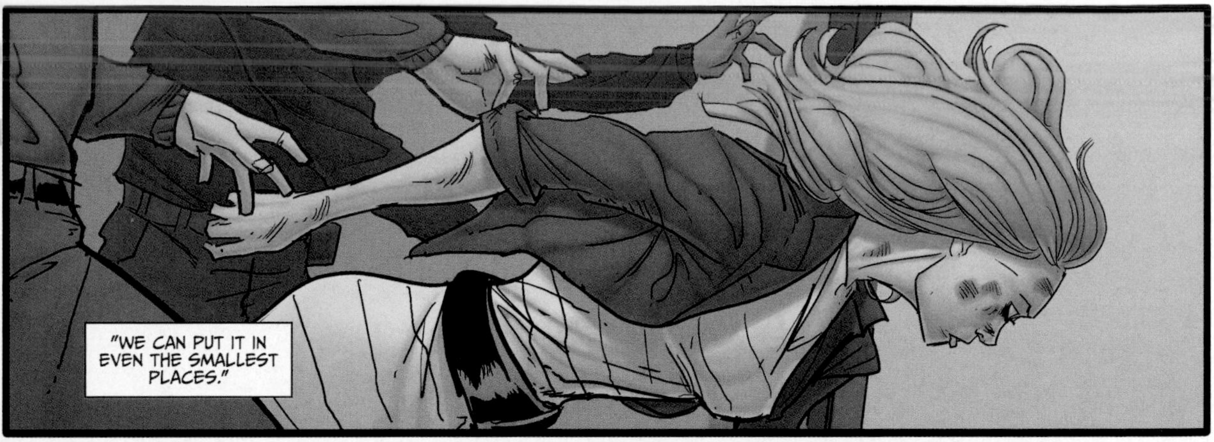
"WE CAN PUT IT IN EVEN THE SMALLEST PLACES."

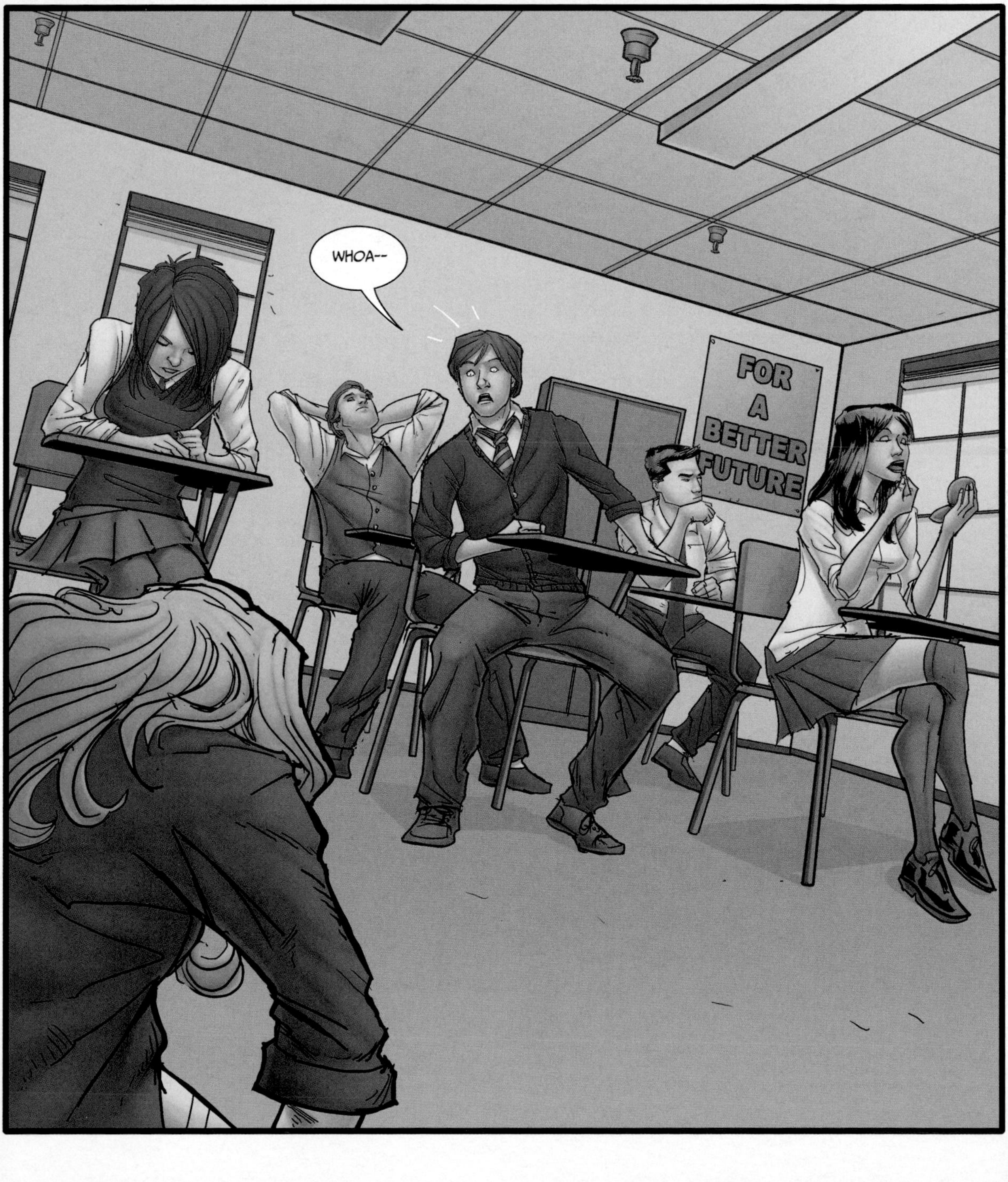
WHOA--
FOR A BETTER FUTURE

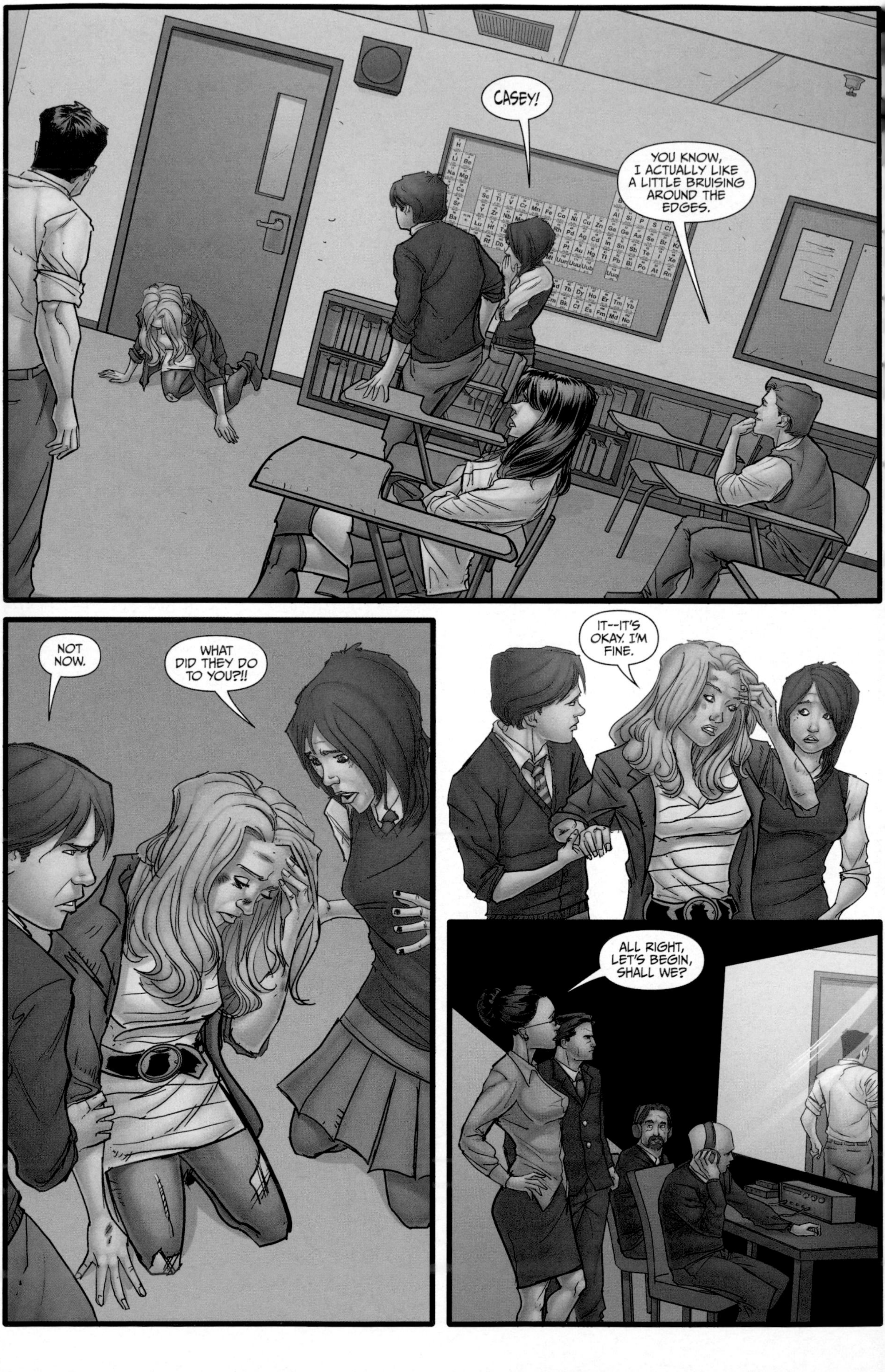
CASEY!
YOU KNOW, I ACTUALLY LIKE A LITTLE BRUISING AROUND THE EDGES.
NOT NOW.
WHAT DID THEY DO TO YOU?!!
IT--IT'S OKAY. I'M FINE.
ALL RIGHT, LET'S BEGIN, SHALL WE?

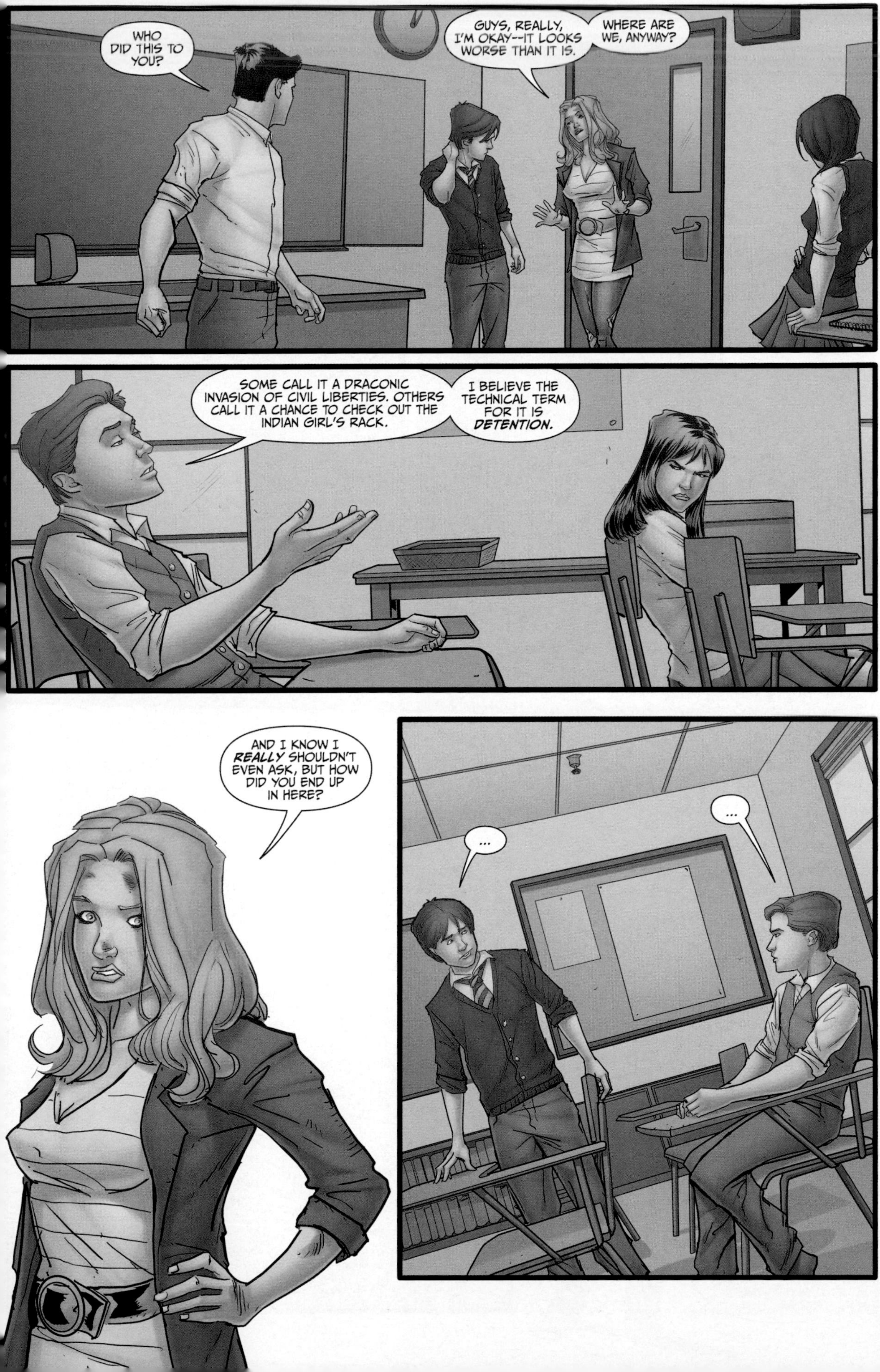
WHO DID THIS TO YOU?
GUYS, REALLY, I'M OKAY--IT LOOKS WORSE THAN IT IS.
WHERE ARE WE, ANYWAY?
SOME CALL IT A DRACONIC INVASION OF CIVIL LIBERTIES. OTHERS CALL IT A CHANCE TO CHECK OUT THE INDIAN GIRL'S RACK.
I BELIEVE THE TECHNICAL TERM FOR IT IS *DETENTION.*
AND I KNOW I *REALLY* SHOULDN'T EVEN ASK, BUT HOW DID YOU END UP IN HERE?
...
...

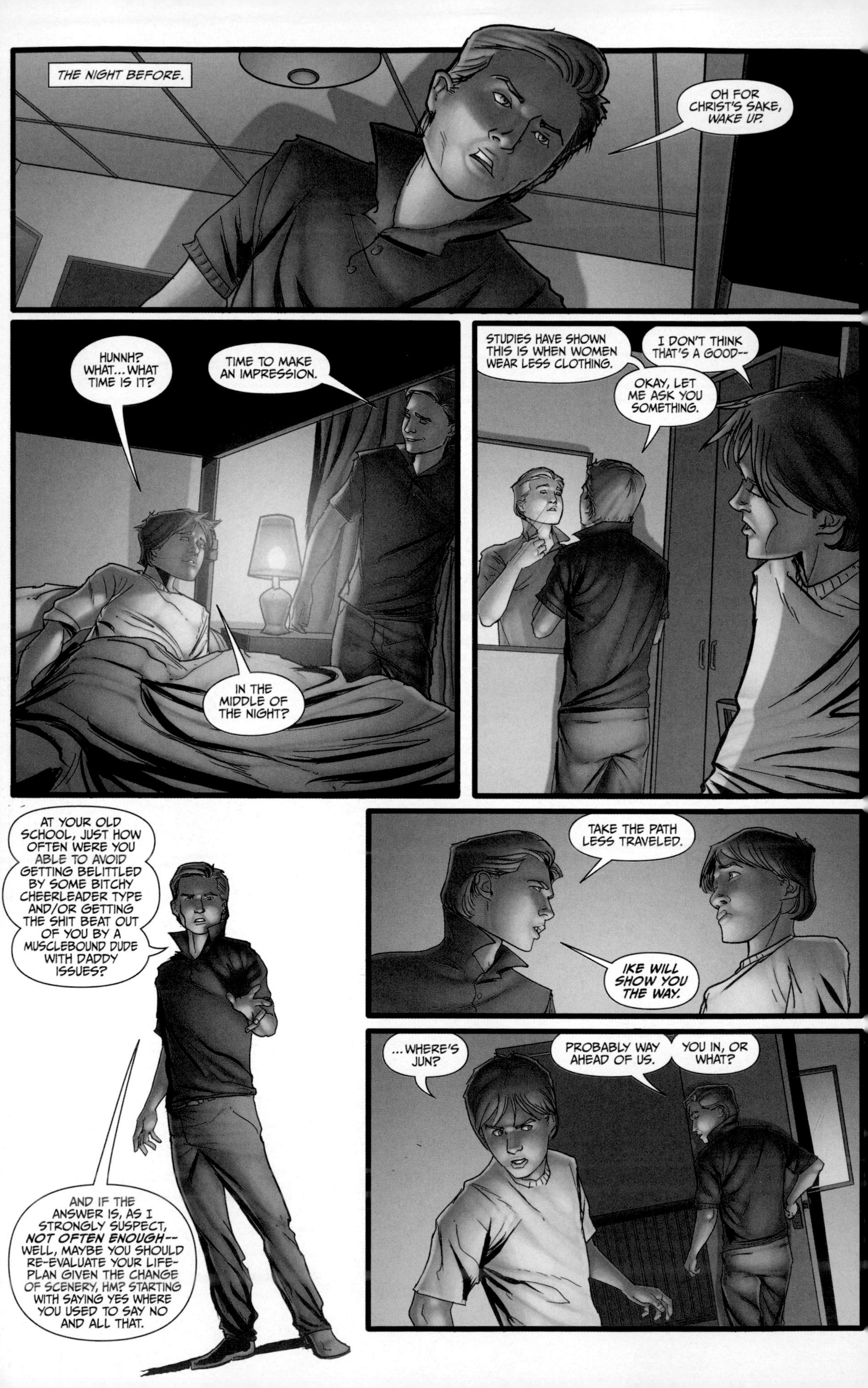
THE NIGHT BEFORE.
OH FOR CHRIST'S SAKE, WAKE UP.
HUNNH? WHAT... WHAT TIME IS IT?
TIME TO MAKE AN IMPRESSION.
IN THE MIDDLE OF THE NIGHT?
STUDIES HAVE SHOWN THIS IS WHEN WOMEN WEAR LESS CLOTHING.
I DON'T THINK THAT'S A GOOD--
OKAY, LET ME ASK YOU SOMETHING.
AT YOUR OLD SCHOOL, JUST HOW OFTEN WERE YOU ABLE TO AVOID GETTING BELITTLED BY SOME BITCHY CHEERLEADER TYPE AND/OR GETTING THE SHIT BEAT OUT OF YOU BY A MUSCLEBOUND DUDE WITH DADDY ISSUES?
AND IF THE ANSWER IS, AS I STRONGLY SUSPECT, NOT OFTEN ENOUGH-- WELL, MAYBE YOU SHOULD RE-EVALUATE YOUR LIFE-PLAN GIVEN THE CHANGE OF SCENERY, HM? STARTING WITH SAYING YES WHERE YOU USED TO SAY NO AND ALL THAT.
TAKE THE PATH LESS TRAVELED.
IKE WILL SHOW YOU THE WAY.
...WHERE'S JUN?
PROBABLY WAY AHEAD OF US.
YOU IN, OR WHAT?

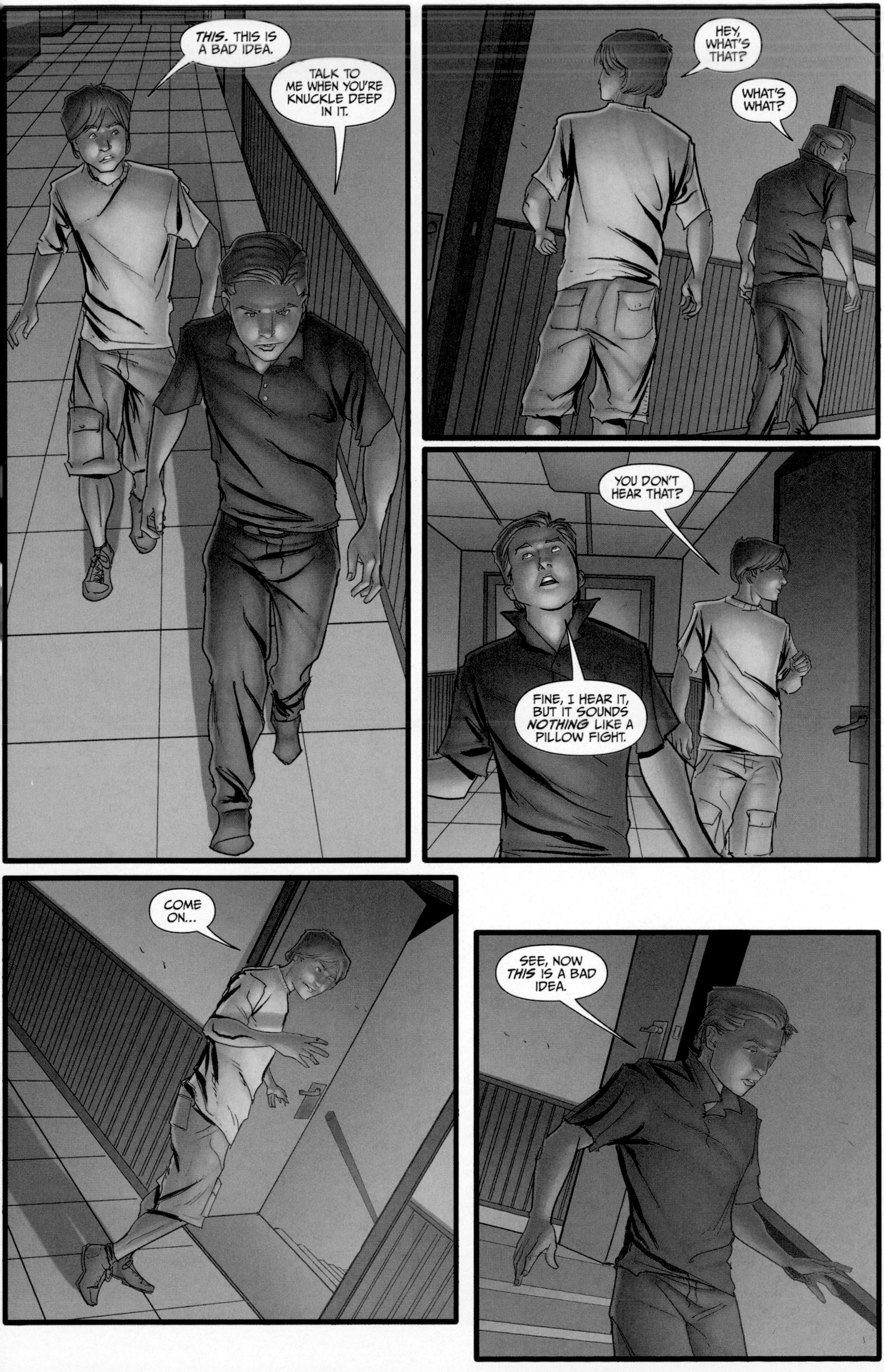
THIS. THIS IS A BAD IDEA.
TALK TO ME WHEN YOU'RE KNUCKLE DEEP IN IT.
HEY, WHAT'S THAT?
WHAT'S WHAT?
YOU DON'T HEAR THAT?
FINE, I HEAR IT, BUT IT SOUNDS NOTHING LIKE A PILLOW FIGHT.
COME ON...
SEE, NOW THIS IS A BAD IDEA.

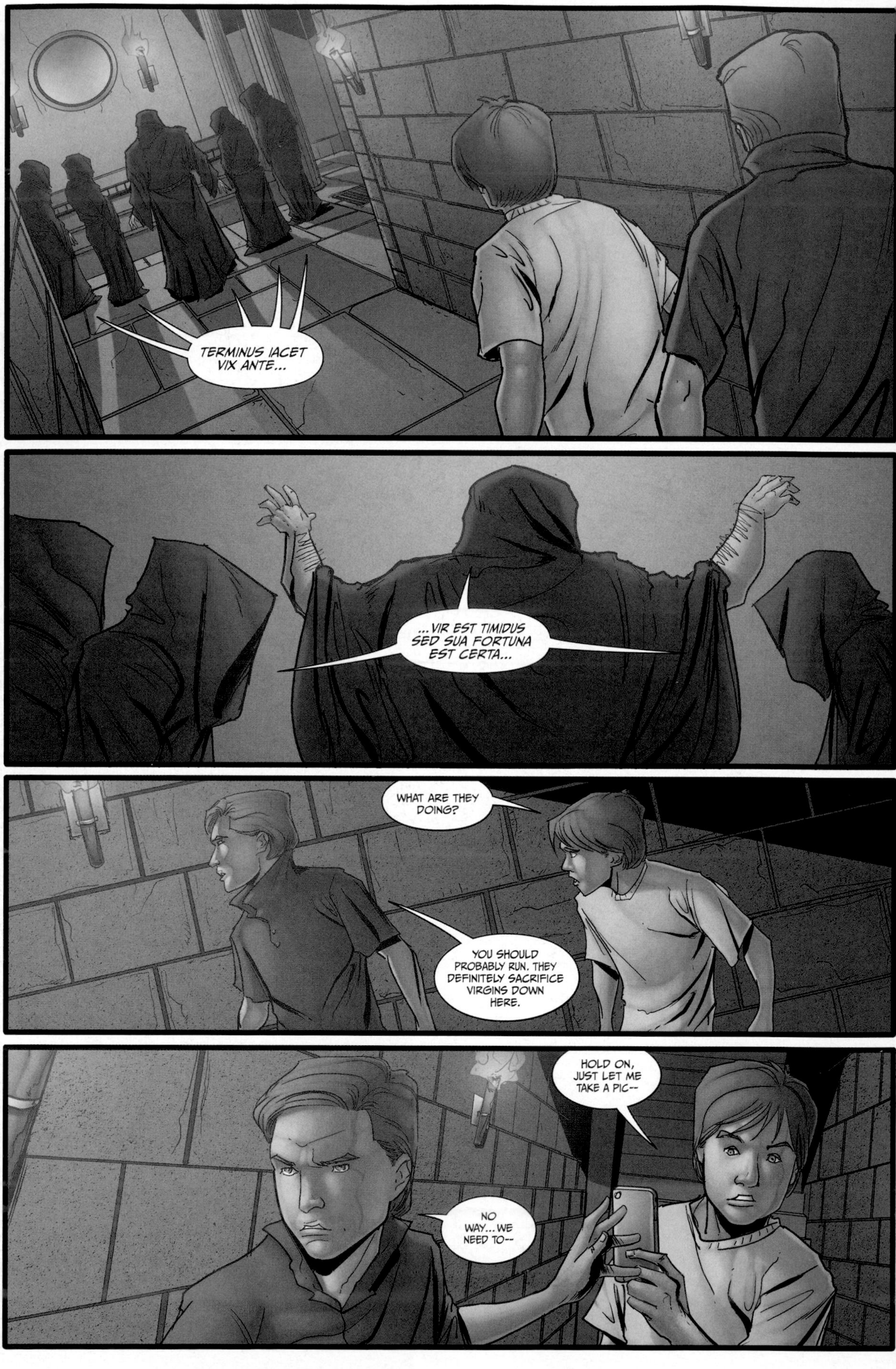
TERMINUS IACET VIX ANTE...
...VIR EST TIMIDUS SED SUA FORTUNA EST CERTA...
WHAT ARE THEY DOING?
YOU SHOULD PROBABLY RUN. THEY DEFINITELY SACRIFICE VIRGINS DOWN HERE.
HOLD ON, JUST LET ME TAKE A PIC--
NO WAY... WE NEED TO--

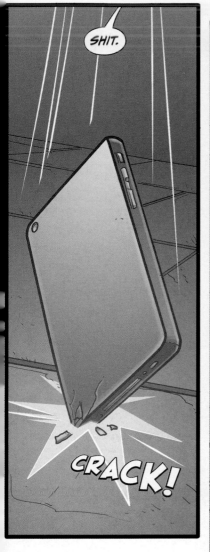

SHIT.

CRACK!

WELL, WHAT DO WE GOT HERE? COUPLE A' VAGABONDS OF THE NIGHT ARE YOU THERE, FELLAS?

HIS IDEA.

I DON'T SUPPOSE A SKULL & BONES PASSWORD CARRIES MUCH WEIGHT AROUND HERE, DOES IT?

'FRAID NOT, BOY. THIS IS ONLY GONNA MEAN TROUBLE. AND THE BEST KIND.

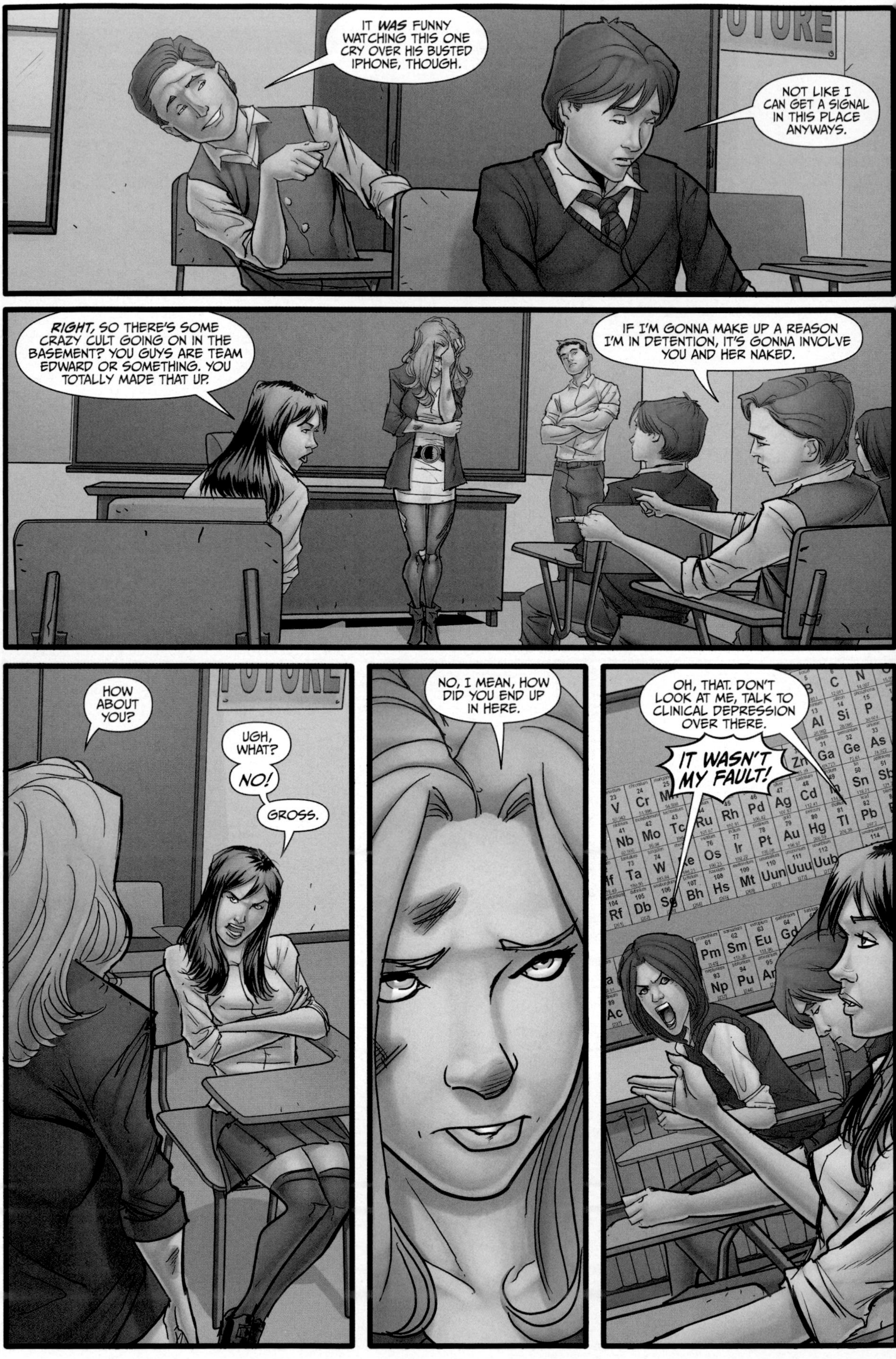
IT WAS FUNNY WATCHING THIS ONE CRY OVER HIS BUSTED IPHONE, THOUGH.
NOT LIKE I CAN GET A SIGNAL IN THIS PLACE ANYWAYS.
RIGHT, SO THERE'S SOME CRAZY CULT GOING ON IN THE BASEMENT? YOU GUYS ARE TEAM EDWARD OR SOMETHING. YOU TOTALLY MADE THAT UP.
IF I'M GONNA MAKE UP A REASON I'M IN DETENTION, IT'S GONNA INVOLVE YOU AND HER NAKED.
HOW ABOUT YOU?
UGH, WHAT?
NO!
GROSS.
NO, I MEAN, HOW DID YOU END UP IN HERE.
OH, THAT. DON'T LOOK AT ME, TALK TO CLINICAL DEPRESSION OVER THERE.
IT WASN'T MY FAULT!

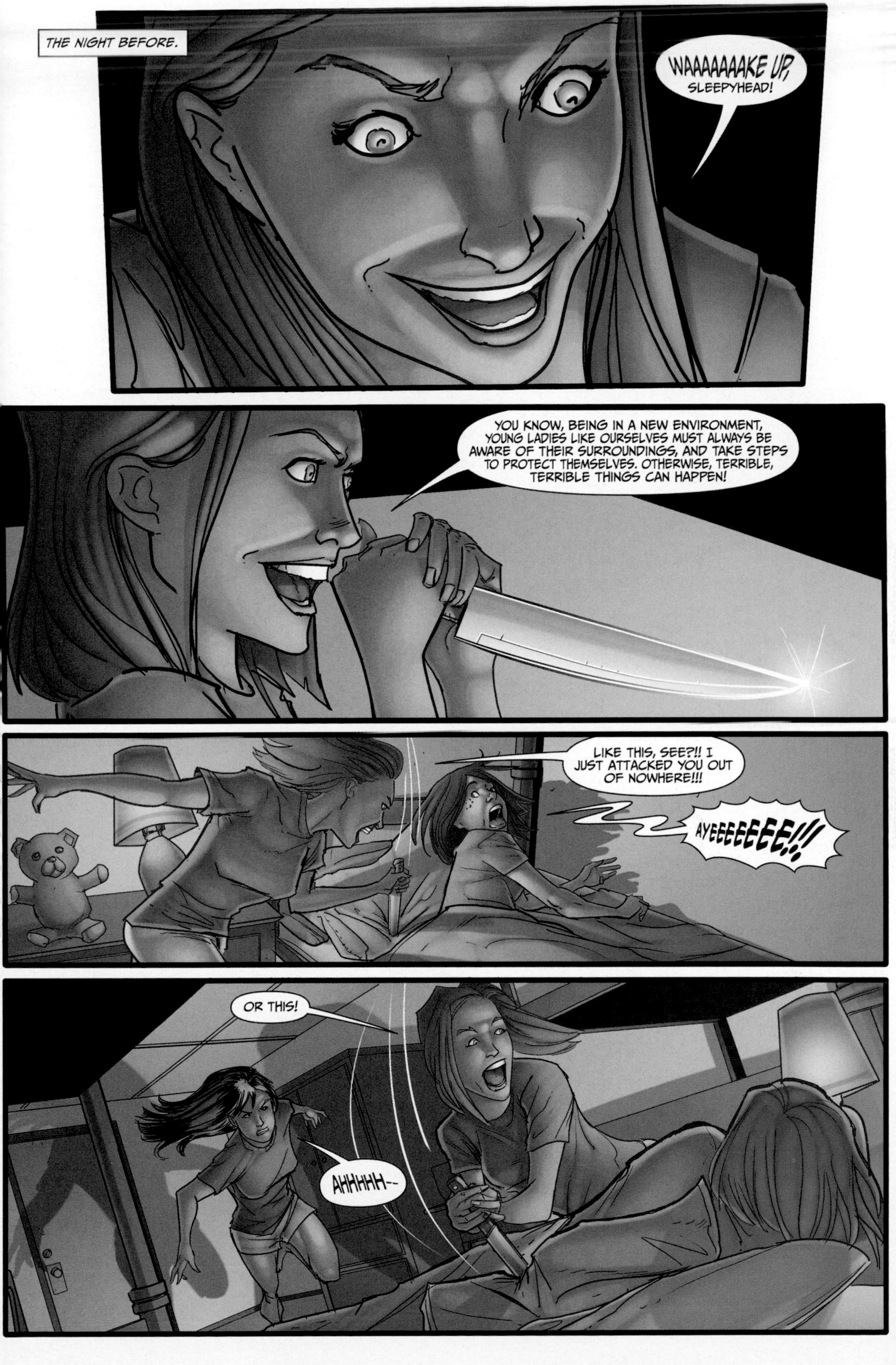
THE NIGHT BEFORE.
WAAAAAAAAKE UP, SLEEPYHEAD!
YOU KNOW, BEING IN A NEW ENVIRONMENT, YOUNG LADIES LIKE OURSELVES MUST ALWAYS BE AWARE OF THEIR SURROUNDINGS, AND TAKE STEPS TO PROTECT THEMSELVES. OTHERWISE, TERRIBLE, TERRIBLE THINGS CAN HAPPEN!
LIKE THIS, SEE?!! I JUST ATTACKED YOU OUT OF NOWHERE!!!
AYEEEEEEEE!!!
OR THIS!
AHHHHH--

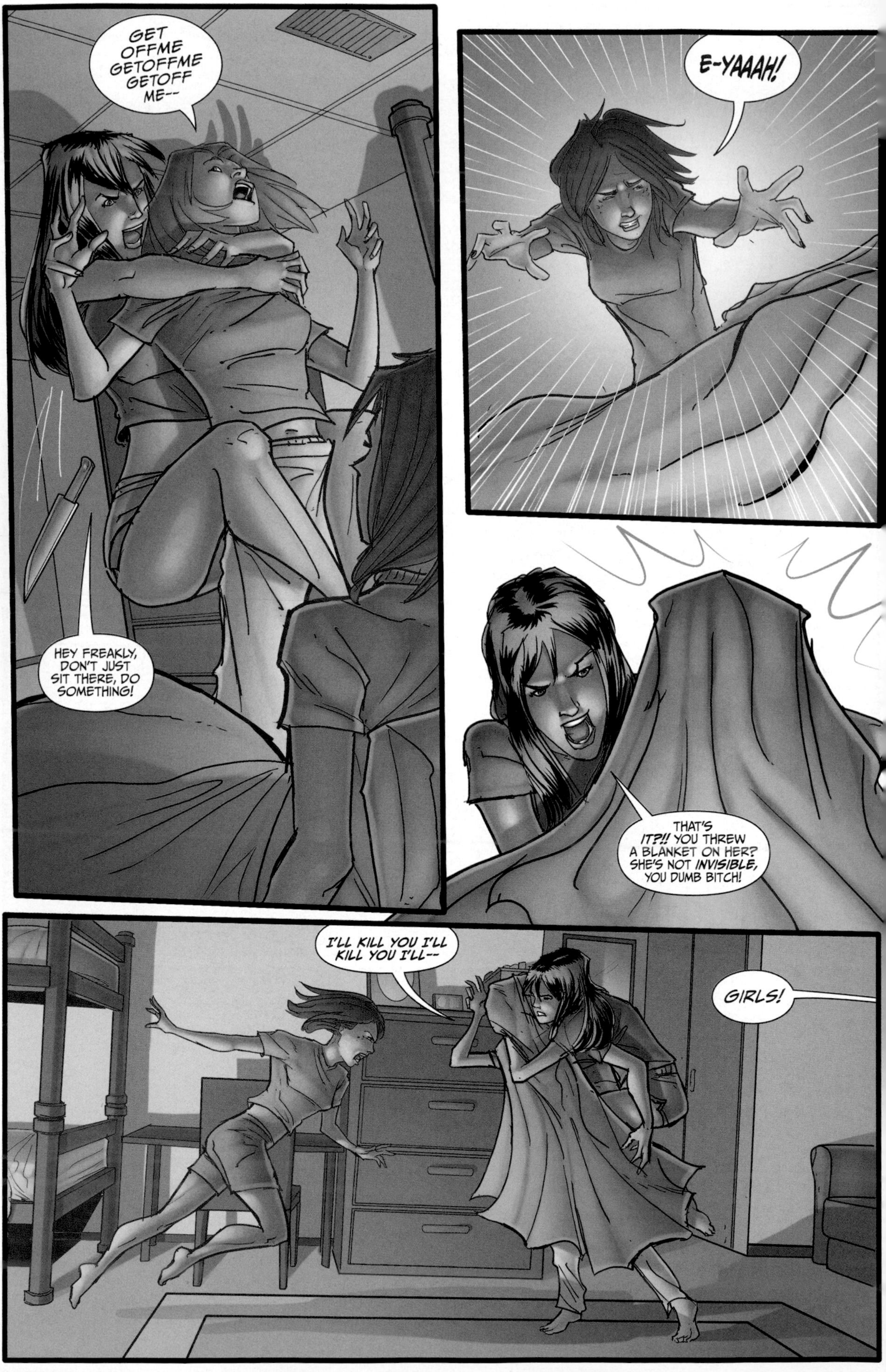
GET OFFME GETOFFME GETOFF ME--
HEY FREAKLY, DON'T JUST SIT THERE, DO SOMETHING!
E-YAAAH!
THAT'S *IT?!!* YOU THREW A BLANKET ON HER? SHE'S NOT *INVISIBLE,* YOU DUMB BITCH!
I'LL KILL YOU I'LL KILL YOU I'LL--
GIRLS!

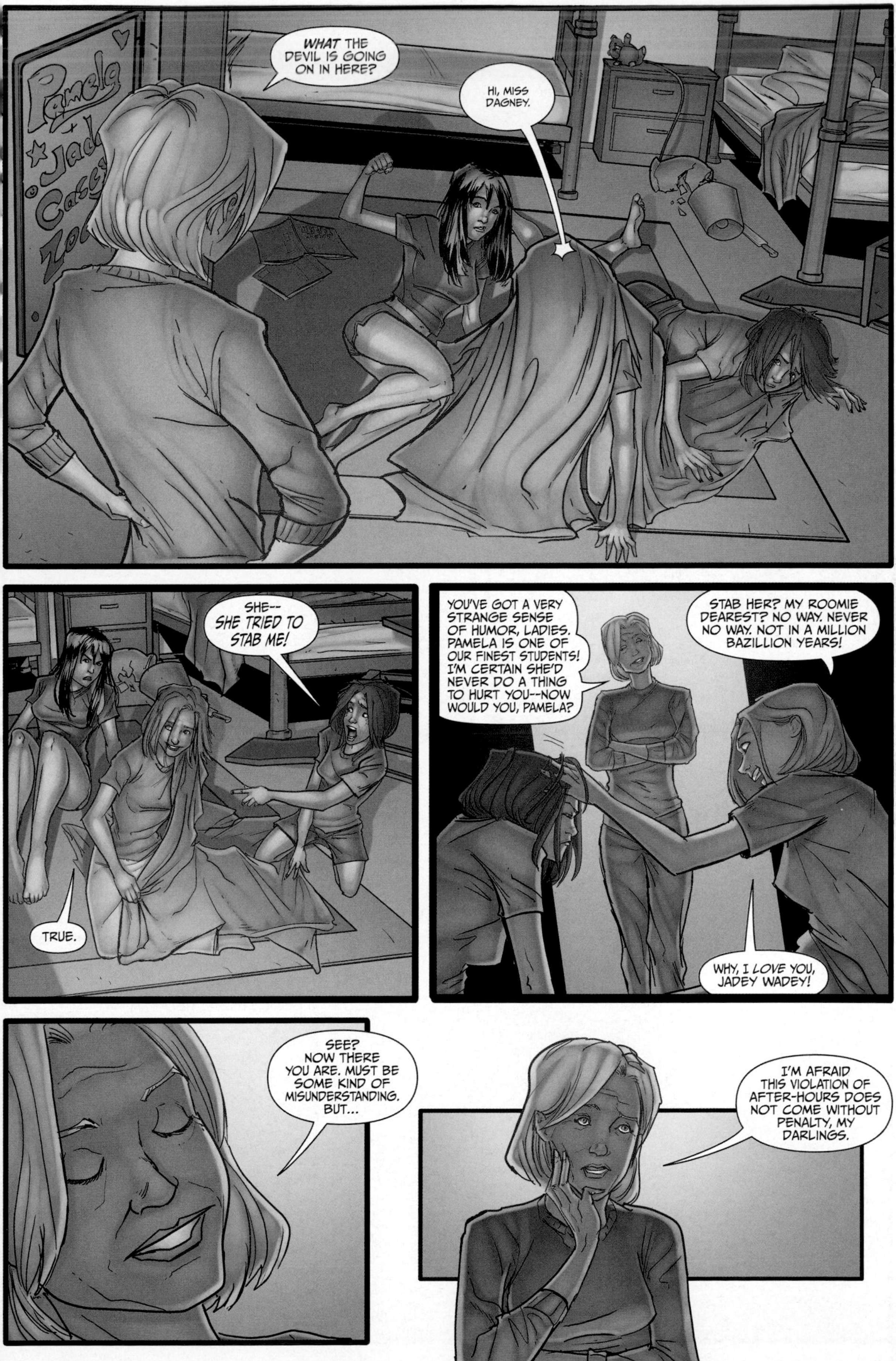
WHAT THE DEVIL IS GOING ON IN HERE?
HI, MISS DAGNEY.
SHE-- SHE TRIED TO STAB ME!
TRUE.
YOU'VE GOT A VERY STRANGE SENSE OF HUMOR, LADIES. PAMELA IS ONE OF OUR FINEST STUDENTS! I'M CERTAIN SHE'D NEVER DO A THING TO HURT YOU--NOW WOULD YOU, PAMELA?
STAB HER? MY ROOMIE DEAREST? NO WAY. NEVER NO WAY. NOT IN A MILLION BAZILLION YEARS!
WHY, I LOVE YOU, JADEY WADEY!
SEE? NOW THERE YOU ARE. MUST BE SOME KIND OF MISUNDERSTANDING. BUT...
I'M AFRAID THIS VIOLATION OF AFTER-HOURS DOES NOT COME WITHOUT PENALTY, MY DARLINGS.

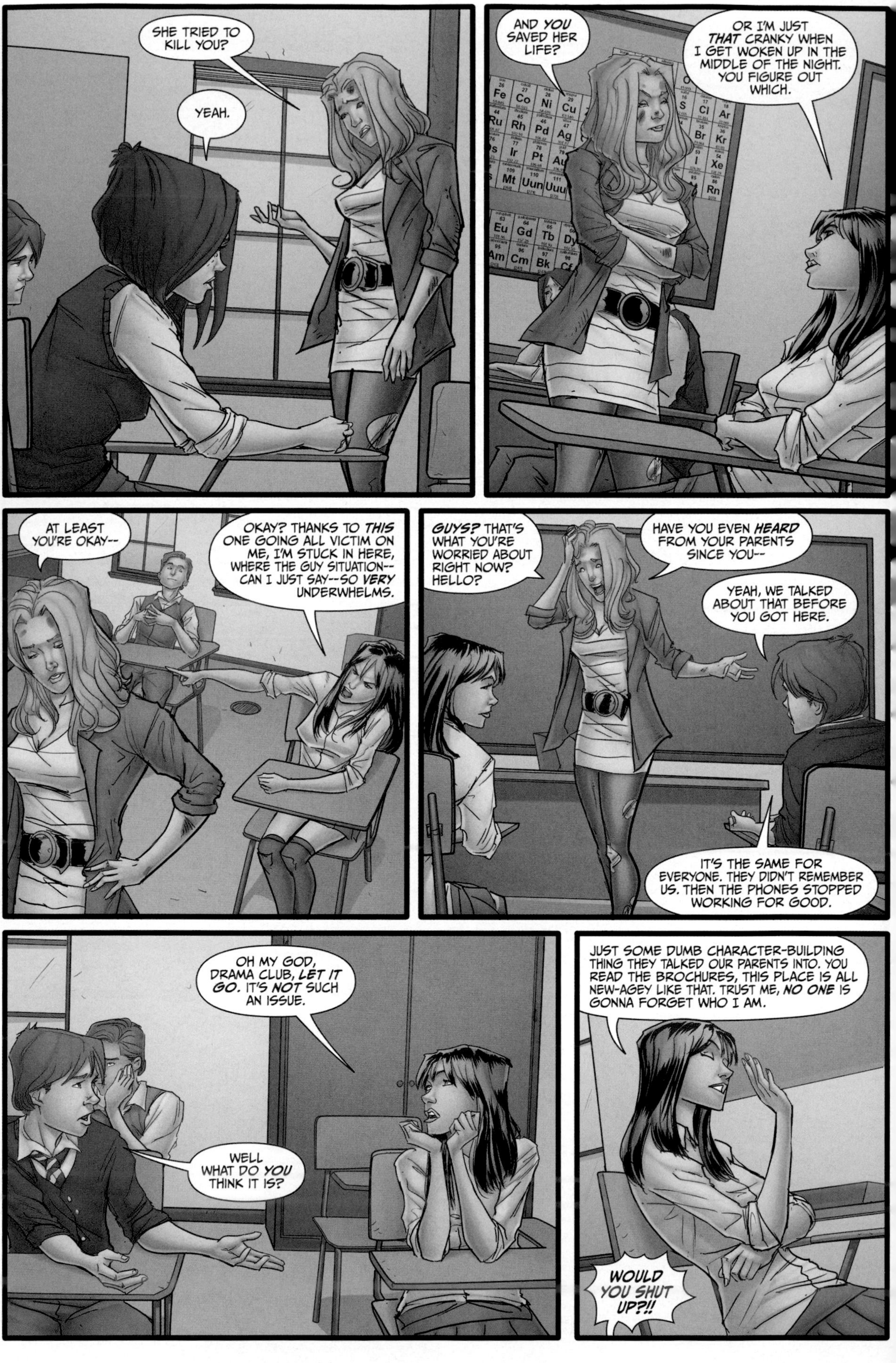
SHE TRIED TO KILL YOU?
YEAH.
AND YOU SAVED HER LIFE?
OR I'M JUST THAT CRANKY WHEN I GET WOKEN UP IN THE MIDDLE OF THE NIGHT. YOU FIGURE OUT WHICH.
AT LEAST YOU'RE OKAY--
OKAY? THANKS TO THIS ONE GOING ALL VICTIM ON ME, I'M STUCK IN HERE, WHERE THE GUY SITUATION-- CAN I JUST SAY--SO VERY UNDERWHELMS.
GUYS? THAT'S WHAT YOU'RE WORRIED ABOUT RIGHT NOW? HELLO?
HAVE YOU EVEN HEARD FROM YOUR PARENTS SINCE YOU--
YEAH, WE TALKED ABOUT THAT BEFORE YOU GOT HERE.
IT'S THE SAME FOR EVERYONE. THEY DIDN'T REMEMBER US. THEN THE PHONES STOPPED WORKING FOR GOOD.
OH MY GOD, DRAMA CLUB, LET IT GO. IT'S NOT SUCH AN ISSUE.
WELL WHAT DO YOU THINK IT IS?
JUST SOME DUMB CHARACTER-BUILDING THING THEY TALKED OUR PARENTS INTO. YOU READ THE BROCHURES, THIS PLACE IS ALL NEW-AGEY LIKE THAT. TRUST ME, NO ONE IS GONNA FORGET WHO I AM.
WOULD YOU SHUT UP?!!

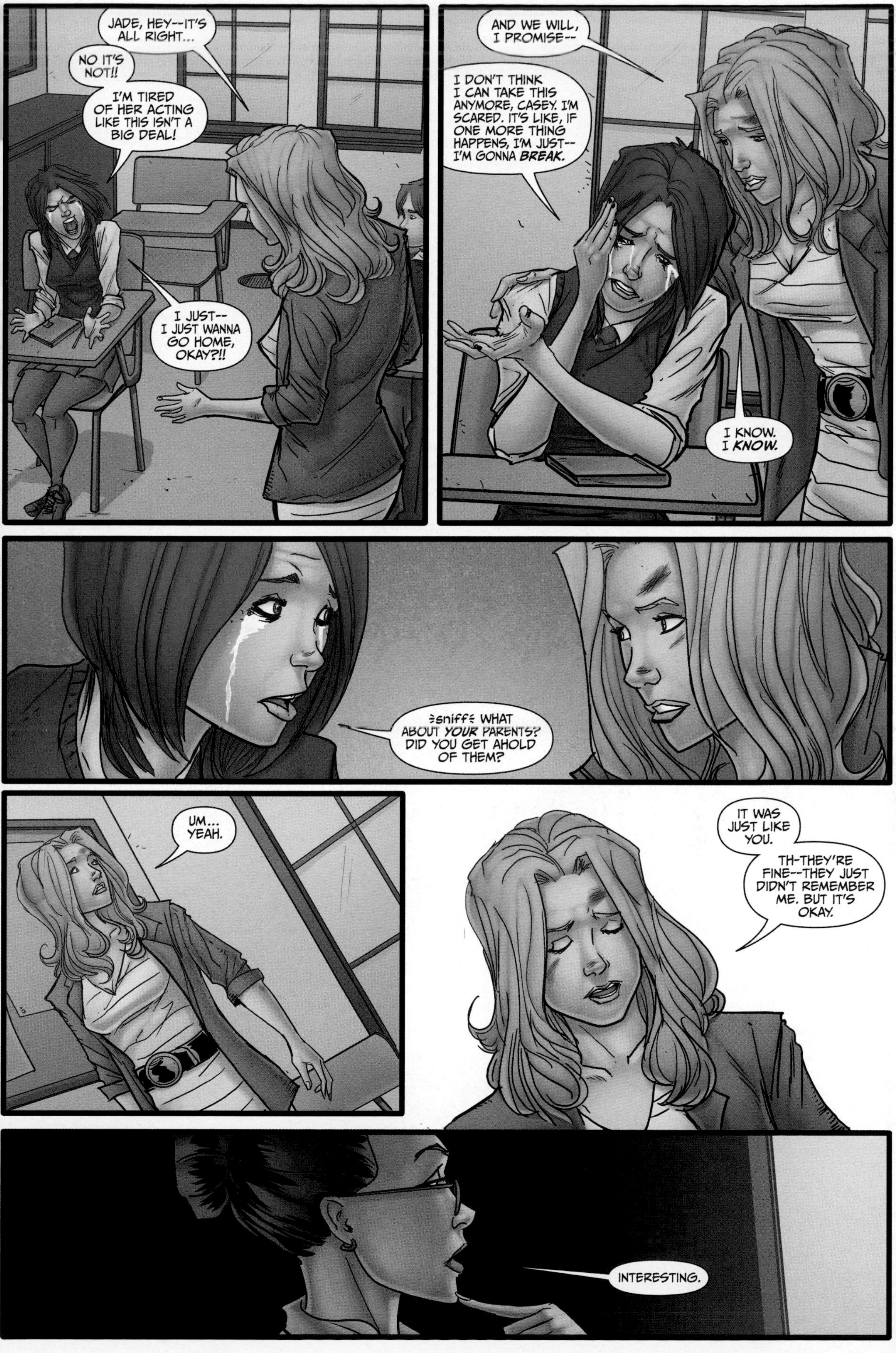
JADE, HEY--IT'S ALL RIGHT...
NO IT'S NOT!!
I'M TIRED OF HER ACTING LIKE THIS ISN'T A BIG DEAL!
I JUST-- I JUST WANNA GO HOME, OKAY?!!
AND WE WILL, I PROMISE--
I DON'T THINK I CAN TAKE THIS ANYMORE, CASEY. I'M SCARED. IT'S LIKE, IF ONE MORE THING HAPPENS, I'M JUST-- I'M GONNA BREAK.
I KNOW. I KNOW.
sniff WHAT ABOUT YOUR PARENTS? DID YOU GET AHOLD OF THEM?
UM... YEAH.
IT WAS JUST LIKE YOU.
TH-THEY'RE FINE--THEY JUST DIDN'T REMEMBER ME. BUT IT'S OKAY.
INTERESTING.

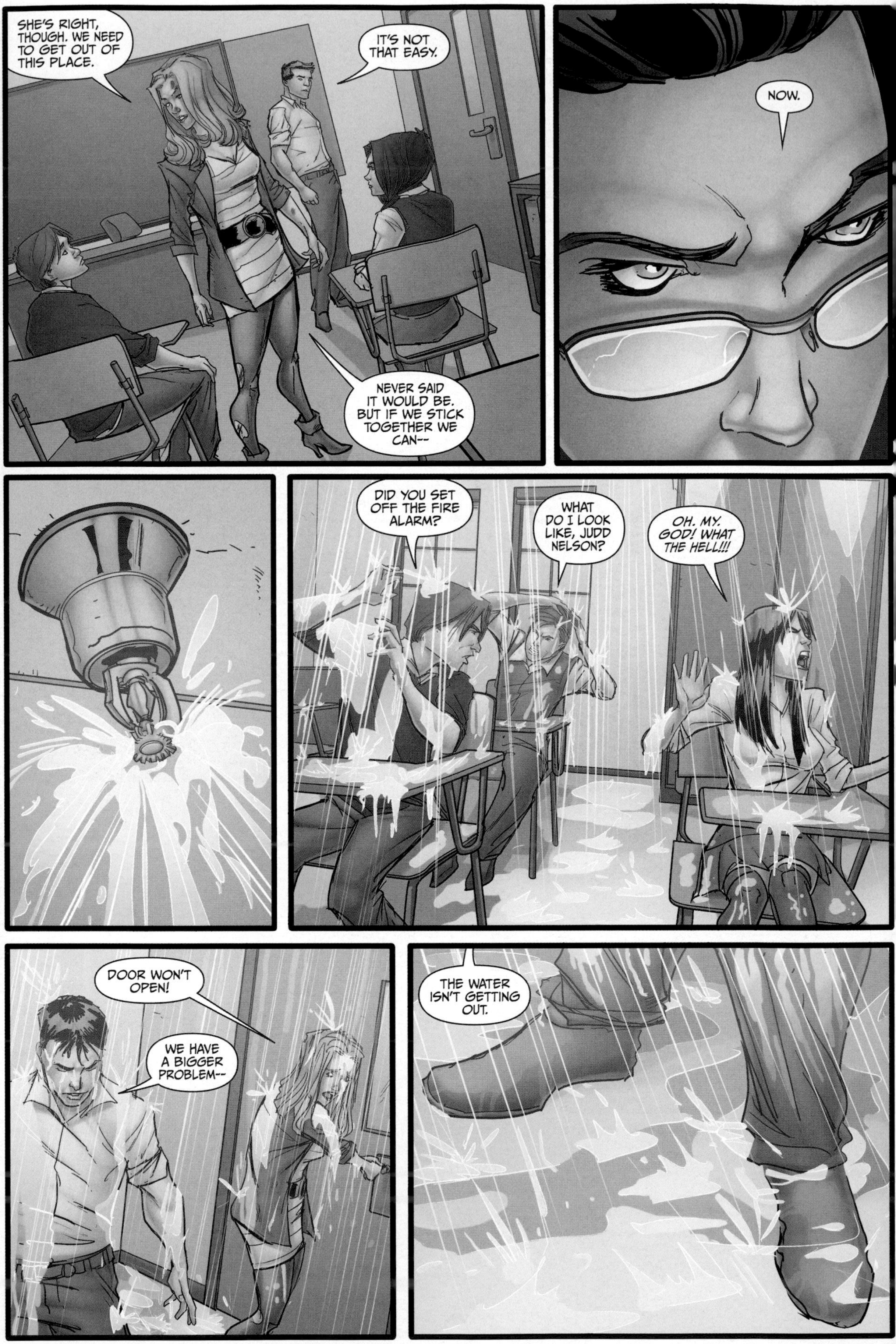
SHE'S RIGHT, THOUGH. WE NEED TO GET OUT OF THIS PLACE.
IT'S NOT THAT EASY.
NEVER SAID IT WOULD BE. BUT IF WE STICK TOGETHER WE CAN--
NOW.
DID YOU SET OFF THE FIRE ALARM?
WHAT DO I LOOK LIKE, JUDD NELSON?
OH. MY. GOD! WHAT THE HELL!!!
DOOR WON'T OPEN!
WE HAVE A BIGGER PROBLEM--
THE WATER ISN'T GETTING OUT.

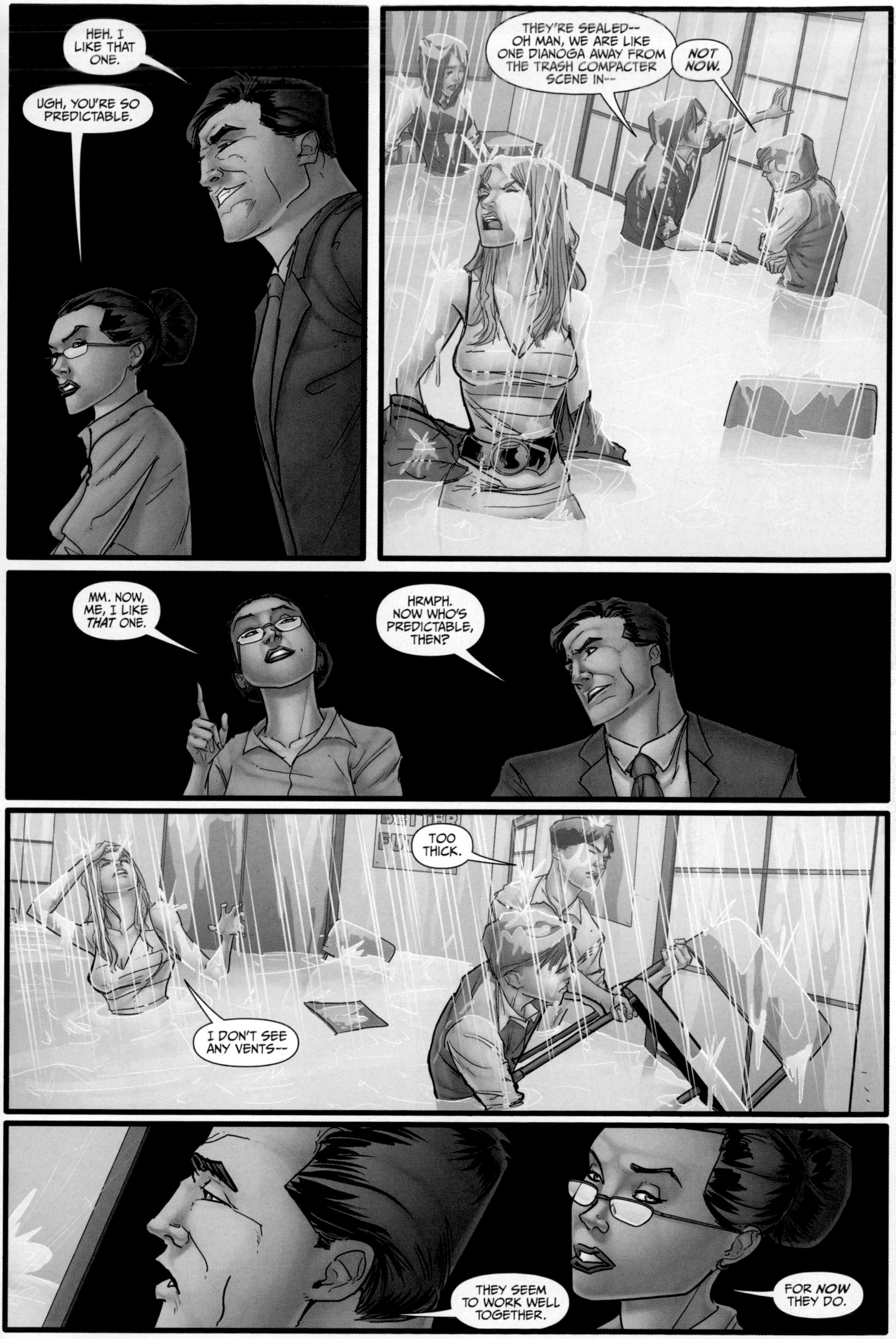
HEH. I LIKE THAT ONE.
UGH, YOU'RE SO PREDICTABLE.
THEY'RE SEALED-- OH MAN, WE ARE LIKE ONE DIANOGA AWAY FROM THE TRASH COMPACTER SCENE IN--
NOT NOW.
MM. NOW, ME, I LIKE THAT ONE.
HRMPH. NOW WHO'S PREDICTABLE, THEN?
TOO THICK.
I DON'T SEE ANY VENTS--
THEY SEEM TO WORK WELL TOGETHER.
FOR NOW THEY DO.

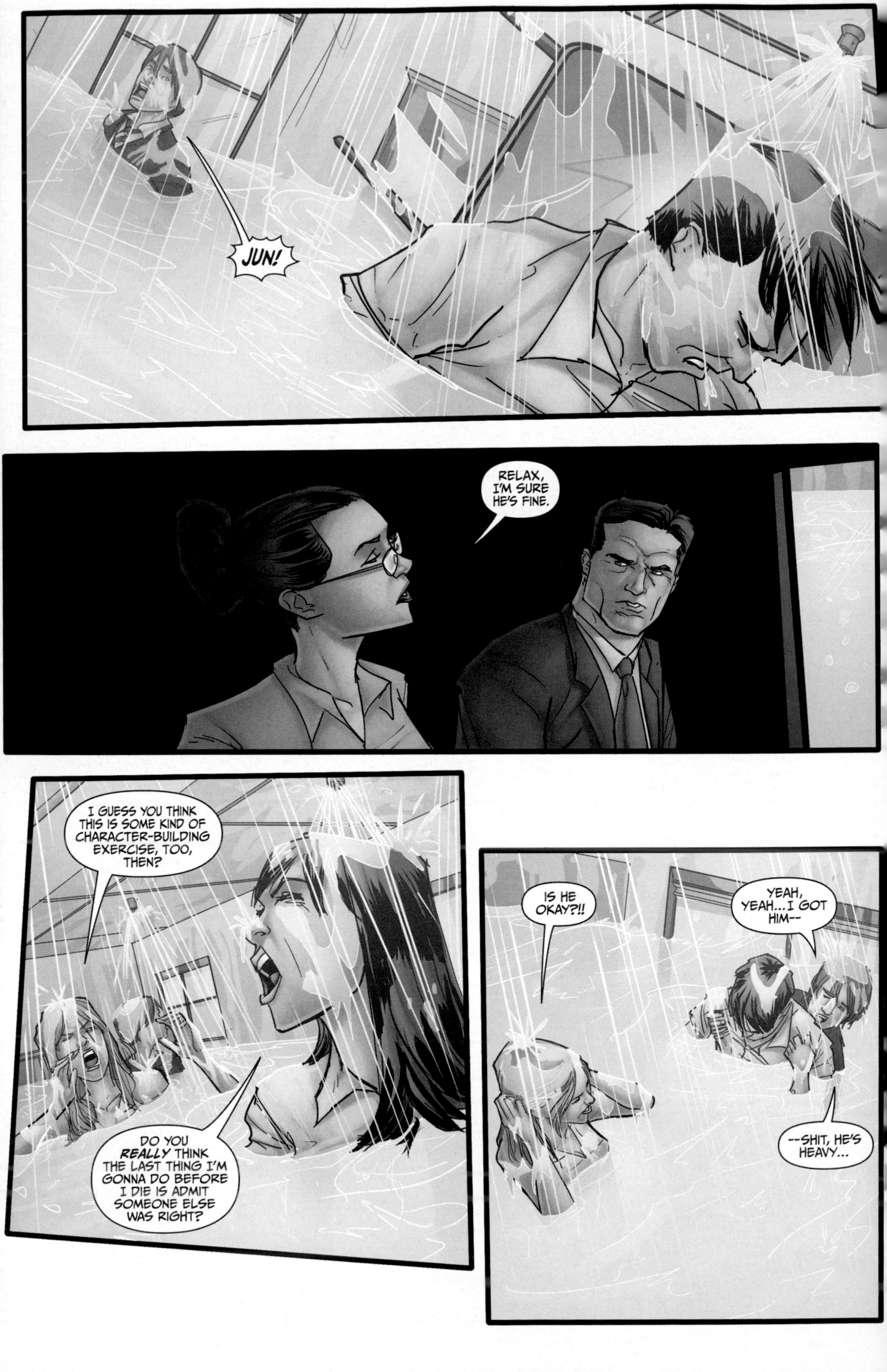
JUN!
RELAX, I'M SURE HE'S FINE.
I GUESS YOU THINK THIS IS SOME KIND OF CHARACTER-BUILDING EXERCISE, TOO, THEN?
DO YOU *REALLY* THINK THE LAST THING I'M GONNA DO BEFORE I DIE IS ADMIT SOMEONE ELSE WAS RIGHT?
IS HE OKAY?!!
YEAH, YEAH...I GOT HIM--
--SHIT, HE'S HEAVY...

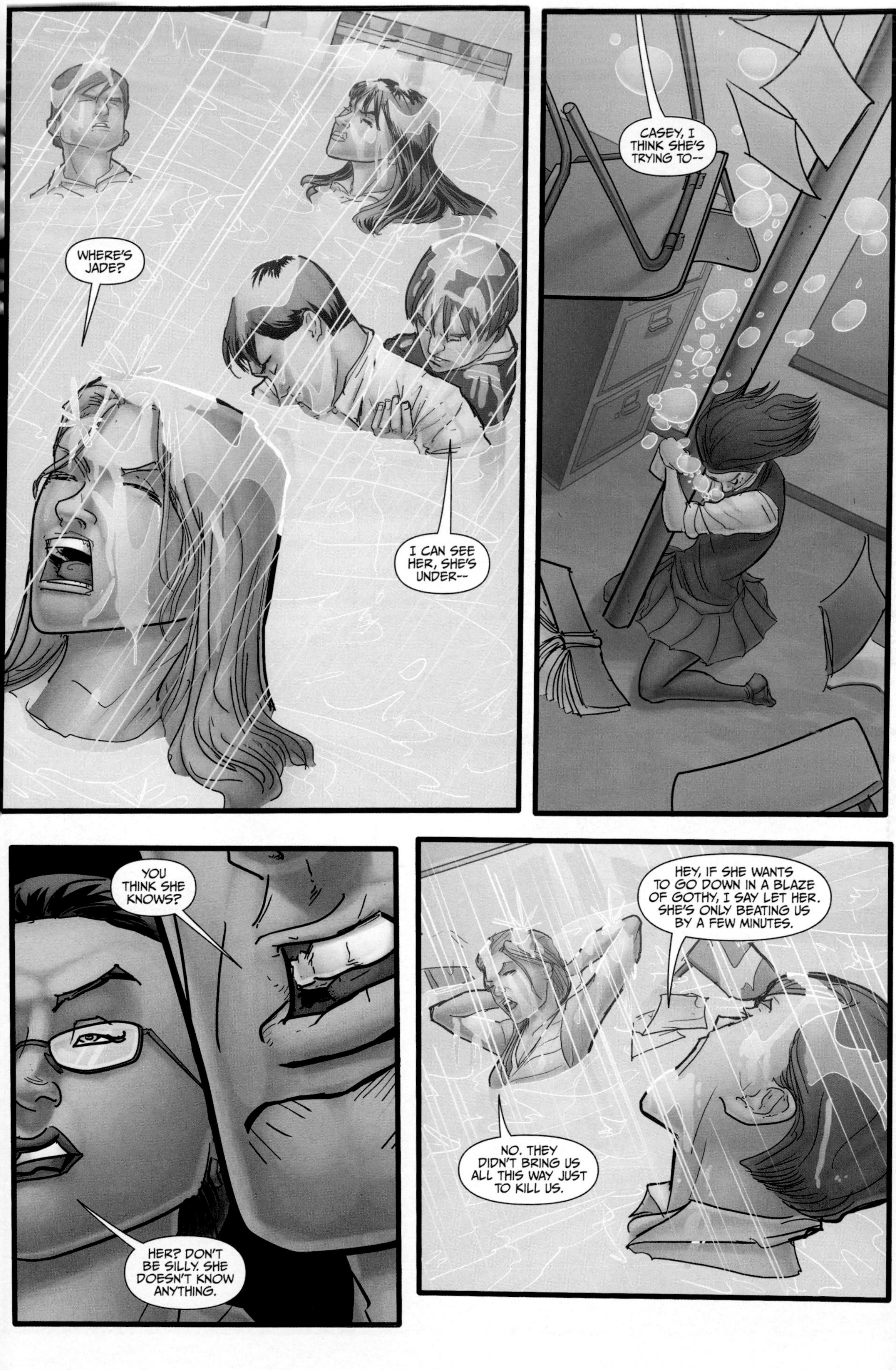
WHERE'S JADE?
I CAN SEE HER, SHE'S UNDER--
CASEY, I THINK SHE'S TRYING TO--
YOU THINK SHE KNOWS?
HER? DON'T BE SILLY. SHE DOESN'T KNOW ANYTHING.
HEY, IF SHE WANTS TO GO DOWN IN A BLAZE OF GOTHY, I SAY LET HER. SHE'S ONLY BEATING US BY A FEW MINUTES.
NO. THEY DIDN'T BRING US ALL THIS WAY JUST TO KILL US.

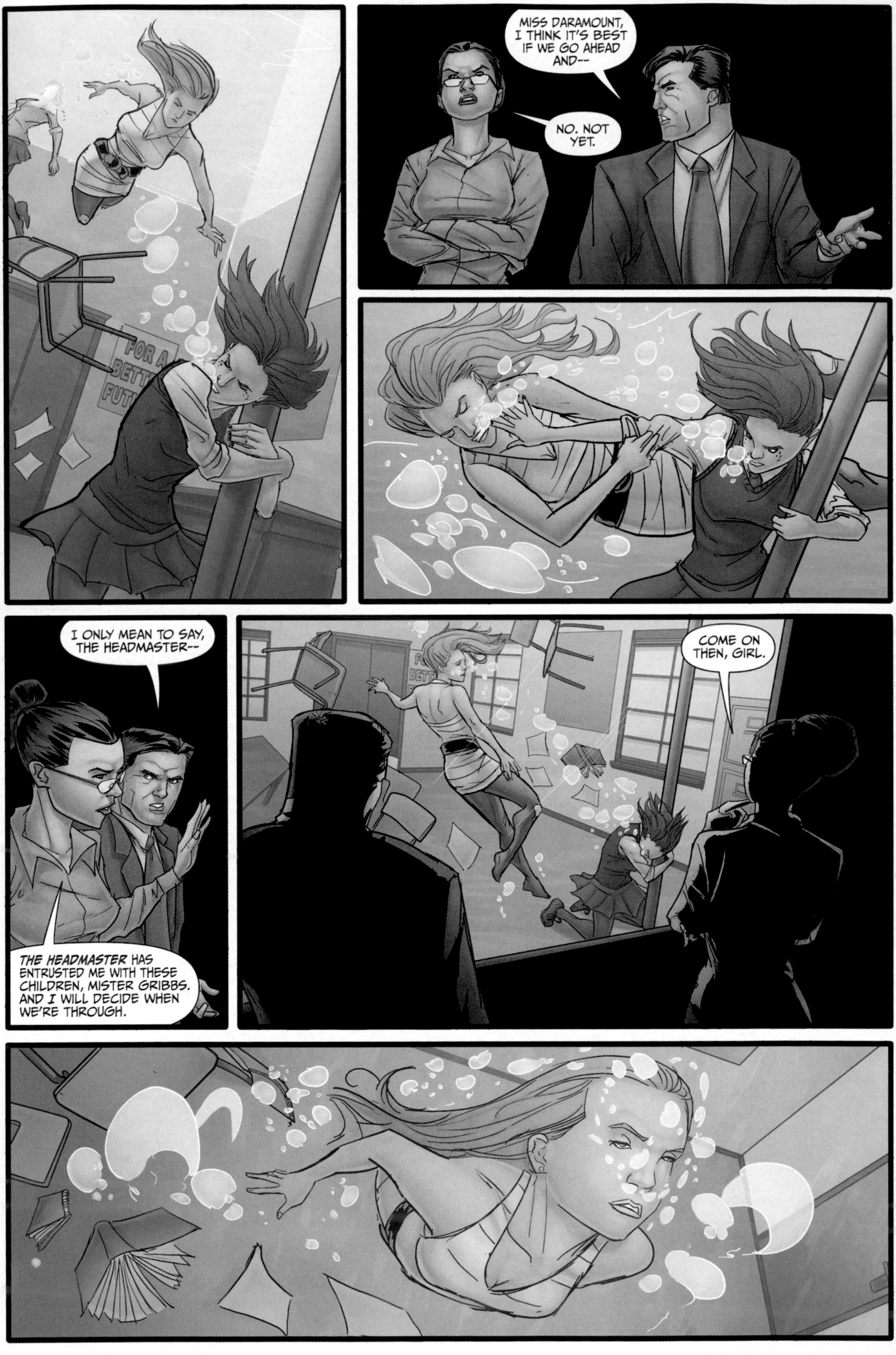
FOR A BETT FUT
MISS DARAMOUNT, I THINK IT'S BEST IF WE GO AHEAD AND--
NO. NOT YET.
I ONLY MEAN TO SAY, THE HEADMASTER--
THE HEADMASTER HAS ENTRUSTED ME WITH THESE CHILDREN, MISTER GRIBBS. AND *I* WILL DECIDE WHEN WE'RE THROUGH.
COME ON THEN, GIRL.

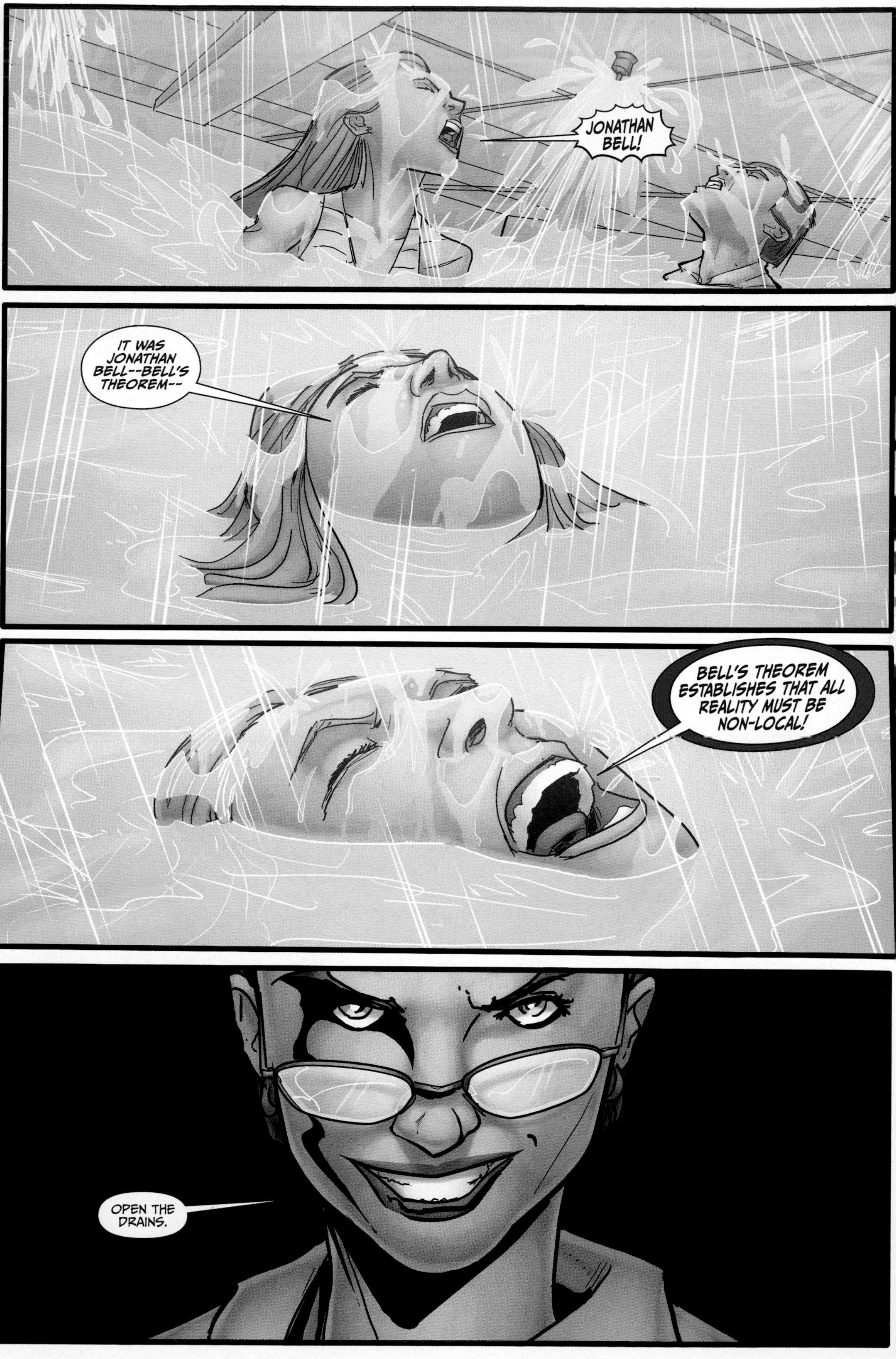
JONATHAN BELL!
IT WAS JONATHAN BELL--BELL'S THEOREM--
BELL'S THEOREM ESTABLISHES THAT ALL REALITY MUST BE NON-LOCAL!
OPEN THE DRAINS.

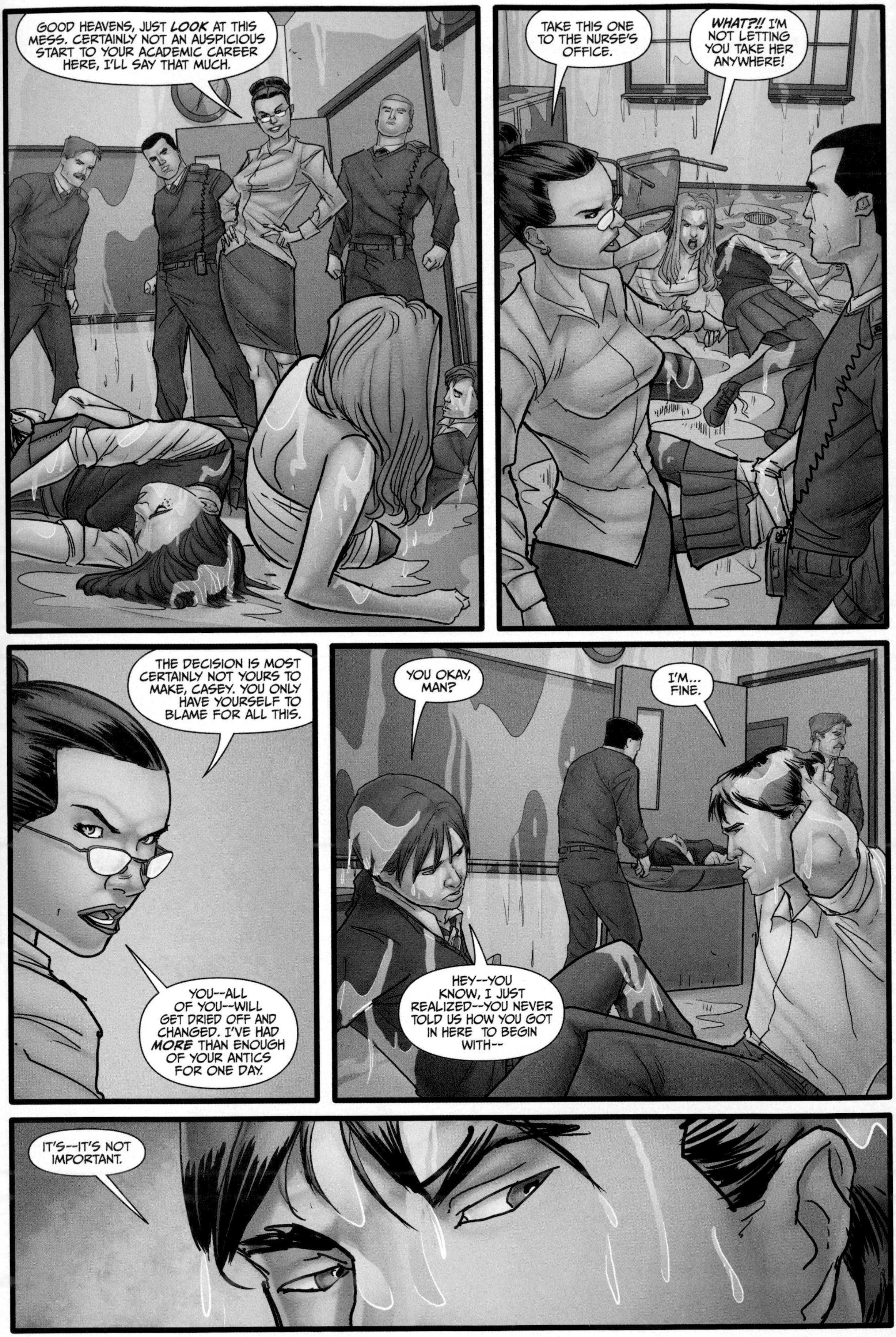
GOOD HEAVENS, JUST LOOK AT THIS MESS. CERTAINLY NOT AN AUSPICIOUS START TO YOUR ACADEMIC CAREER HERE, I'LL SAY THAT MUCH.
TAKE THIS ONE TO THE NURSE'S OFFICE.
WHAT?!! I'M NOT LETTING YOU TAKE HER ANYWHERE!
THE DECISION IS MOST CERTAINLY NOT YOURS TO MAKE, CASEY. YOU ONLY HAVE YOURSELF TO BLAME FOR ALL THIS.
YOU--ALL OF YOU--WILL GET DRIED OFF AND CHANGED. I'VE HAD MORE THAN ENOUGH OF YOUR ANTICS FOR ONE DAY.
YOU OKAY, MAN?
I'M... FINE.
HEY--YOU KNOW, I JUST REALIZED--YOU NEVER TOLD US HOW YOU GOT IN HERE TO BEGIN WITH--
IT'S--IT'S NOT IMPORTANT.

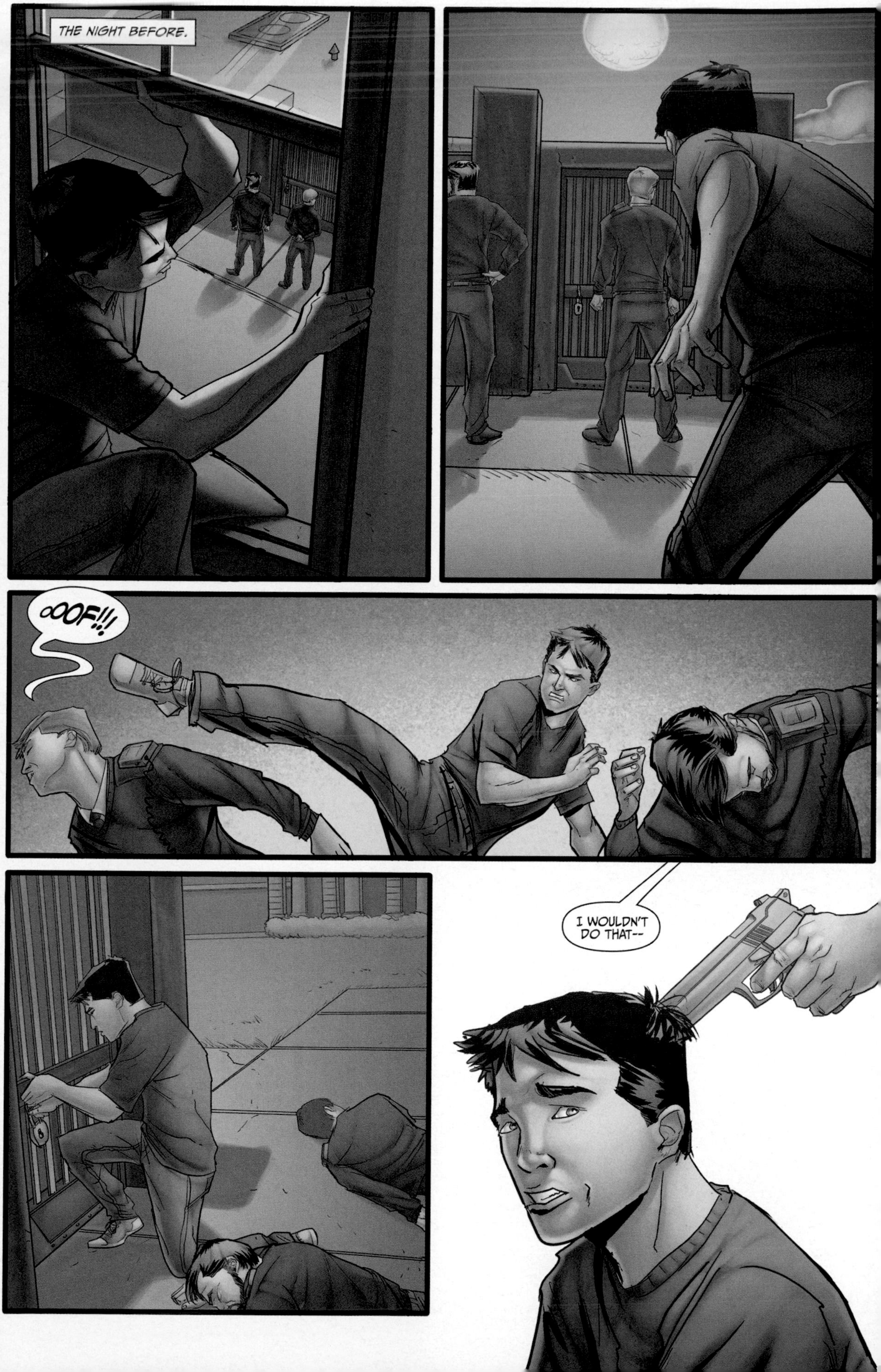
THE NIGHT BEFORE.
OOOF!!!
I WOULDN'T DO THAT--

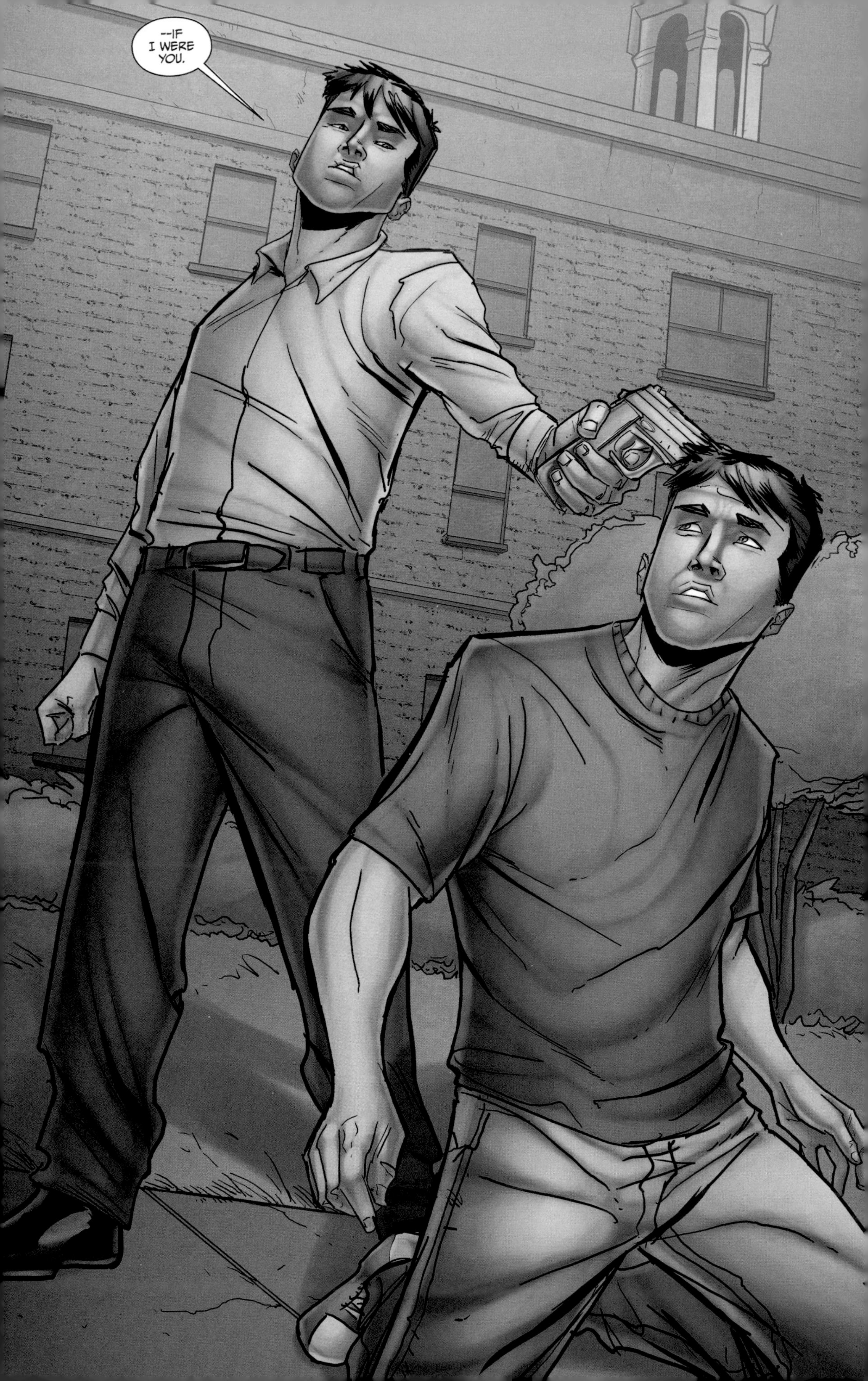
--IF I WERE YOU.

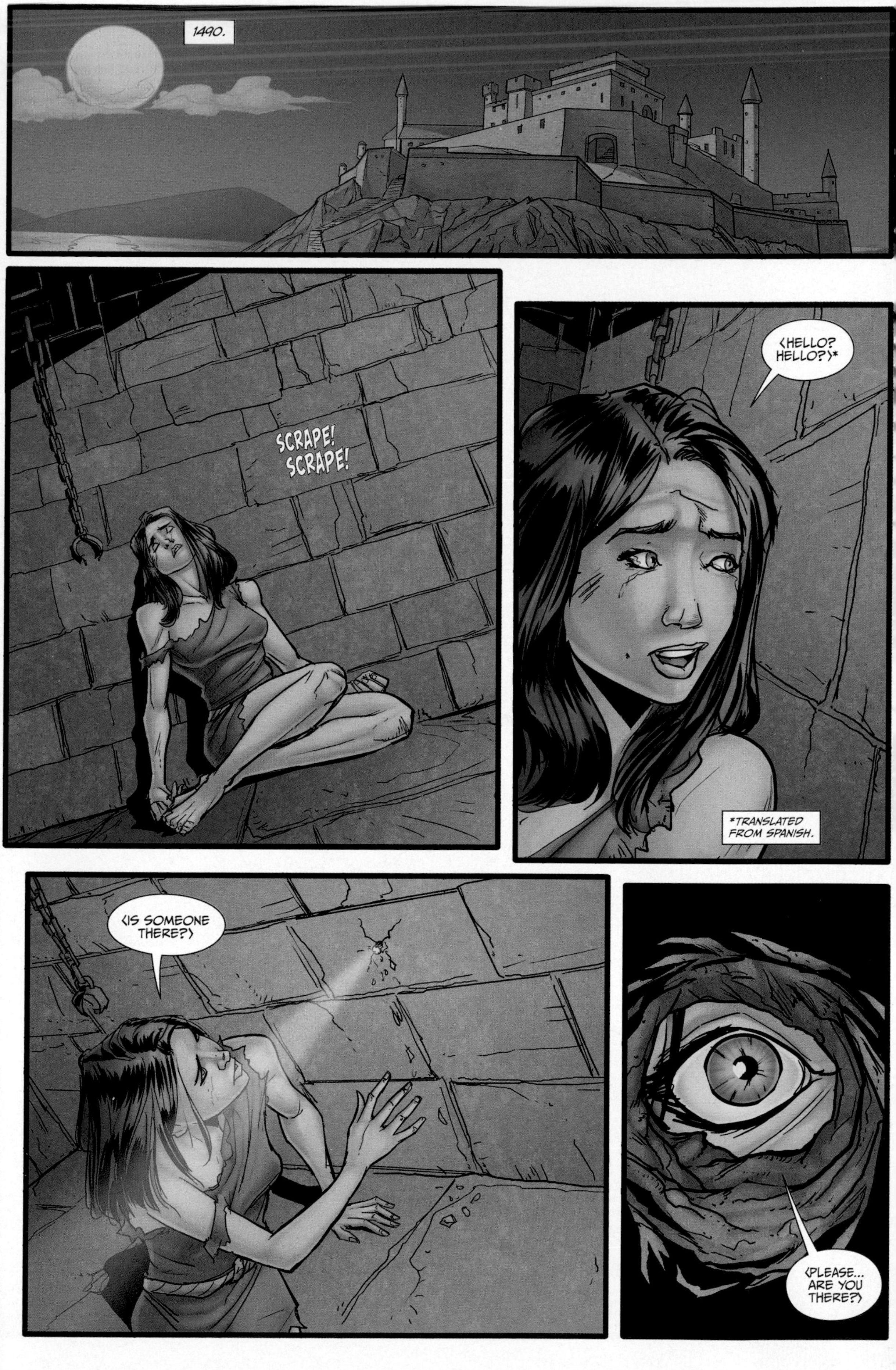
1490.
SCRAPE! SCRAPE!
<HELLO? HELLO?>*
*TRANSLATED FROM SPANISH.
<IS SOMEONE THERE?>
<PLEASE... ARE YOU THERE?>

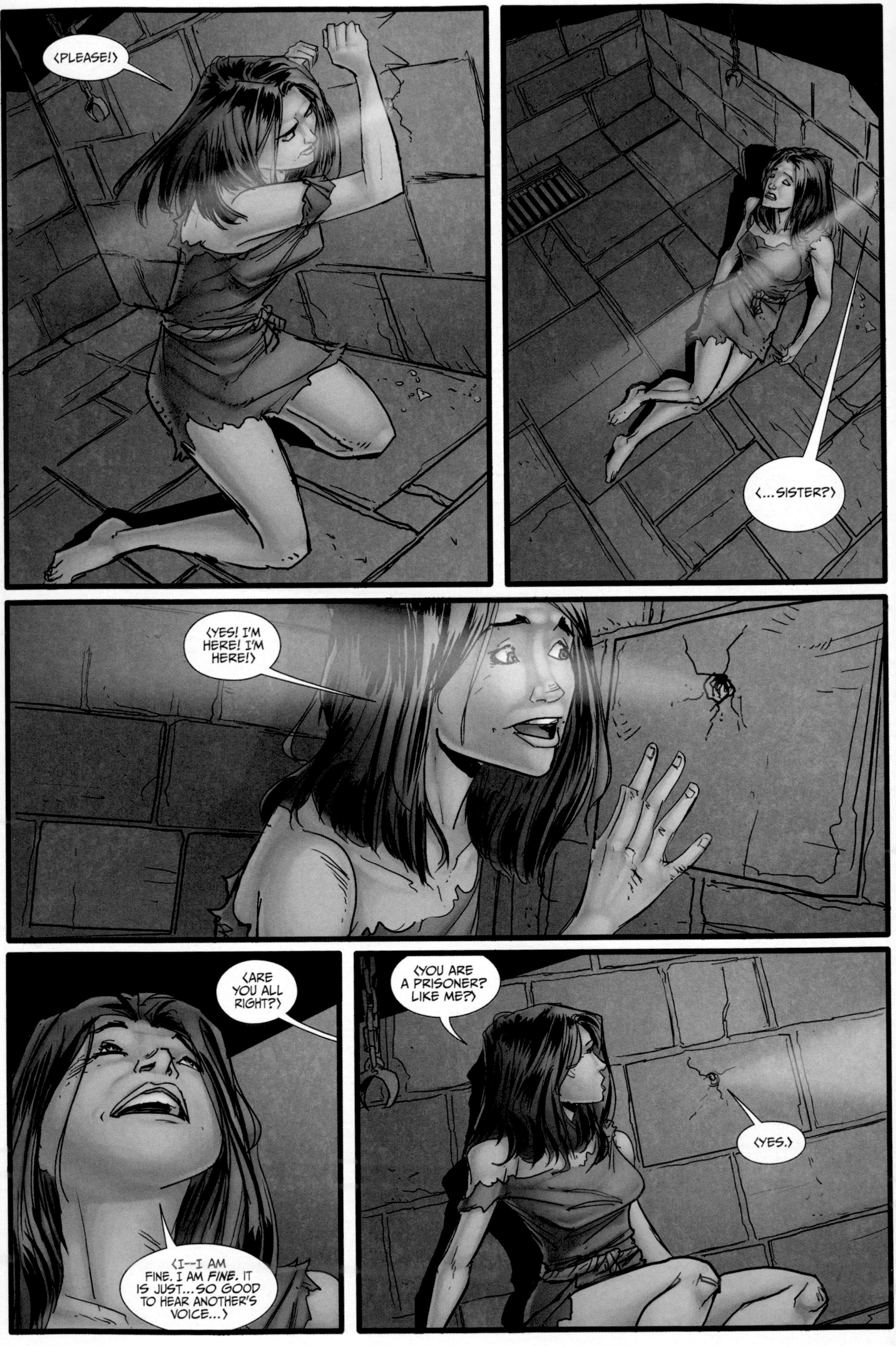

‹PLEASE!›
‹...SISTER?›
‹YES! I'M HERE! I'M HERE!›
‹ARE YOU ALL RIGHT?›
‹I--I AM FINE. I AM *FINE.* IT IS JUST...SO GOOD TO HEAR ANOTHER'S VOICE...›
‹YOU ARE A PRISONER? LIKE ME?›
‹YES.›

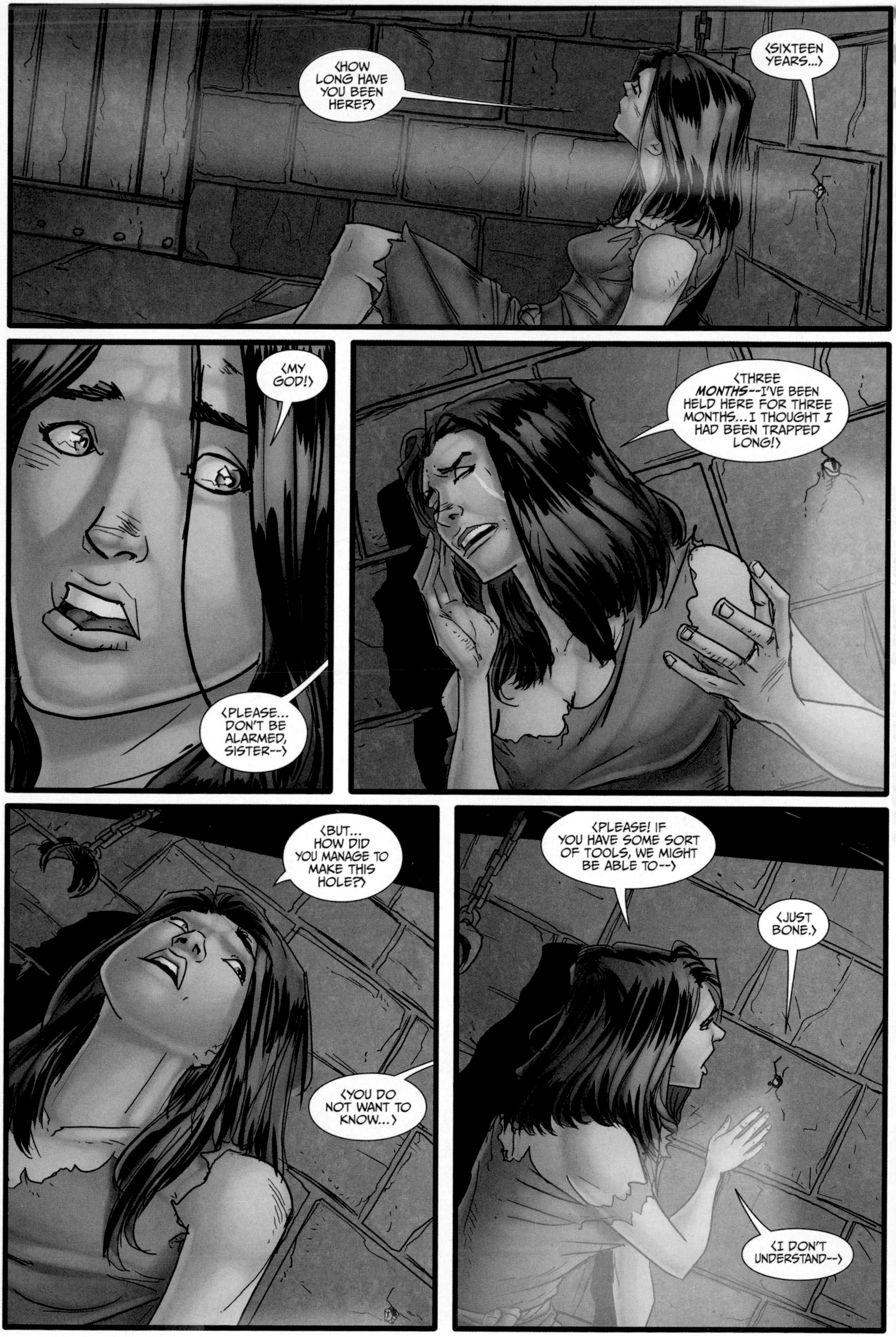

‹HOW LONG HAVE YOU BEEN HERE?›
‹SIXTEEN YEARS...›
‹MY GOD!›
‹PLEASE... DON'T BE ALARMED, SISTER--›
‹THREE *MONTHS*--I'VE BEEN HELD HERE FOR THREE MONTHS...I THOUGHT *I* HAD BEEN TRAPPED LONG!›
‹BUT... HOW DID YOU MANAGE TO MAKE THIS HOLE?›
‹YOU DO NOT WANT TO KNOW...›
‹PLEASE! IF YOU HAVE SOME SORT OF TOOLS, WE MIGHT BE ABLE TO--›
‹JUST BONE.›
‹I DON'T UNDERSTAND--›

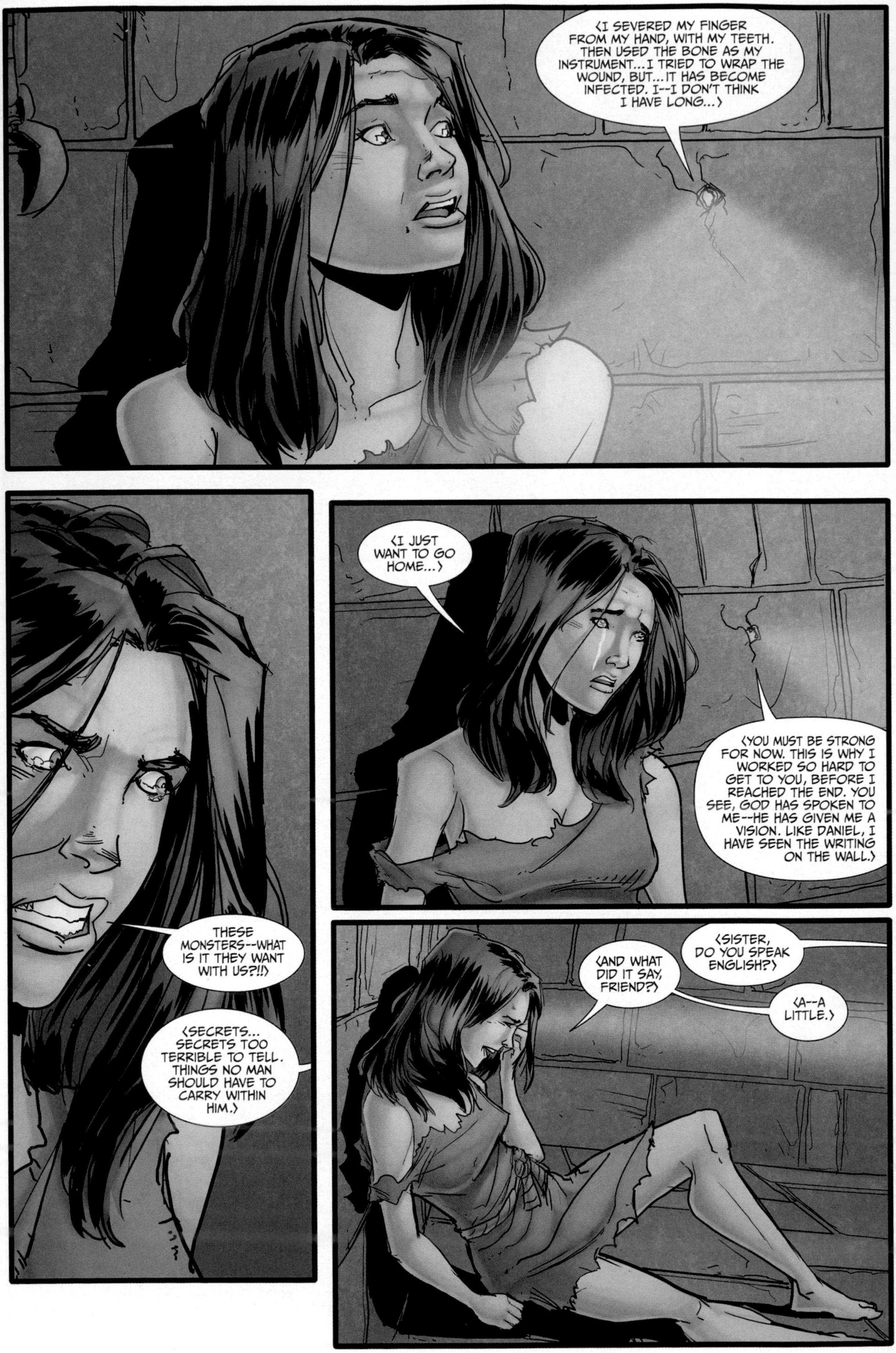
‹I SEVERED MY FINGER FROM MY HAND, WITH MY TEETH. THEN USED THE BONE AS MY INSTRUMENT...I TRIED TO WRAP THE WOUND, BUT...IT HAS BECOME INFECTED. I--I DON'T THINK I HAVE LONG...›
‹I JUST WANT TO GO HOME...›
‹YOU MUST BE STRONG FOR NOW. THIS IS WHY I WORKED SO HARD TO GET TO YOU, BEFORE I REACHED THE END. YOU SEE, GOD HAS SPOKEN TO ME--HE HAS GIVEN ME A VISION. LIKE DANIEL, I HAVE SEEN THE WRITING ON THE WALL.›
THESE MONSTERS--WHAT IS IT THEY WANT WITH US?!!›
‹SECRETS... SECRETS TOO TERRIBLE TO TELL. THINGS NO MAN SHOULD HAVE TO CARRY WITHIN HIM.›
‹AND WHAT DID IT SAY, FRIEND?›
‹SISTER, DO YOU SPEAK ENGLISH?›
‹A--A LITTLE.›

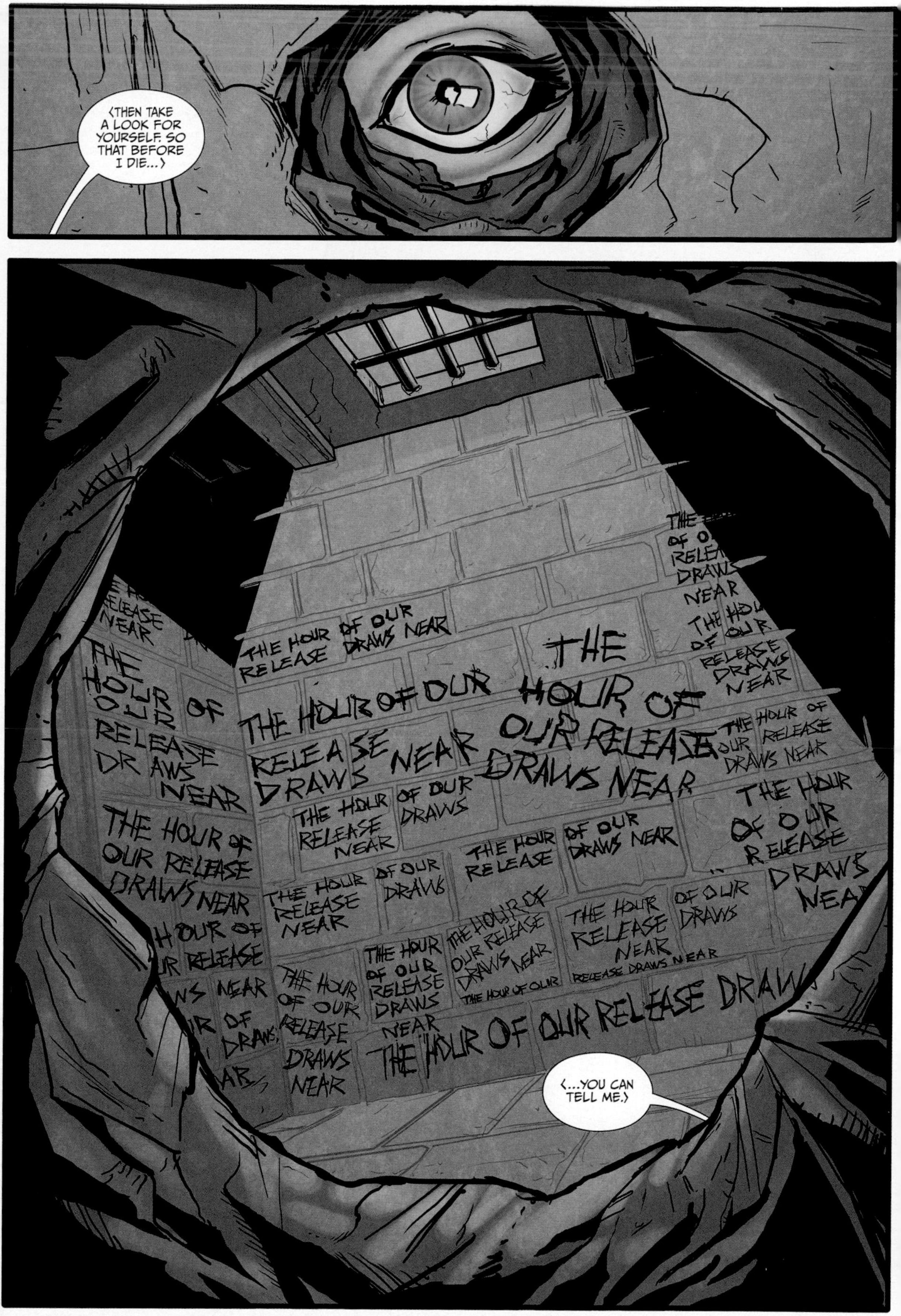

‹THEN TAKE A LOOK FOR YOURSELF. SO THAT BEFORE I DIE...›
THE HOUR OF OUR RELEASE DRAWS NEAR
THE HOUR OF OUR RELEASE DRAWS NEAR
THE HOUR OF OUR RELEASE DRAWS
THE HOUR OF OUR
‹...YOU CAN TELL ME.›

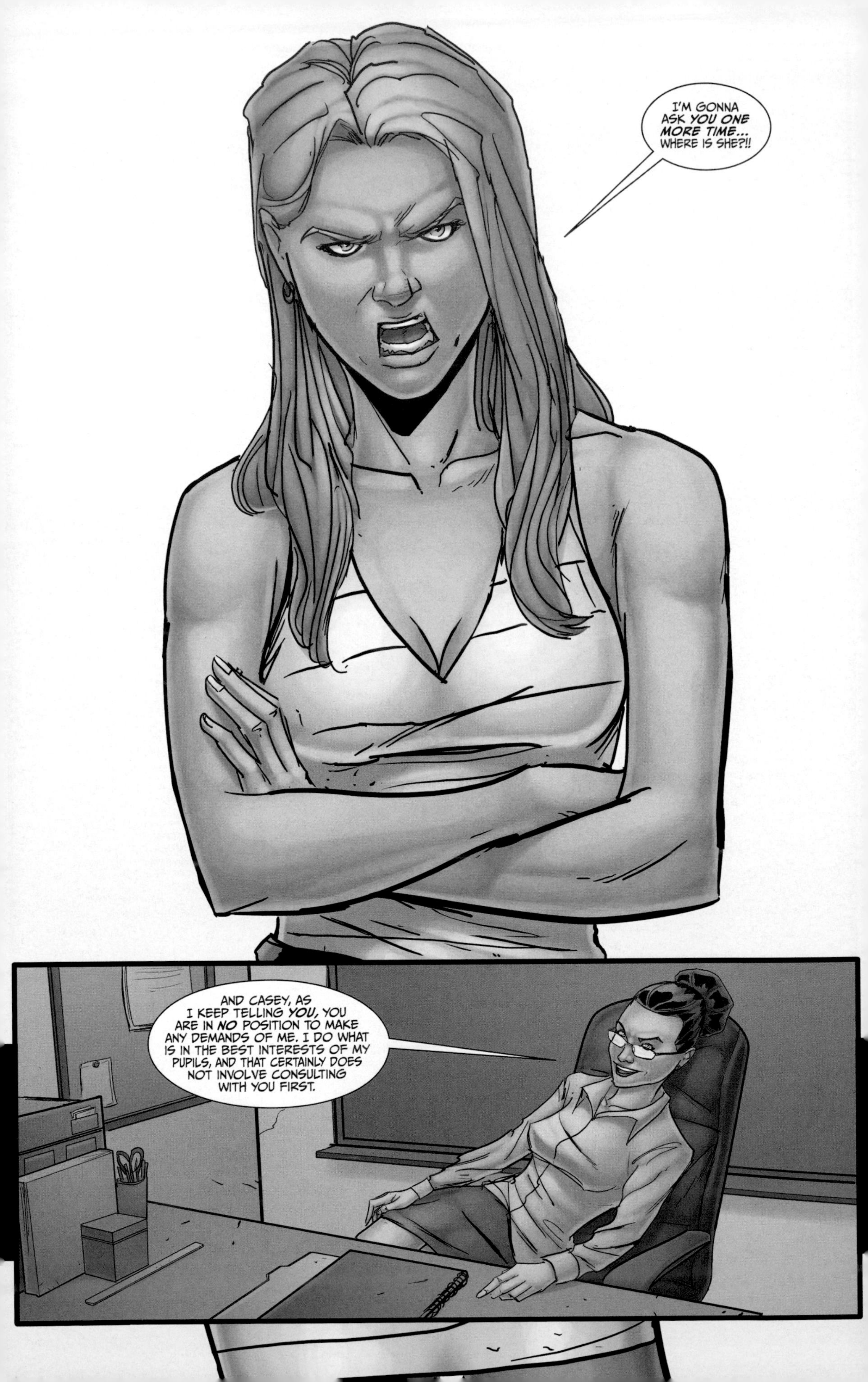
I'M GONNA ASK YOU ONE MORE TIME... WHERE IS SHE?!!
AND CASEY, AS I KEEP TELLING YOU, YOU ARE IN NO POSITION TO MAKE ANY DEMANDS OF ME. I DO WHAT IS IN THE BEST INTERESTS OF MY PUPILS, AND THAT CERTAINLY DOES NOT INVOLVE CONSULTING WITH YOU FIRST.

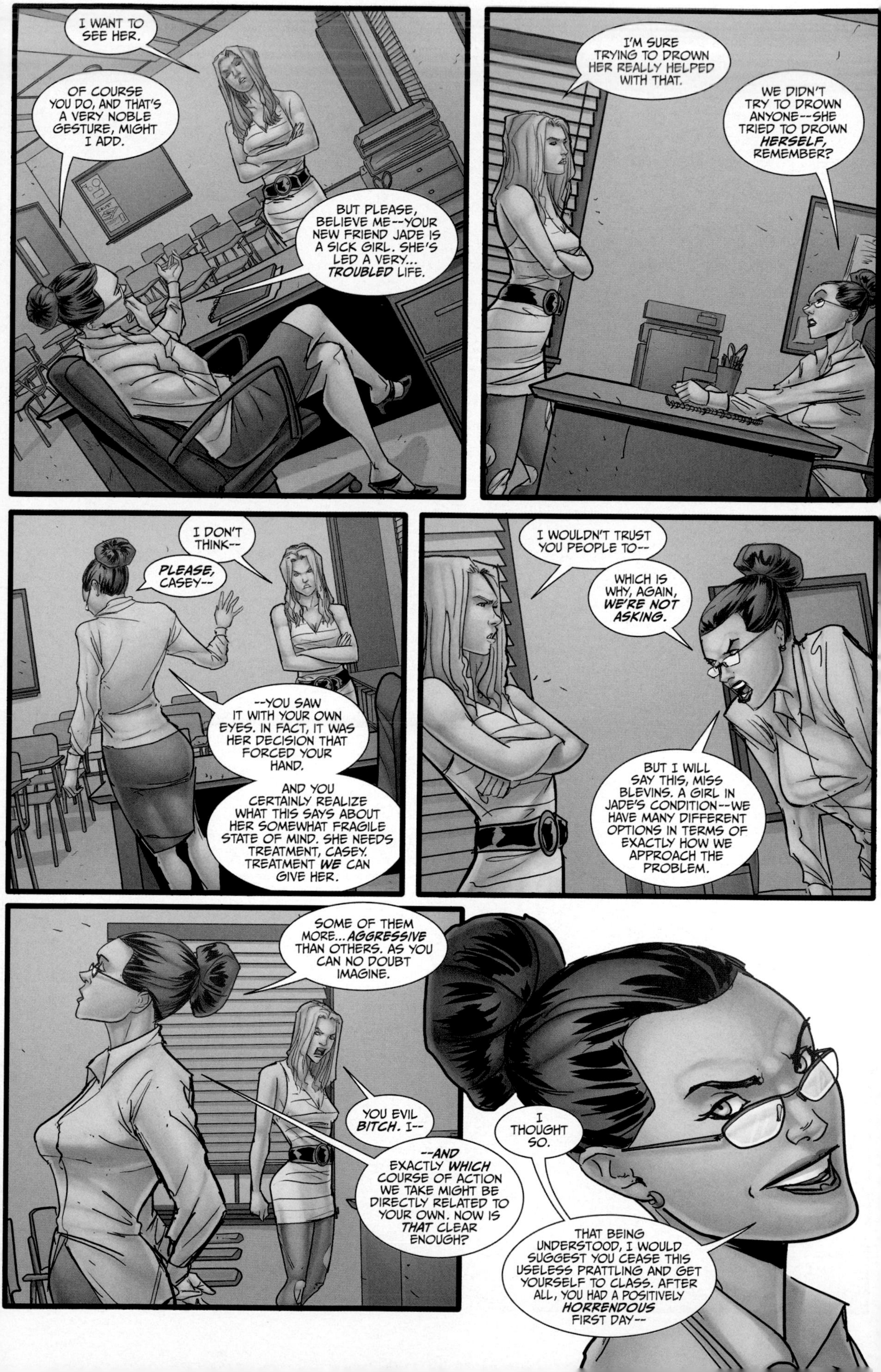
I WANT TO SEE HER.
OF COURSE YOU DO, AND THAT'S A VERY NOBLE GESTURE, MIGHT I ADD.
BUT PLEASE, BELIEVE ME--YOUR NEW FRIEND JADE IS A SICK GIRL. SHE'S LED A VERY... *TROUBLED* LIFE.
I'M SURE TRYING TO DROWN HER REALLY HELPED WITH THAT.
WE DIDN'T TRY TO DROWN ANYONE--SHE TRIED TO DROWN *HERSELF*, REMEMBER?
I DON'T THINK--
PLEASE, CASEY--
--YOU SAW IT WITH YOUR OWN EYES. IN FACT, IT WAS HER DECISION THAT FORCED YOUR HAND.
AND YOU CERTAINLY REALIZE WHAT THIS SAYS ABOUT HER SOMEWHAT FRAGILE STATE OF MIND. SHE NEEDS TREATMENT, CASEY. TREATMENT *WE* CAN GIVE HER.
I WOULDN'T TRUST YOU PEOPLE TO--
WHICH IS WHY, AGAIN, *WE'RE NOT ASKING.*
BUT I WILL SAY THIS, MISS BLEVINS. A GIRL IN JADE'S CONDITION--WE HAVE MANY DIFFERENT OPTIONS IN TERMS OF EXACTLY HOW WE APPROACH THE PROBLEM.
SOME OF THEM MORE... *AGGRESSIVE* THAN OTHERS. AS YOU CAN NO DOUBT IMAGINE.
YOU EVIL *BITCH*. I--
--AND EXACTLY *WHICH* COURSE OF ACTION WE TAKE MIGHT BE DIRECTLY RELATED TO YOUR OWN. NOW IS *THAT* CLEAR ENOUGH?
I THOUGHT SO.
THAT BEING UNDERSTOOD, I WOULD SUGGEST YOU CEASE THIS USELESS PRATTLING AND GET YOURSELF TO CLASS. AFTER ALL, YOU HAD A POSITIVELY *HORRENDOUS* FIRST DAY--

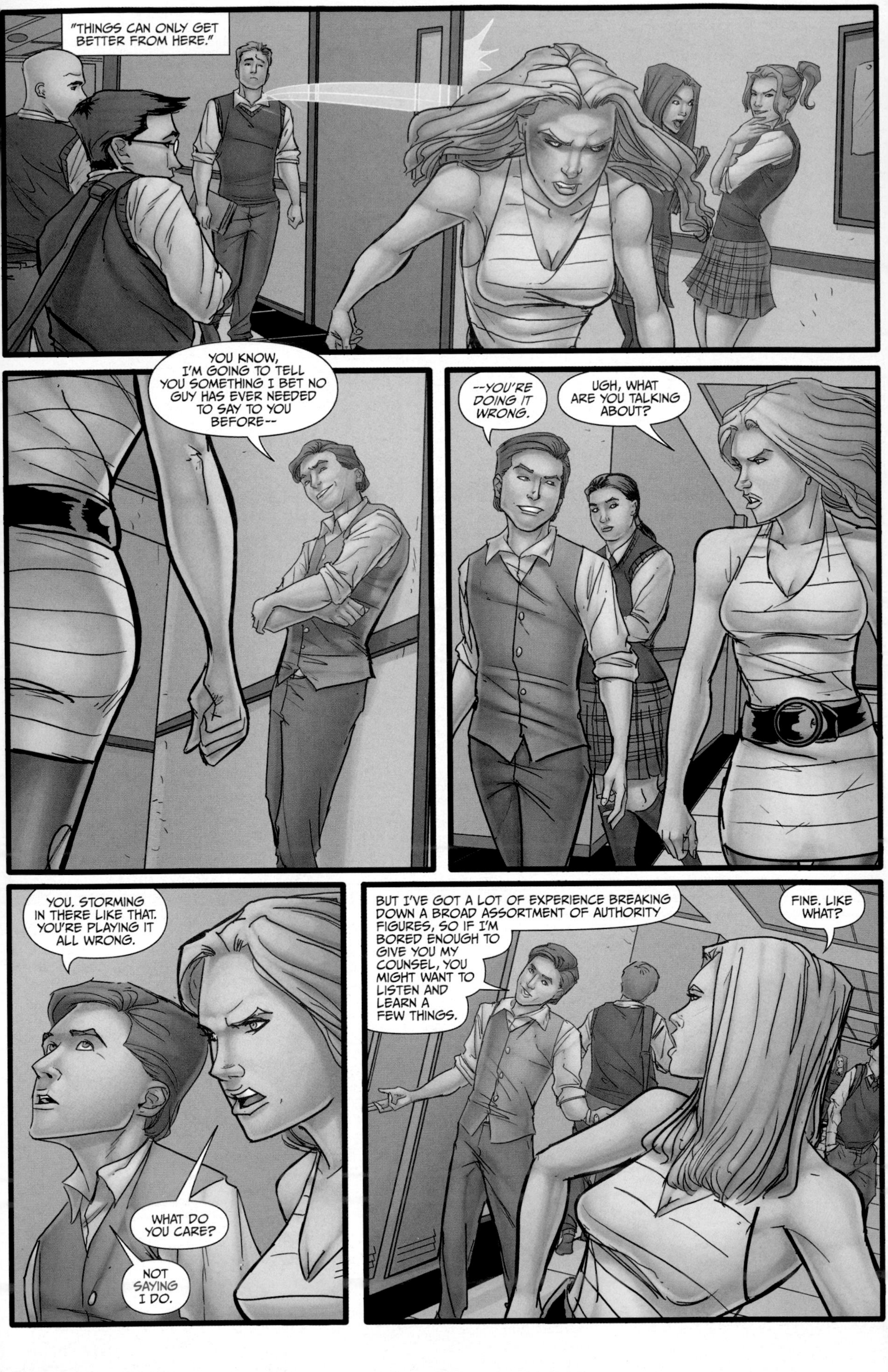
"THINGS CAN ONLY GET BETTER FROM HERE."
YOU KNOW, I'M GOING TO TELL YOU SOMETHING I BET NO GUY HAS EVER NEEDED TO SAY TO YOU BEFORE--
--YOU'RE DOING IT WRONG.
UGH, WHAT ARE YOU TALKING ABOUT?
YOU. STORMING IN THERE LIKE THAT. YOU'RE PLAYING IT ALL WRONG.
WHAT DO YOU CARE?
NOT SAYING I DO.
BUT I'VE GOT A LOT OF EXPERIENCE BREAKING DOWN A BROAD ASSORTMENT OF AUTHORITY FIGURES, SO IF I'M BORED ENOUGH TO GIVE YOU MY COUNSEL, YOU MIGHT WANT TO LISTEN AND LEARN A FEW THINGS.
FINE. LIKE WHAT?

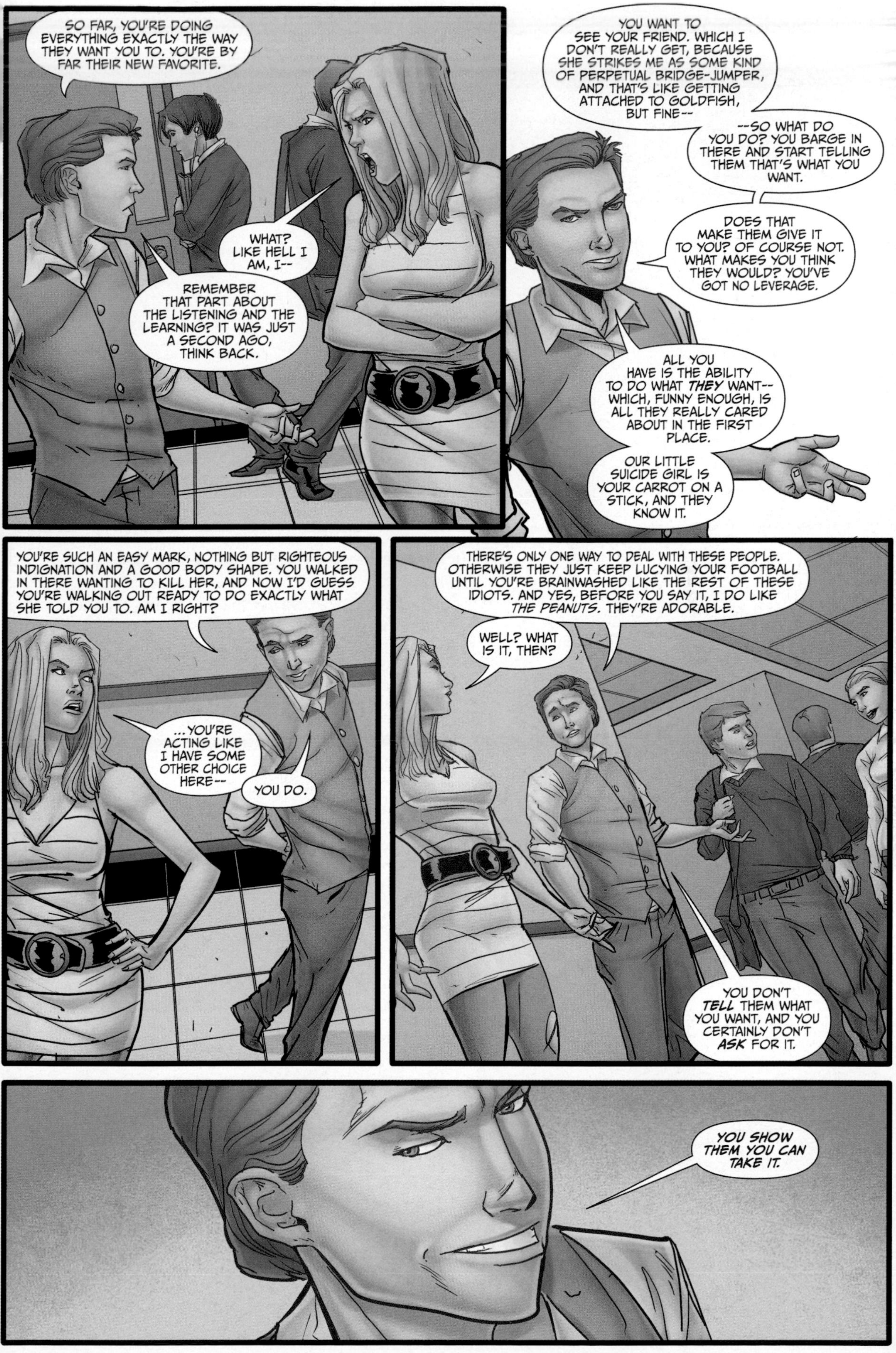
SO FAR, YOU'RE DOING EVERYTHING EXACTLY THE WAY THEY WANT YOU TO. YOU'RE BY FAR THEIR NEW FAVORITE.
WHAT? LIKE HELL I AM, I--
REMEMBER THAT PART ABOUT THE LISTENING AND THE LEARNING? IT WAS JUST A SECOND AGO, THINK BACK.
YOU WANT TO SEE YOUR FRIEND. WHICH I DON'T REALLY GET, BECAUSE SHE STRIKES ME AS SOME KIND OF PERPETUAL BRIDGE-JUMPER, AND THAT'S LIKE GETTING ATTACHED TO GOLDFISH, BUT FINE--
--SO WHAT DO YOU DO? YOU BARGE IN THERE AND START TELLING THEM THAT'S WHAT YOU WANT.
DOES THAT MAKE THEM GIVE IT TO YOU? OF COURSE NOT. WHAT MAKES YOU THINK THEY WOULD? YOU'VE GOT NO LEVERAGE.
ALL YOU HAVE IS THE ABILITY TO DO WHAT *THEY* WANT-- WHICH, FUNNY ENOUGH, IS ALL THEY REALLY CARED ABOUT IN THE FIRST PLACE.
OUR LITTLE SUICIDE GIRL IS YOUR CARROT ON A STICK, AND THEY KNOW IT.
YOU'RE SUCH AN EASY MARK, NOTHING BUT RIGHTEOUS INDIGNATION AND A GOOD BODY SHAPE. YOU WALKED IN THERE WANTING TO KILL HER, AND NOW I'D GUESS YOU'RE WALKING OUT READY TO DO EXACTLY WHAT SHE TOLD YOU TO. AM I RIGHT?
...YOU'RE ACTING LIKE I HAVE SOME OTHER CHOICE HERE--
YOU DO.
THERE'S ONLY ONE WAY TO DEAL WITH THESE PEOPLE. OTHERWISE THEY JUST KEEP LUCYING YOUR FOOTBALL UNTIL YOU'RE BRAINWASHED LIKE THE REST OF THESE IDIOTS. AND YES, BEFORE YOU SAY IT, I DO LIKE *THE PEANUTS*. THEY'RE ADORABLE.
WELL? WHAT IS IT, THEN?
YOU DON'T ***TELL*** THEM WHAT YOU WANT, AND YOU CERTAINLY DON'T ***ASK*** FOR IT.
YOU SHOW THEM YOU CAN TAKE IT.

[redacted]

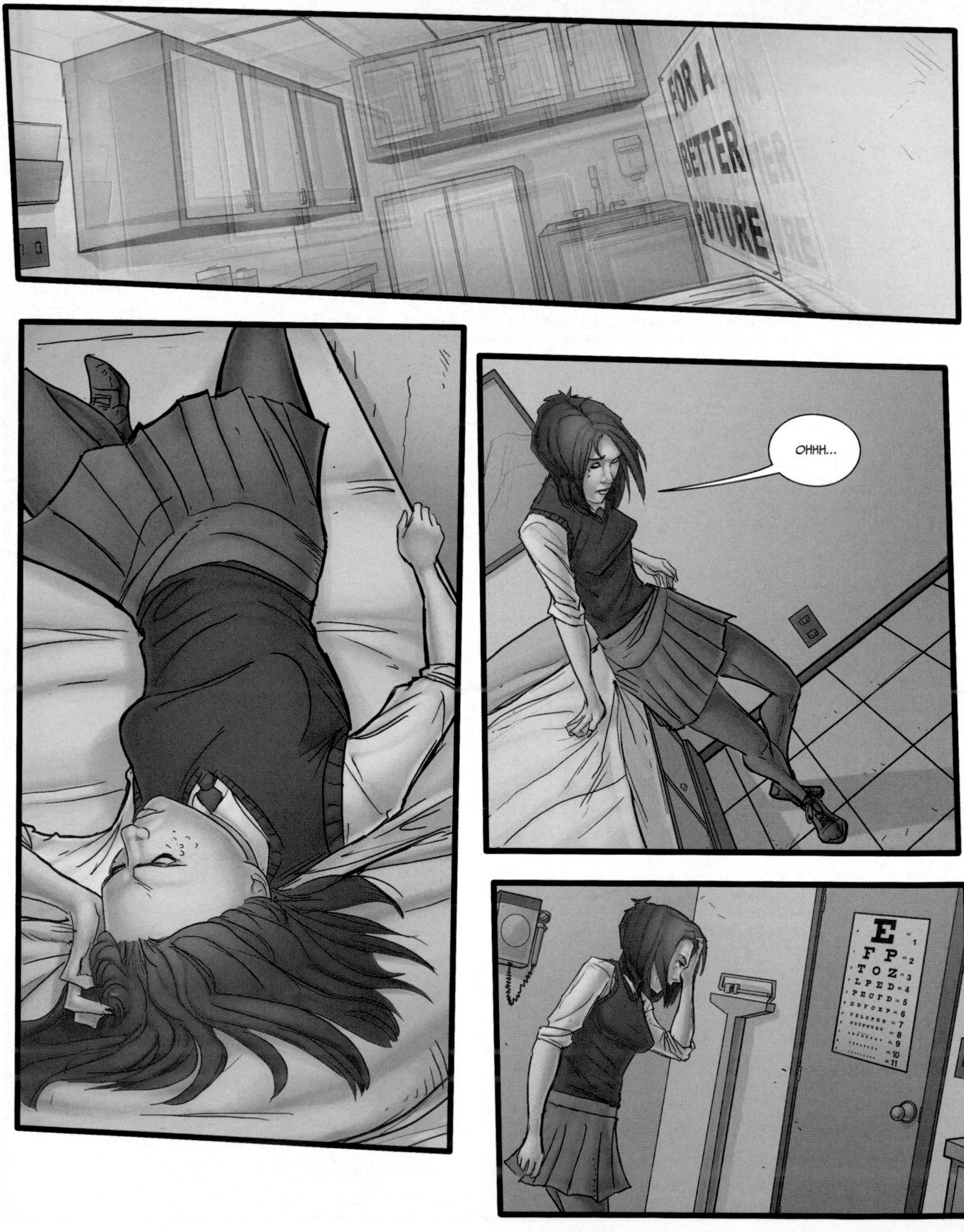
FOR A BETTER FUTURE
OHHH...
E
F P
T O Z
L P E D

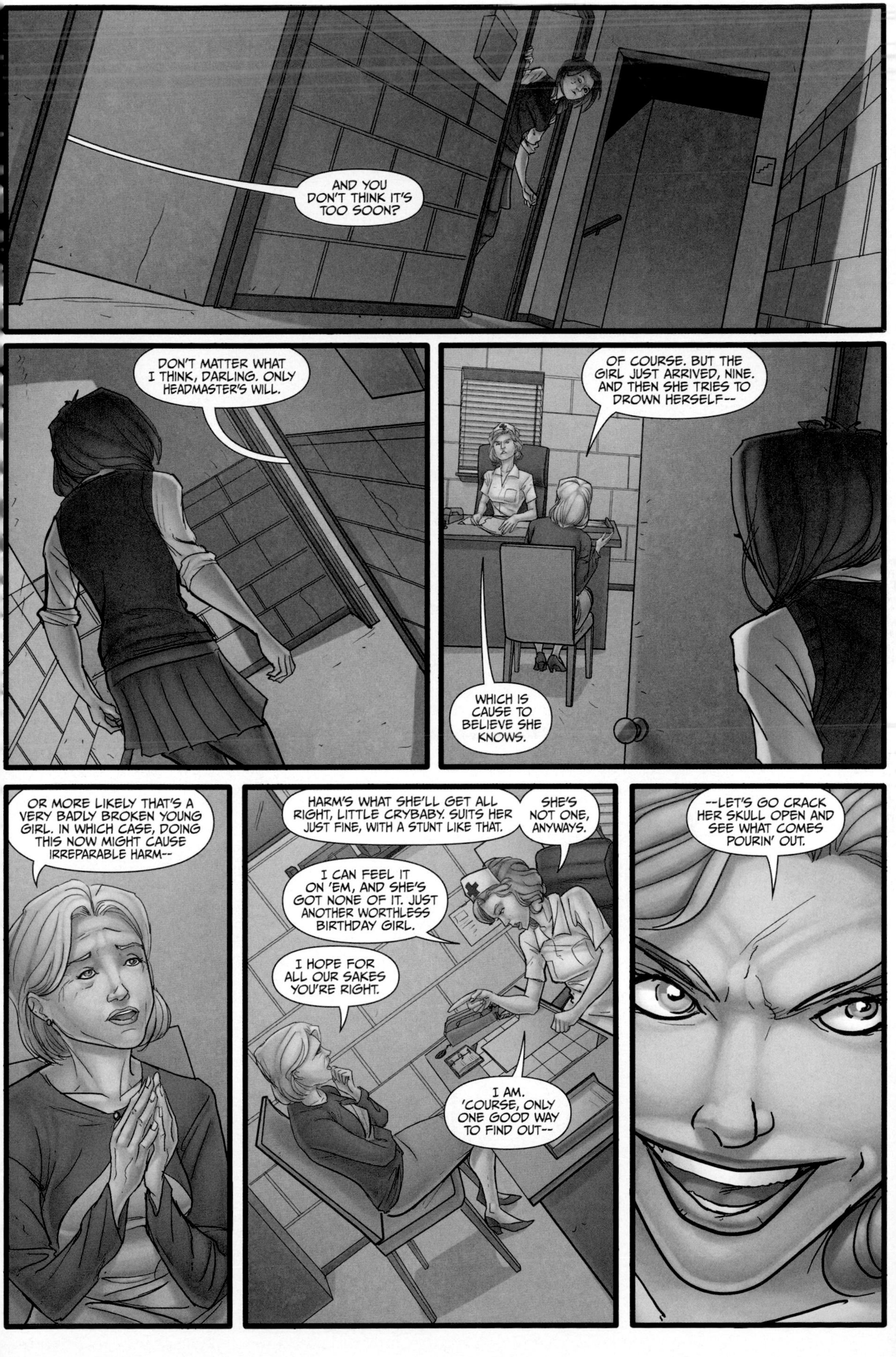
AND YOU DON'T THINK IT'S TOO SOON?
DON'T MATTER WHAT I THINK, DARLING. ONLY HEADMASTER'S WILL.
OF COURSE. BUT THE GIRL JUST ARRIVED, NINE. AND THEN SHE TRIES TO DROWN HERSELF--
WHICH IS CAUSE TO BELIEVE SHE KNOWS.
OR MORE LIKELY THAT'S A VERY BADLY BROKEN YOUNG GIRL. IN WHICH CASE, DOING THIS NOW MIGHT CAUSE IRREPARABLE HARM--
HARM'S WHAT SHE'LL GET ALL RIGHT, LITTLE CRYBABY. SUITS HER JUST FINE, WITH A STUNT LIKE THAT.
SHE'S NOT ONE, ANYWAYS.
I CAN FEEL IT ON 'EM, AND SHE'S GOT NONE OF IT. JUST ANOTHER WORTHLESS BIRTHDAY GIRL.
I HOPE FOR ALL OUR SAKES YOU'RE RIGHT.
I AM. 'COURSE, ONLY ONE GOOD WAY TO FIND OUT--
--LET'S GO CRACK HER SKULL OPEN AND SEE WHAT COMES POURIN' OUT.

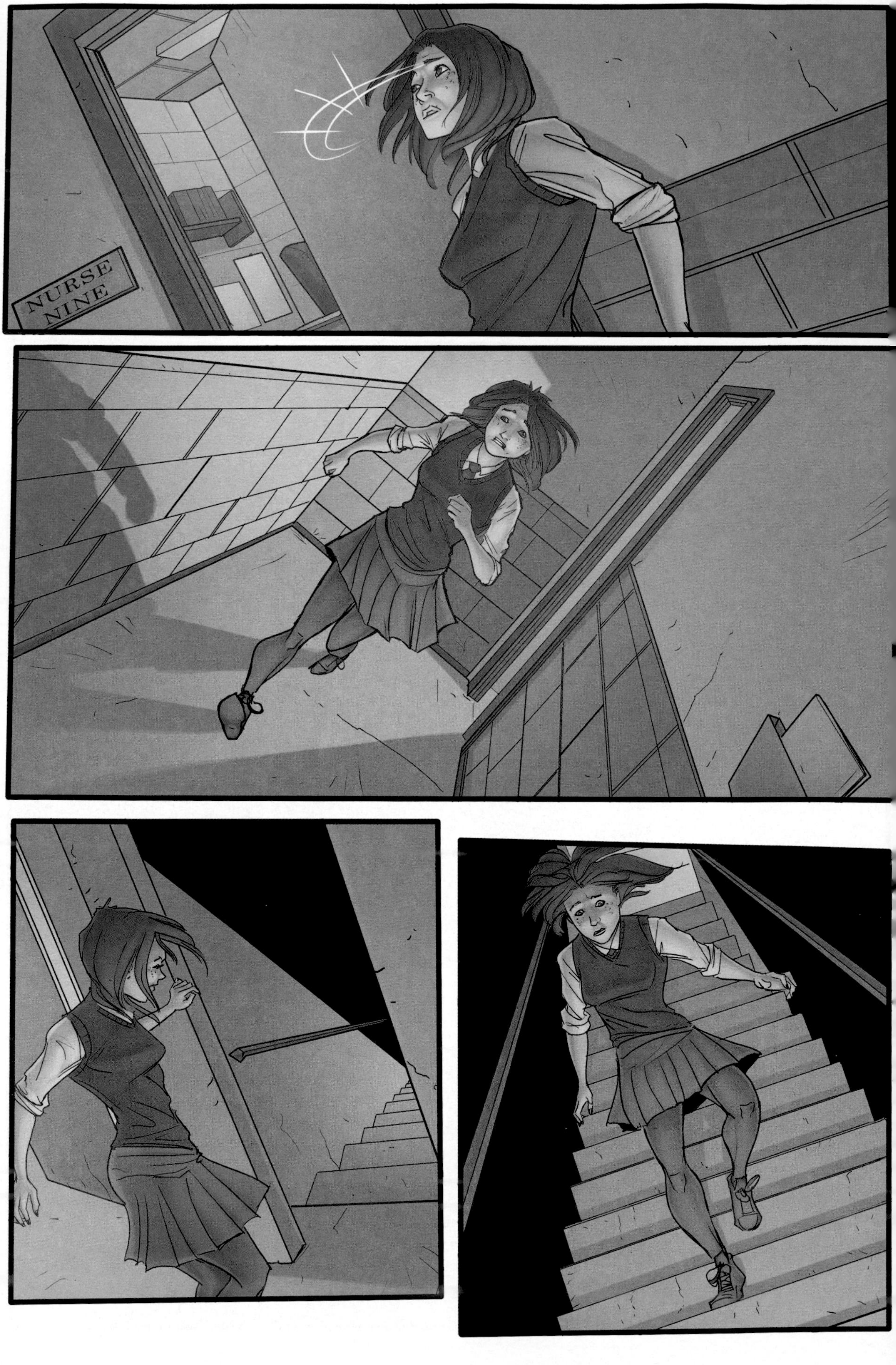
NURSE
NINE

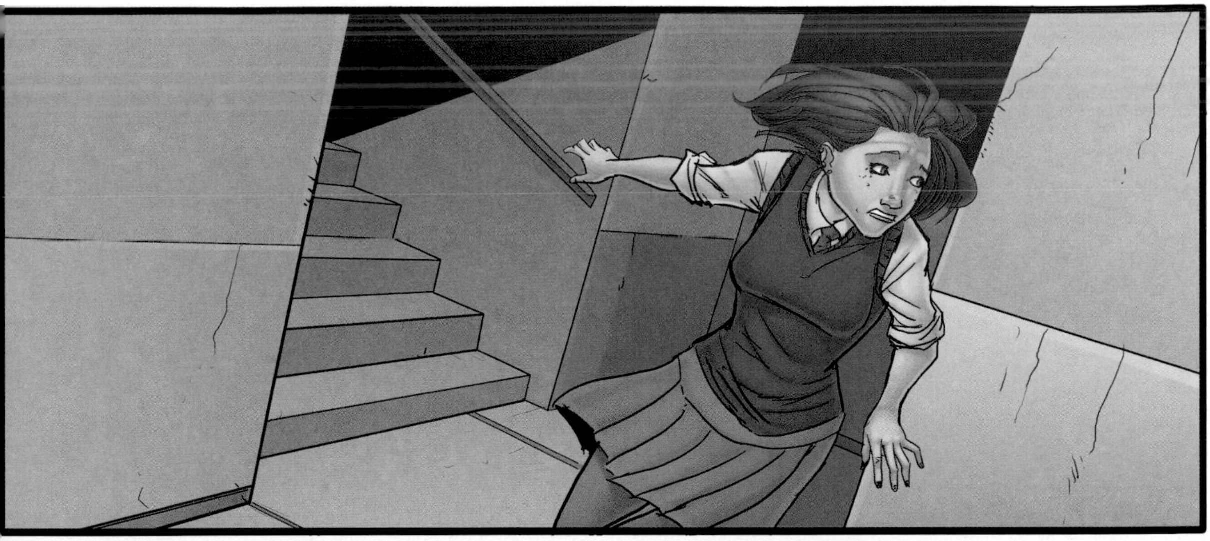
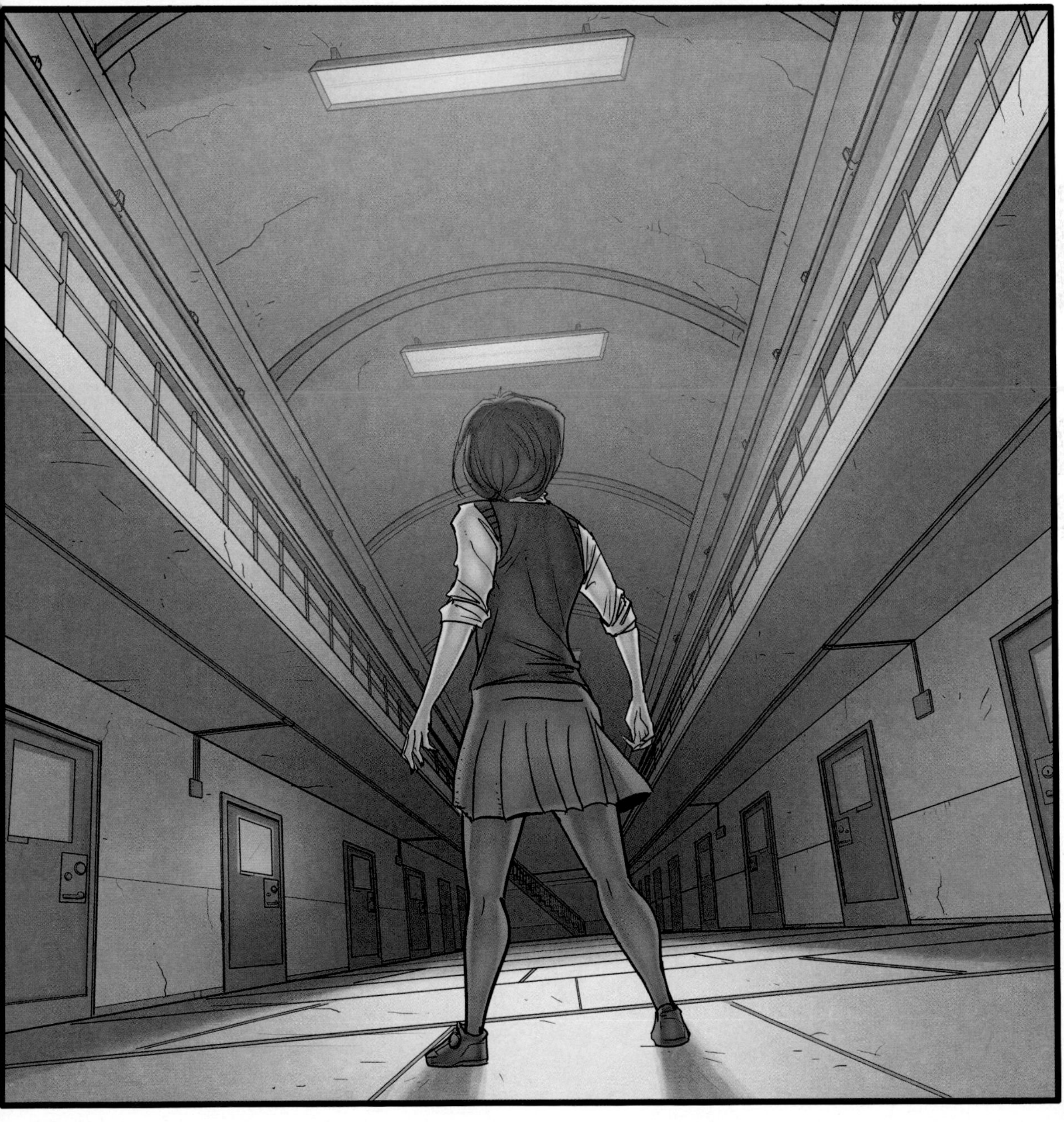

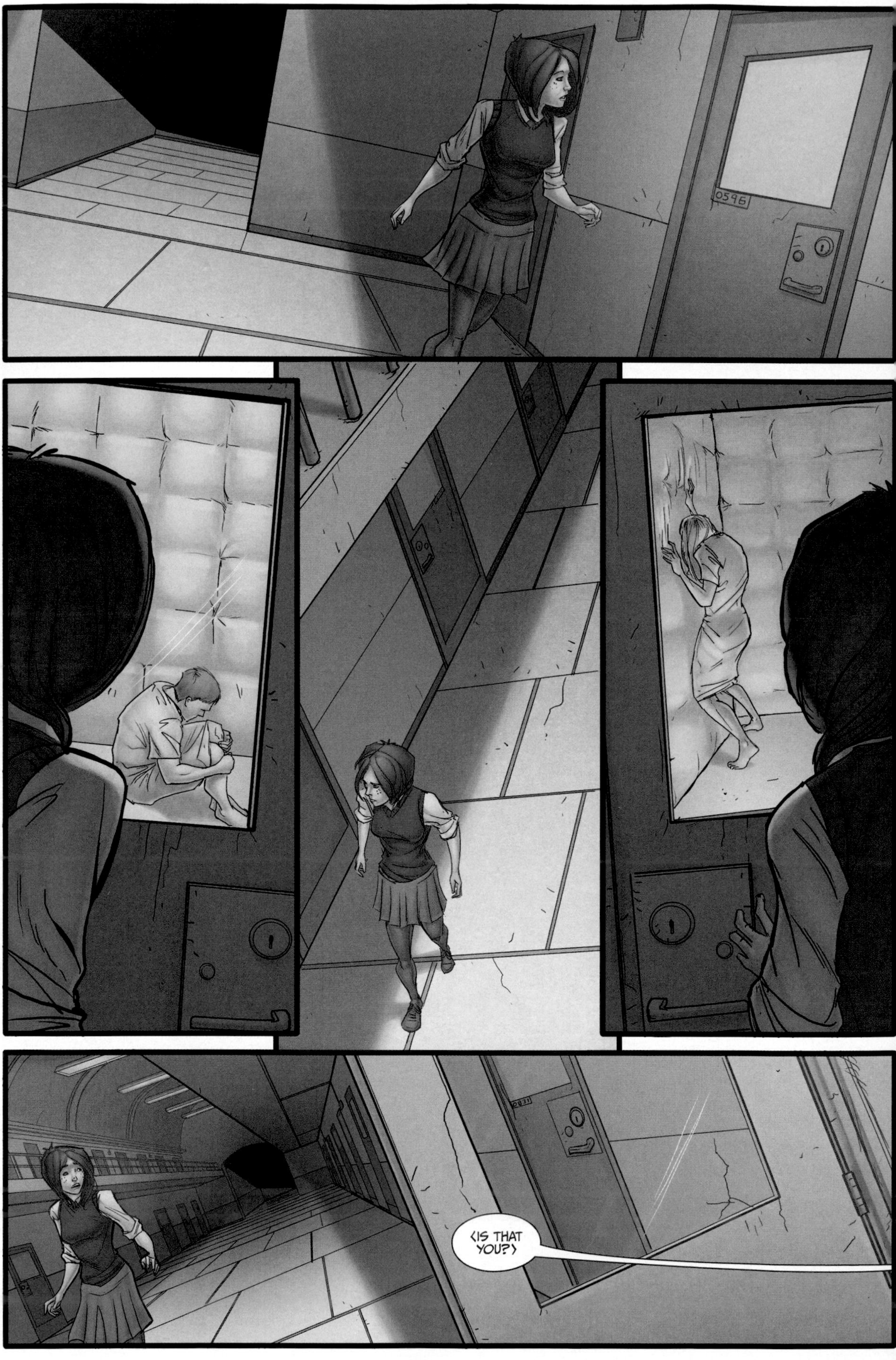
0596
⟨IS THAT YOU?⟩

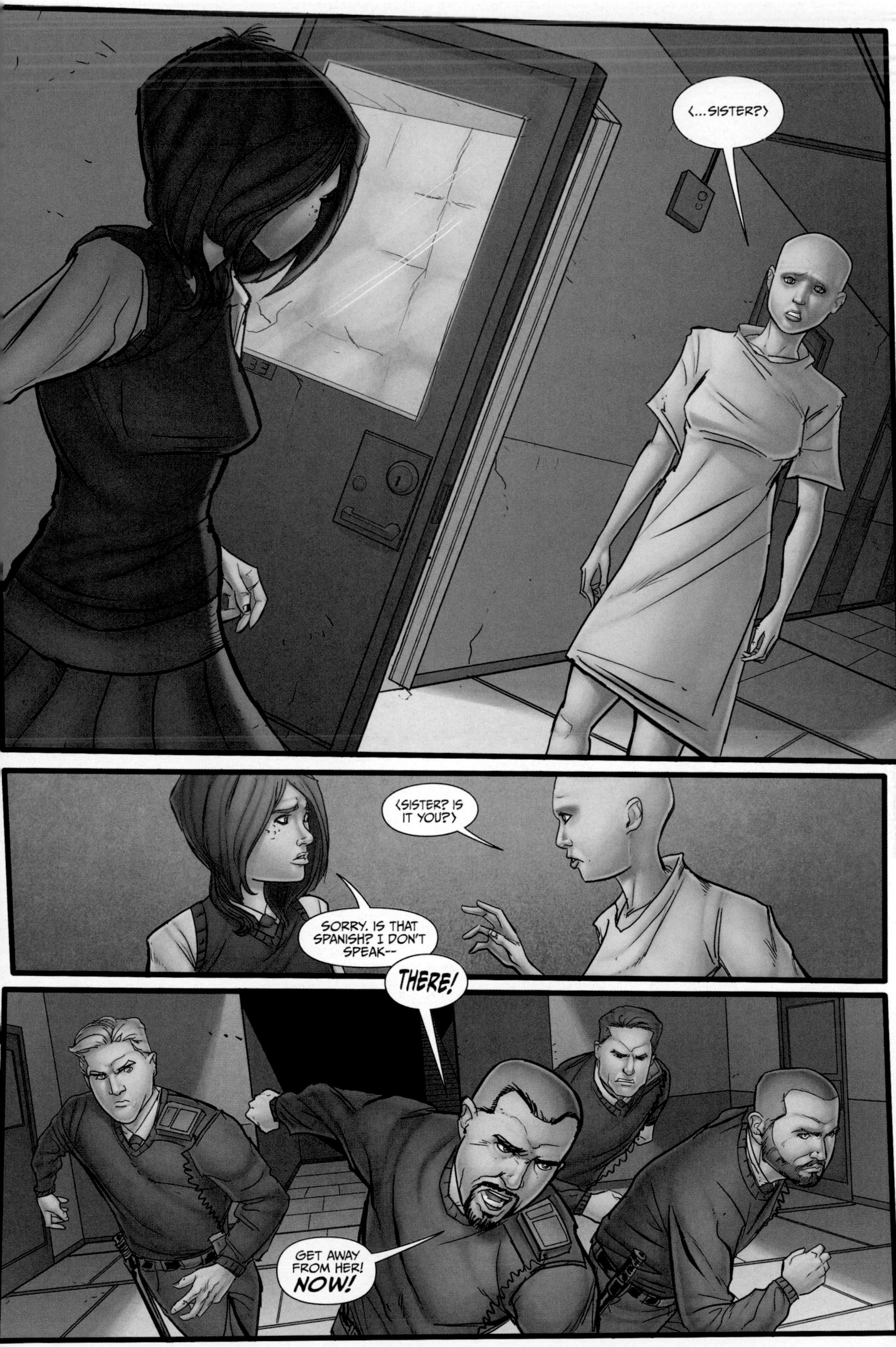

‹...SISTER?›
‹SISTER? IS IT YOU?›
SORRY. IS THAT SPANISH? I DON'T SPEAK--
THERE!
GET AWAY FROM HER! NOW!

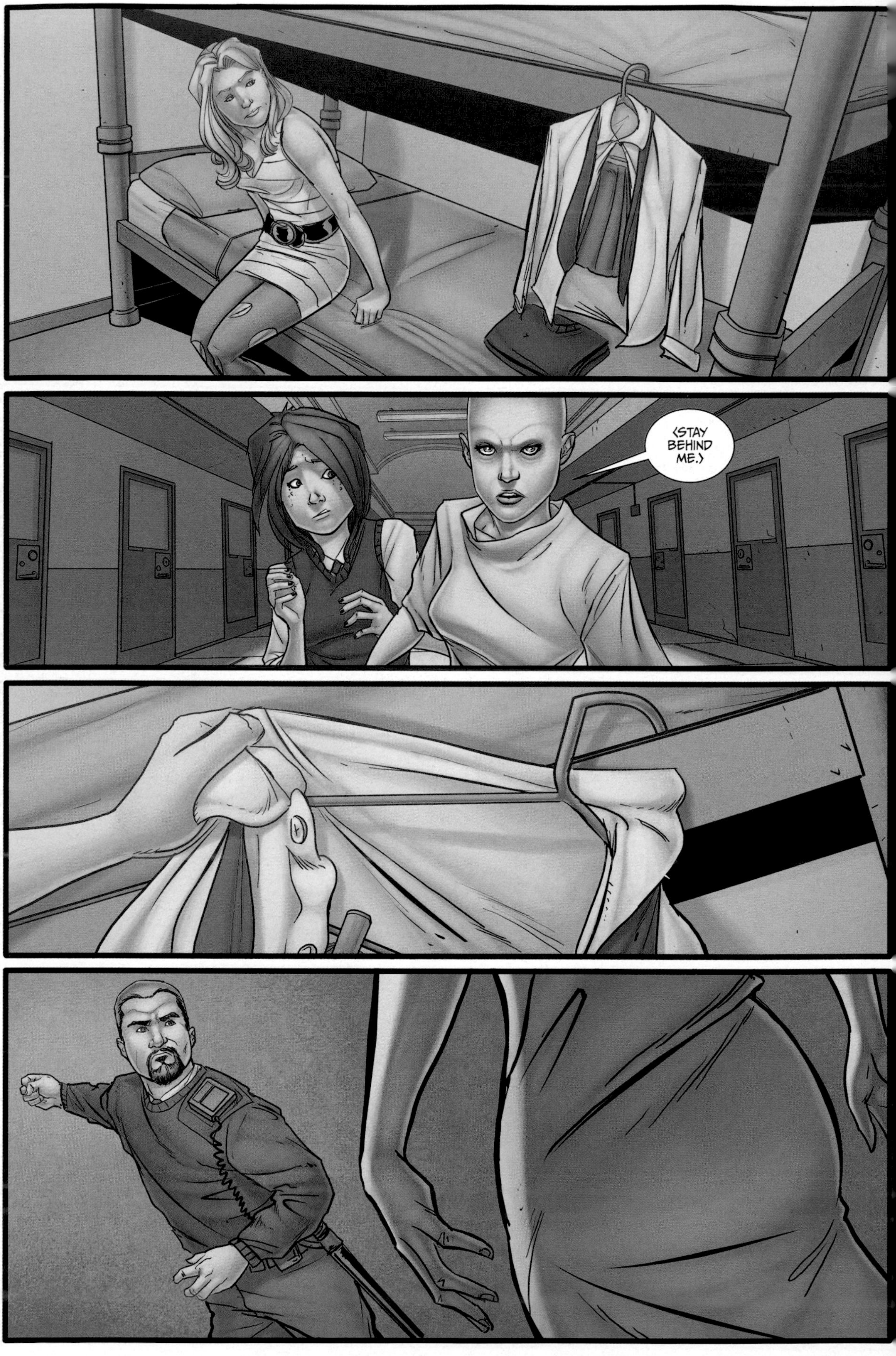
<STAY BEHIND ME.>

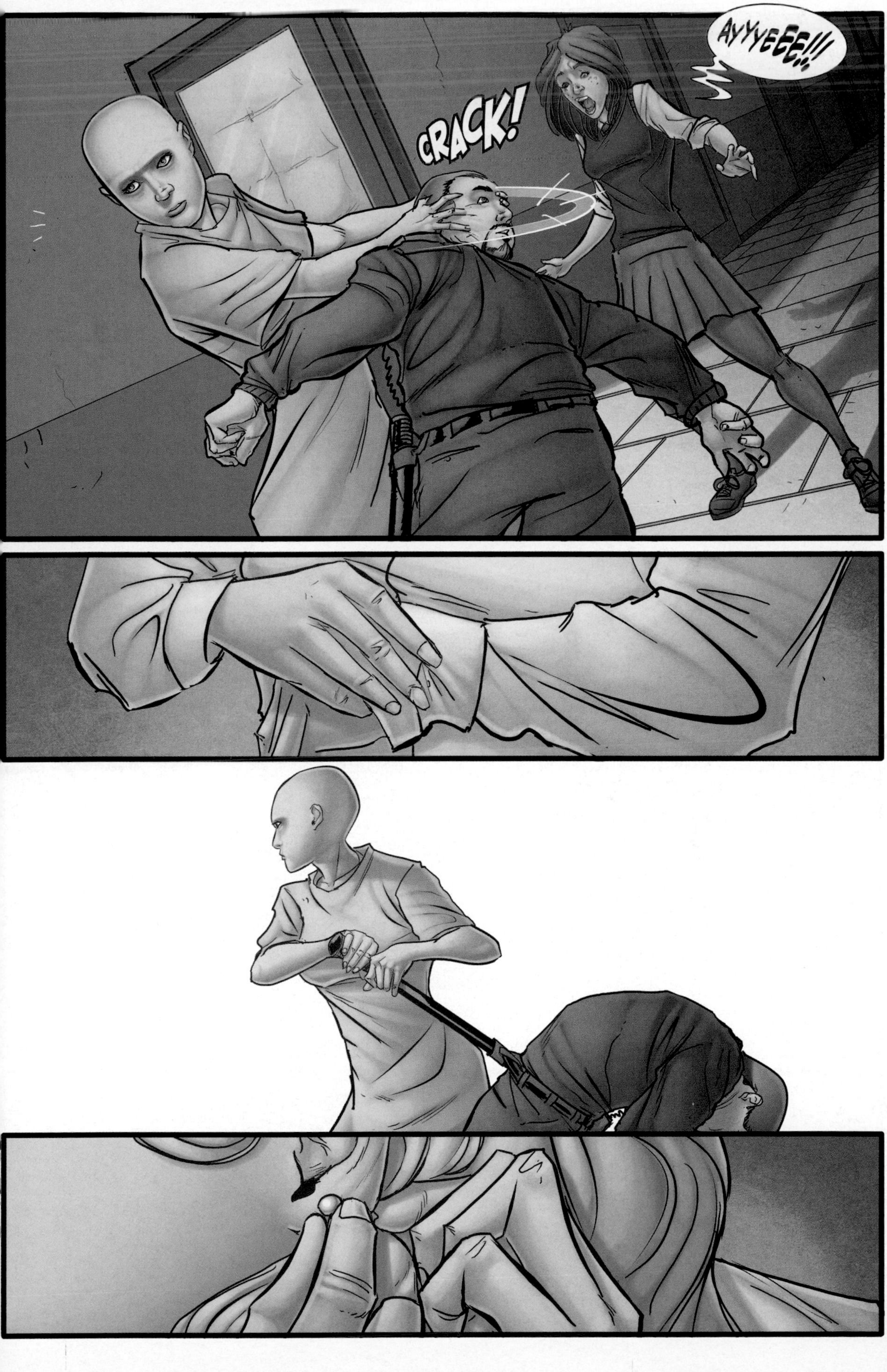
AYYYEEE!!!
CRACK!

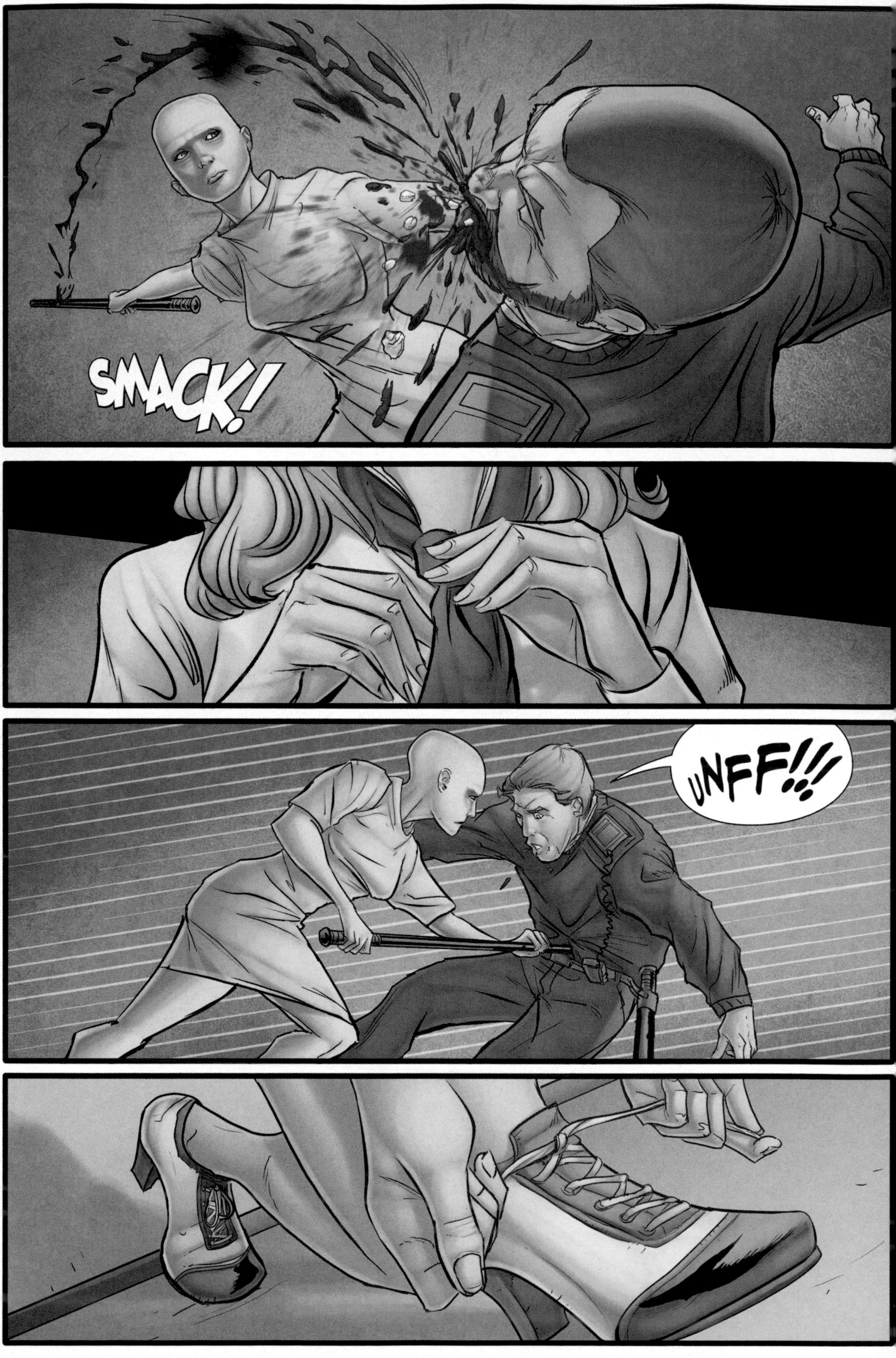
SMACK!
UNFF!!!

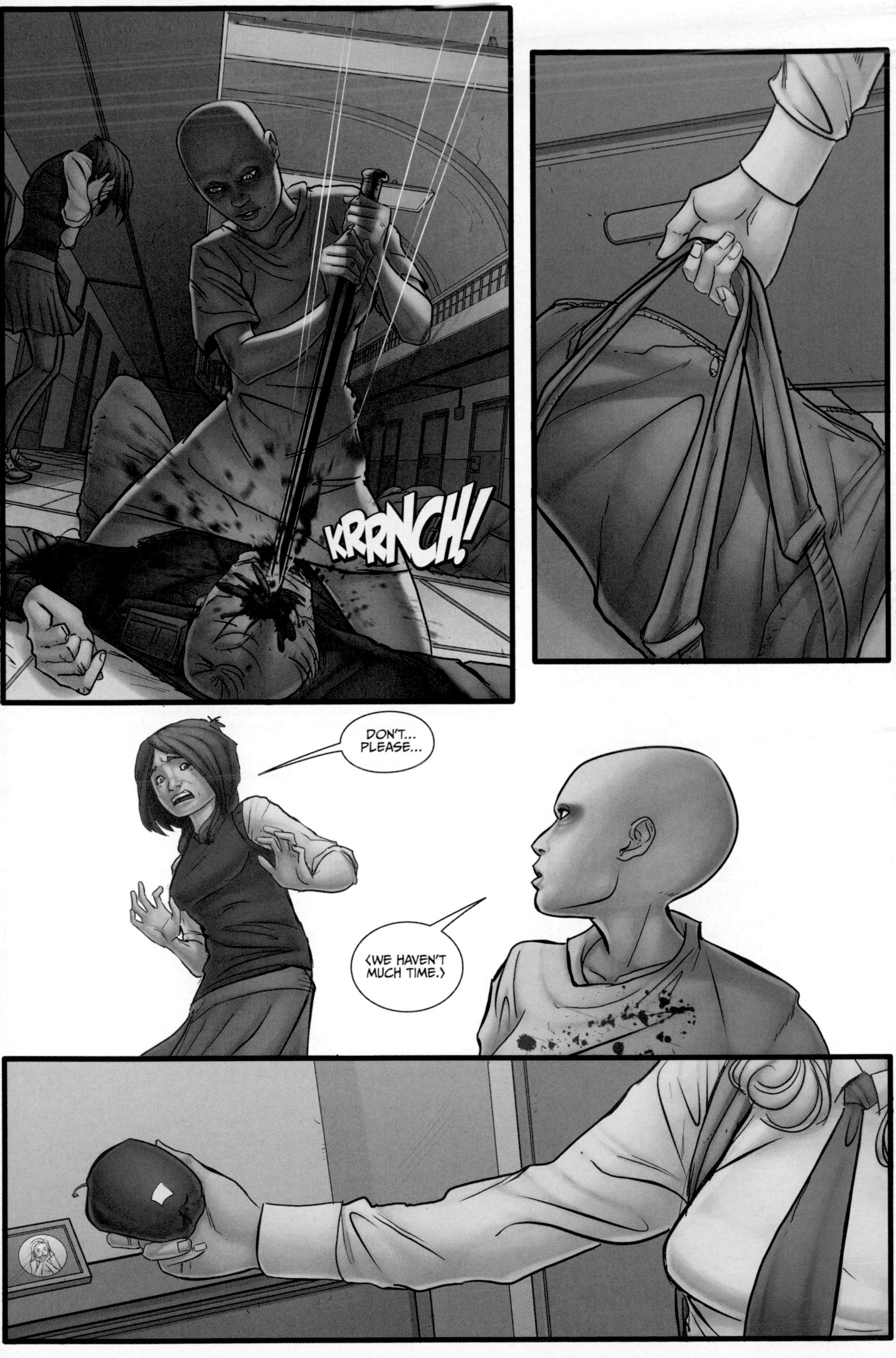
KRRNCH!
DON'T... PLEASE...
‹WE HAVEN'T MUCH TIME.›

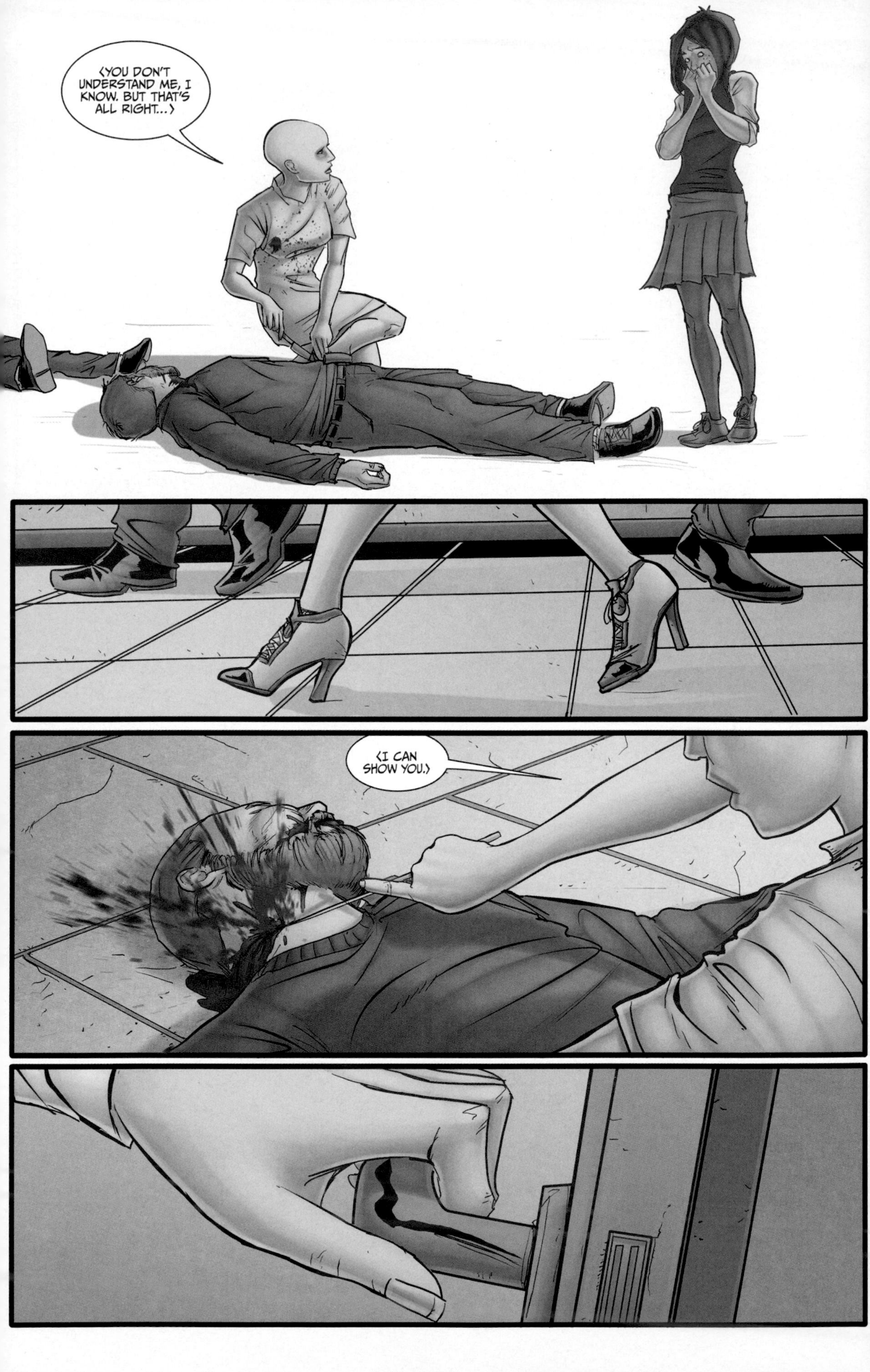
‹YOU DON'T UNDERSTAND ME, I KNOW. BUT THAT'S ALL RIGHT...›
‹I CAN SHOW YOU.›

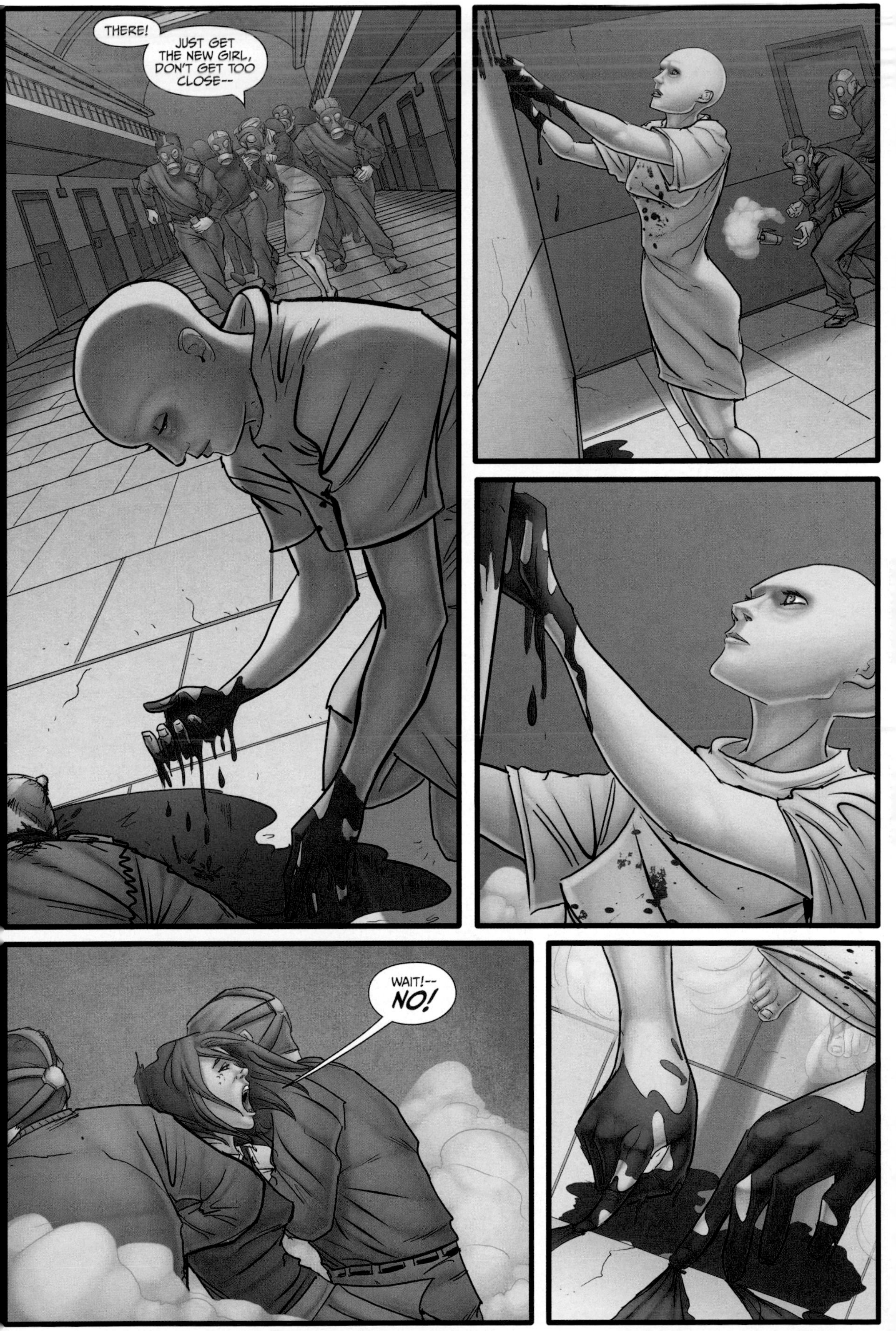
THERE!
JUST GET THE NEW GIRL, DON'T GET TOO CLOSE--
WAIT!-- NO!

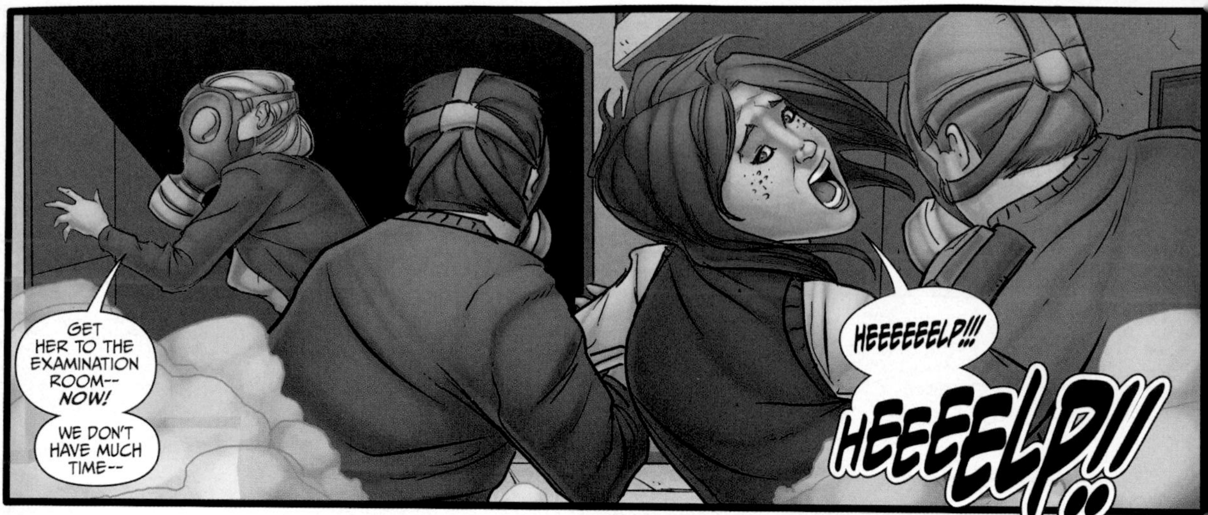
GET HER TO THE EXAMINATION ROOM-- NOW!
WE DON'T HAVE MUCH TIME--
HEEEEEELP!!!
HEEEEELP!!

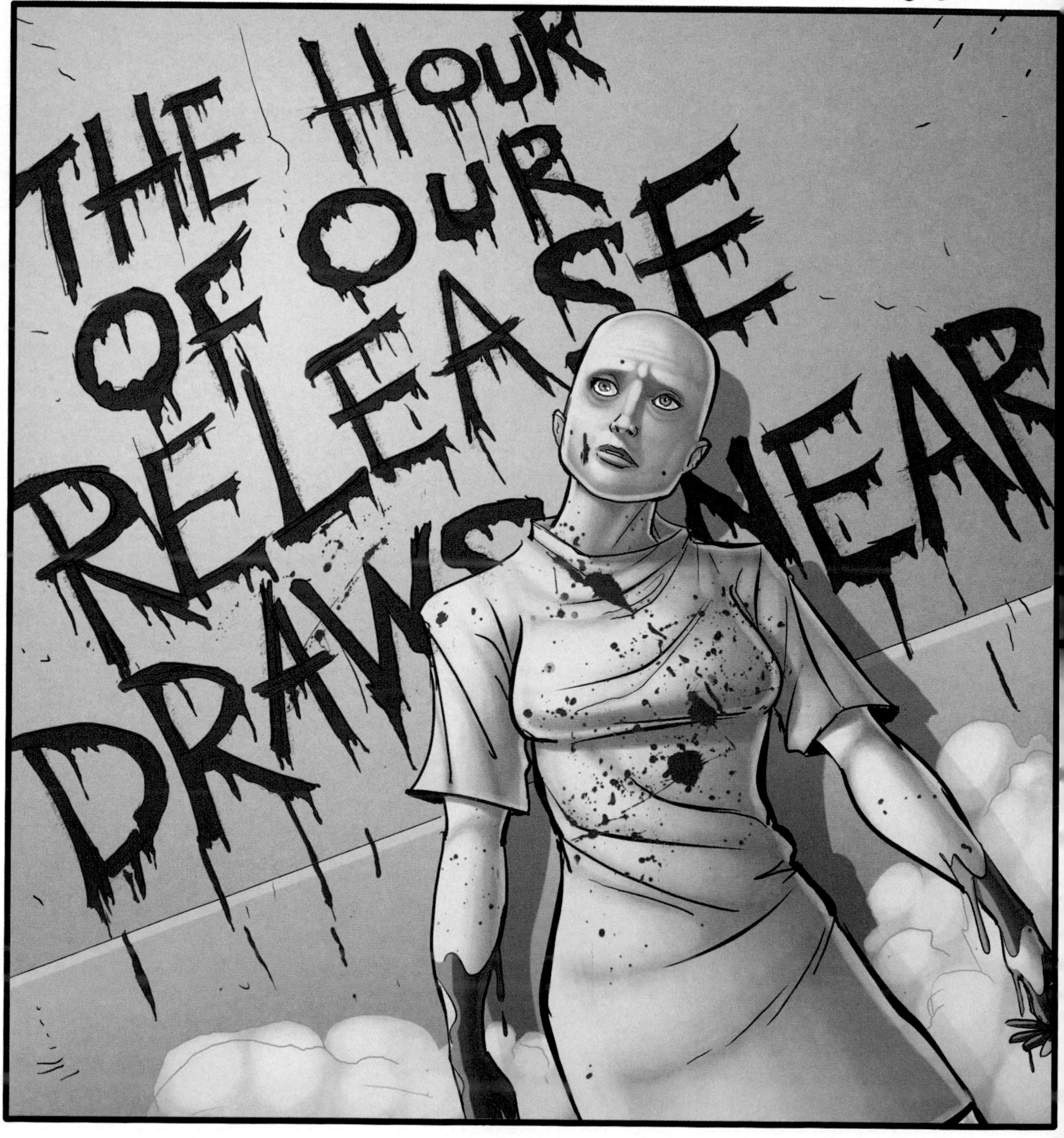
THE HOUR OF OUR RELEASE DRAWS NEAR

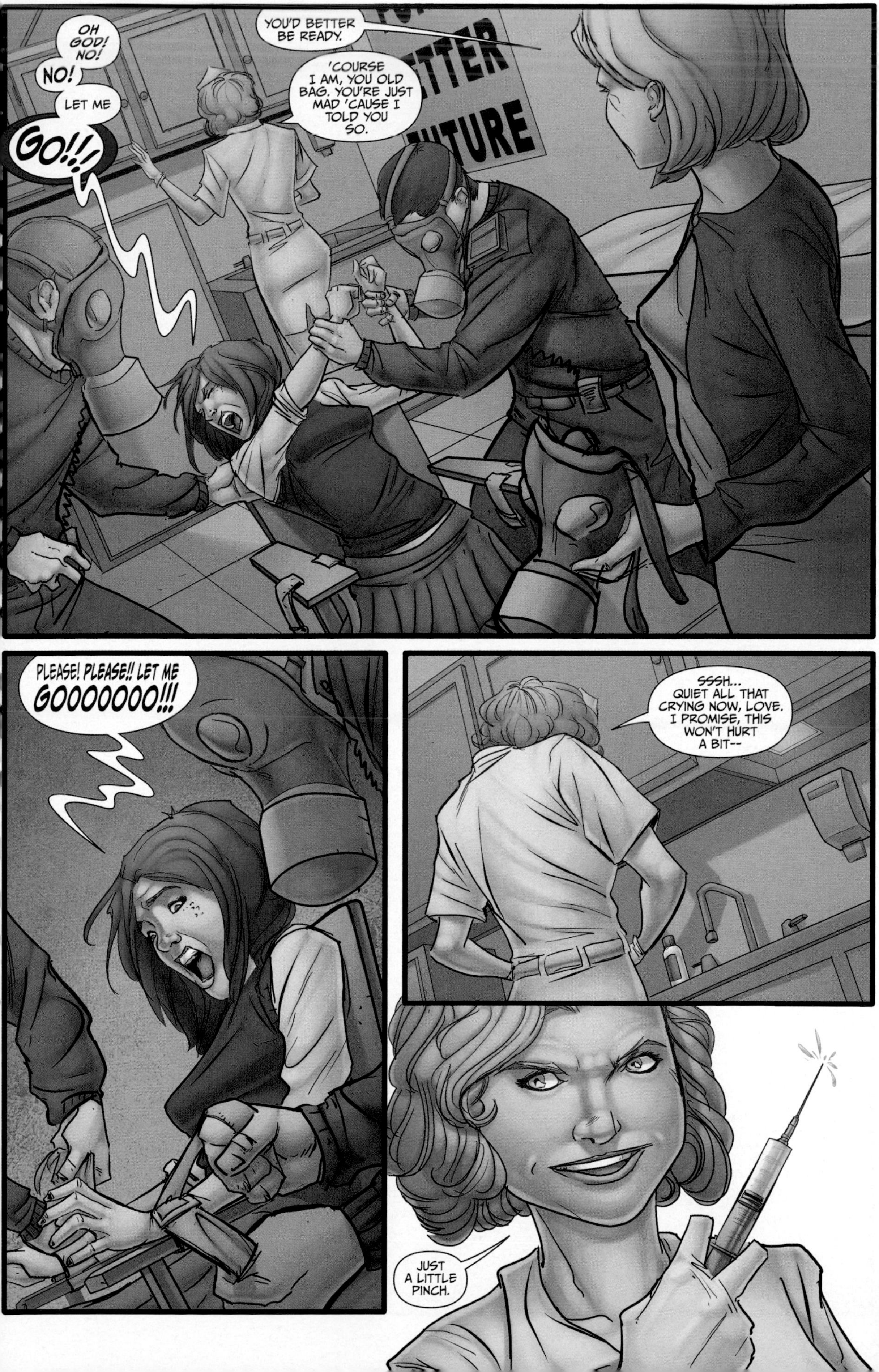

OH GOD! NO!
NO!
LET ME
GO!!!
YOU'D BETTER BE READY.
'COURSE I AM, YOU OLD BAG. YOU'RE JUST MAD 'CAUSE I TOLD YOU SO.
PLEASE! PLEASE!! LET ME GOOOOOOO!!!
SSSH... QUIET ALL THAT CRYING NOW, LOVE. I PROMISE, THIS WON'T HURT A BIT--
JUST A LITTLE PINCH.

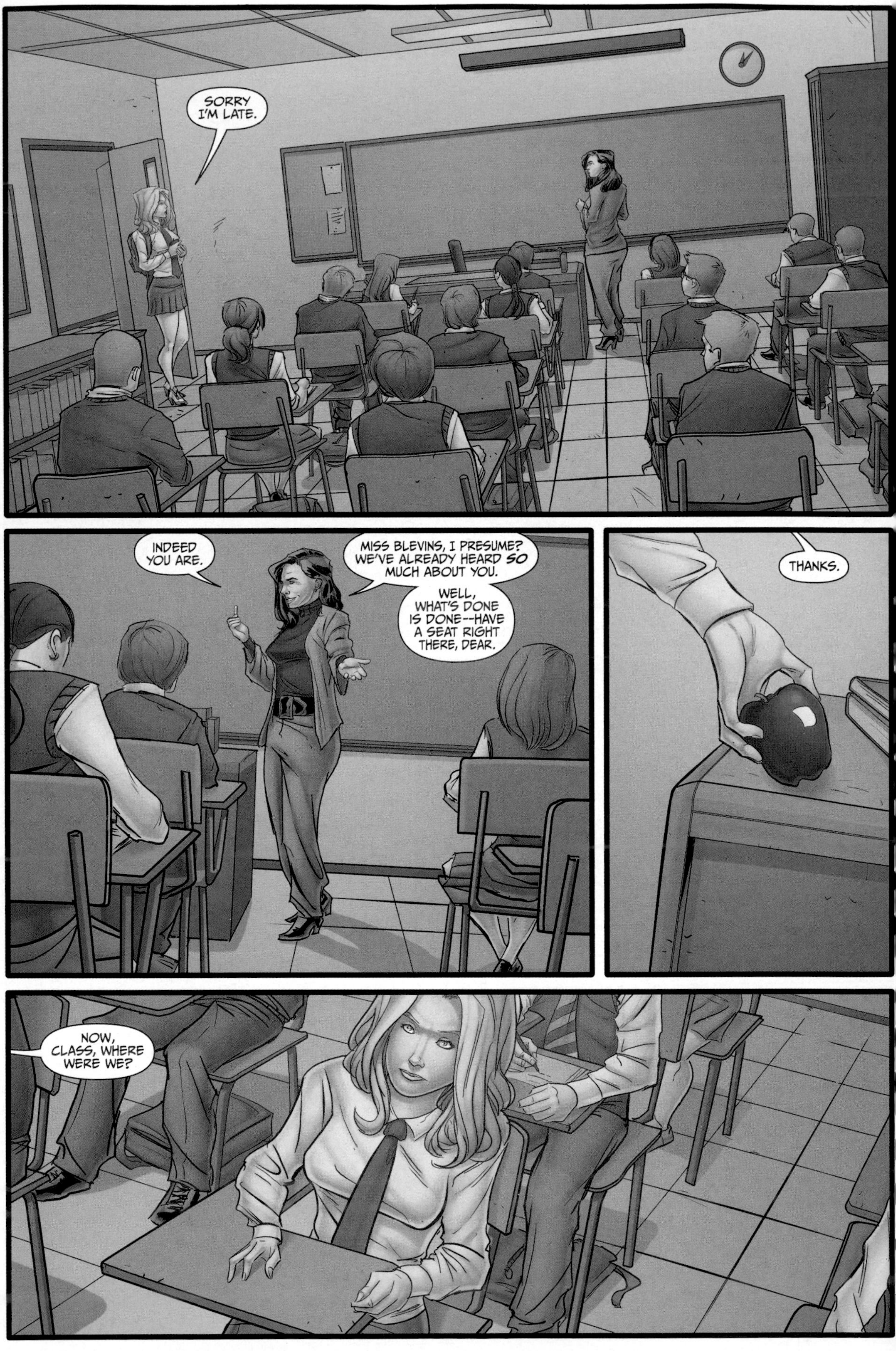
SORRY I'M LATE.
INDEED YOU ARE.
MISS BLEVINS, I PRESUME? WE'VE ALREADY HEARD SO MUCH ABOUT YOU.
WELL, WHAT'S DONE IS DONE--HAVE A SEAT RIGHT THERE, DEAR.
THANKS.
NOW, CLASS, WHERE WERE WE?

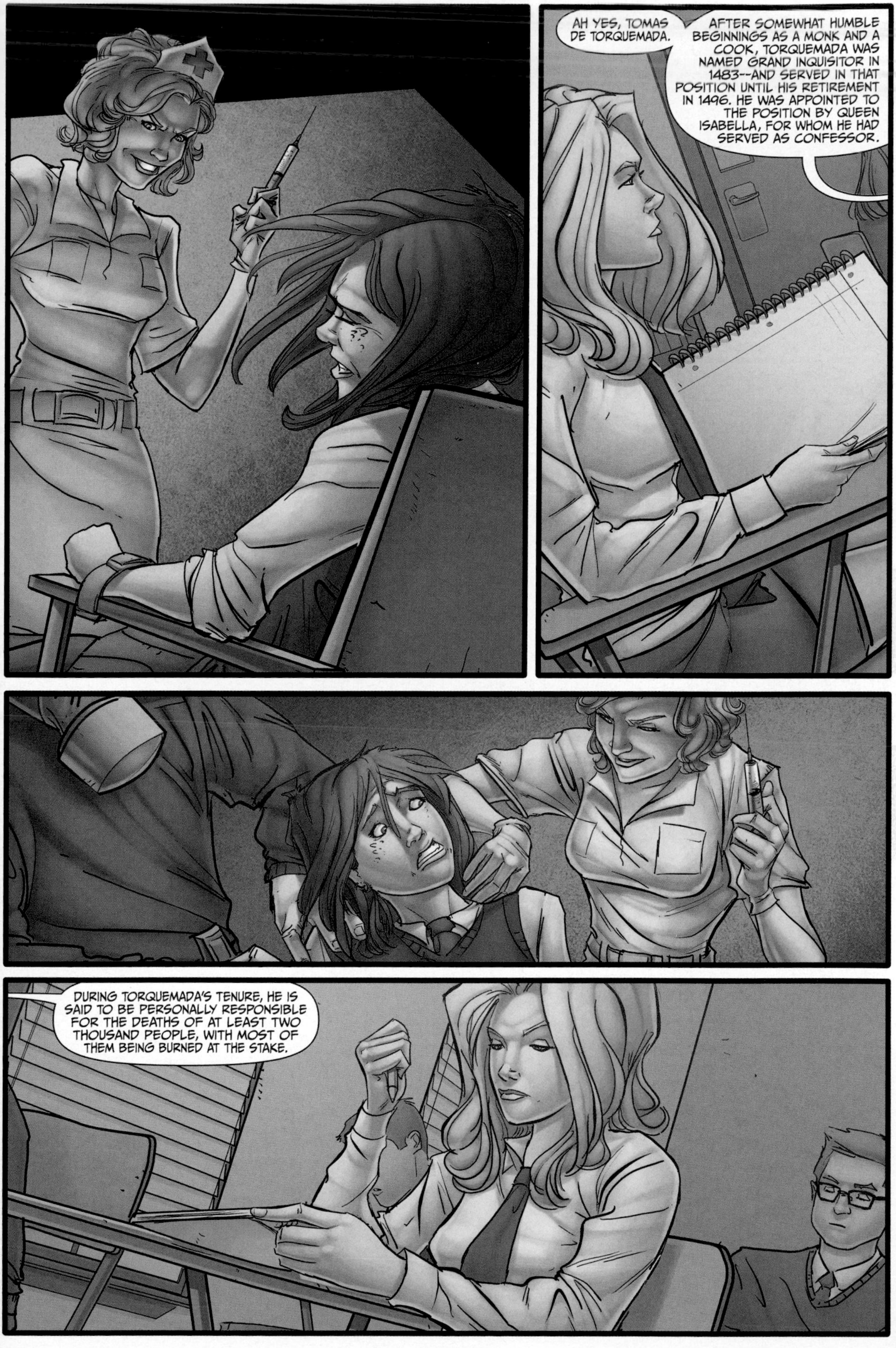
AH YES, TOMAS DE TORQUEMADA.
AFTER SOMEWHAT HUMBLE BEGINNINGS AS A MONK AND A COOK, TORQUEMADA WAS NAMED GRAND INQUISITOR IN 1483--AND SERVED IN THAT POSITION UNTIL HIS RETIREMENT IN 1496. HE WAS APPOINTED TO THE POSITION BY QUEEN ISABELLA, FOR WHOM HE HAD SERVED AS CONFESSOR.
DURING TORQUEMADA'S TENURE, HE IS SAID TO BE PERSONALLY RESPONSIBLE FOR THE DEATHS OF AT LEAST TWO THOUSAND PEOPLE, WITH MOST OF THEM BEING BURNED AT THE STAKE.

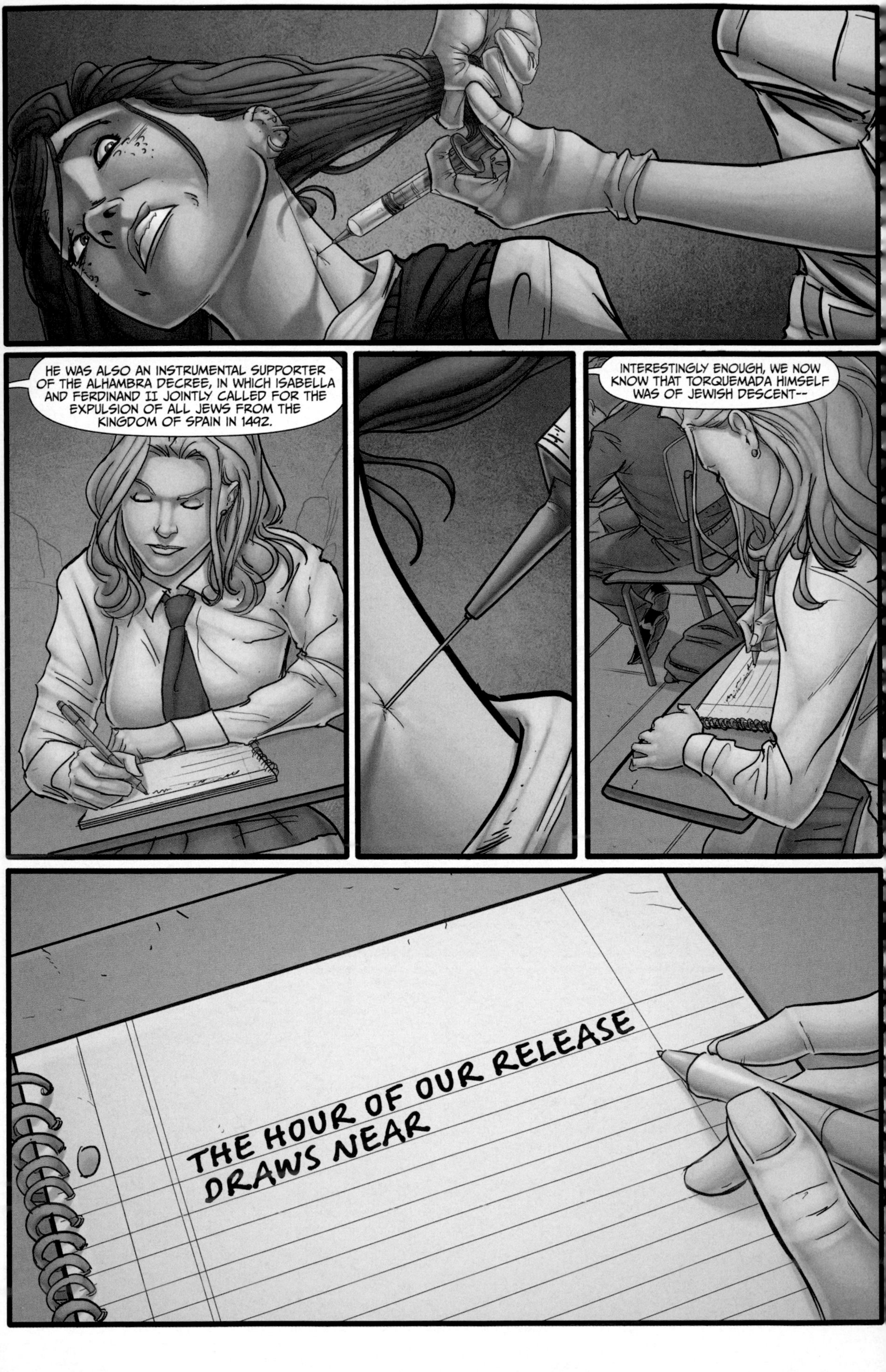
HE WAS ALSO AN INSTRUMENTAL SUPPORTER OF THE ALHAMBRA DECREE, IN WHICH ISABELLA AND FERDINAND II JOINTLY CALLED FOR THE EXPULSION OF ALL JEWS FROM THE KINGDOM OF SPAIN IN 1492.
INTERESTINGLY ENOUGH, WE NOW KNOW THAT TORQUEMADA HIMSELF WAS OF JEWISH DESCENT--
THE HOUR OF OUR RELEASE DRAWS NEAR

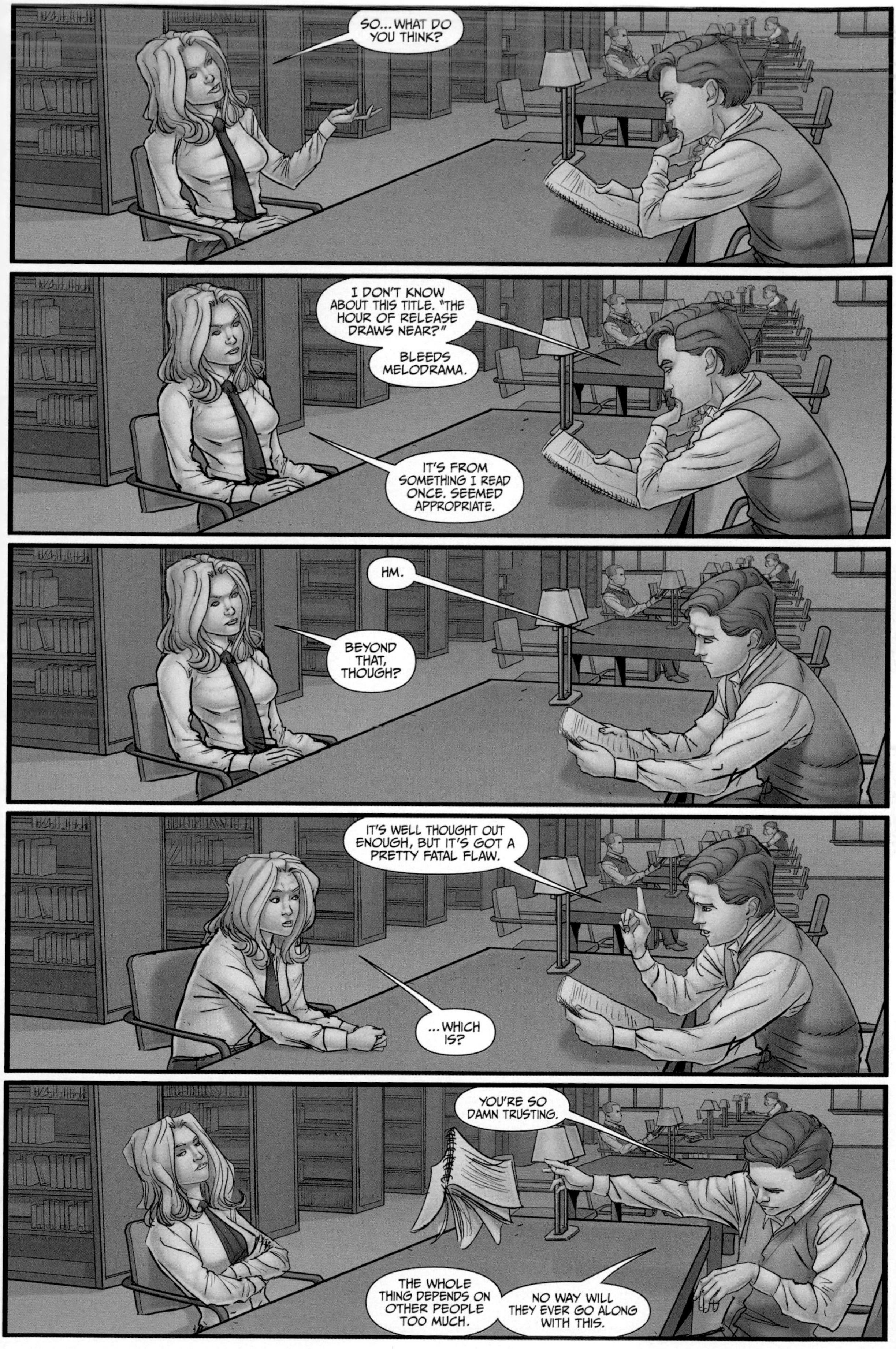
SO... WHAT DO YOU THINK?
I DON'T KNOW ABOUT THIS TITLE. "THE HOUR OF RELEASE DRAWS NEAR?"
BLEEDS MELODRAMA.
IT'S FROM SOMETHING I READ ONCE. SEEMED APPROPRIATE.
HM.
BEYOND THAT, THOUGH?
IT'S WELL THOUGHT OUT ENOUGH, BUT IT'S GOT A PRETTY FATAL FLAW.
...WHICH IS?
YOU'RE SO DAMN TRUSTING.
THE WHOLE THING DEPENDS ON OTHER PEOPLE TOO MUCH.
NO WAY WILL THEY EVER GO ALONG WITH THIS.

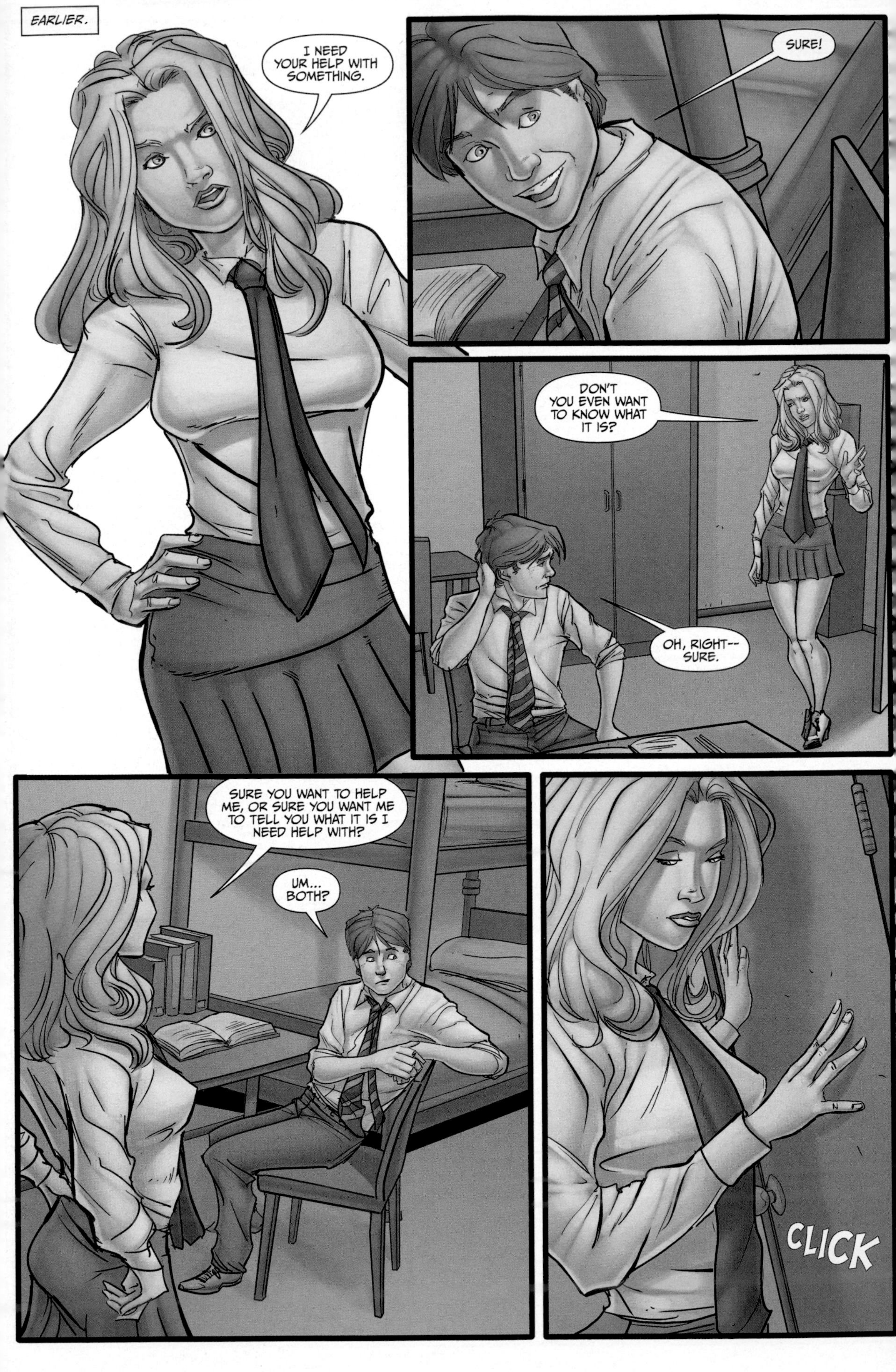
EARLIER.
I NEED YOUR HELP WITH SOMETHING.
SURE!
DON'T YOU EVEN WANT TO KNOW WHAT IT IS?
OH, RIGHT-- SURE.
SURE YOU WANT TO HELP ME, OR SURE YOU WANT ME TO TELL YOU WHAT IT IS I NEED HELP WITH?
UM... BOTH?
CLICK

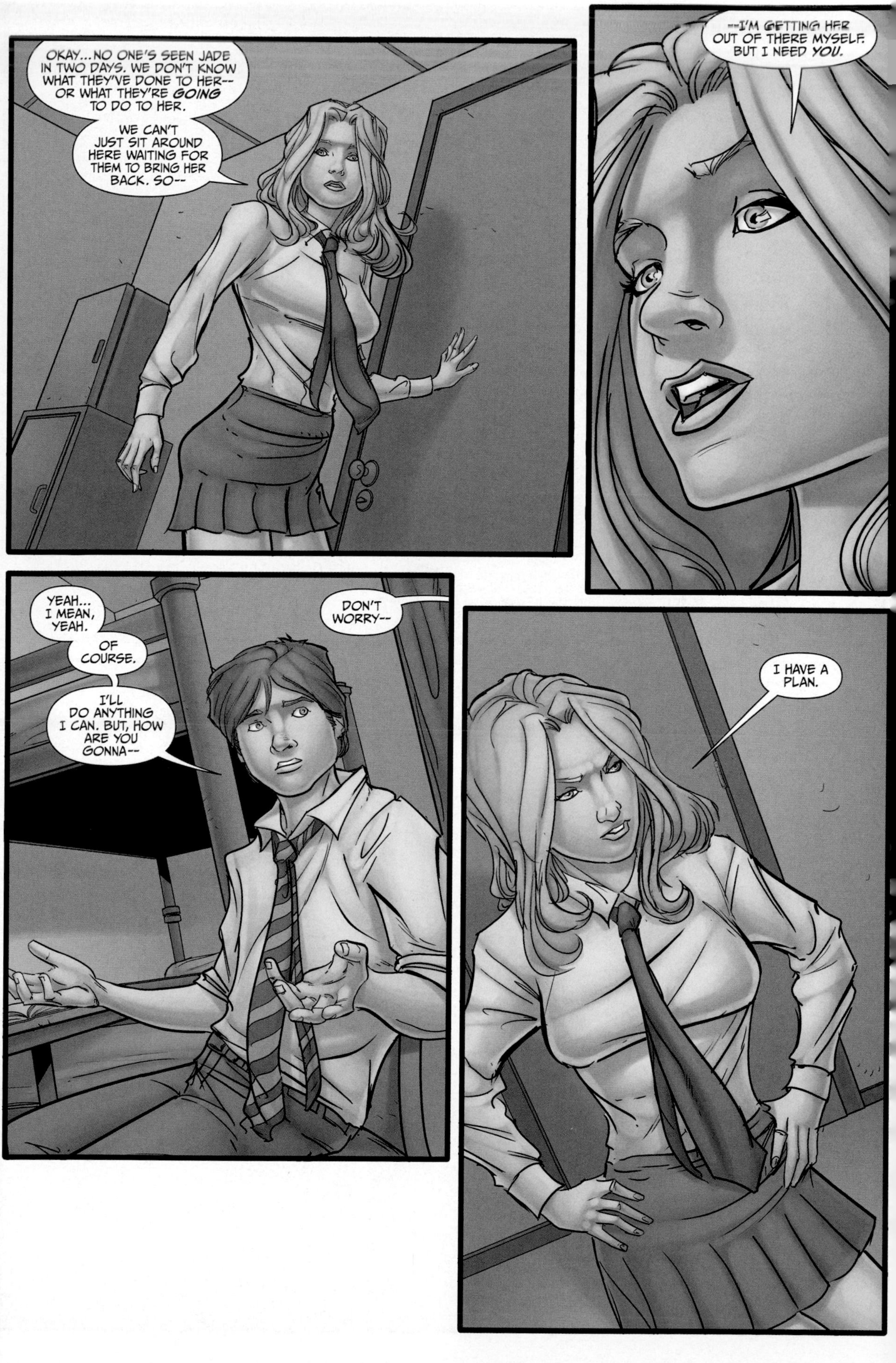
OKAY...NO ONE'S SEEN JADE IN TWO DAYS. WE DON'T KNOW WHAT THEY'VE DONE TO HER-- OR WHAT THEY'RE GOING TO DO TO HER.
WE CAN'T JUST SIT AROUND HERE WAITING FOR THEM TO BRING HER BACK. SO--
--I'M GETTING HER OUT OF THERE MYSELF. BUT I NEED YOU.
YEAH... I MEAN, YEAH.
OF COURSE.
I'LL DO ANYTHING I CAN. BUT, HOW ARE YOU GONNA--
DON'T WORRY--
I HAVE A PLAN.

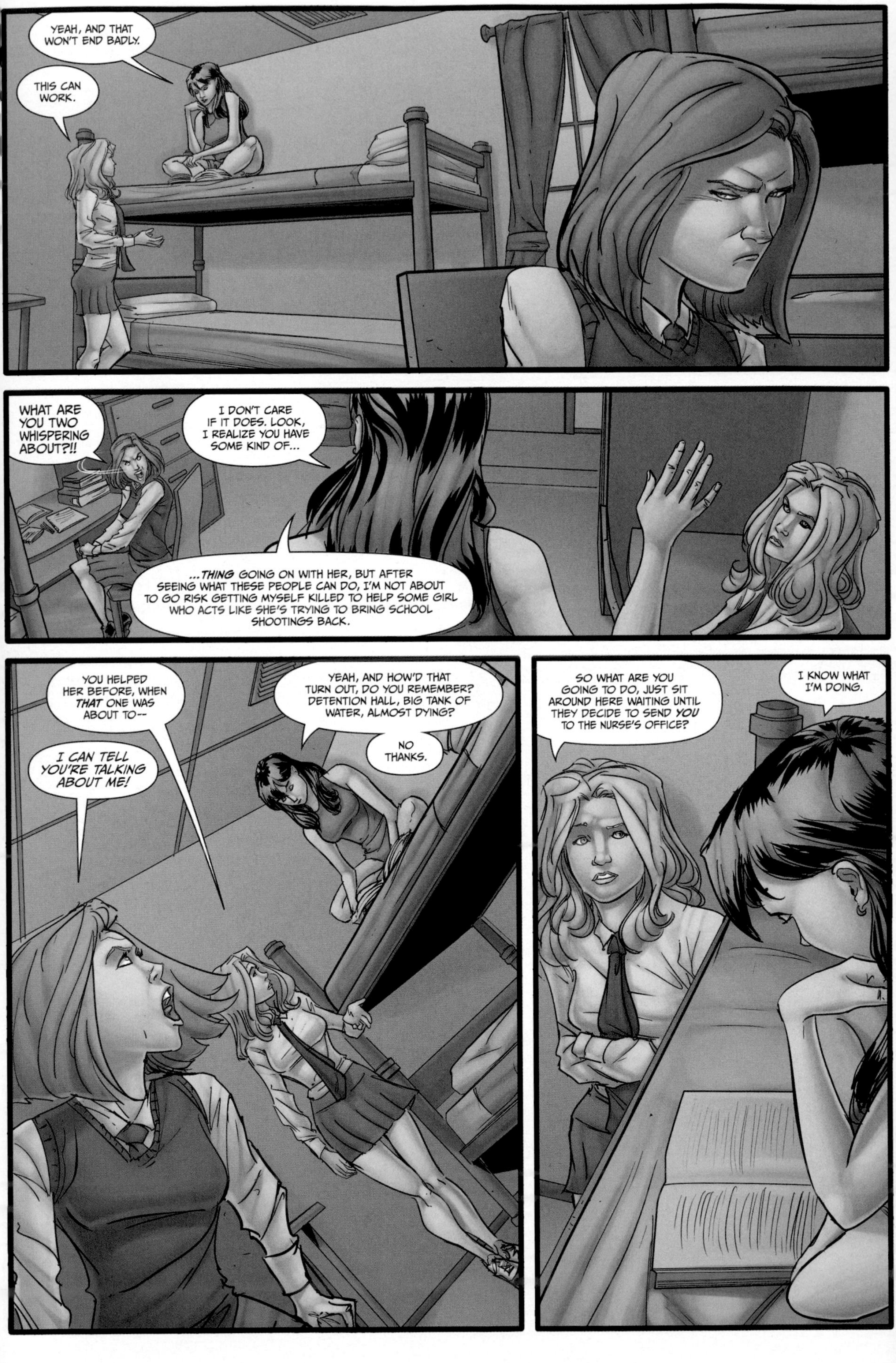
YEAH, AND THAT WON'T END BADLY.
THIS CAN WORK.
WHAT ARE YOU TWO WHISPERING ABOUT?!!
I DON'T CARE IF IT DOES. LOOK, I REALIZE YOU HAVE SOME KIND OF...
...THING GOING ON WITH HER, BUT AFTER SEEING WHAT THESE PEOPLE CAN DO, I'M NOT ABOUT TO GO RISK GETTING MYSELF KILLED TO HELP SOME GIRL WHO ACTS LIKE SHE'S TRYING TO BRING SCHOOL SHOOTINGS BACK.
YOU HELPED HER BEFORE, WHEN THAT ONE WAS ABOUT TO--
I CAN TELL YOU'RE TALKING ABOUT ME!
YEAH, AND HOW'D THAT TURN OUT, DO YOU REMEMBER? DETENTION HALL, BIG TANK OF WATER, ALMOST DYING?
NO THANKS.
SO WHAT ARE YOU GOING TO DO, JUST SIT AROUND HERE WAITING UNTIL THEY DECIDE TO SEND YOU TO THE NURSE'S OFFICE?
I KNOW WHAT I'M DOING.

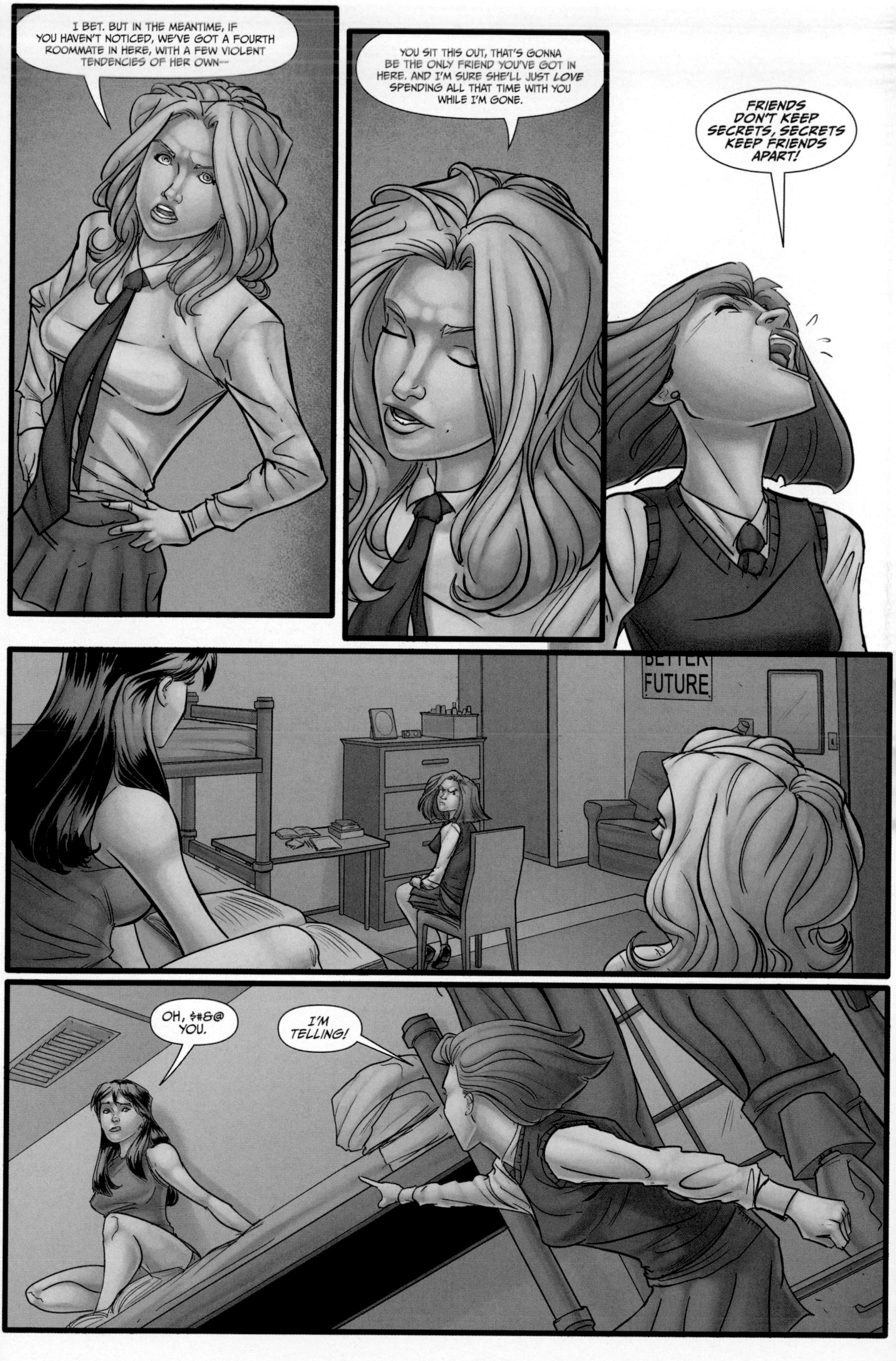
I BET. BUT IN THE MEANTIME, IF YOU HAVEN'T NOTICED, WE'VE GOT A FOURTH ROOMMATE IN HERE, WITH A FEW VIOLENT TENDENCIES OF HER OWN--
YOU SIT THIS OUT, THAT'S GONNA BE THE ONLY FRIEND YOU'VE GOT IN HERE. AND I'M SURE SHE'LL JUST LOVE SPENDING ALL THAT TIME WITH YOU WHILE I'M GONE.
FRIENDS DON'T KEEP SECRETS, SECRETS KEEP FRIENDS APART!
BETTER FUTURE
OH, $#&@ YOU.
I'M TELLING!

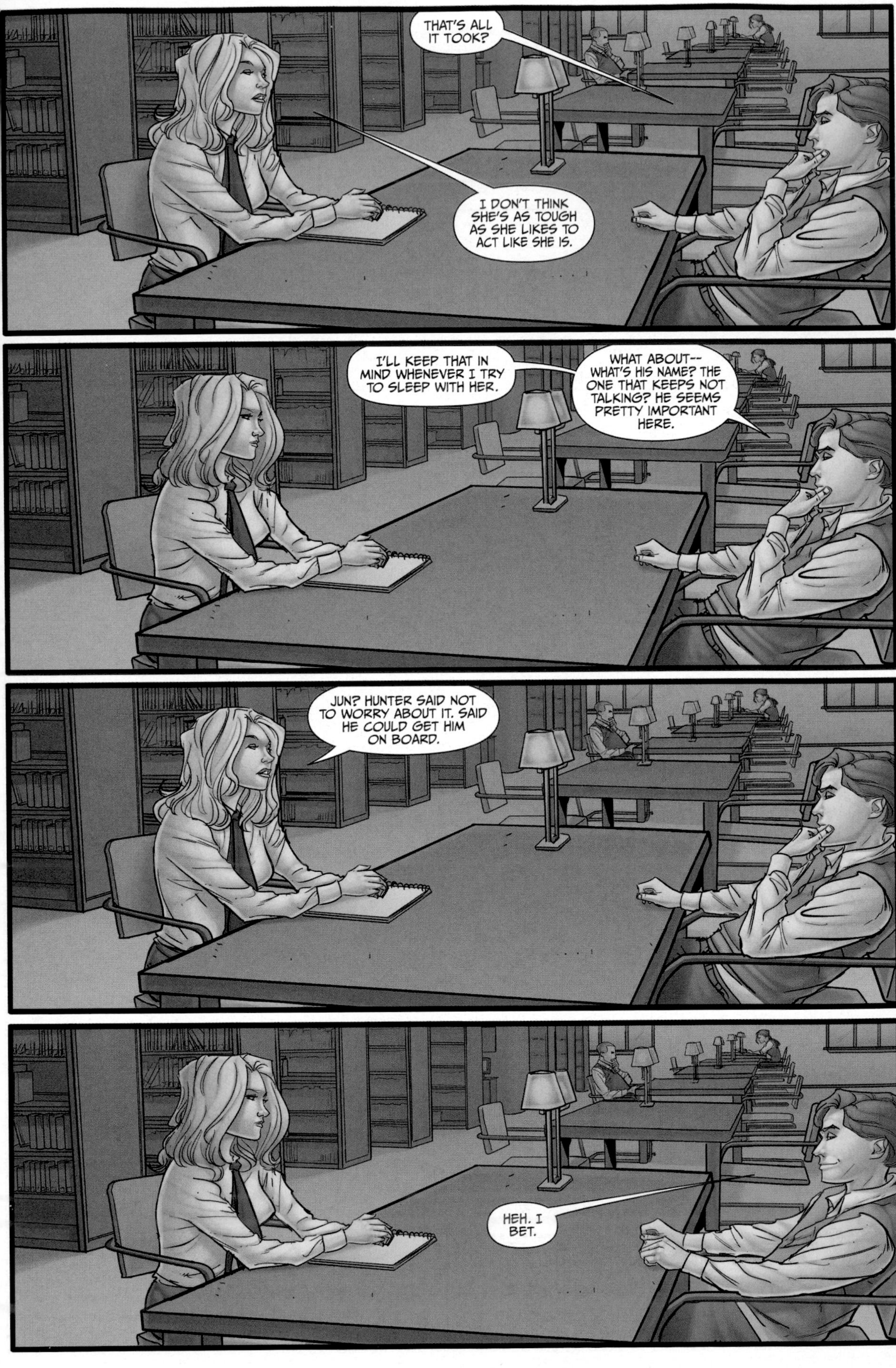
THAT'S ALL IT TOOK?
I DON'T THINK SHE'S AS TOUGH AS SHE LIKES TO ACT LIKE SHE IS.
I'LL KEEP THAT IN MIND WHENEVER I TRY TO SLEEP WITH HER.
WHAT ABOUT-- WHAT'S HIS NAME? THE ONE THAT KEEPS NOT TALKING? HE SEEMS PRETTY IMPORTANT HERE.
JUN? HUNTER SAID NOT TO WORRY ABOUT IT. SAID HE COULD GET HIM ON BOARD.
HEH. I BET.

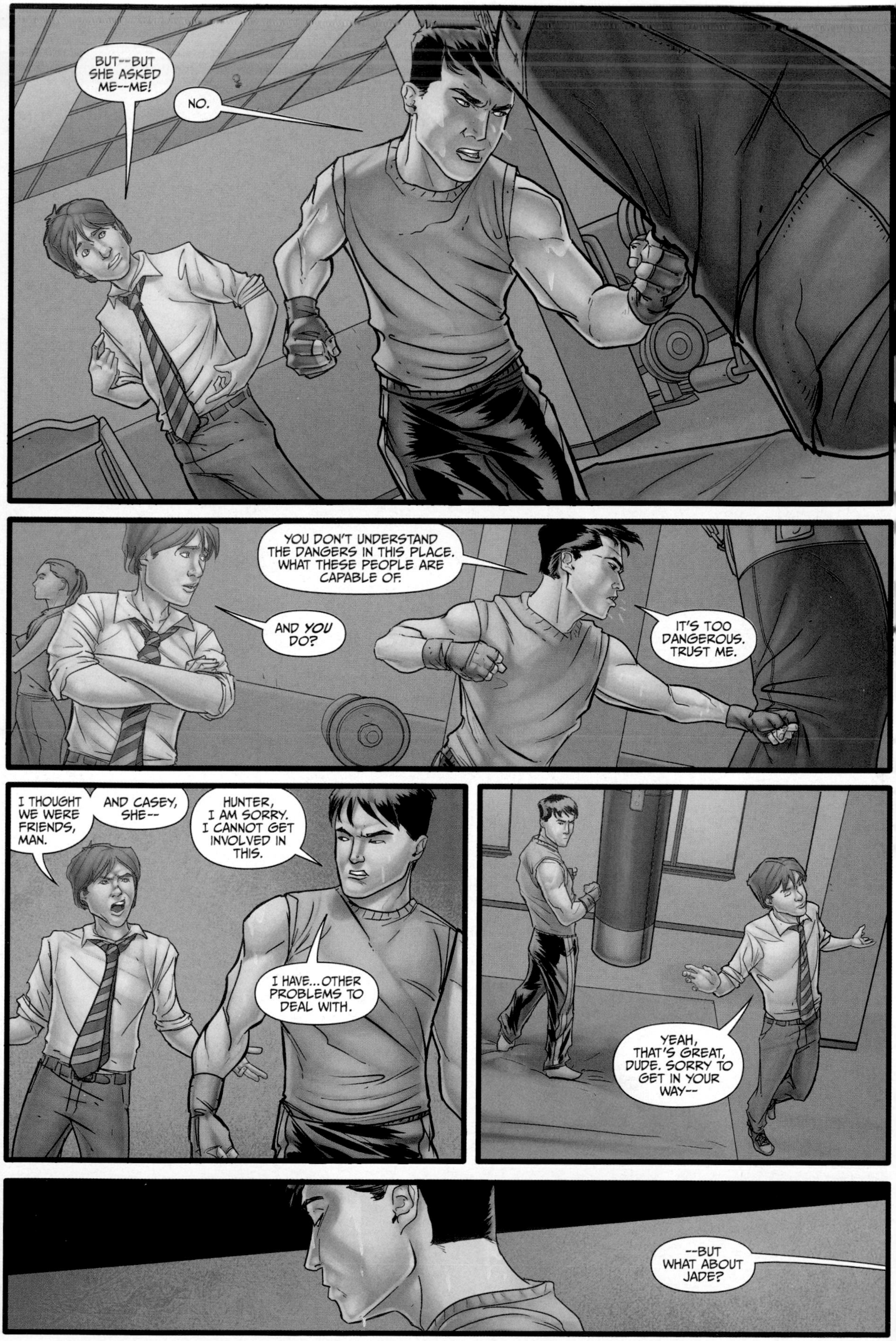
BUT--BUT SHE ASKED ME--ME!
NO.
YOU DON'T UNDERSTAND THE DANGERS IN THIS PLACE. WHAT THESE PEOPLE ARE CAPABLE OF.
AND *YOU* DO?
IT'S TOO DANGEROUS. TRUST ME.
I THOUGHT WE WERE FRIENDS, MAN.
AND CASEY, SHE--
HUNTER, I AM SORRY. I CANNOT GET INVOLVED IN THIS.
I HAVE...OTHER PROBLEMS TO DEAL WITH.
YEAH, THAT'S GREAT, DUDE. SORRY TO GET IN YOUR WAY--
--BUT WHAT ABOUT JADE?

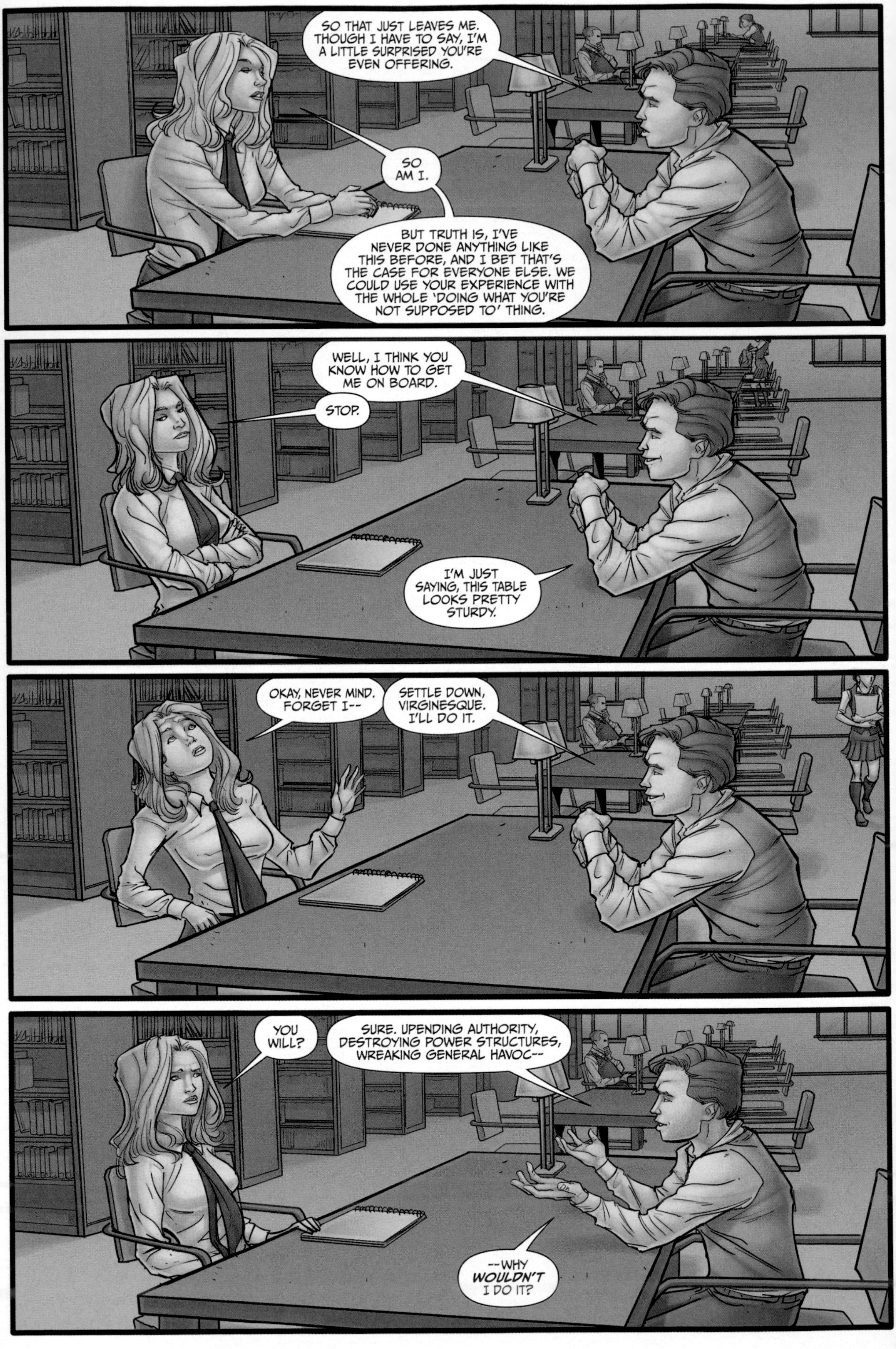
SO THAT JUST LEAVES ME. THOUGH I HAVE TO SAY, I'M A LITTLE SURPRISED YOU'RE EVEN OFFERING.
SO AM I.
BUT TRUTH IS, I'VE NEVER DONE ANYTHING LIKE THIS BEFORE, AND I BET THAT'S THE CASE FOR EVERYONE ELSE. WE COULD USE YOUR EXPERIENCE WITH THE WHOLE 'DOING WHAT YOU'RE NOT SUPPOSED TO' THING.
WELL, I THINK YOU KNOW HOW TO GET ME ON BOARD.
STOP.
I'M JUST SAYING, THIS TABLE LOOKS PRETTY STURDY.
OKAY, NEVER MIND. FORGET I--
SETTLE DOWN, VIRGINESQUE. I'LL DO IT.
YOU WILL?
SURE. UPENDING AUTHORITY, DESTROYING POWER STRUCTURES, WREAKING GENERAL HAVOC--
--WHY *WOULDN'T* I DO IT?

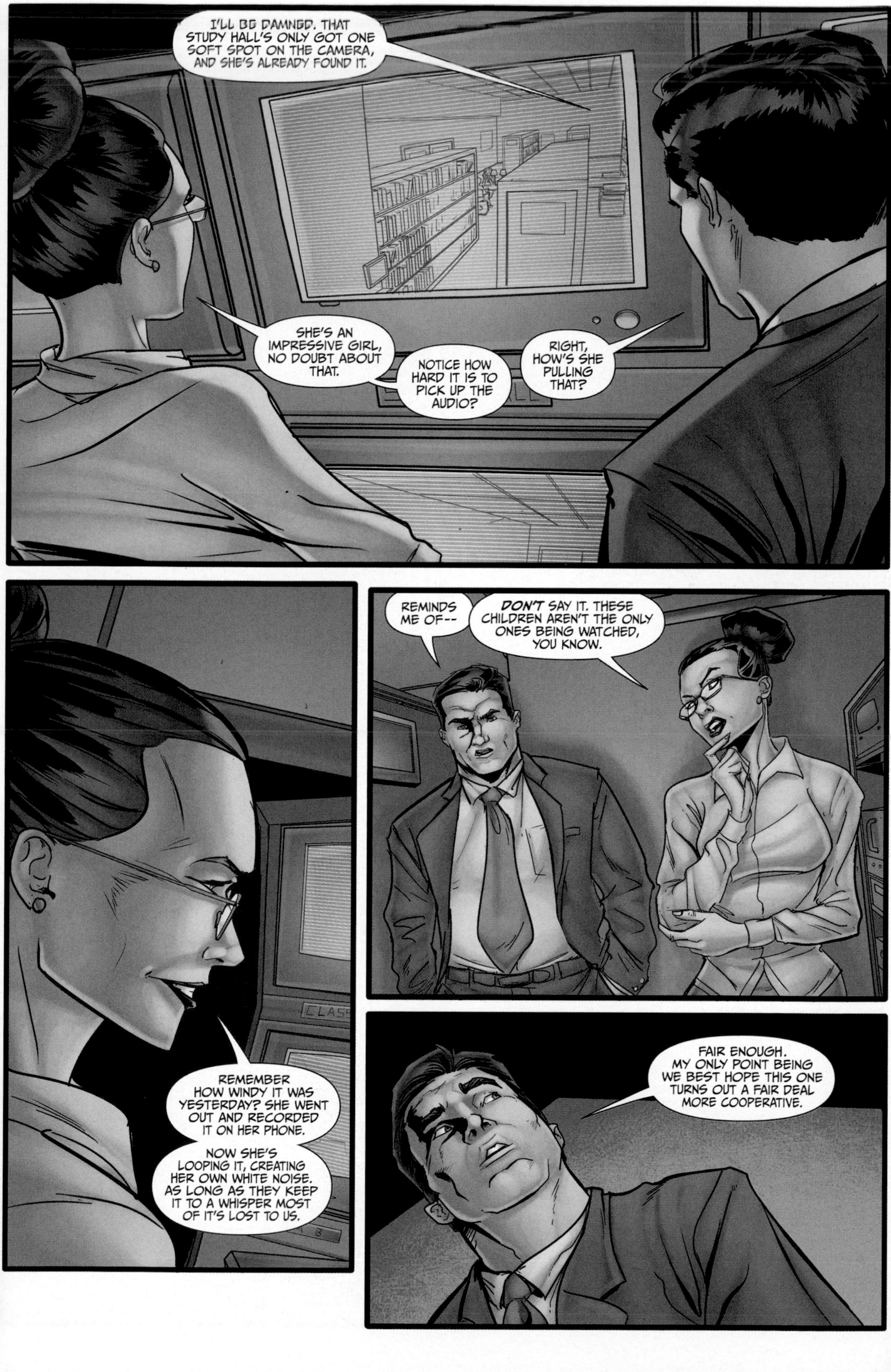
I'LL BE DAMNED. THAT STUDY HALL'S ONLY GOT ONE SOFT SPOT ON THE CAMERA, AND SHE'S ALREADY FOUND IT.
SHE'S AN IMPRESSIVE GIRL, NO DOUBT ABOUT THAT.
NOTICE HOW HARD IT IS TO PICK UP THE AUDIO?
RIGHT, HOW'S SHE PULLING THAT?
REMEMBER HOW WINDY IT WAS YESTERDAY? SHE WENT OUT AND RECORDED IT ON HER PHONE.
NOW SHE'S LOOPING IT, CREATING HER OWN WHITE NOISE. AS LONG AS THEY KEEP IT TO A WHISPER MOST OF IT'S LOST TO US.
REMINDS ME OF--
DON'T SAY IT. THESE CHILDREN AREN'T THE ONLY ONES BEING WATCHED, YOU KNOW.
FAIR ENOUGH. MY ONLY POINT BEING WE BEST HOPE THIS ONE TURNS OUT A FAIR DEAL MORE COOPERATIVE.

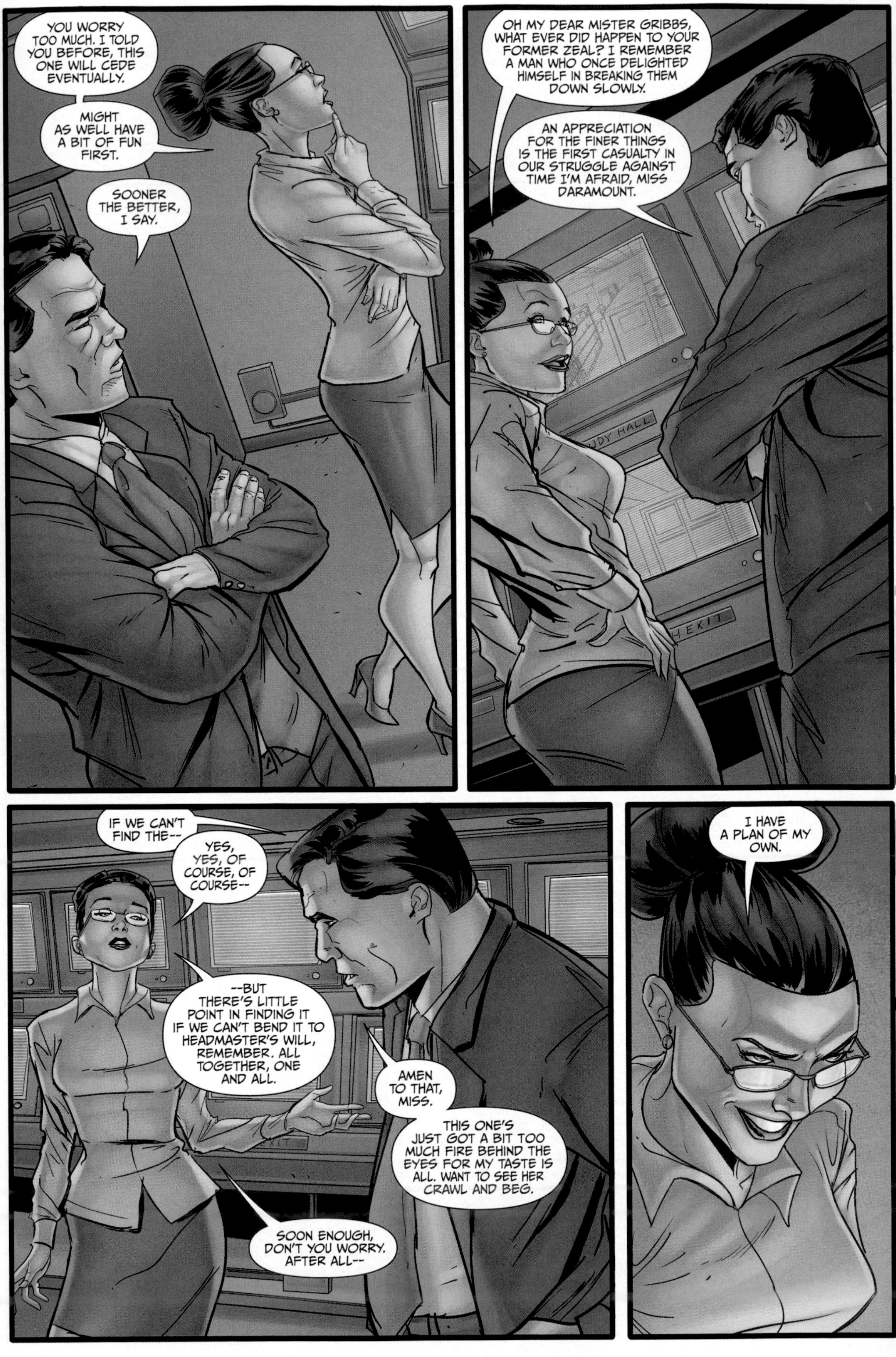
YOU WORRY TOO MUCH. I TOLD YOU BEFORE, THIS ONE WILL CEDE EVENTUALLY.
MIGHT AS WELL HAVE A BIT OF FUN FIRST.
SOONER THE BETTER, I SAY.
OH MY DEAR MISTER GRIBBS, WHAT EVER DID HAPPEN TO YOUR FORMER ZEAL? I REMEMBER A MAN WHO ONCE DELIGHTED HIMSELF IN BREAKING THEM DOWN SLOWLY.
AN APPRECIATION FOR THE FINER THINGS IS THE FIRST CASUALTY IN OUR STRUGGLE AGAINST TIME I'M AFRAID, MISS DARAMOUNT.
IF WE CAN'T FIND THE--
YES, YES, OF COURSE, OF COURSE--
--BUT THERE'S LITTLE POINT IN FINDING IT IF WE CAN'T BEND IT TO HEADMASTER'S WILL, REMEMBER. ALL TOGETHER, ONE AND ALL.
AMEN TO THAT, MISS.
THIS ONE'S JUST GOT A BIT TOO MUCH FIRE BEHIND THE EYES FOR MY TASTE IS ALL. WANT TO SEE HER CRAWL AND BEG.
SOON ENOUGH, DON'T YOU WORRY. AFTER ALL--
I HAVE A PLAN OF MY OWN.

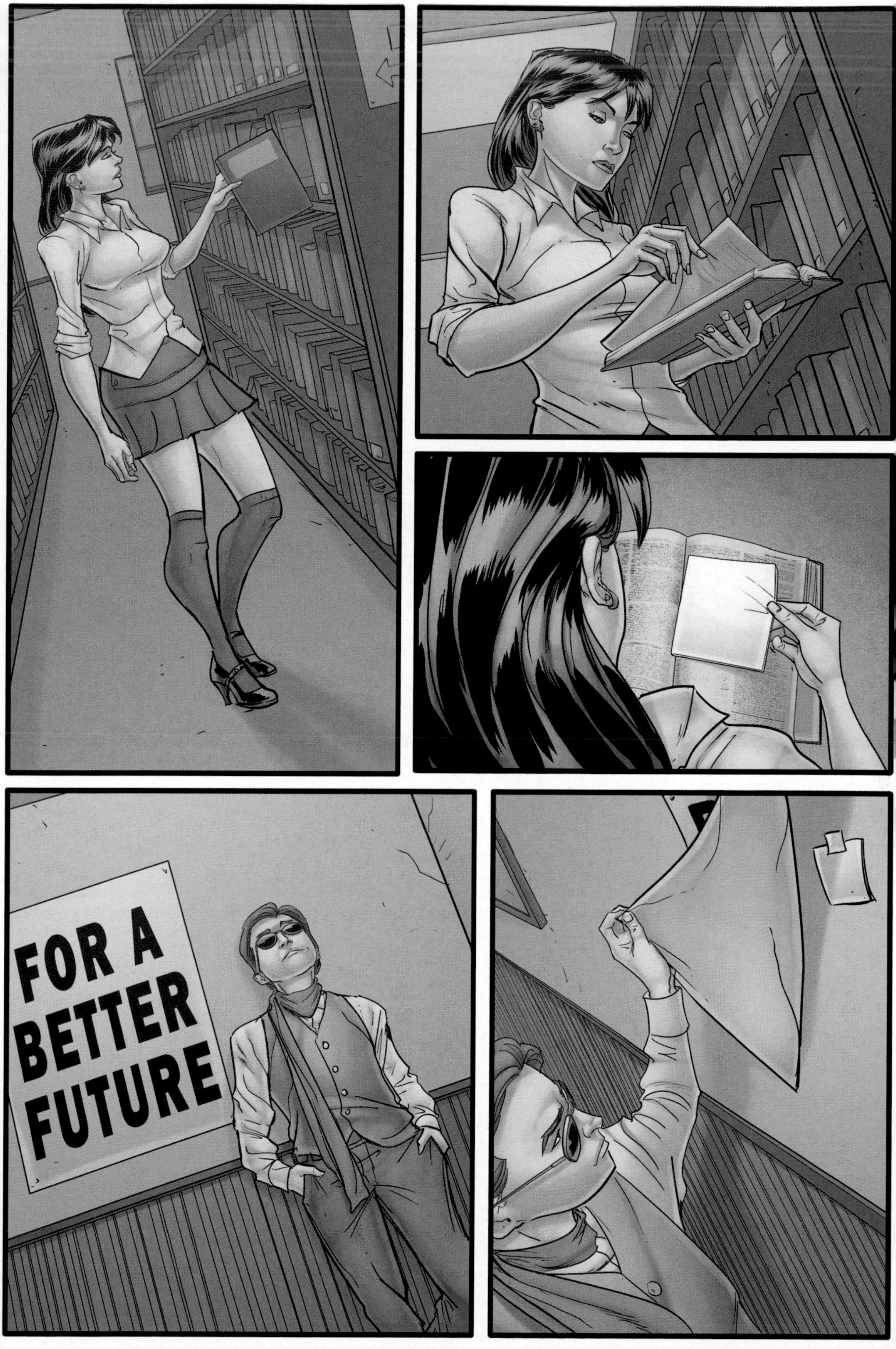
FOR A BETTER FUTURE

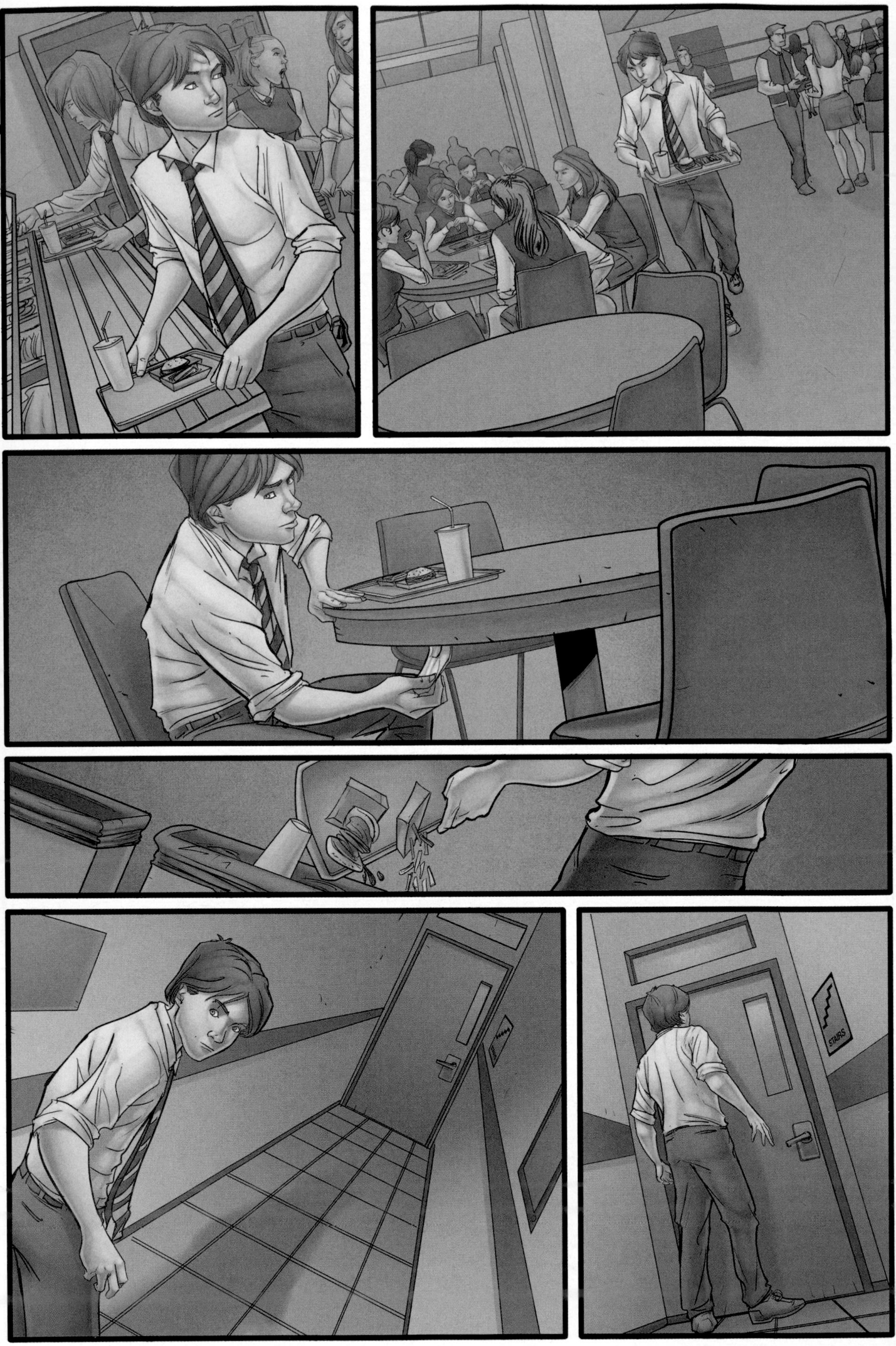
STAIRS

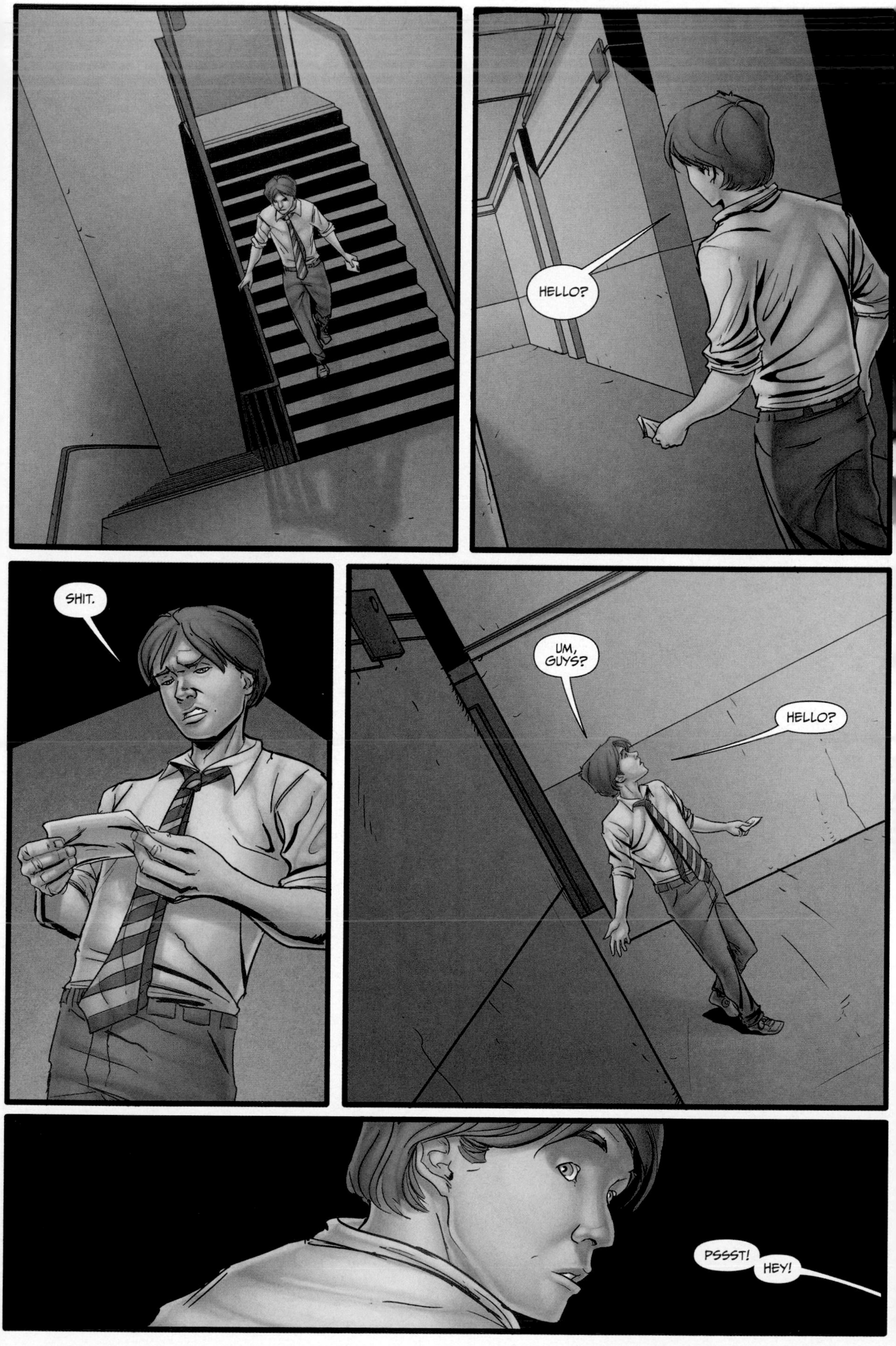
HELLO?
SHIT.
UM, GUYS?
HELLO?
PSSST!
HEY!

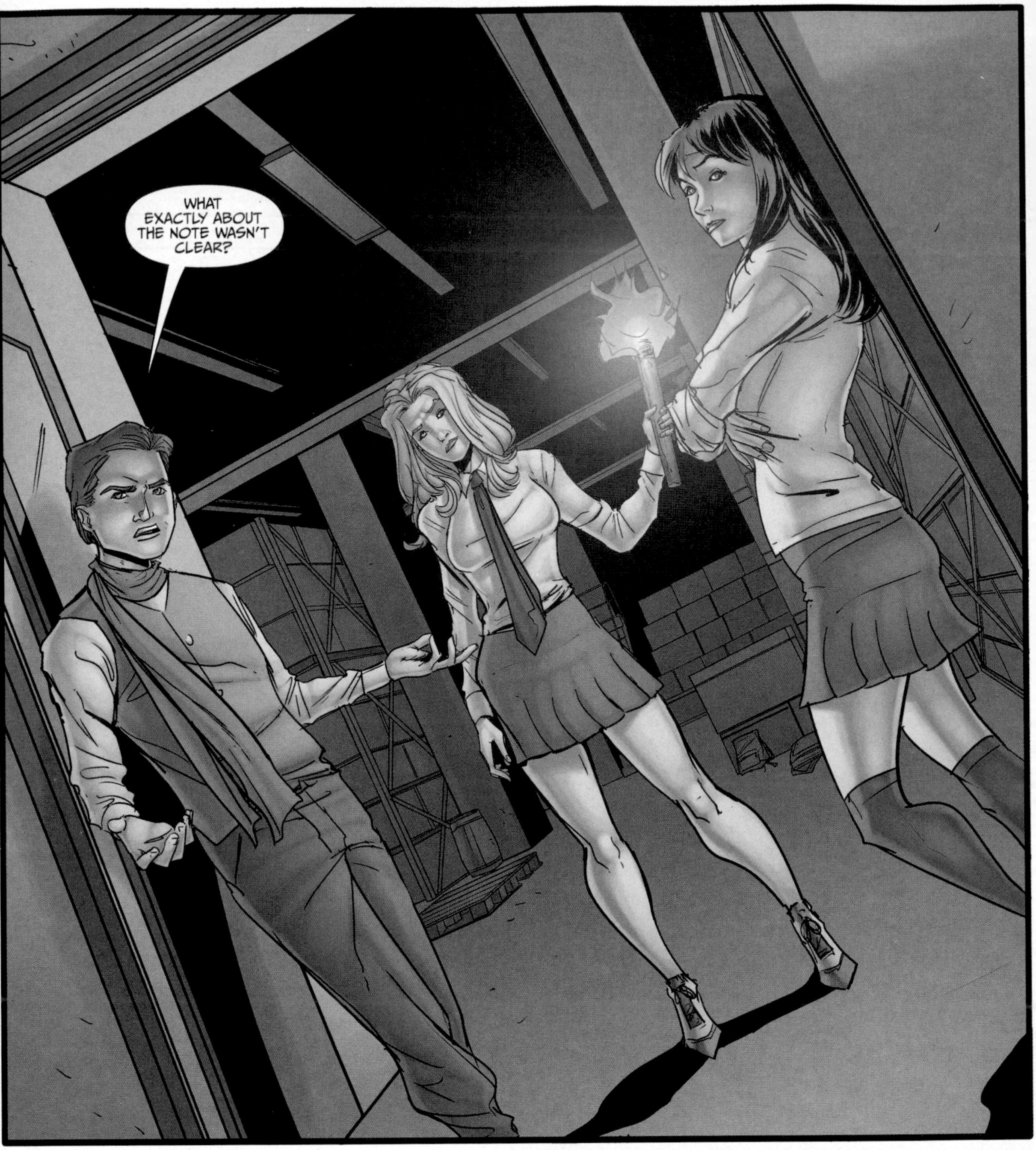
WHAT EXACTLY ABOUT THE NOTE WASN'T CLEAR?

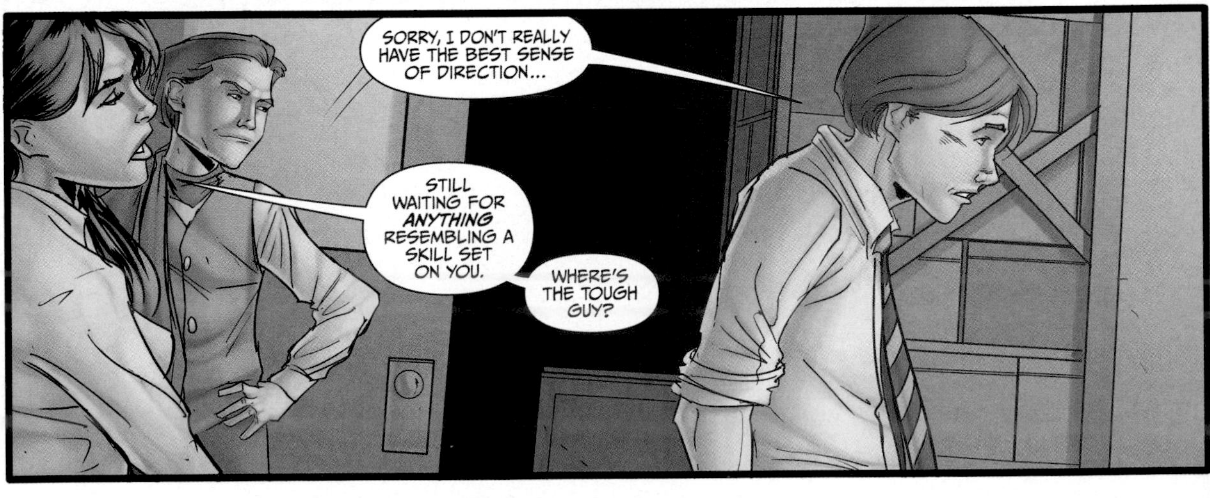
SORRY, I DON'T REALLY HAVE THE BEST SENSE OF DIRECTION...
STILL WAITING FOR *ANYTHING* RESEMBLING A SKILL SET ON YOU.
WHERE'S THE TOUGH GUY?

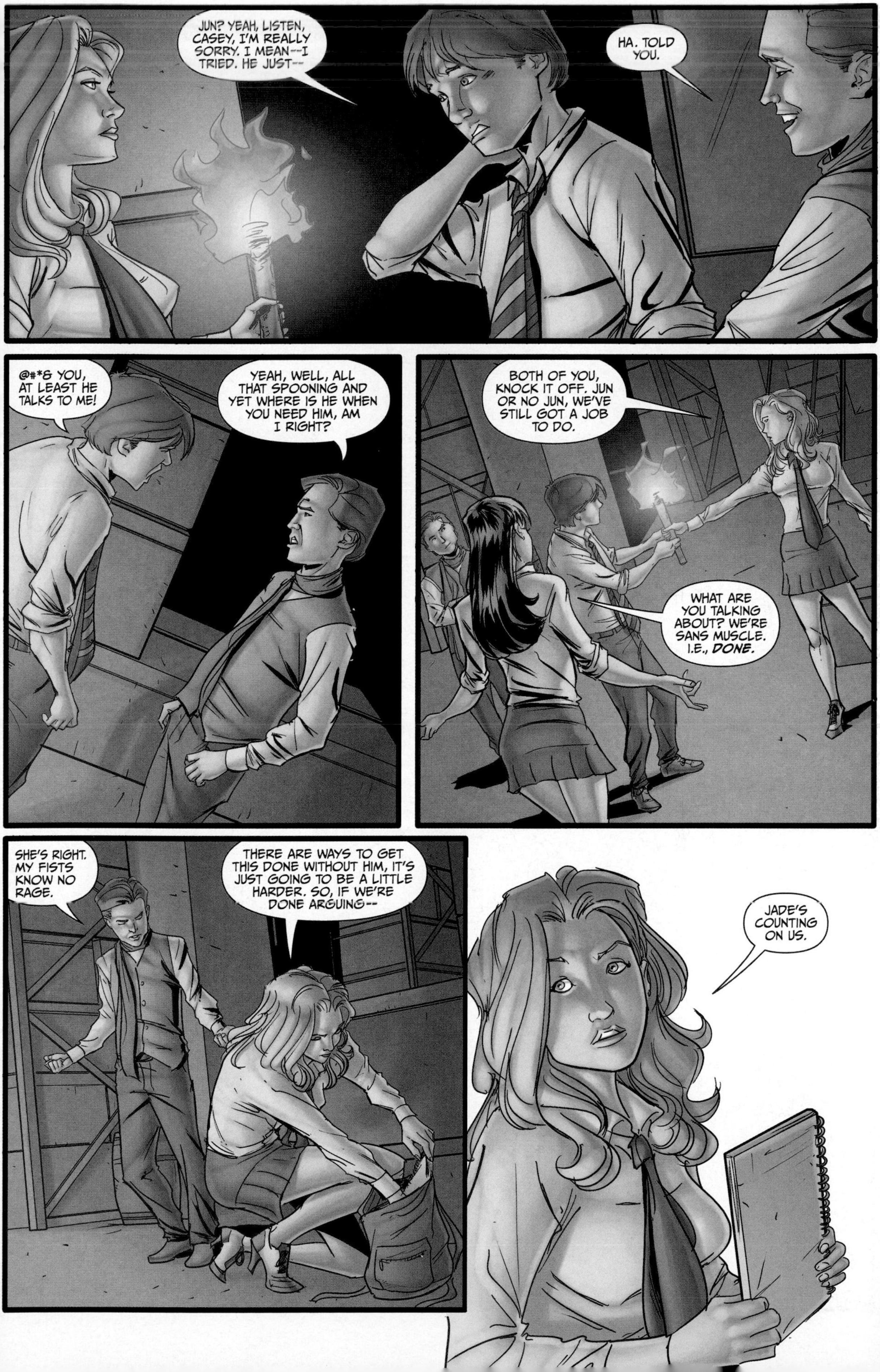
JUN? YEAH, LISTEN, CASEY, I'M REALLY SORRY. I MEAN--I TRIED. HE JUST--
HA. TOLD YOU.
@#*& YOU, AT LEAST HE TALKS TO ME!
YEAH, WELL, ALL THAT SPOONING AND YET WHERE IS HE WHEN YOU NEED HIM, AM I RIGHT?
BOTH OF YOU, KNOCK IT OFF. JUN OR NO JUN, WE'VE STILL GOT A JOB TO DO.
WHAT ARE YOU TALKING ABOUT? WE'RE SANS MUSCLE. I.E., DONE.
SHE'S RIGHT. MY FISTS KNOW NO RAGE.
THERE ARE WAYS TO GET THIS DONE WITHOUT HIM, IT'S JUST GOING TO BE A LITTLE HARDER. SO, IF WE'RE DONE ARGUING--
JADE'S COUNTING ON US.

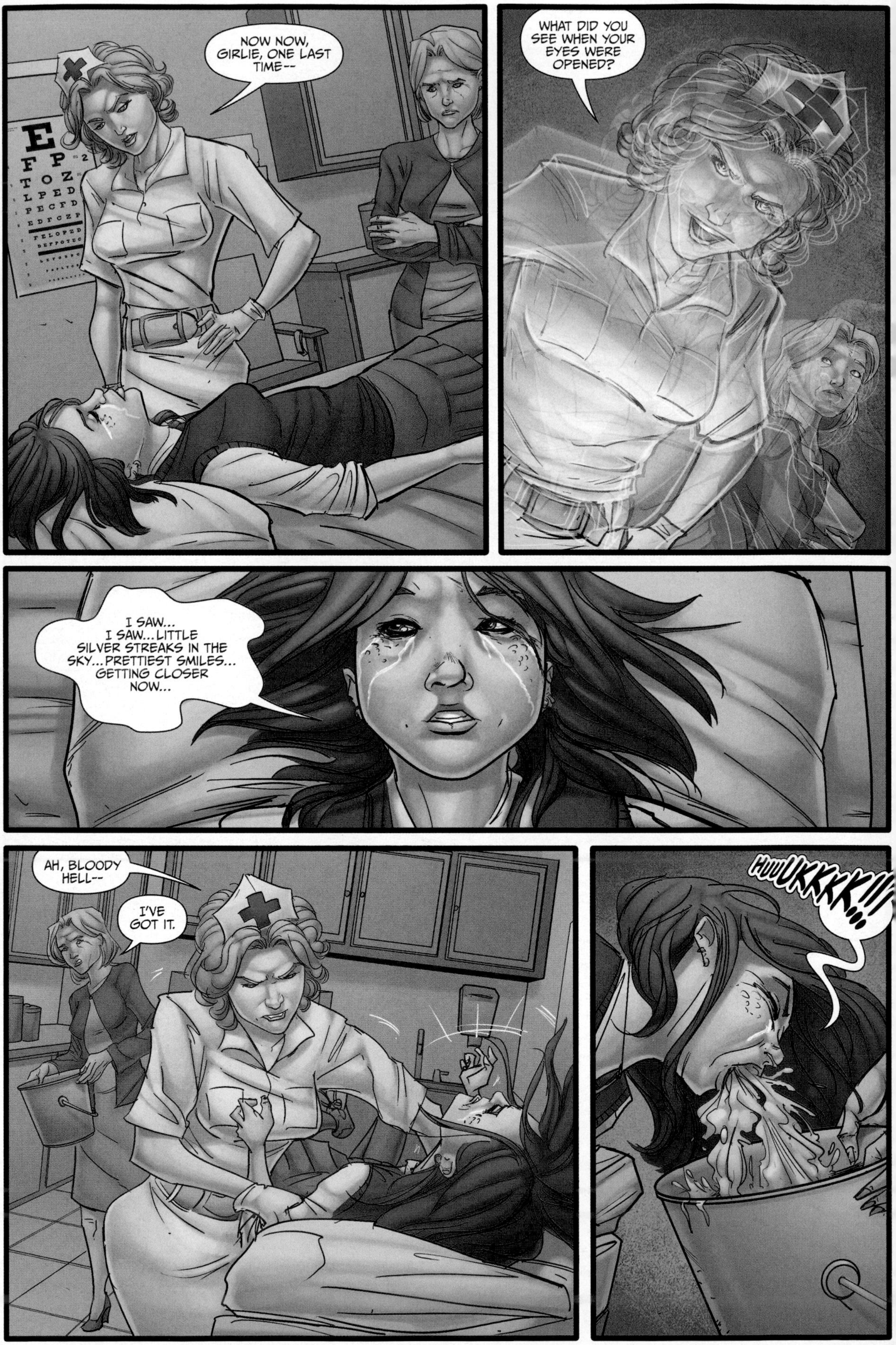
NOW NOW, GIRLIE, ONE LAST TIME--
E F P T O Z L P E D P E C F D E D F C Z P F E L O P Z D D E F P O T E C
WHAT DID YOU SEE WHEN YOUR EYES WERE OPENED?
I SAW... I SAW...LITTLE SILVER STREAKS IN THE SKY...PRETTIEST SMILES... GETTING CLOSER NOW...
AH, BLOODY HELL--
I'VE GOT IT.
HUUUKKKK!!!

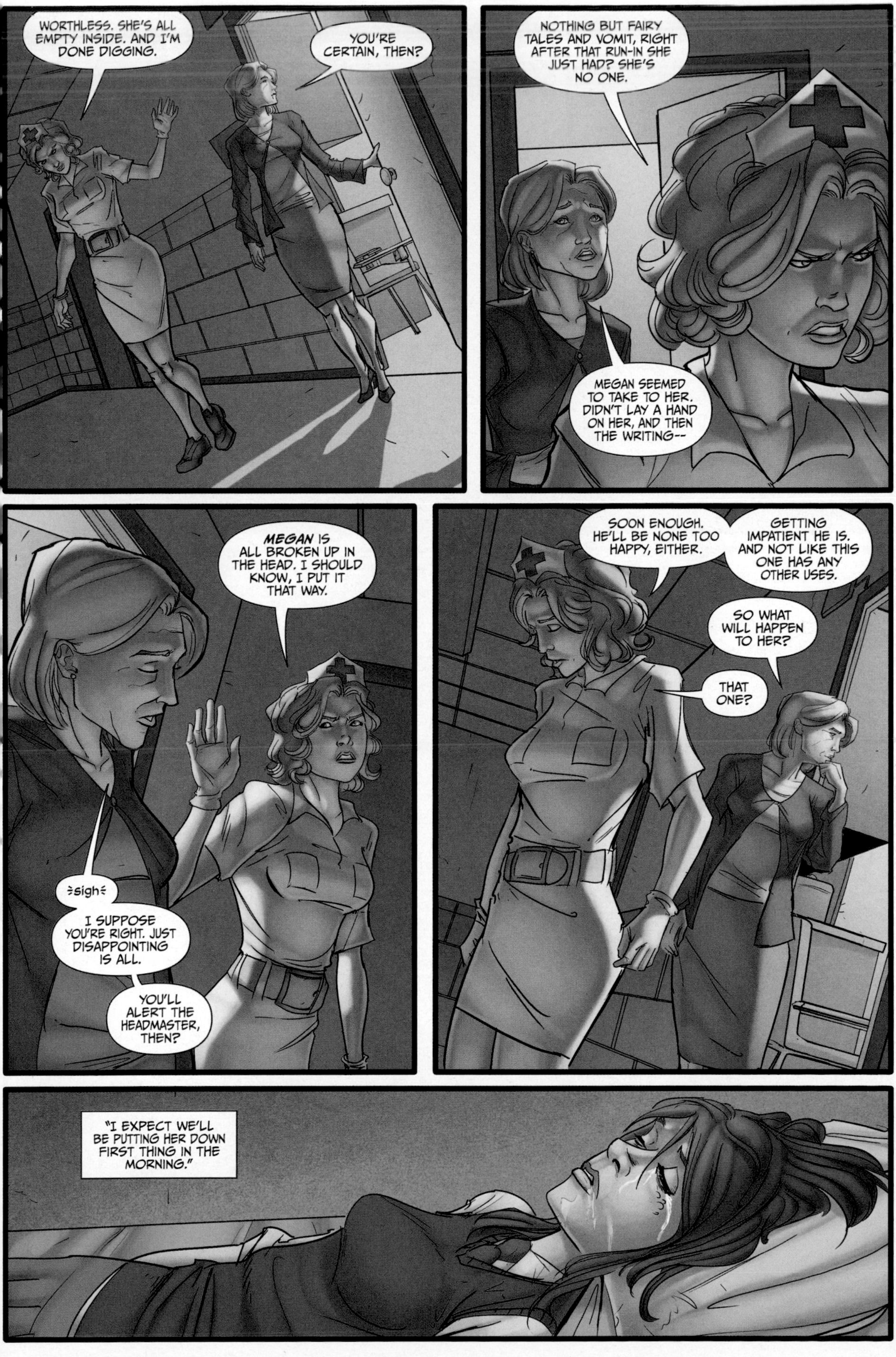
WORTHLESS. SHE'S ALL EMPTY INSIDE. AND I'M DONE DIGGING.
YOU'RE CERTAIN, THEN?
NOTHING BUT FAIRY TALES AND VOMIT, RIGHT AFTER THAT RUN-IN SHE JUST HAD? SHE'S NO ONE.
MEGAN SEEMED TO TAKE TO HER. DIDN'T LAY A HAND ON HER, AND THEN THE WRITING--
MEGAN IS ALL BROKEN UP IN THE HEAD. I SHOULD KNOW, I PUT IT THAT WAY.
sigh
I SUPPOSE YOU'RE RIGHT. JUST DISAPPOINTING IS ALL.
YOU'LL ALERT THE HEADMASTER, THEN?
SOON ENOUGH. HE'LL BE NONE TOO HAPPY, EITHER.
GETTING IMPATIENT HE IS. AND NOT LIKE THIS ONE HAS ANY OTHER USES.
SO WHAT WILL HAPPEN TO HER?
THAT ONE?
"I EXPECT WE'LL BE PUTTING HER DOWN FIRST THING IN THE MORNING."

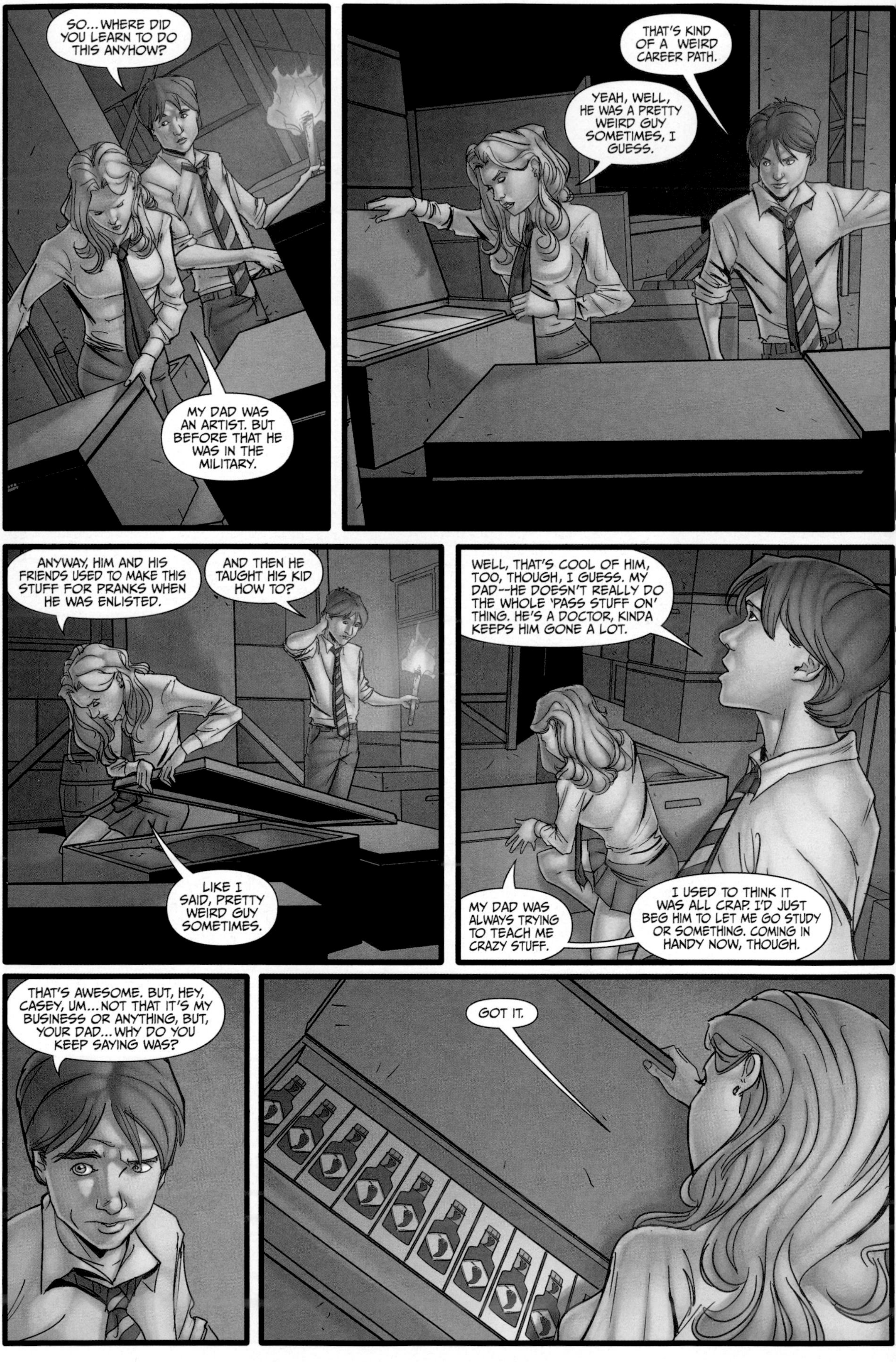
SO... WHERE DID YOU LEARN TO DO THIS ANYHOW?
MY DAD WAS AN ARTIST. BUT BEFORE THAT HE WAS IN THE MILITARY.
THAT'S KIND OF A WEIRD CAREER PATH.
YEAH, WELL, HE WAS A PRETTY WEIRD GUY SOMETIMES, I GUESS.
ANYWAY, HIM AND HIS FRIENDS USED TO MAKE THIS STUFF FOR PRANKS WHEN HE WAS ENLISTED.
AND THEN HE TAUGHT HIS KID HOW TO?
LIKE I SAID, PRETTY WEIRD GUY SOMETIMES.
WELL, THAT'S COOL OF HIM, TOO, THOUGH, I GUESS. MY DAD--HE DOESN'T REALLY DO THE WHOLE 'PASS STUFF ON' THING. HE'S A DOCTOR, KINDA KEEPS HIM GONE A LOT.
MY DAD WAS ALWAYS TRYING TO TEACH ME CRAZY STUFF.
I USED TO THINK IT WAS ALL CRAP. I'D JUST BEG HIM TO LET ME GO STUDY OR SOMETHING. COMING IN HANDY NOW, THOUGH.
THAT'S AWESOME. BUT, HEY, CASEY, UM... NOT THAT IT'S MY BUSINESS OR ANYTHING, BUT, YOUR DAD... WHY DO YOU KEEP SAYING WAS?
GOT IT.

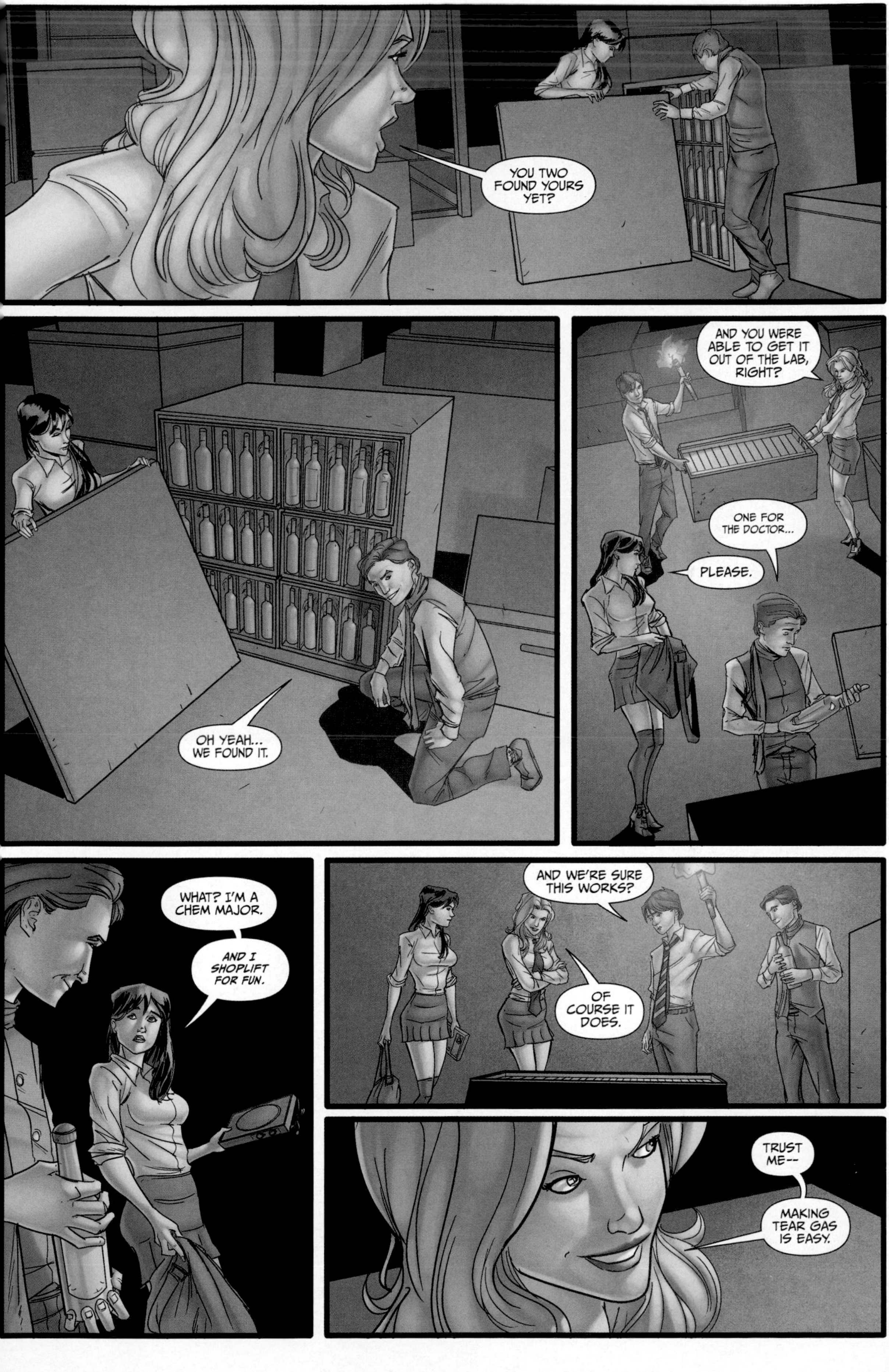
YOU TWO FOUND YOURS YET?
OH YEAH... WE FOUND IT.
AND YOU WERE ABLE TO GET IT OUT OF THE LAB, RIGHT?
ONE FOR THE DOCTOR...
PLEASE.
WHAT? I'M A CHEM MAJOR.
AND I SHOPLIFT FOR FUN.
AND WE'RE SURE THIS WORKS?
OF COURSE IT DOES.
TRUST ME--
MAKING TEAR GAS IS EASY.

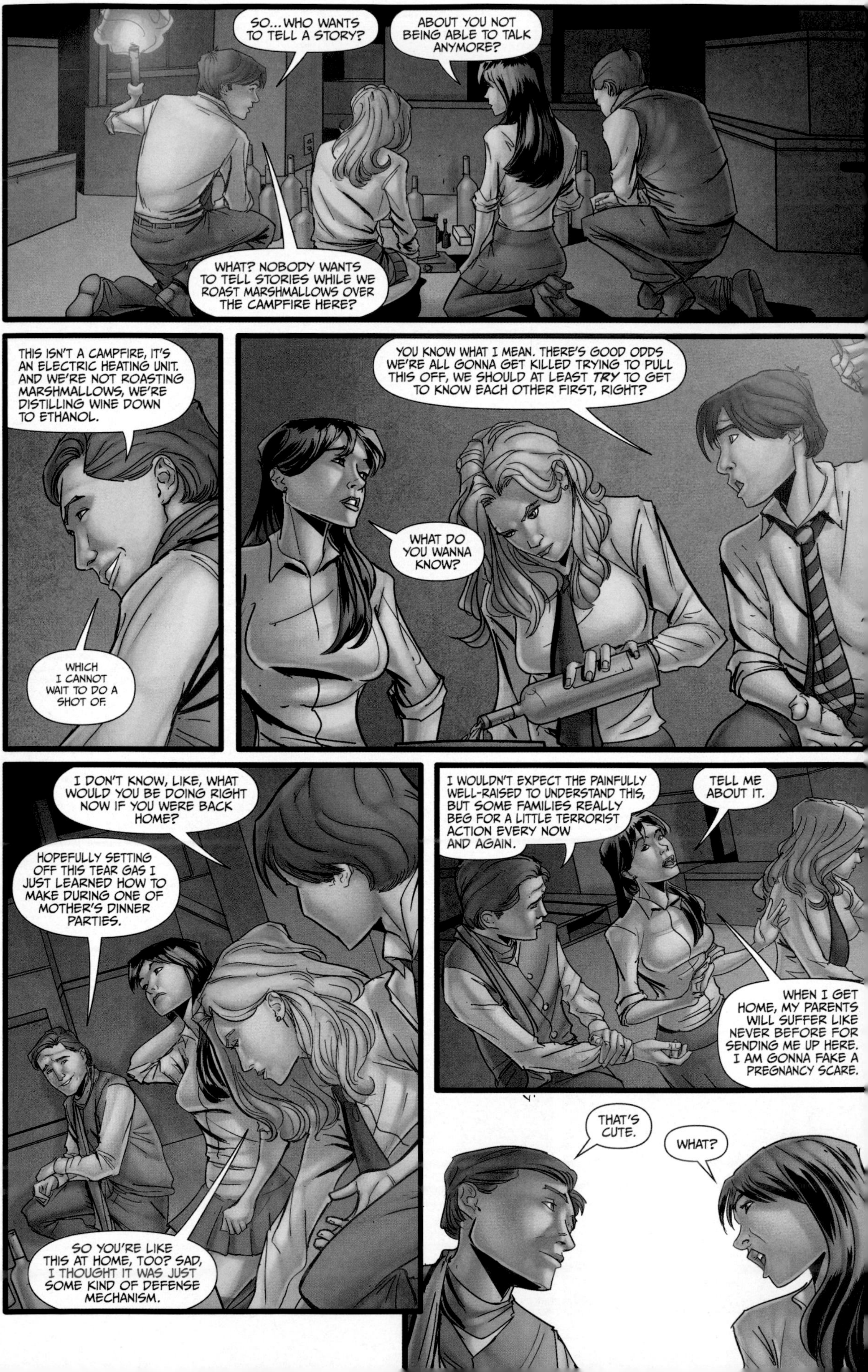

SO... WHO WANTS TO TELL A STORY?
ABOUT YOU NOT BEING ABLE TO TALK ANYMORE?
WHAT? NOBODY WANTS TO TELL STORIES WHILE WE ROAST MARSHMALLOWS OVER THE CAMPFIRE HERE?
THIS ISN'T A CAMPFIRE, IT'S AN ELECTRIC HEATING UNIT. AND WE'RE NOT ROASTING MARSHMALLOWS, WE'RE DISTILLING WINE DOWN TO ETHANOL.
WHICH I CANNOT WAIT TO DO A SHOT OF.
YOU KNOW WHAT I MEAN. THERE'S GOOD ODDS WE'RE ALL GONNA GET KILLED TRYING TO PULL THIS OFF, WE SHOULD AT LEAST TRY TO GET TO KNOW EACH OTHER FIRST, RIGHT?
WHAT DO YOU WANNA KNOW?
I DON'T KNOW, LIKE, WHAT WOULD YOU BE DOING RIGHT NOW IF YOU WERE BACK HOME?
HOPEFULLY SETTING OFF THIS TEAR GAS I JUST LEARNED HOW TO MAKE DURING ONE OF MOTHER'S DINNER PARTIES.
SO YOU'RE LIKE THIS AT HOME, TOO? SAD, I THOUGHT IT WAS JUST SOME KIND OF DEFENSE MECHANISM.
I WOULDN'T EXPECT THE PAINFULLY WELL-RAISED TO UNDERSTAND THIS, BUT SOME FAMILIES REALLY BEG FOR A LITTLE TERRORIST ACTION EVERY NOW AND AGAIN.
TELL ME ABOUT IT.
WHEN I GET HOME, MY PARENTS WILL SUFFER LIKE NEVER BEFORE FOR SENDING ME UP HERE. I AM GONNA FAKE A PREGNANCY SCARE.
THAT'S CUTE.
WHAT?

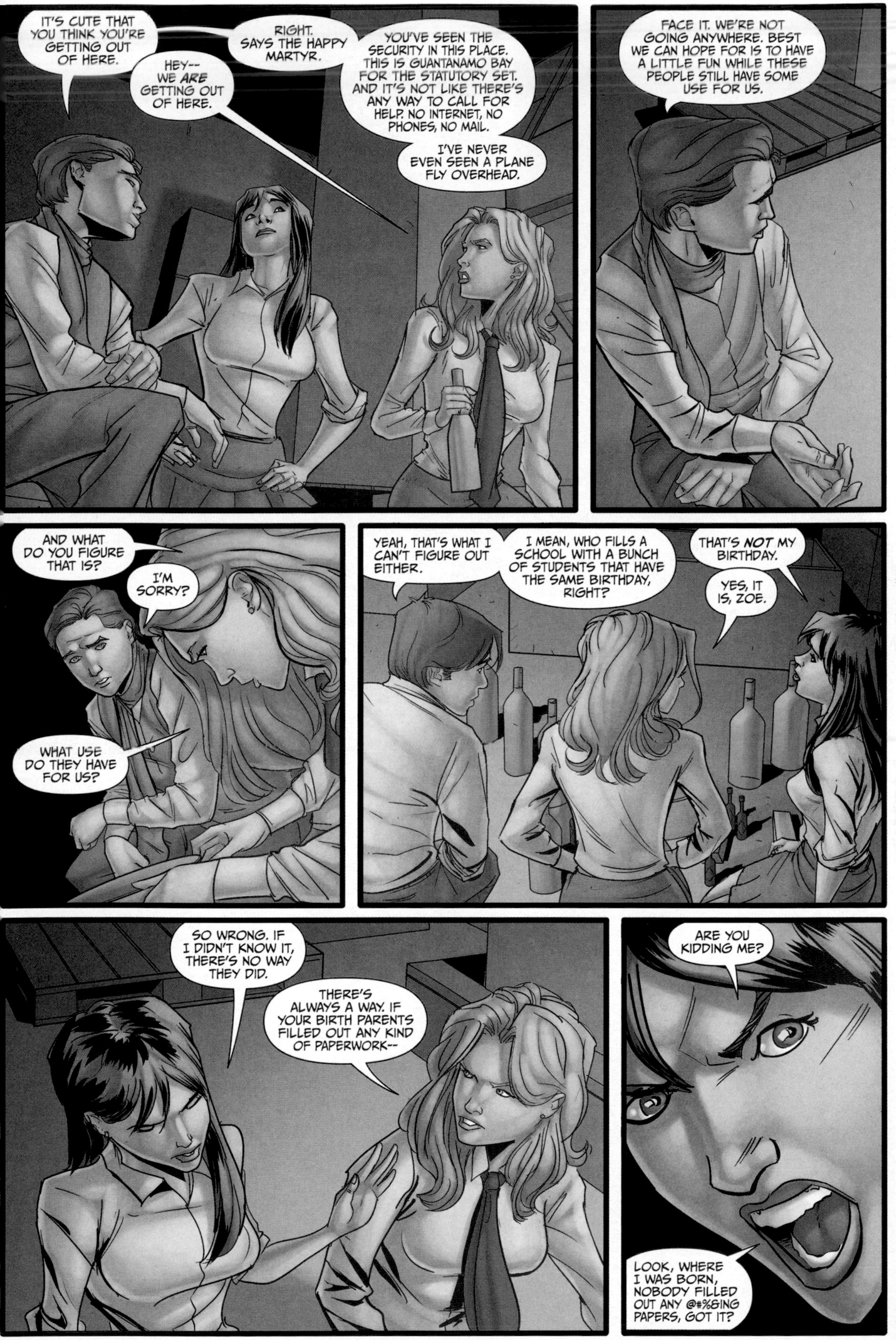
IT'S CUTE THAT YOU THINK YOU'RE GETTING OUT OF HERE.
RIGHT. SAYS THE HAPPY MARTYR.
HEY-- WE ARE GETTING OUT OF HERE.
YOU'VE SEEN THE SECURITY IN THIS PLACE. THIS IS GUANTANAMO BAY FOR THE STATUTORY SET. AND IT'S NOT LIKE THERE'S ANY WAY TO CALL FOR HELP. NO INTERNET, NO PHONES, NO MAIL.
I'VE NEVER EVEN SEEN A PLANE FLY OVERHEAD.
FACE IT. WE'RE NOT GOING ANYWHERE. BEST WE CAN HOPE FOR IS TO HAVE A LITTLE FUN WHILE THESE PEOPLE STILL HAVE SOME USE FOR US.
AND WHAT DO YOU FIGURE THAT IS?
I'M SORRY?
WHAT USE DO THEY HAVE FOR US?
YEAH, THAT'S WHAT I CAN'T FIGURE OUT EITHER.
I MEAN, WHO FILLS A SCHOOL WITH A BUNCH OF STUDENTS THAT HAVE THE SAME BIRTHDAY, RIGHT?
THAT'S NOT MY BIRTHDAY.
YES, IT IS, ZOE.
SO WRONG. IF I DIDN'T KNOW IT, THERE'S NO WAY THEY DID.
THERE'S ALWAYS A WAY. IF YOUR BIRTH PARENTS FILLED OUT ANY KIND OF PAPERWORK--
ARE YOU KIDDING ME?
LOOK, WHERE I WAS BORN, NOBODY FILLED OUT ANY @#%&ING PAPERS, GOT IT?

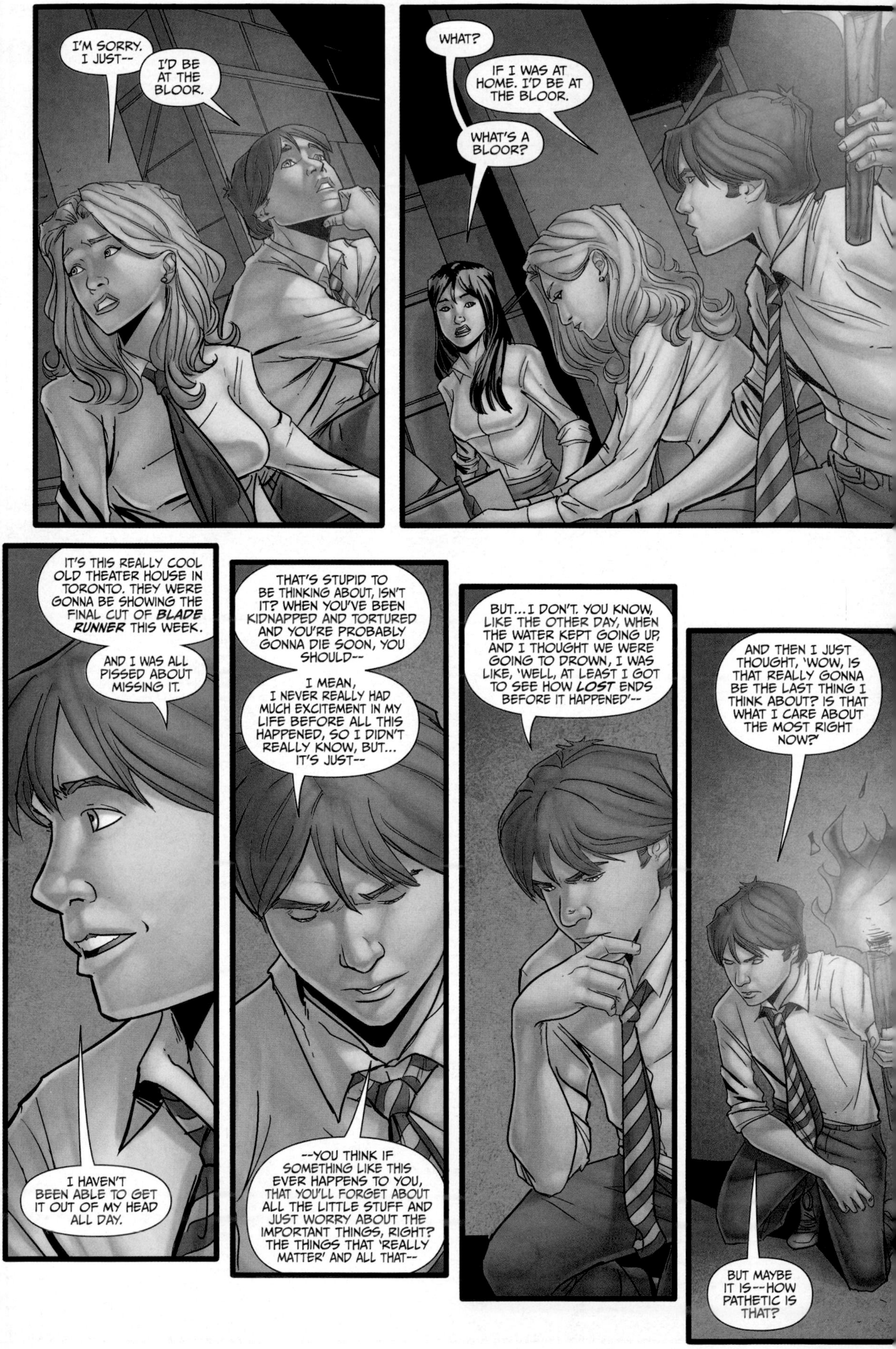
I'M SORRY. I JUST--
I'D BE AT THE BLOOR.
WHAT?
IF I WAS AT HOME. I'D BE AT THE BLOOR.
WHAT'S A BLOOR?
IT'S THIS REALLY COOL OLD THEATER HOUSE IN TORONTO. THEY WERE GONNA BE SHOWING THE FINAL CUT OF **BLADE RUNNER** THIS WEEK.
AND I WAS ALL PISSED ABOUT MISSING IT.
I HAVEN'T BEEN ABLE TO GET IT OUT OF MY HEAD ALL DAY.
THAT'S STUPID TO BE THINKING ABOUT, ISN'T IT? WHEN YOU'VE BEEN KIDNAPPED AND TORTURED AND YOU'RE PROBABLY GONNA DIE SOON, YOU SHOULD--
I MEAN, I NEVER REALLY HAD MUCH EXCITEMENT IN MY LIFE BEFORE ALL THIS HAPPENED, SO I DIDN'T REALLY KNOW, BUT... IT'S JUST--
--YOU THINK IF SOMETHING LIKE THIS EVER HAPPENS TO YOU, THAT YOU'LL FORGET ABOUT ALL THE LITTLE STUFF AND JUST WORRY ABOUT THE IMPORTANT THINGS, RIGHT? THE THINGS THAT 'REALLY MATTER' AND ALL THAT--
BUT... I DON'T. YOU KNOW, LIKE THE OTHER DAY, WHEN THE WATER KEPT GOING UP, AND I THOUGHT WE WERE GOING TO DROWN, I WAS LIKE, 'WELL, AT LEAST I GOT TO SEE HOW **LOST** ENDS BEFORE IT HAPPENED'--
AND THEN I JUST THOUGHT, 'WOW, IS THAT REALLY GONNA BE THE LAST THING I THINK ABOUT? IS THAT WHAT I CARE ABOUT THE MOST RIGHT NOW?'
BUT MAYBE IT IS--HOW PATHETIC IS THAT?

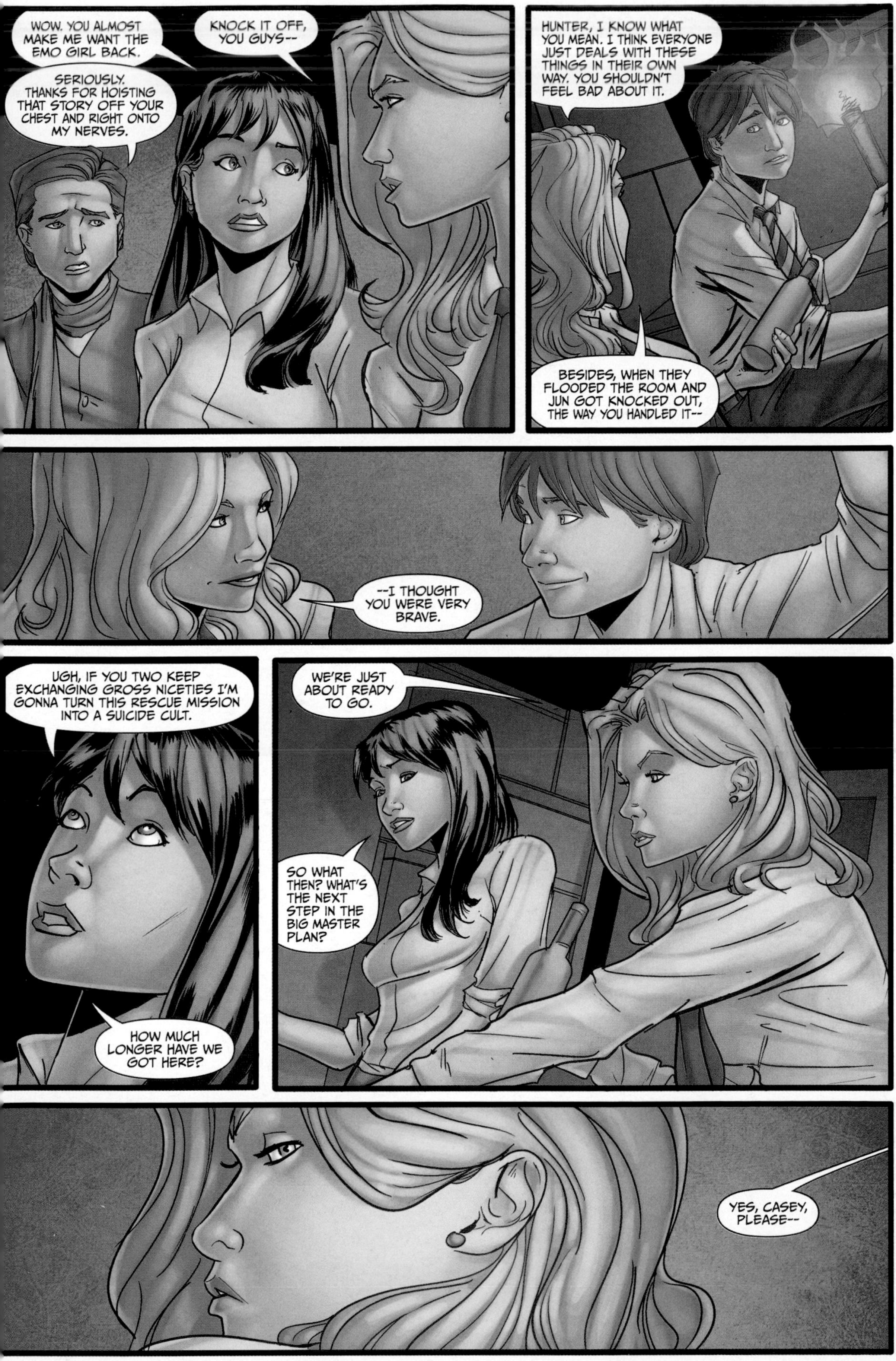
WOW. YOU ALMOST MAKE ME WANT THE EMO GIRL BACK.
KNOCK IT OFF, YOU GUYS--
SERIOUSLY. THANKS FOR HOISTING THAT STORY OFF YOUR CHEST AND RIGHT ONTO MY NERVES.
HUNTER, I KNOW WHAT YOU MEAN. I THINK EVERYONE JUST DEALS WITH THESE THINGS IN THEIR OWN WAY. YOU SHOULDN'T FEEL BAD ABOUT IT.
BESIDES, WHEN THEY FLOODED THE ROOM AND JUN GOT KNOCKED OUT, THE WAY YOU HANDLED IT--
--I THOUGHT YOU WERE VERY BRAVE.
UGH, IF YOU TWO KEEP EXCHANGING GROSS NICETIES I'M GONNA TURN THIS RESCUE MISSION INTO A SUICIDE CULT.
HOW MUCH LONGER HAVE WE GOT HERE?
WE'RE JUST ABOUT READY TO GO.
SO WHAT THEN? WHAT'S THE NEXT STEP IN THE BIG MASTER PLAN?
YES, CASEY, PLEASE--

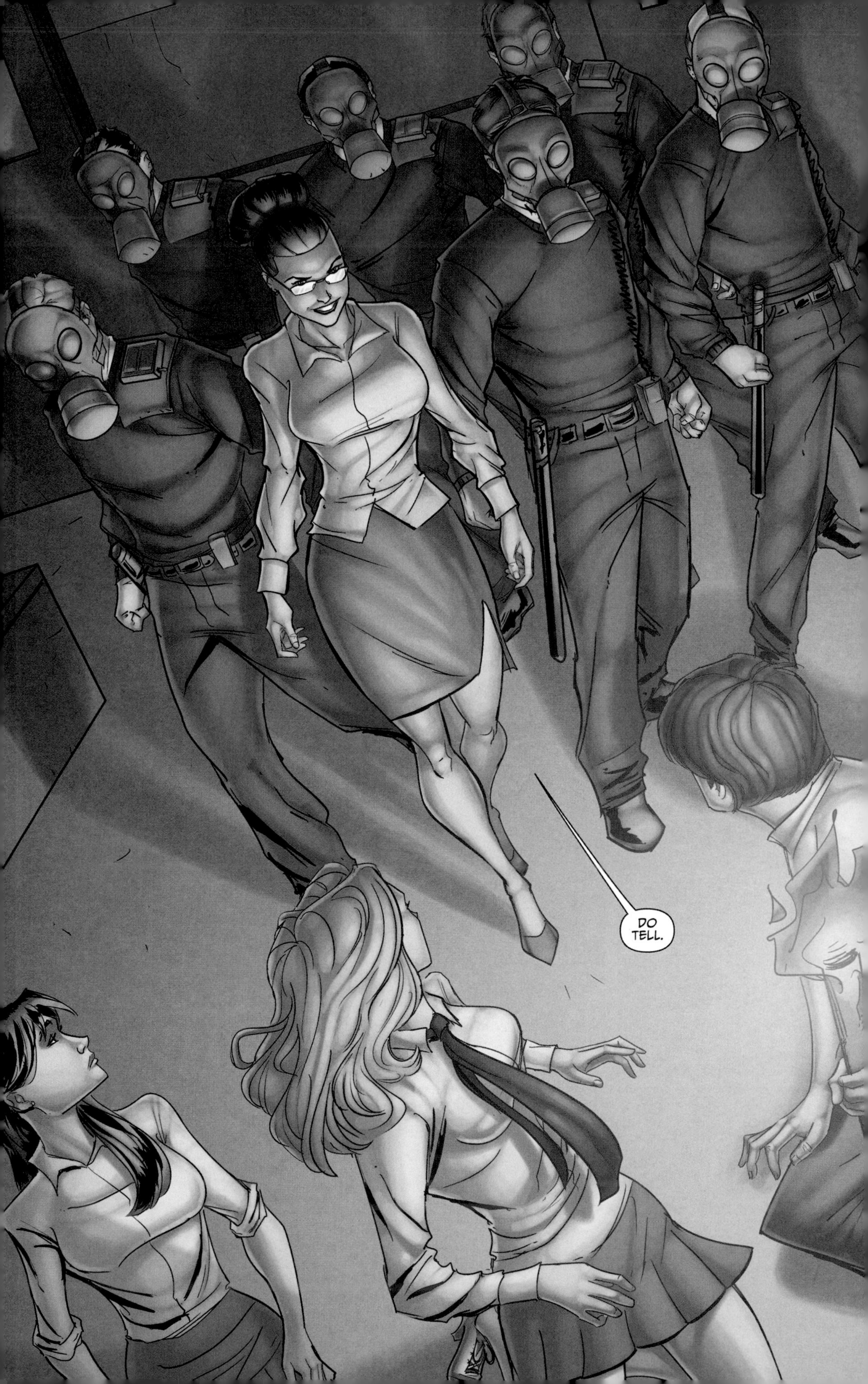
DO TELL.

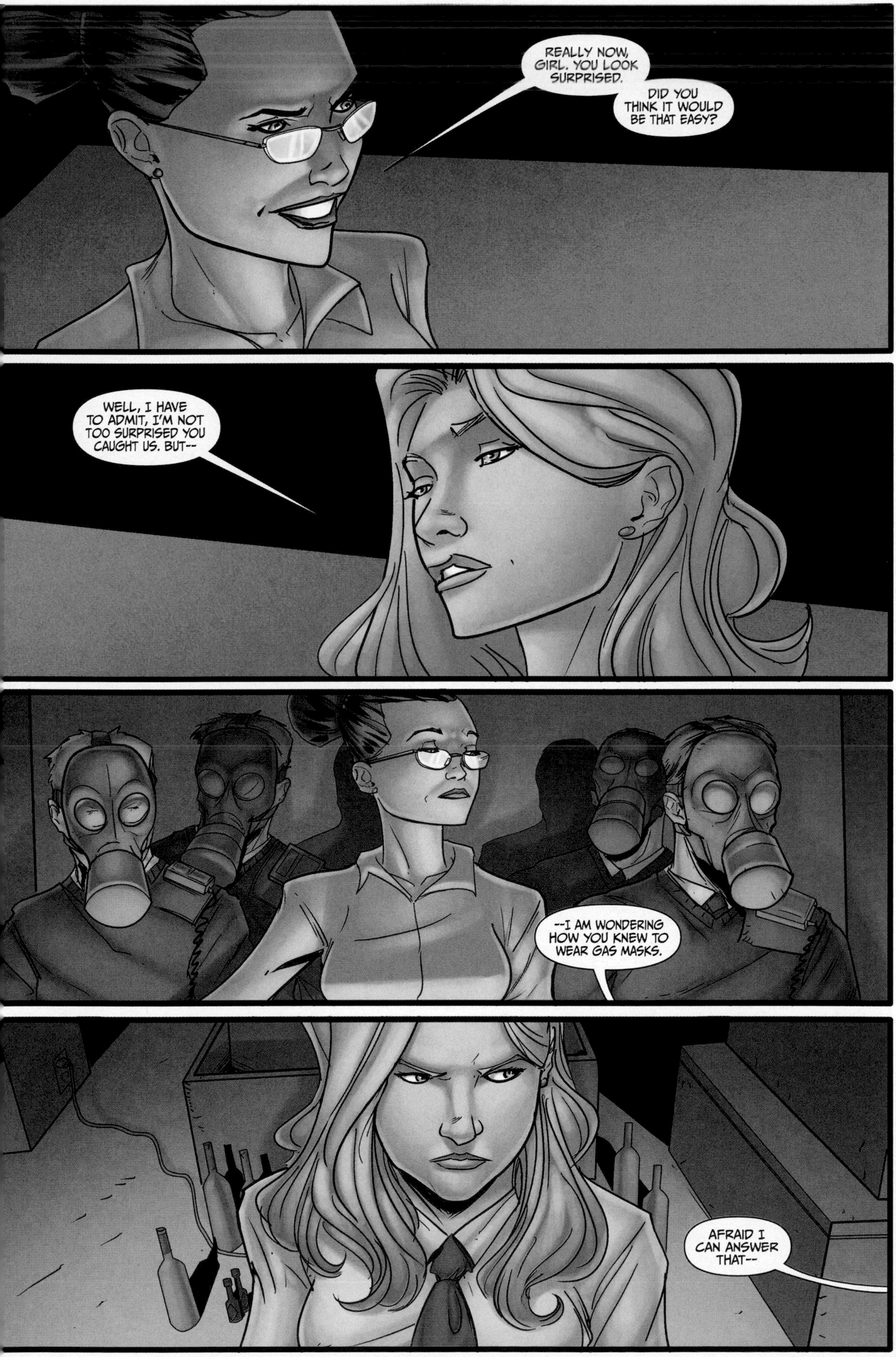
REALLY NOW, GIRL. YOU LOOK SURPRISED.
DID YOU THINK IT WOULD BE THAT EASY?
WELL, I HAVE TO ADMIT, I'M NOT TOO SURPRISED YOU CAUGHT US. BUT--
--I AM WONDERING HOW YOU KNEW TO WEAR GAS MASKS.
AFRAID I CAN ANSWER THAT--

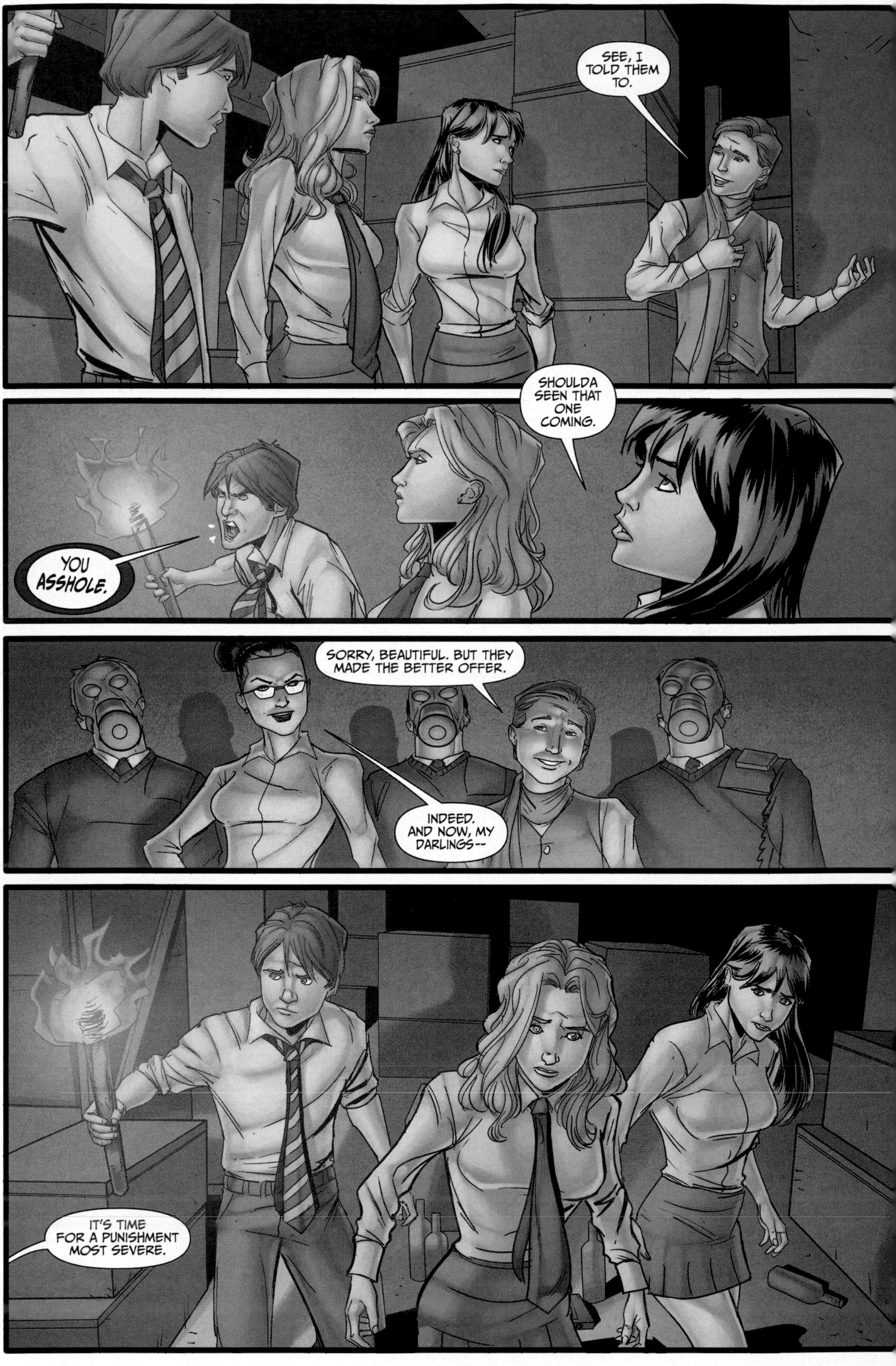
SEE, I TOLD THEM TO.
YOU ASSHOLE.
SHOULDA SEEN THAT ONE COMING.
SORRY, BEAUTIFUL. BUT THEY MADE THE BETTER OFFER.
INDEED. AND NOW, MY DARLINGS--
IT'S TIME FOR A PUNISHMENT MOST SEVERE.

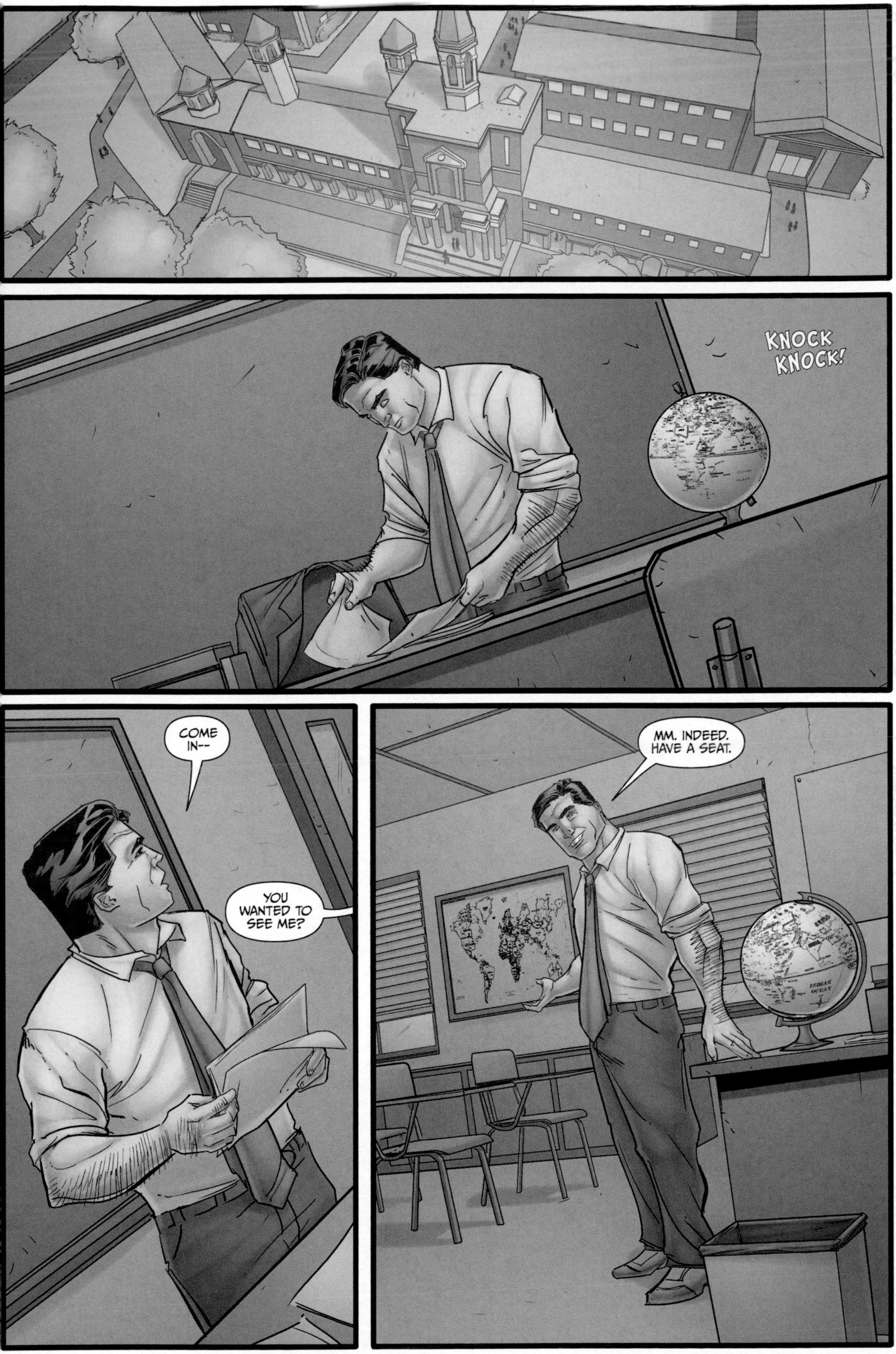
KNOCK KNOCK!
COME IN--
YOU WANTED TO SEE ME?
MM. INDEED. HAVE A SEAT.
INDIAN OCEAN

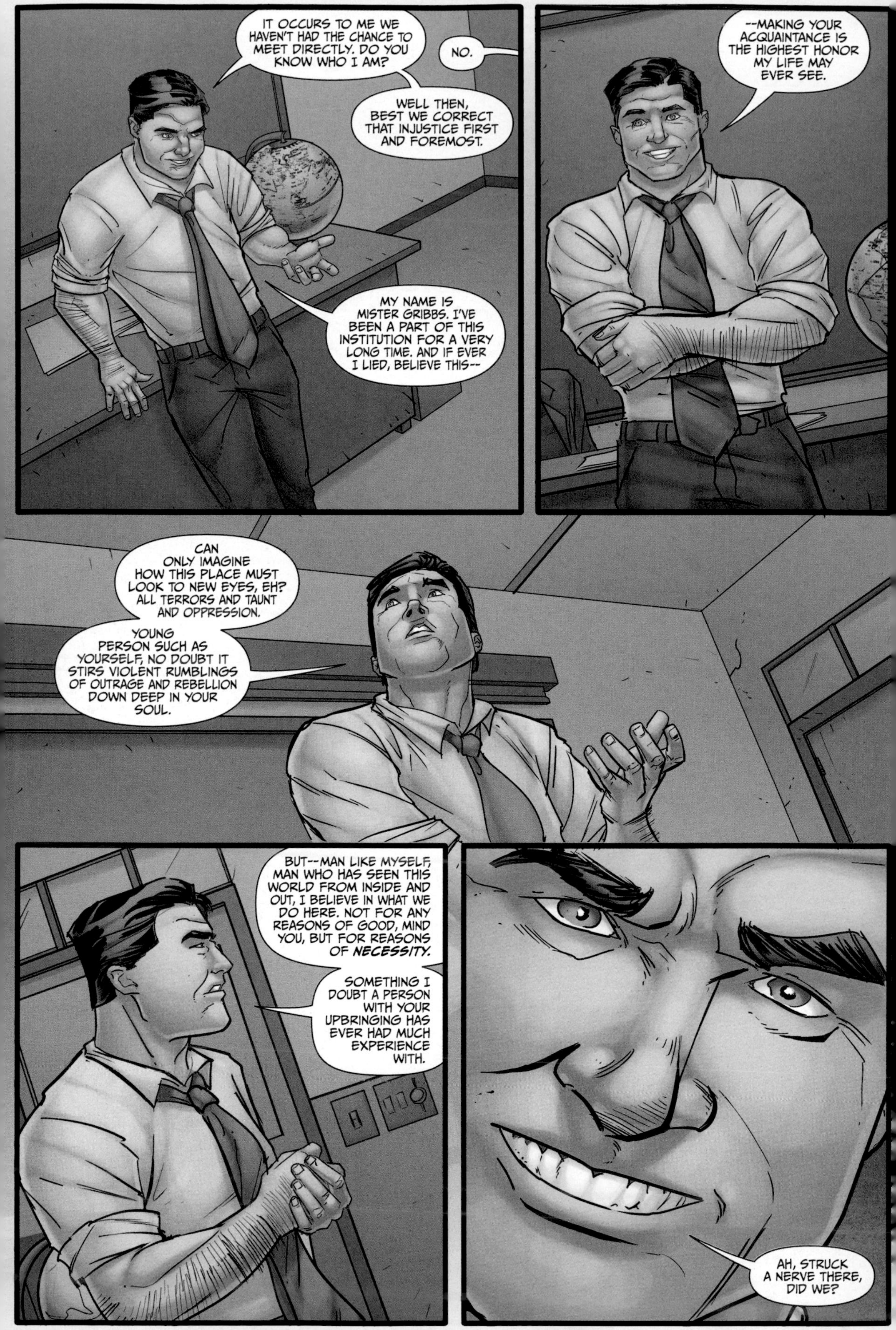
IT OCCURS TO ME WE HAVEN'T HAD THE CHANCE TO MEET DIRECTLY. DO YOU KNOW WHO I AM?
NO.
WELL THEN, BEST WE CORRECT THAT INJUSTICE FIRST AND FOREMOST.
MY NAME IS MISTER GRIBBS. I'VE BEEN A PART OF THIS INSTITUTION FOR A VERY LONG TIME. AND IF EVER I LIED, BELIEVE THIS--
--MAKING YOUR ACQUAINTANCE IS THE HIGHEST HONOR MY LIFE MAY EVER SEE.
CAN ONLY IMAGINE HOW THIS PLACE MUST LOOK TO NEW EYES, EH? ALL TERRORS AND TAUNT AND OPPRESSION.
YOUNG PERSON SUCH AS YOURSELF, NO DOUBT IT STIRS VIOLENT RUMBLINGS OF OUTRAGE AND REBELLION DOWN DEEP IN YOUR SOUL.
BUT--MAN LIKE MYSELF, MAN WHO HAS SEEN THIS WORLD FROM INSIDE AND OUT, I BELIEVE IN WHAT WE DO HERE. NOT FOR ANY REASONS OF GOOD, MIND YOU, BUT FOR REASONS OF *NECESSITY.*
SOMETHING I DOUBT A PERSON WITH YOUR UPBRINGING HAS EVER HAD MUCH EXPERIENCE WITH.
AH, STRUCK A NERVE THERE, DID WE?

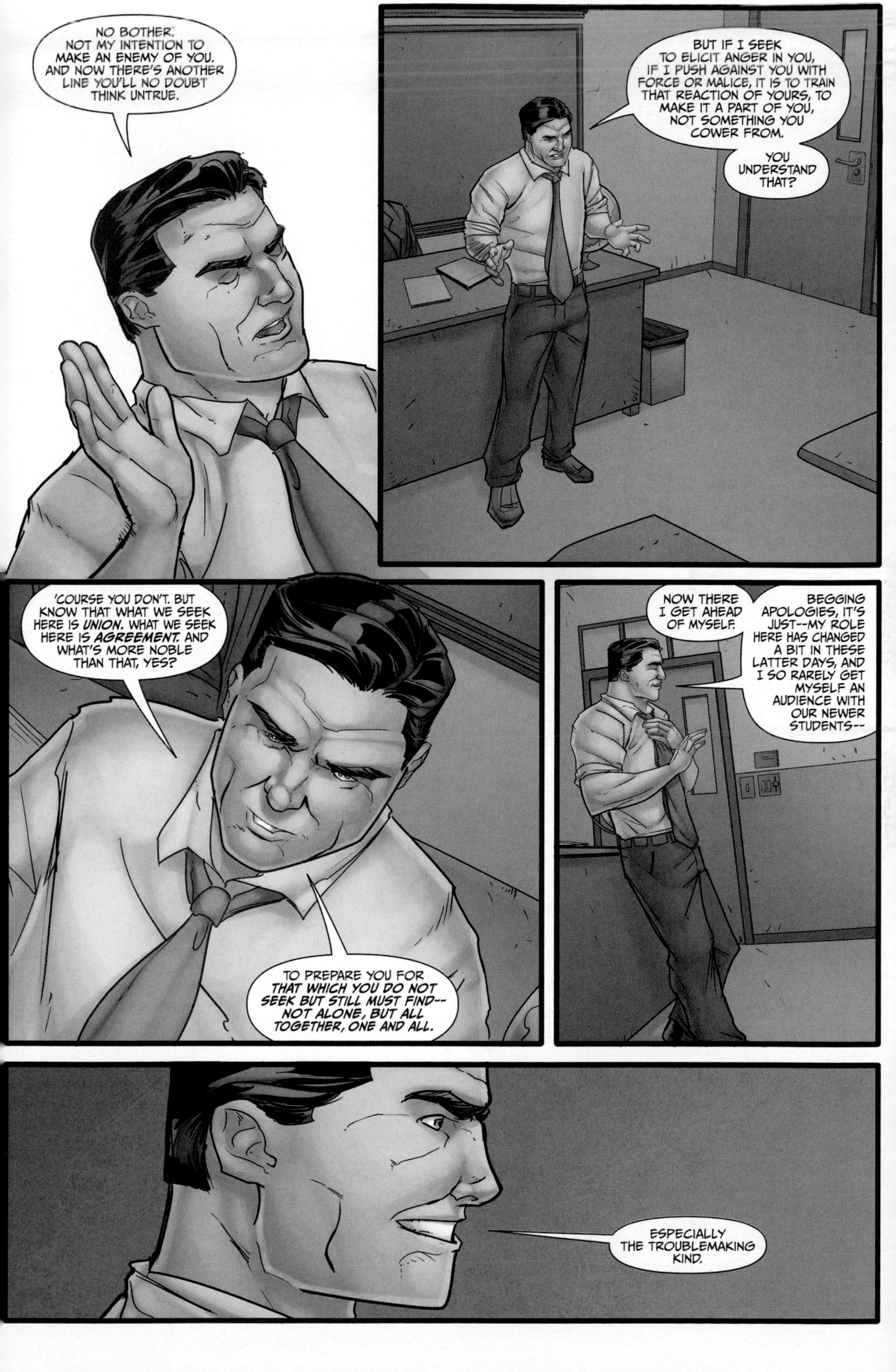
NO BOTHER. NOT MY INTENTION TO MAKE AN ENEMY OF YOU. AND NOW THERE'S ANOTHER LINE YOU'LL NO DOUBT THINK UNTRUE.
BUT IF I SEEK TO ELICIT ANGER IN YOU, IF I PUSH AGAINST YOU WITH FORCE OR MALICE, IT IS TO TRAIN THAT REACTION OF YOURS, TO MAKE IT A PART OF YOU, NOT SOMETHING YOU COWER FROM.
YOU UNDERSTAND THAT?
'COURSE YOU DON'T. BUT KNOW THAT WHAT WE SEEK HERE IS UNION. WHAT WE SEEK HERE IS AGREEMENT. AND WHAT'S MORE NOBLE THAN THAT, YES?
TO PREPARE YOU FOR THAT WHICH YOU DO NOT SEEK BUT STILL MUST FIND-- NOT ALONE, BUT ALL TOGETHER, ONE AND ALL.
NOW THERE I GET AHEAD OF MYSELF.
BEGGING APOLOGIES, IT'S JUST--MY ROLE HERE HAS CHANGED A BIT IN THESE LATTER DAYS, AND I SO RARELY GET MYSELF AN AUDIENCE WITH OUR NEWER STUDENTS--
ESPECIALLY THE TROUBLEMAKING KIND.

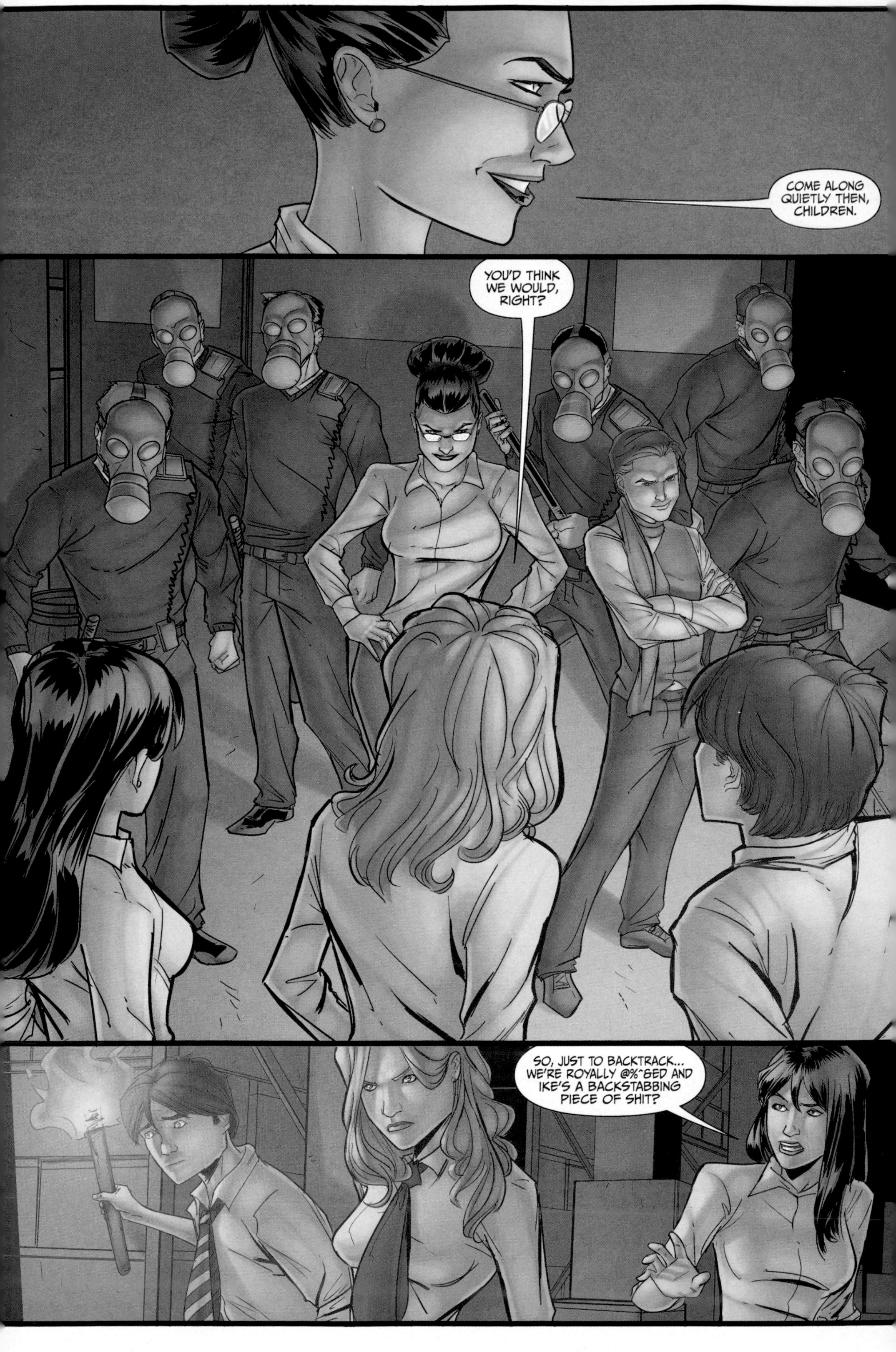
COME ALONG QUIETLY THEN, CHILDREN.
YOU'D THINK WE WOULD, RIGHT?
SO, JUST TO BACKTRACK... WE'RE ROYALLY @%^&ED AND IKE'S A BACKSTABBING PIECE OF SHIT?

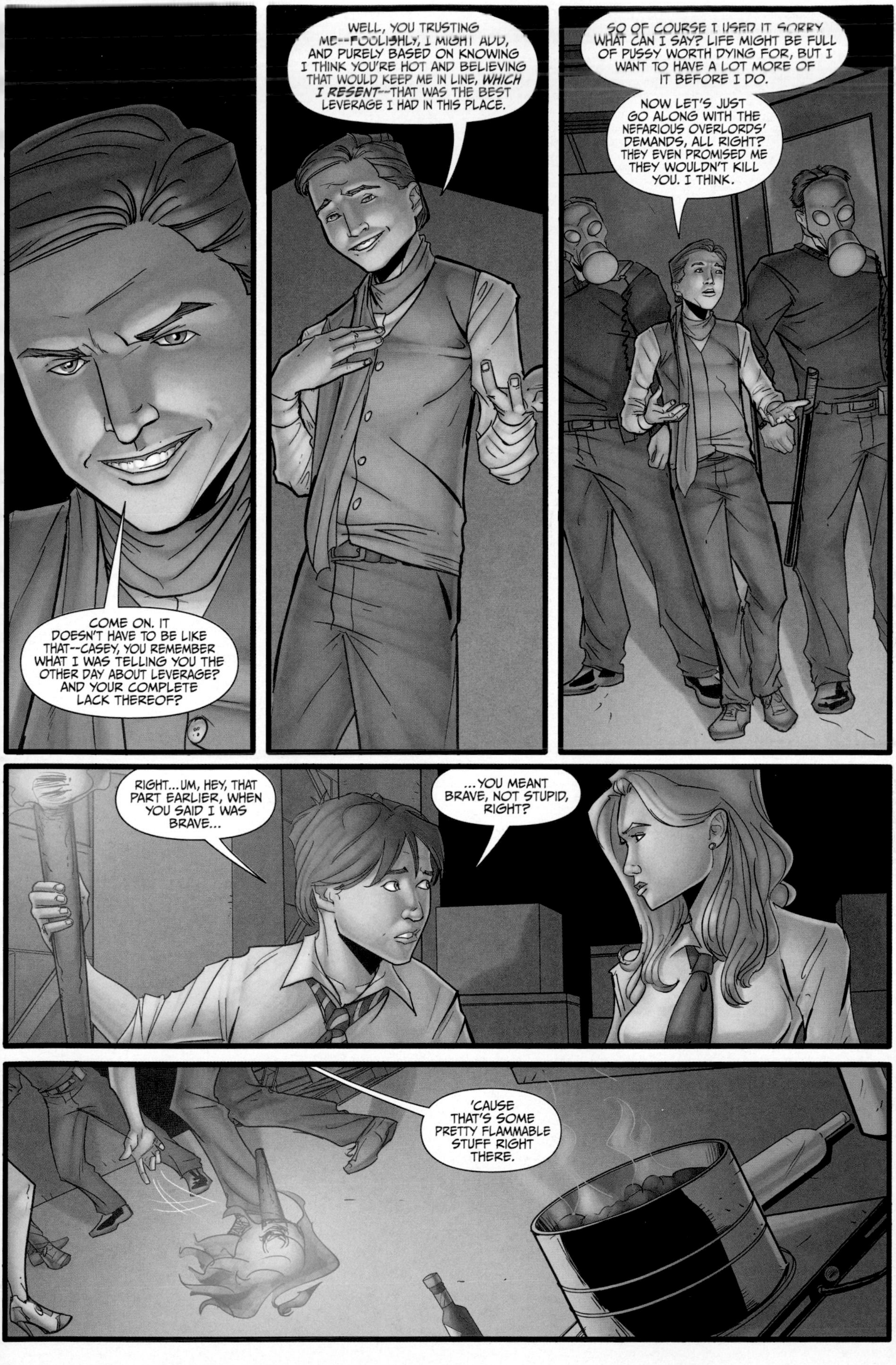
COME ON. IT DOESN'T HAVE TO BE LIKE THAT--CASEY, YOU REMEMBER WHAT I WAS TELLING YOU THE OTHER DAY ABOUT LEVERAGE? AND YOUR COMPLETE LACK THEREOF?
WELL, YOU TRUSTING ME--FOOLISHLY, I MIGHT ADD, AND PURELY BASED ON KNOWING I THINK YOU'RE HOT AND BELIEVING THAT WOULD KEEP ME IN LINE, *WHICH I RESENT*--THAT WAS THE BEST LEVERAGE I HAD IN THIS PLACE.
SO OF COURSE I USED IT. SORRY. WHAT CAN I SAY? LIFE MIGHT BE FULL OF PUSSY WORTH DYING FOR, BUT I WANT TO HAVE A LOT MORE OF IT BEFORE I DO.
NOW LET'S JUST GO ALONG WITH THE NEFARIOUS OVERLORDS' DEMANDS, ALL RIGHT? THEY EVEN PROMISED ME THEY WOULDN'T KILL YOU. I THINK.
RIGHT...UM, HEY, THAT PART EARLIER, WHEN YOU SAID I WAS BRAVE...
...YOU MEANT BRAVE, NOT STUPID, RIGHT?
'CAUSE THAT'S SOME PRETTY FLAMMABLE STUFF RIGHT THERE.

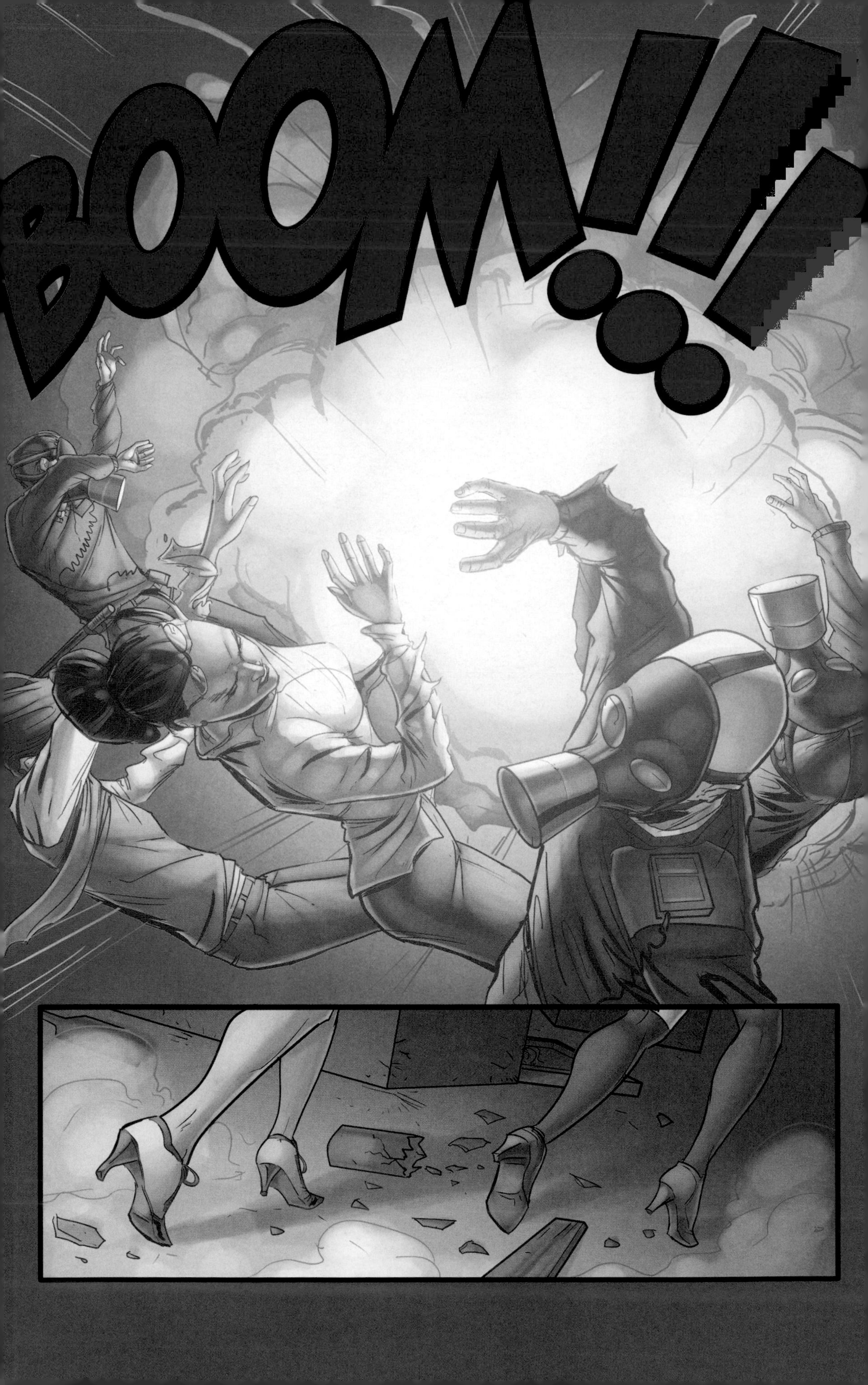
BOOM!!...

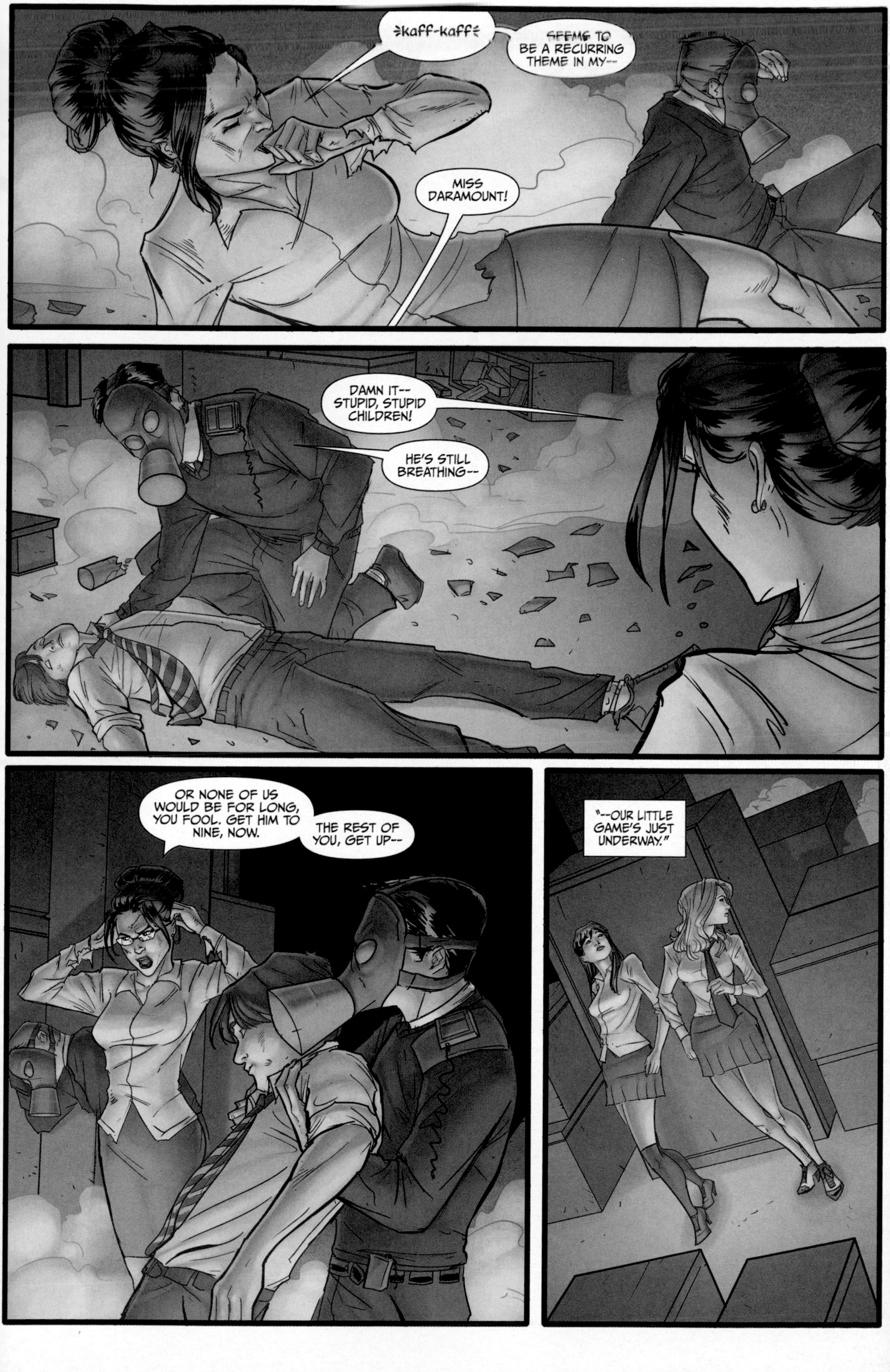
kaff-kaff
SEEMS TO BE A RECURRING THEME IN MY--
MISS DARAMOUNT!
DAMN IT-- STUPID, STUPID CHILDREN!
HE'S STILL BREATHING--
OR NONE OF US WOULD BE FOR LONG, YOU FOOL. GET HIM TO NINE, NOW.
THE REST OF YOU, GET UP--
"--OUR LITTLE GAME'S JUST UNDERWAY."

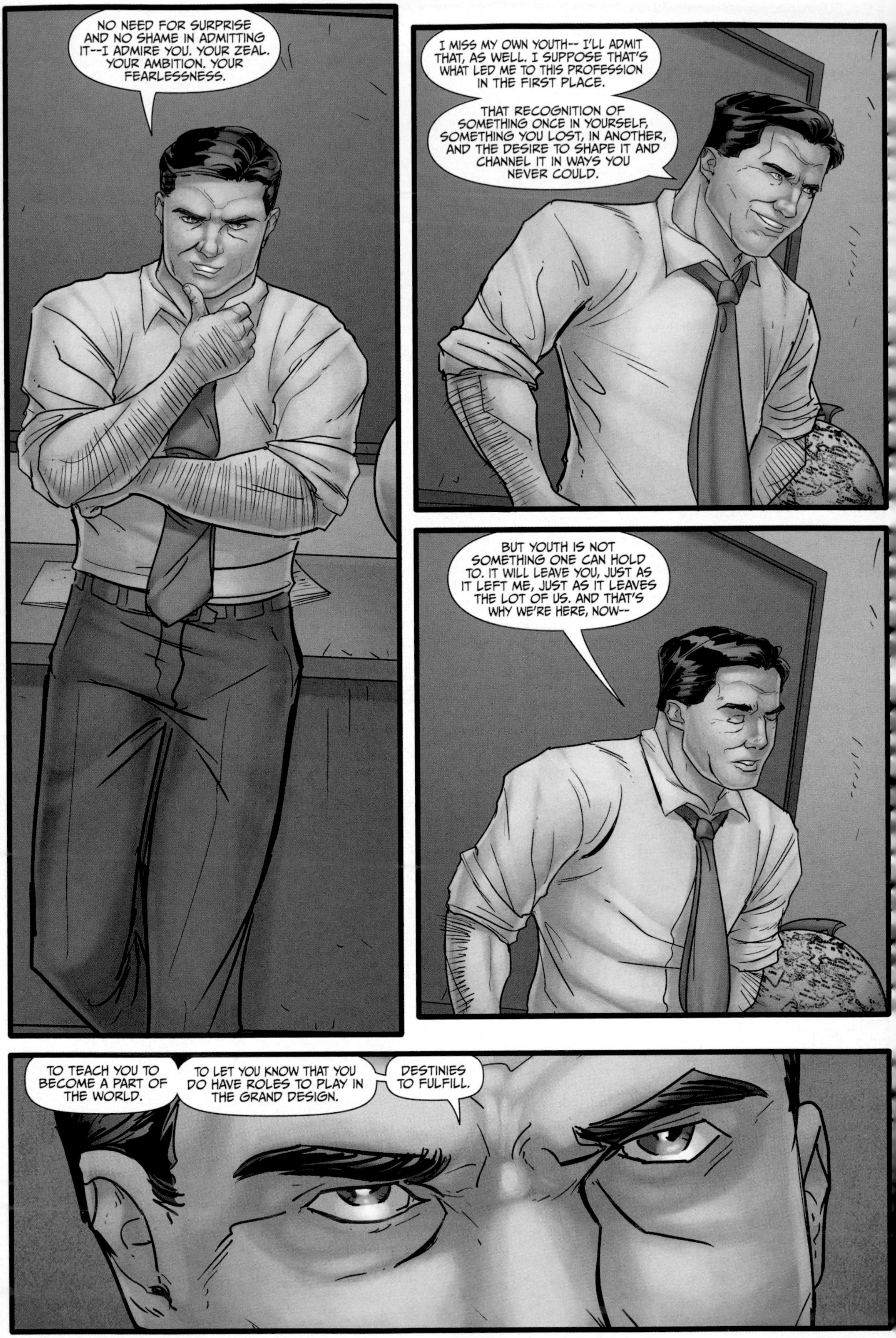
NO NEED FOR SURPRISE AND NO SHAME IN ADMITTING IT--I ADMIRE YOU. YOUR ZEAL. YOUR AMBITION. YOUR FEARLESSNESS.
I MISS MY OWN YOUTH-- I'LL ADMIT THAT, AS WELL. I SUPPOSE THAT'S WHAT LED ME TO THIS PROFESSION IN THE FIRST PLACE.
THAT RECOGNITION OF SOMETHING ONCE IN YOURSELF, SOMETHING YOU LOST, IN ANOTHER, AND THE DESIRE TO SHAPE IT AND CHANNEL IT IN WAYS YOU NEVER COULD.
BUT YOUTH IS NOT SOMETHING ONE CAN HOLD TO. IT WILL LEAVE YOU, JUST AS IT LEFT ME, JUST AS IT LEAVES THE LOT OF US. AND THAT'S WHY WE'RE HERE, NOW--
TO TEACH YOU TO BECOME A PART OF THE WORLD.
TO LET YOU KNOW THAT YOU DO HAVE ROLES TO PLAY IN THE GRAND DESIGN.
DESTINIES TO FULFILL.

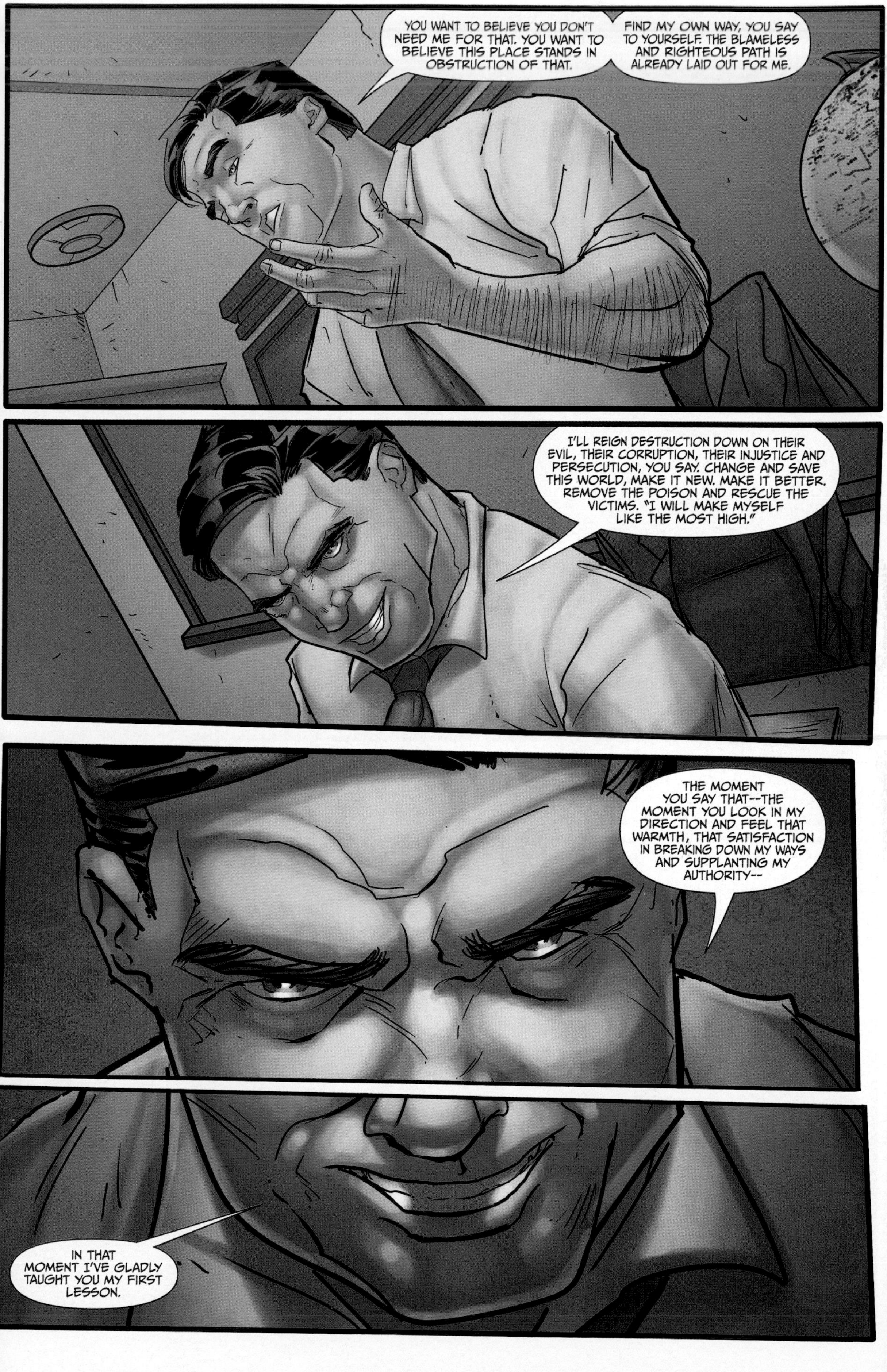
YOU WANT TO BELIEVE YOU DON'T NEED ME FOR THAT. YOU WANT TO BELIEVE THIS PLACE STANDS IN OBSTRUCTION OF THAT.
FIND MY OWN WAY, YOU SAY TO YOURSELF. THE BLAMELESS AND RIGHTEOUS PATH IS ALREADY LAID OUT FOR ME.
I'LL REIGN DESTRUCTION DOWN ON THEIR EVIL, THEIR CORRUPTION, THEIR INJUSTICE AND PERSECUTION, YOU SAY. CHANGE AND SAVE THIS WORLD, MAKE IT NEW. MAKE IT BETTER. REMOVE THE POISON AND RESCUE THE VICTIMS. "I WILL MAKE MYSELF LIKE THE MOST HIGH."
THE MOMENT YOU SAY THAT--THE MOMENT YOU LOOK IN MY DIRECTION AND FEEL THAT WARMTH, THAT SATISFACTION IN BREAKING DOWN MY WAYS AND SUPPLANTING MY AUTHORITY--
IN THAT MOMENT I'VE GLADLY TAUGHT YOU MY FIRST LESSON.

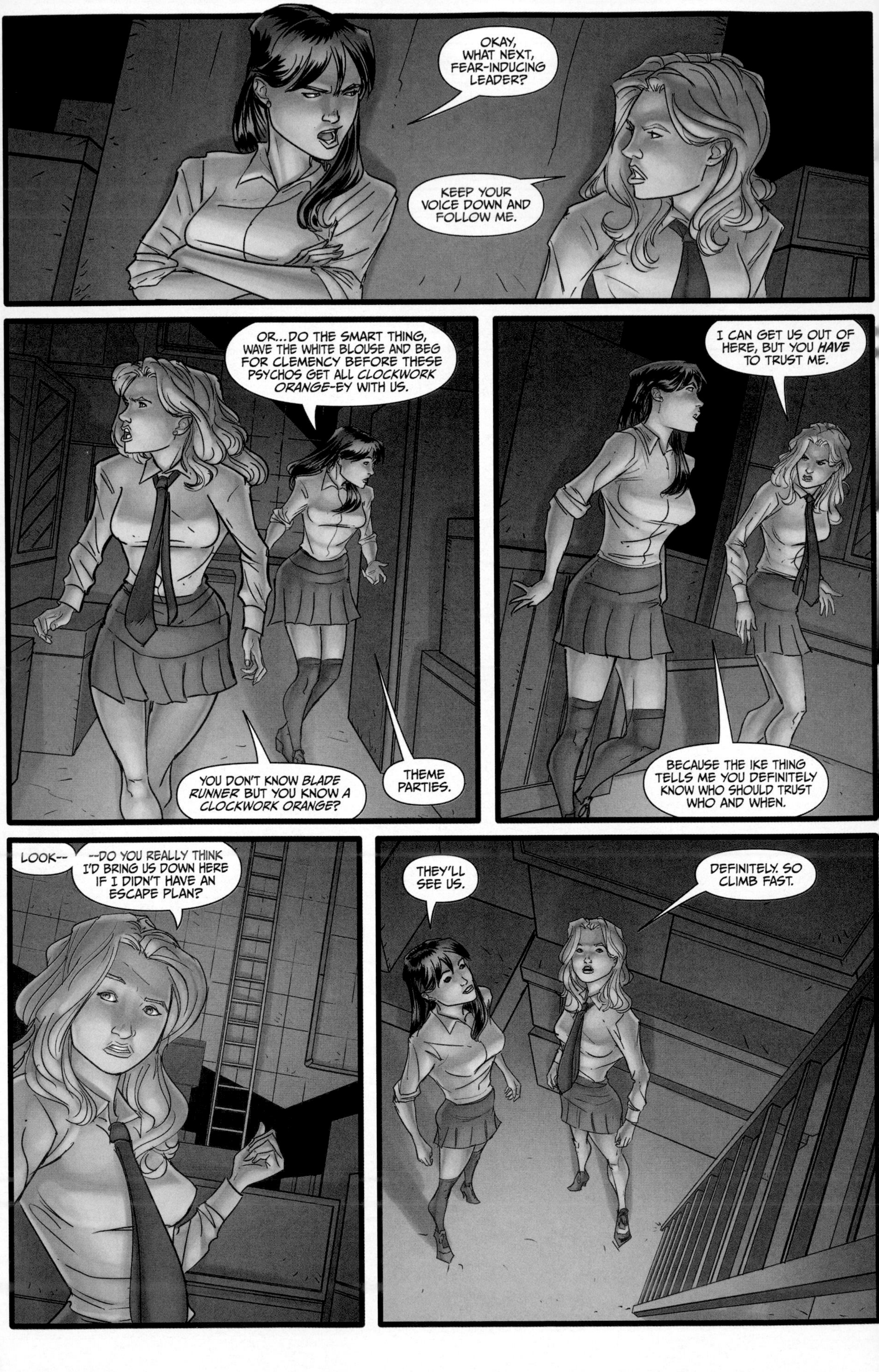
OKAY, WHAT NEXT, FEAR-INDUCING LEADER?
KEEP YOUR VOICE DOWN AND FOLLOW ME.
OR...DO THE SMART THING, WAVE THE WHITE BLOUSE AND BEG FOR CLEMENCY BEFORE THESE PSYCHOS GET ALL *CLOCKWORK ORANGE*-EY WITH US.
YOU DON'T KNOW *BLADE RUNNER* BUT YOU KNOW A *CLOCKWORK ORANGE?*
THEME PARTIES.
I CAN GET US OUT OF HERE, BUT YOU *HAVE* TO TRUST ME.
BECAUSE THE IKE THING TELLS ME YOU DEFINITELY KNOW WHO SHOULD TRUST WHO AND WHEN.
LOOK--
--DO YOU REALLY THINK I'D BRING US DOWN HERE IF I DIDN'T HAVE AN ESCAPE PLAN?
THEY'LL SEE US.
DEFINITELY. SO CLIMB FAST.

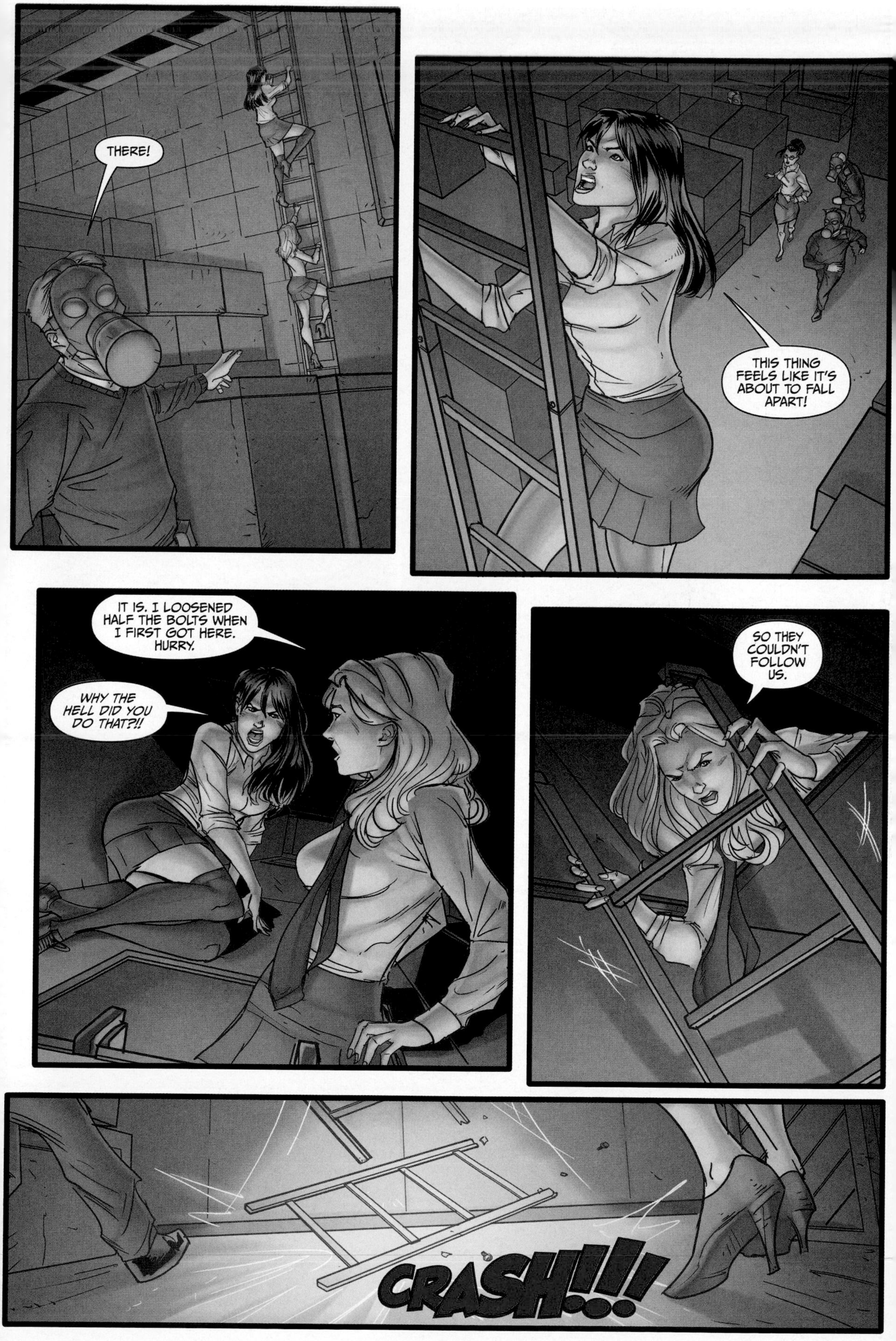
THERE!
THIS THING FEELS LIKE IT'S ABOUT TO FALL APART!
IT IS. I LOOSENED HALF THE BOLTS WHEN I FIRST GOT HERE. HURRY.
WHY THE HELL DID YOU DO THAT?!!
SO THEY COULDN'T FOLLOW US.
CRASH!!!

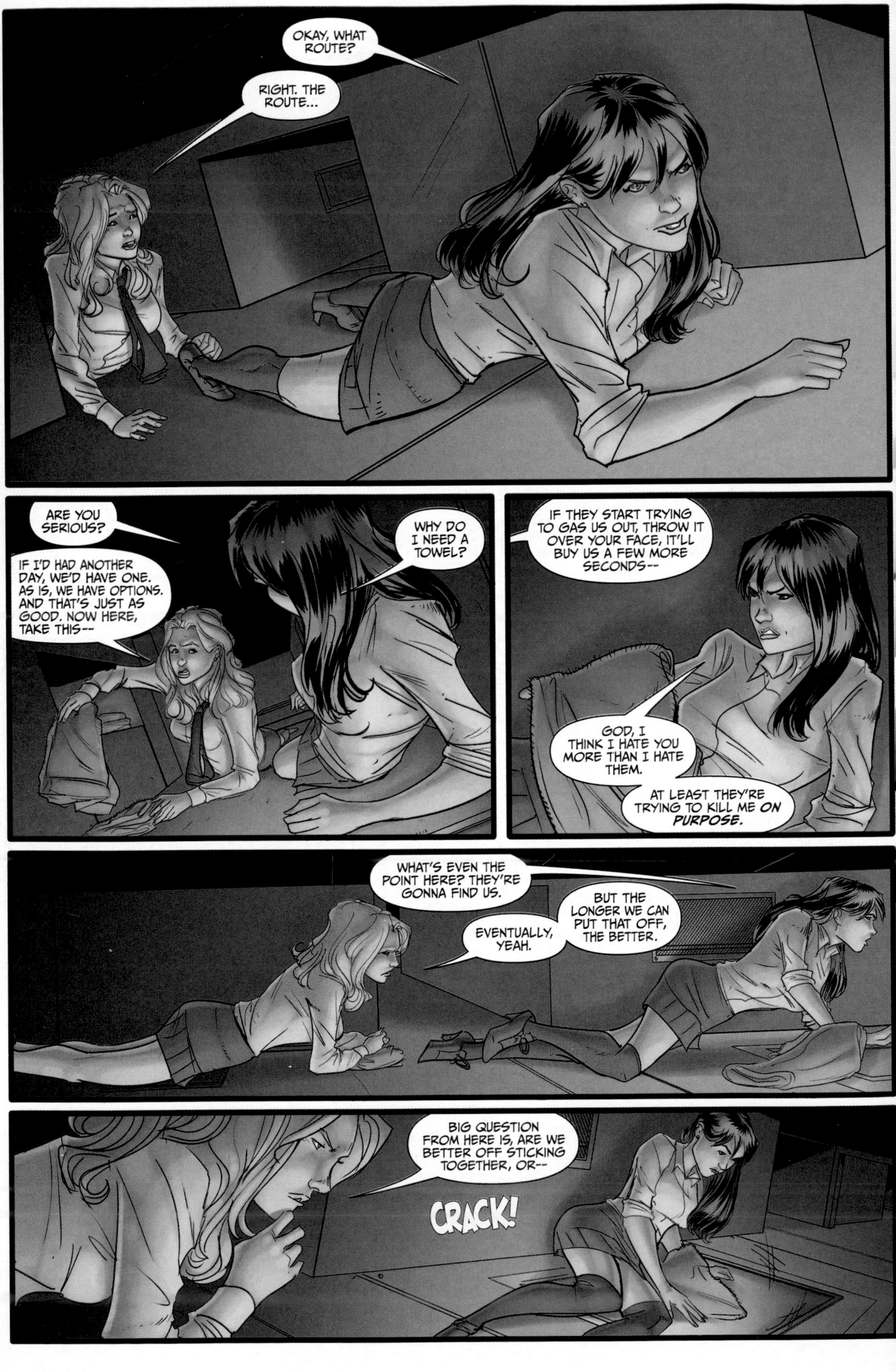
OKAY, WHAT ROUTE?
RIGHT. THE ROUTE...
ARE YOU SERIOUS?
IF I'D HAD ANOTHER DAY, WE'D HAVE ONE. AS IS, WE HAVE OPTIONS. AND THAT'S JUST AS GOOD. NOW HERE, TAKE THIS--
WHY DO I NEED A TOWEL?
IF THEY START TRYING TO GAS US OUT, THROW IT OVER YOUR FACE, IT'LL BUY US A FEW MORE SECONDS--
GOD, I THINK I HATE YOU MORE THAN I HATE THEM.
AT LEAST THEY'RE TRYING TO KILL ME *ON PURPOSE*.
WHAT'S EVEN THE POINT HERE? THEY'RE GONNA FIND US.
EVENTUALLY, YEAH.
BUT THE LONGER WE CAN PUT THAT OFF, THE BETTER.
BIG QUESTION FROM HERE IS, ARE WE BETTER OFF STICKING TOGETHER, OR--
CRACK!

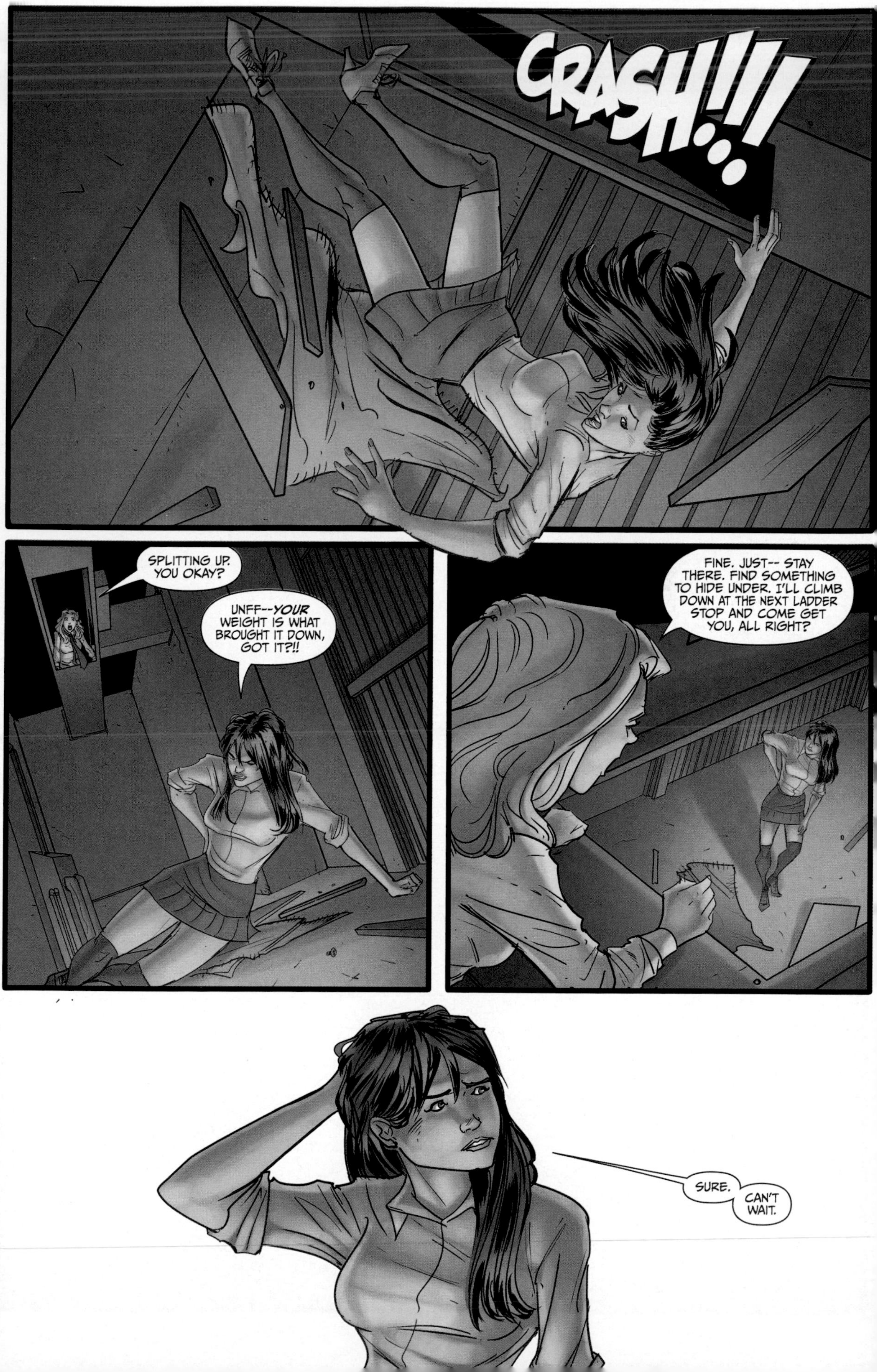
CRASH!!!
SPLITTING UP. YOU OKAY?
UNFF--YOUR WEIGHT IS WHAT BROUGHT IT DOWN, GOT IT?!!
FINE. JUST-- STAY THERE. FIND SOMETHING TO HIDE UNDER. I'LL CLIMB DOWN AT THE NEXT LADDER STOP AND COME GET YOU, ALL RIGHT?
SURE.
CAN'T WAIT.

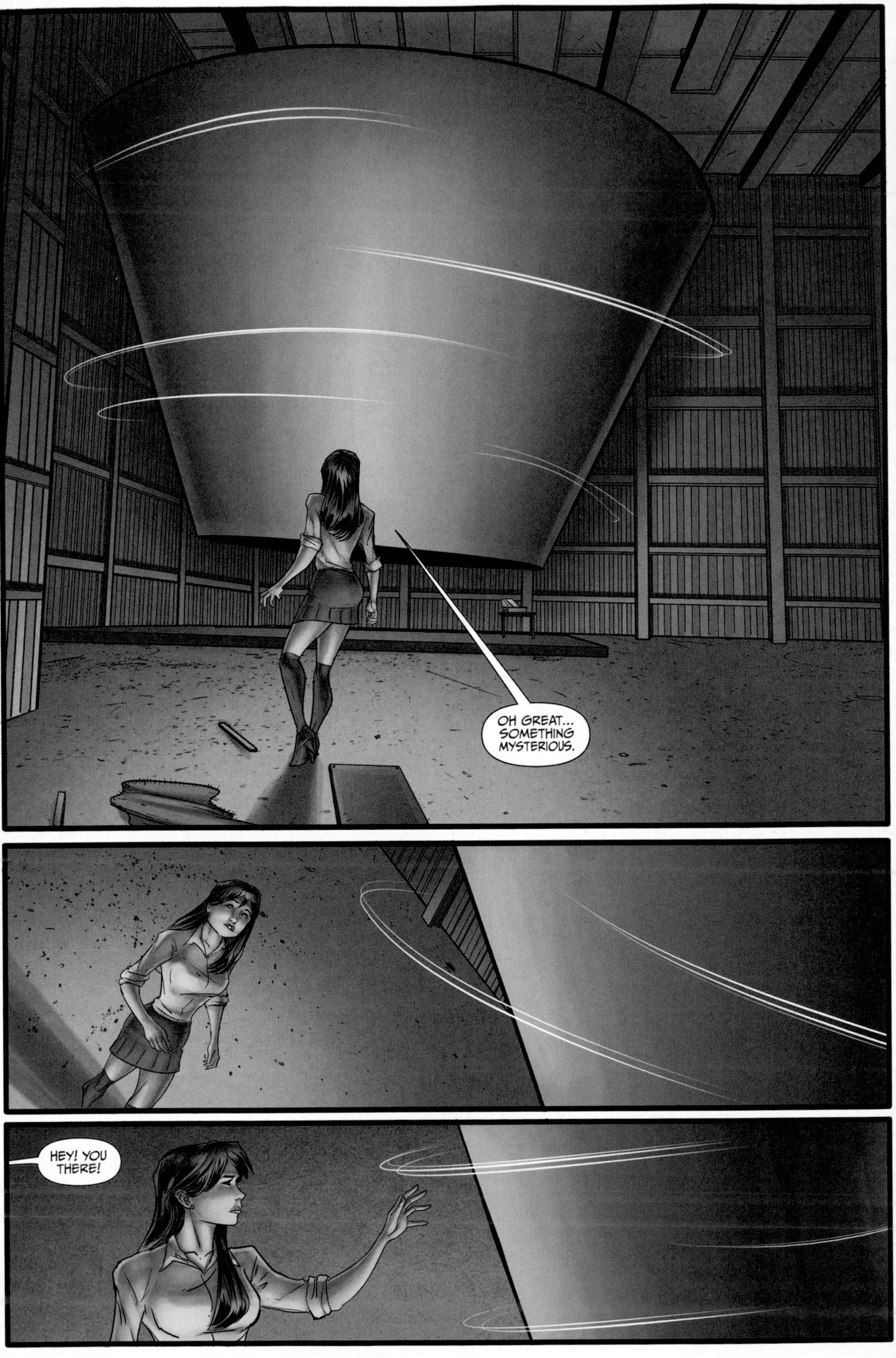
OH GREAT... SOMETHING MYSTERIOUS.
HEY! YOU THERE!

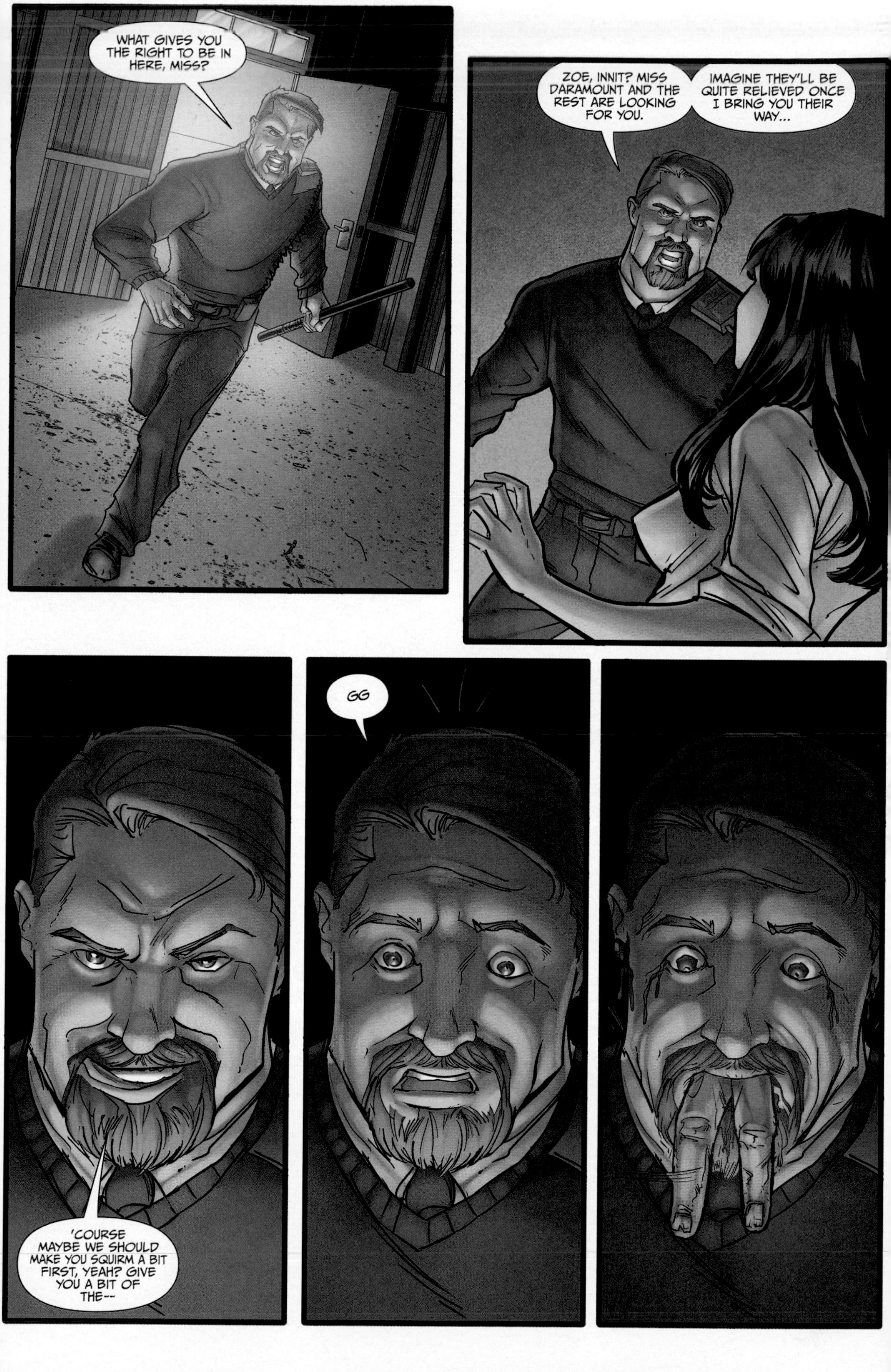
WHAT GIVES YOU THE RIGHT TO BE IN HERE, MISS?
ZOE, INNIT? MISS DARAMOUNT AND THE REST ARE LOOKING FOR YOU.
IMAGINE THEY'LL BE QUITE RELIEVED ONCE I BRING YOU THEIR WAY...
'COURSE MAYBE WE SHOULD MAKE YOU SQUIRM A BIT FIRST, YEAH? GIVE YOU A BIT OF THE--
GG

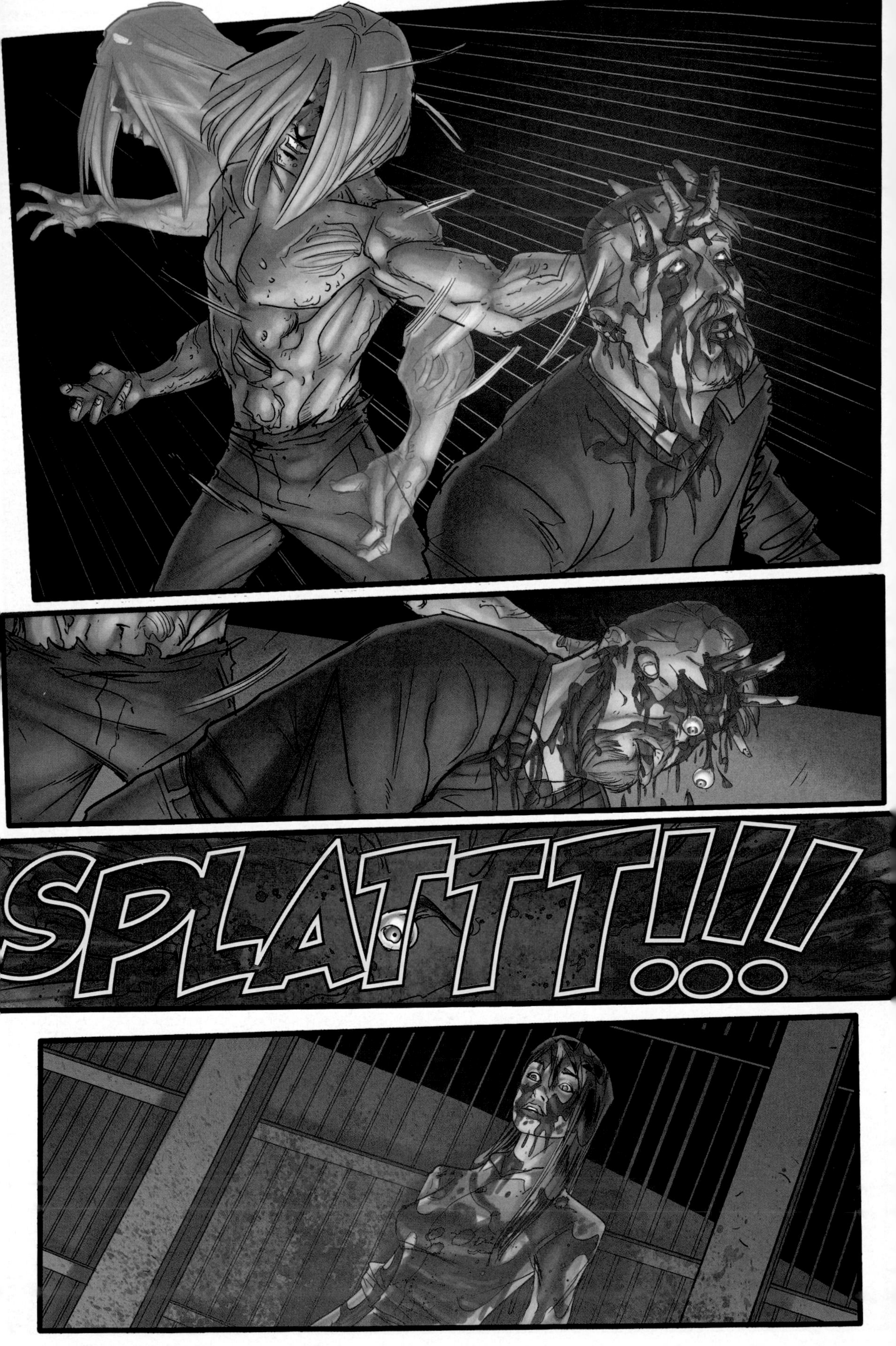
SPLATTT!!!...

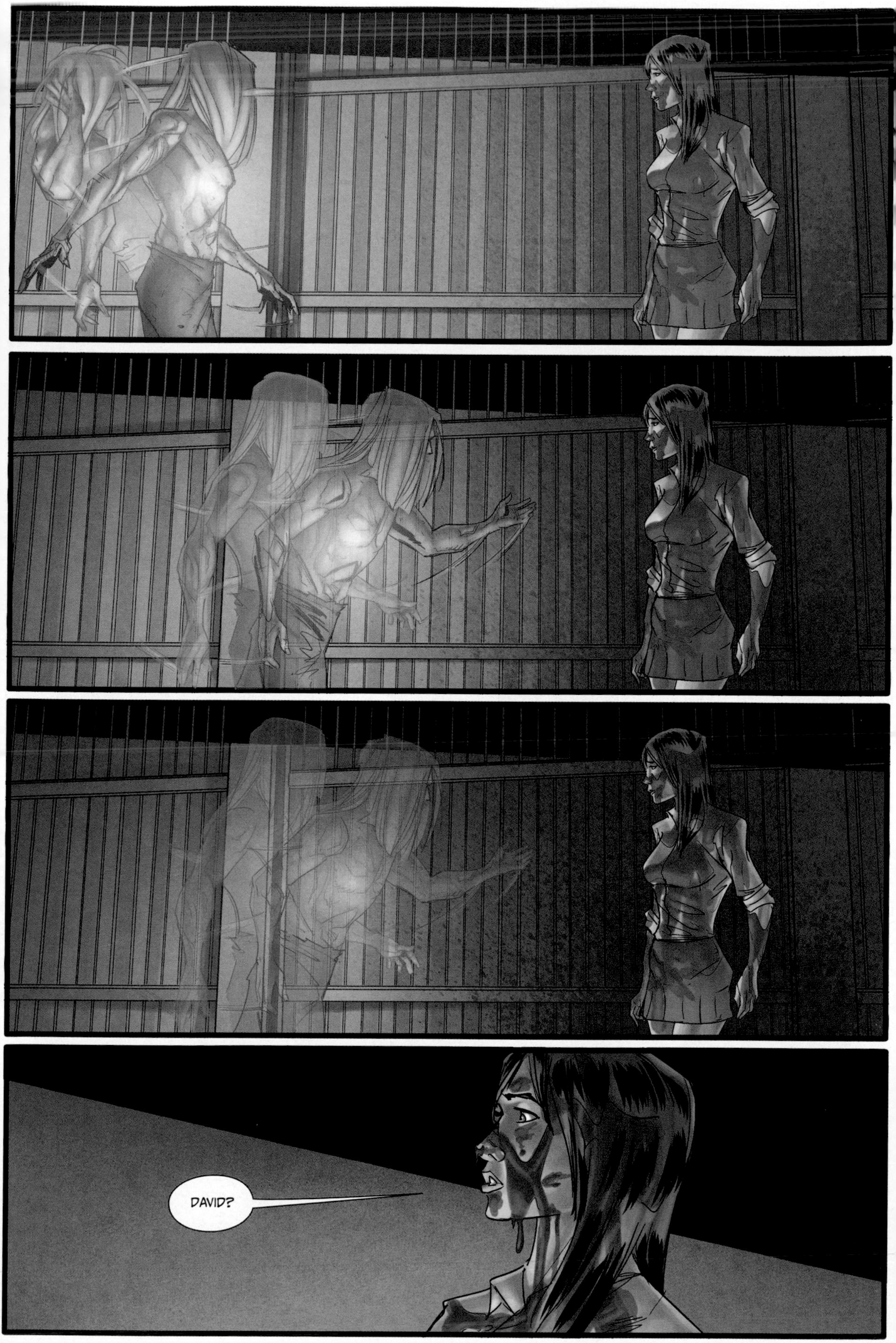
DAVID?

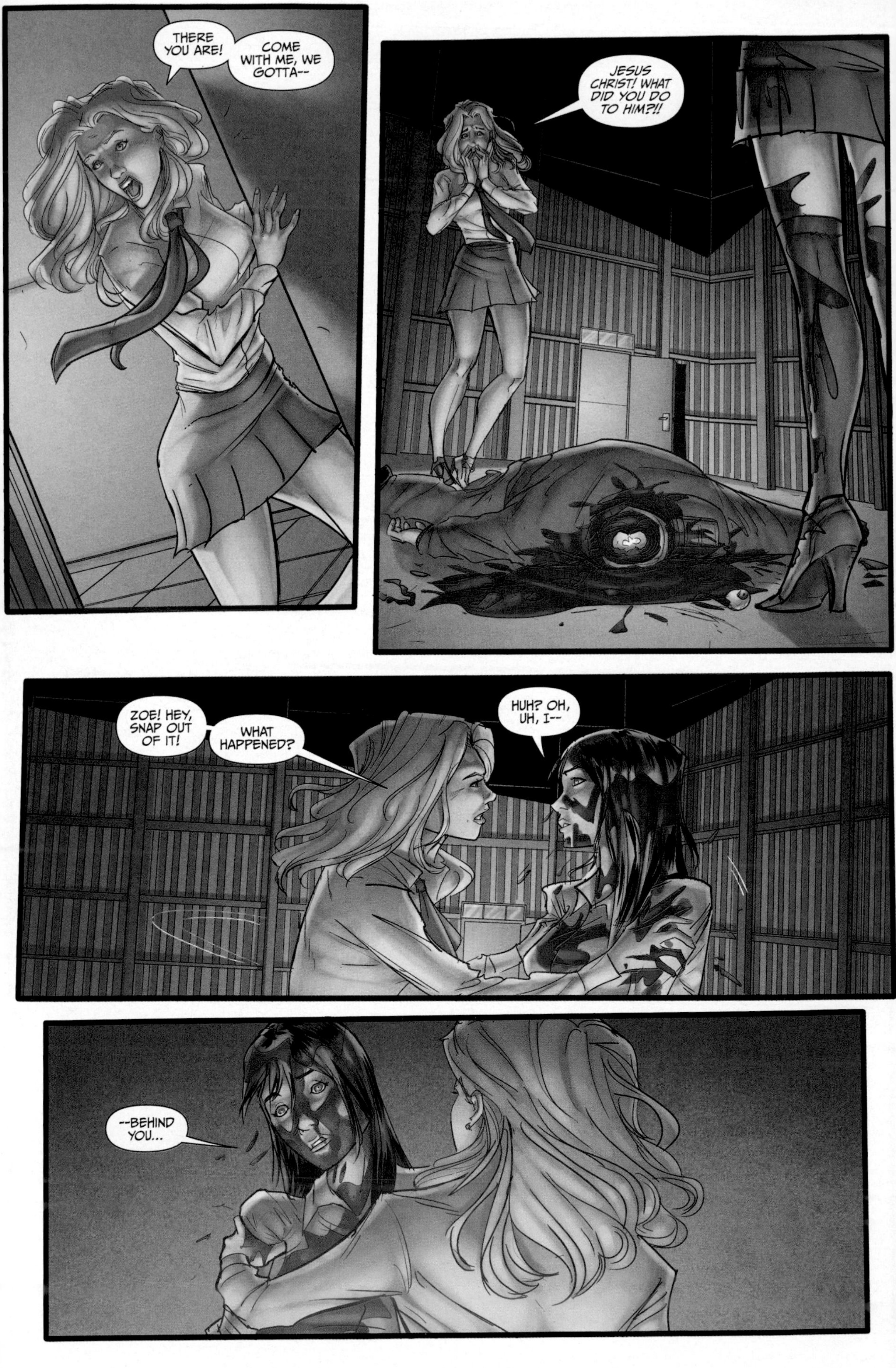
THERE YOU ARE!
COME WITH ME, WE GOTTA--
JESUS CHRIST! WHAT DID YOU DO TO HIM?!!
ZOE! HEY, SNAP OUT OF IT!
WHAT HAPPENED?
HUH? OH, UH, I--
--BEHIND YOU...

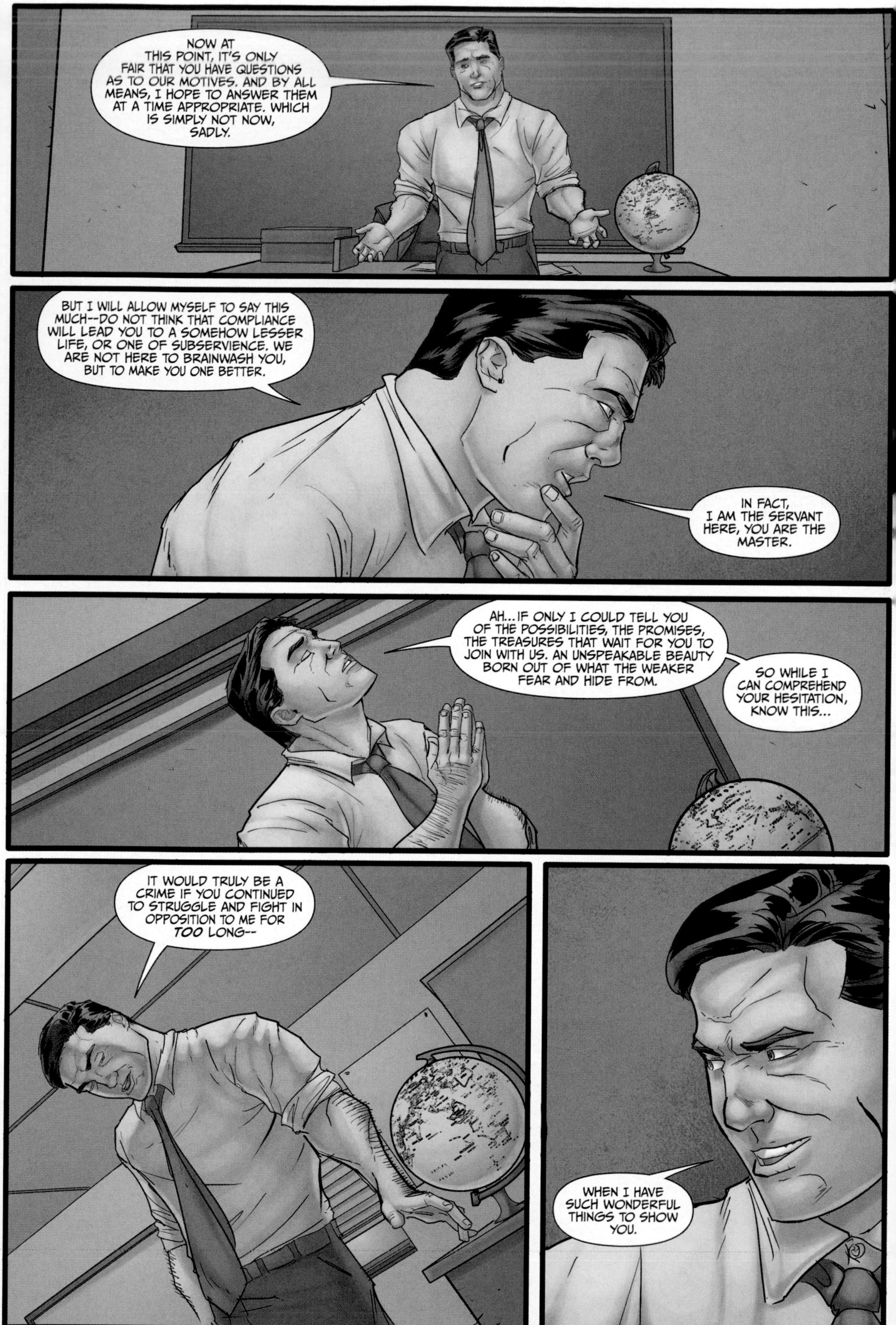
NOW AT THIS POINT, IT'S ONLY FAIR THAT YOU HAVE QUESTIONS AS TO OUR MOTIVES. AND BY ALL MEANS, I HOPE TO ANSWER THEM AT A TIME APPROPRIATE. WHICH IS SIMPLY NOT NOW, SADLY.
BUT I WILL ALLOW MYSELF TO SAY THIS MUCH--DO NOT THINK THAT COMPLIANCE WILL LEAD YOU TO A SOMEHOW LESSER LIFE, OR ONE OF SUBSERVIENCE. WE ARE NOT HERE TO BRAINWASH YOU, BUT TO MAKE YOU ONE BETTER.
IN FACT, I AM THE SERVANT HERE, YOU ARE THE MASTER.
AH... IF ONLY I COULD TELL YOU OF THE POSSIBILITIES, THE PROMISES, THE TREASURES THAT WAIT FOR YOU TO JOIN WITH US. AN UNSPEAKABLE BEAUTY BORN OUT OF WHAT THE WEAKER FEAR AND HIDE FROM.
SO WHILE I CAN COMPREHEND YOUR HESITATION, KNOW THIS...
IT WOULD TRULY BE A CRIME IF YOU CONTINUED TO STRUGGLE AND FIGHT IN OPPOSITION TO ME FOR *TOO* LONG--
WHEN I HAVE SUCH WONDERFUL THINGS TO SHOW YOU.

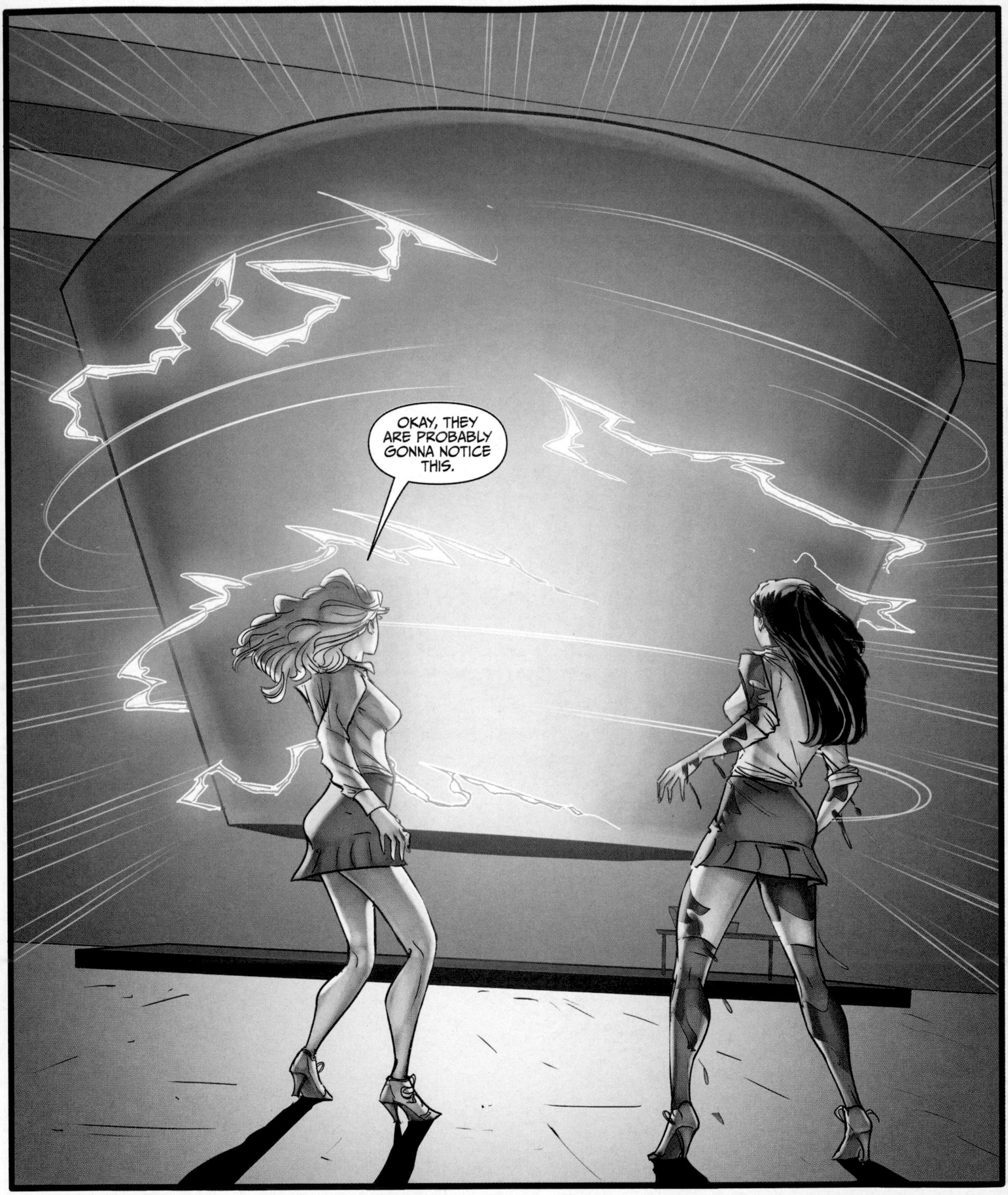
OKAY, THEY ARE PROBABLY GONNA NOTICE THIS.

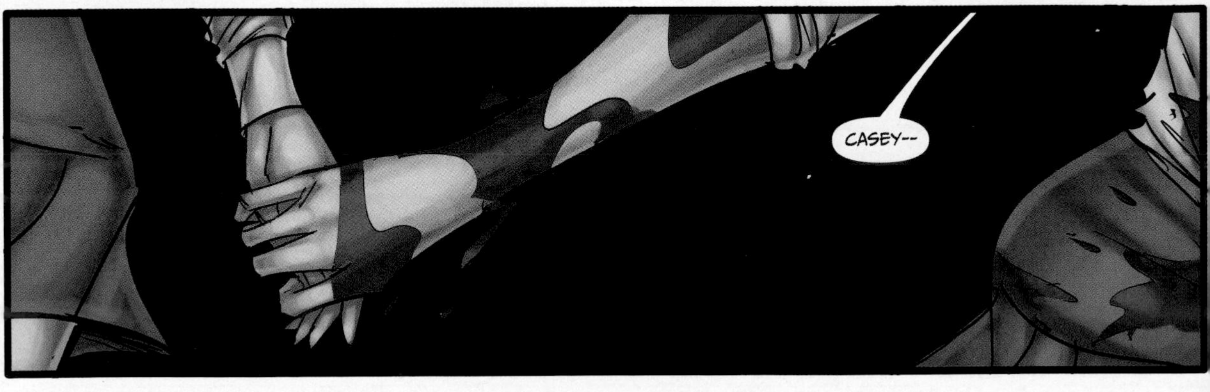
CASEY--

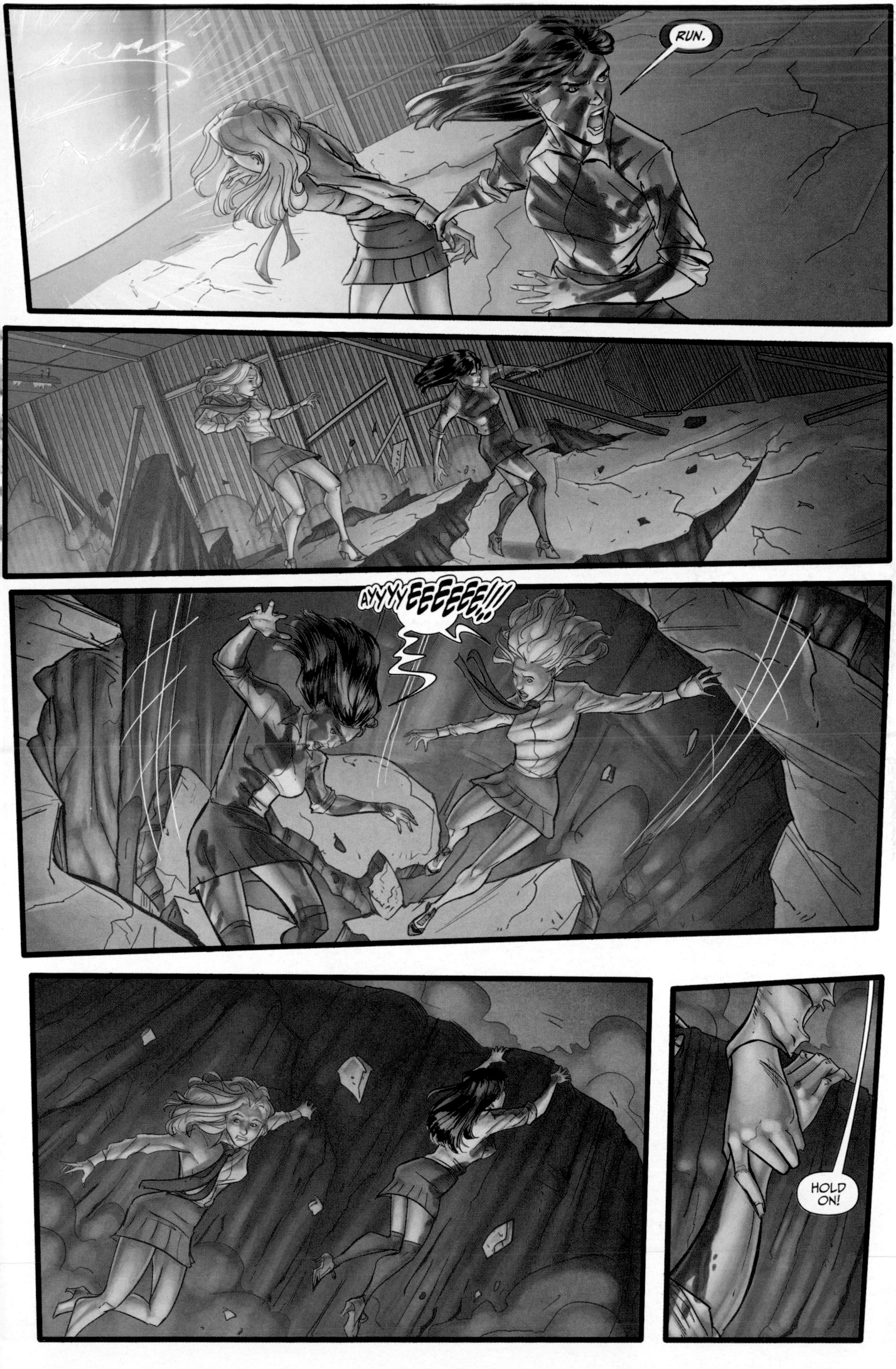
RUN.
AYYYYEEEEEE!!!
HOLD ON!

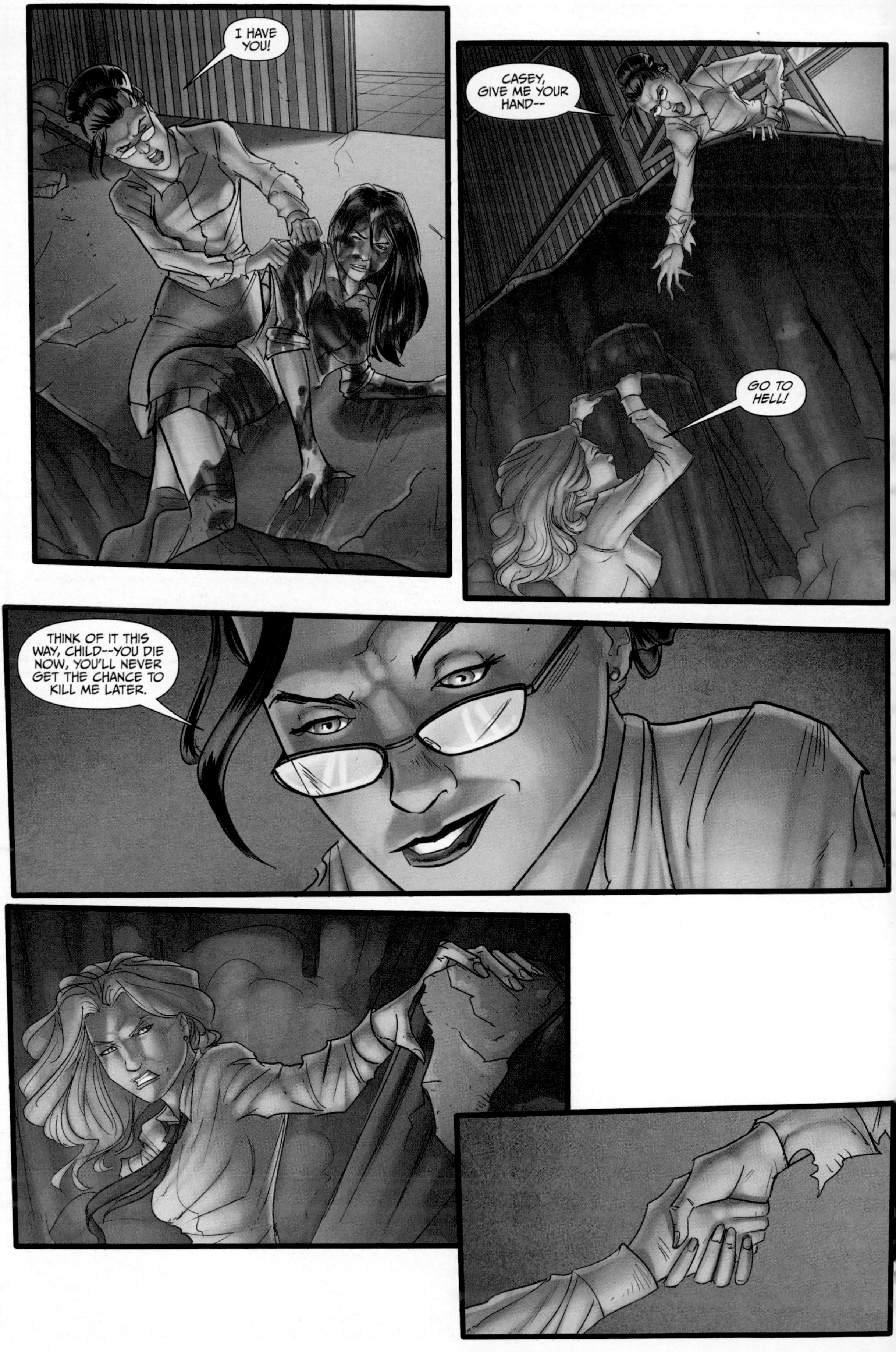
I HAVE YOU!
CASEY, GIVE ME YOUR HAND--
GO TO HELL!
THINK OF IT THIS WAY, CHILD--YOU DIE NOW, YOU'LL NEVER GET THE CHANCE TO KILL ME LATER.

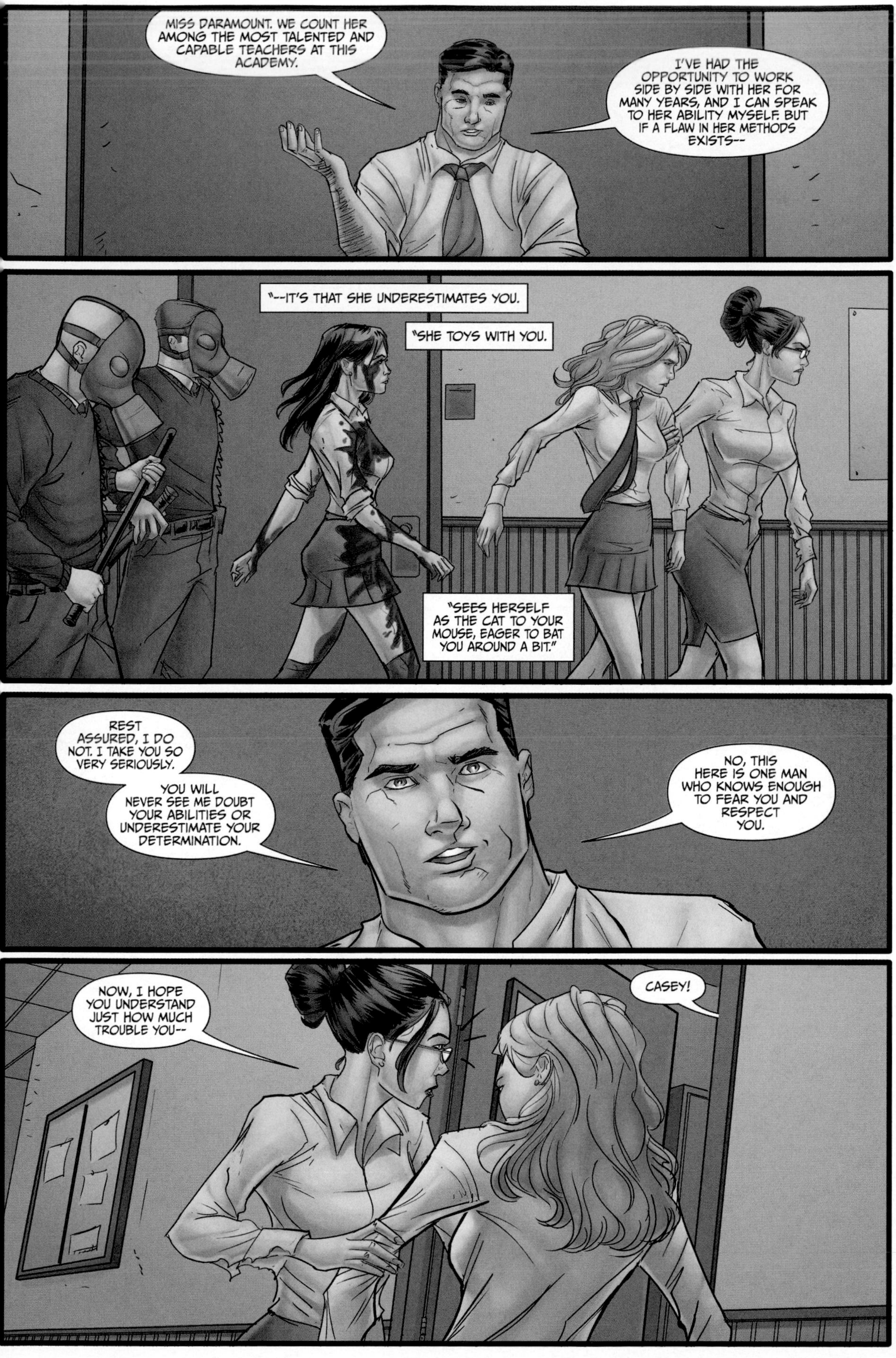
MISS DARAMOUNT. WE COUNT HER AMONG THE MOST TALENTED AND CAPABLE TEACHERS AT THIS ACADEMY.
I'VE HAD THE OPPORTUNITY TO WORK SIDE BY SIDE WITH HER FOR MANY YEARS, AND I CAN SPEAK TO HER ABILITY MYSELF. BUT IF A FLAW IN HER METHODS EXISTS--
"--IT'S THAT SHE UNDERESTIMATES YOU.
"SHE TOYS WITH YOU.
"SEES HERSELF AS THE CAT TO YOUR MOUSE, EAGER TO BAT YOU AROUND A BIT."
REST ASSURED, I DO NOT. I TAKE YOU SO VERY SERIOUSLY.
YOU WILL NEVER SEE ME DOUBT YOUR ABILITIES OR UNDERESTIMATE YOUR DETERMINATION.
NO, THIS HERE IS ONE MAN WHO KNOWS ENOUGH TO FEAR YOU AND RESPECT YOU.
NOW, I HOPE YOU UNDERSTAND JUST HOW MUCH TROUBLE YOU--
CASEY!

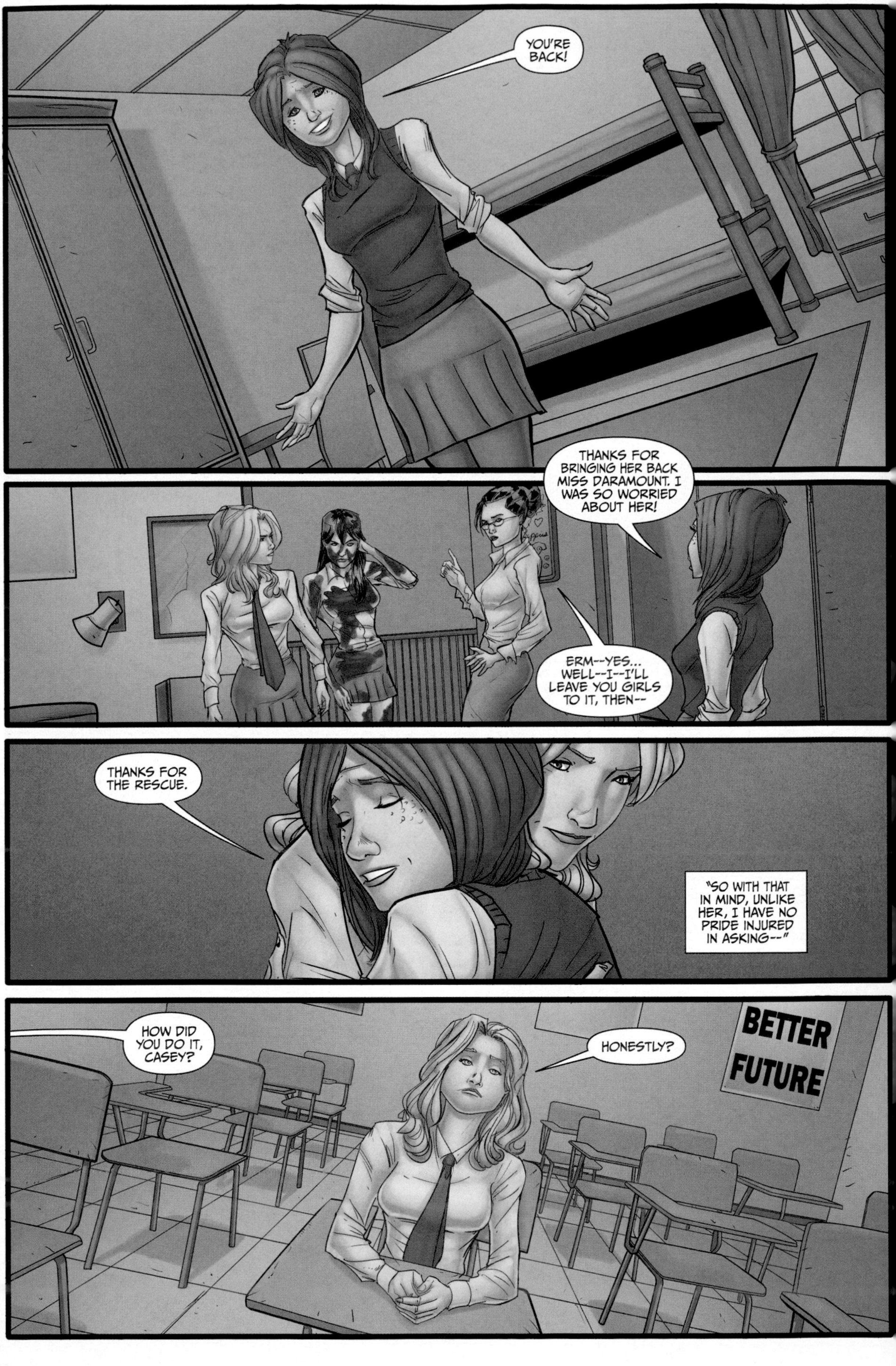
YOU'RE BACK!
THANKS FOR BRINGING HER BACK MISS DARAMOUNT. I WAS SO WORRIED ABOUT HER!
ERM--YES... WELL--I--I'LL LEAVE YOU GIRLS TO IT, THEN--
THANKS FOR THE RESCUE.
"SO WITH THAT IN MIND, UNLIKE HER, I HAVE NO PRIDE INJURED IN ASKING--"
HOW DID YOU DO IT, CASEY?
HONESTLY?
BETTER FUTURE

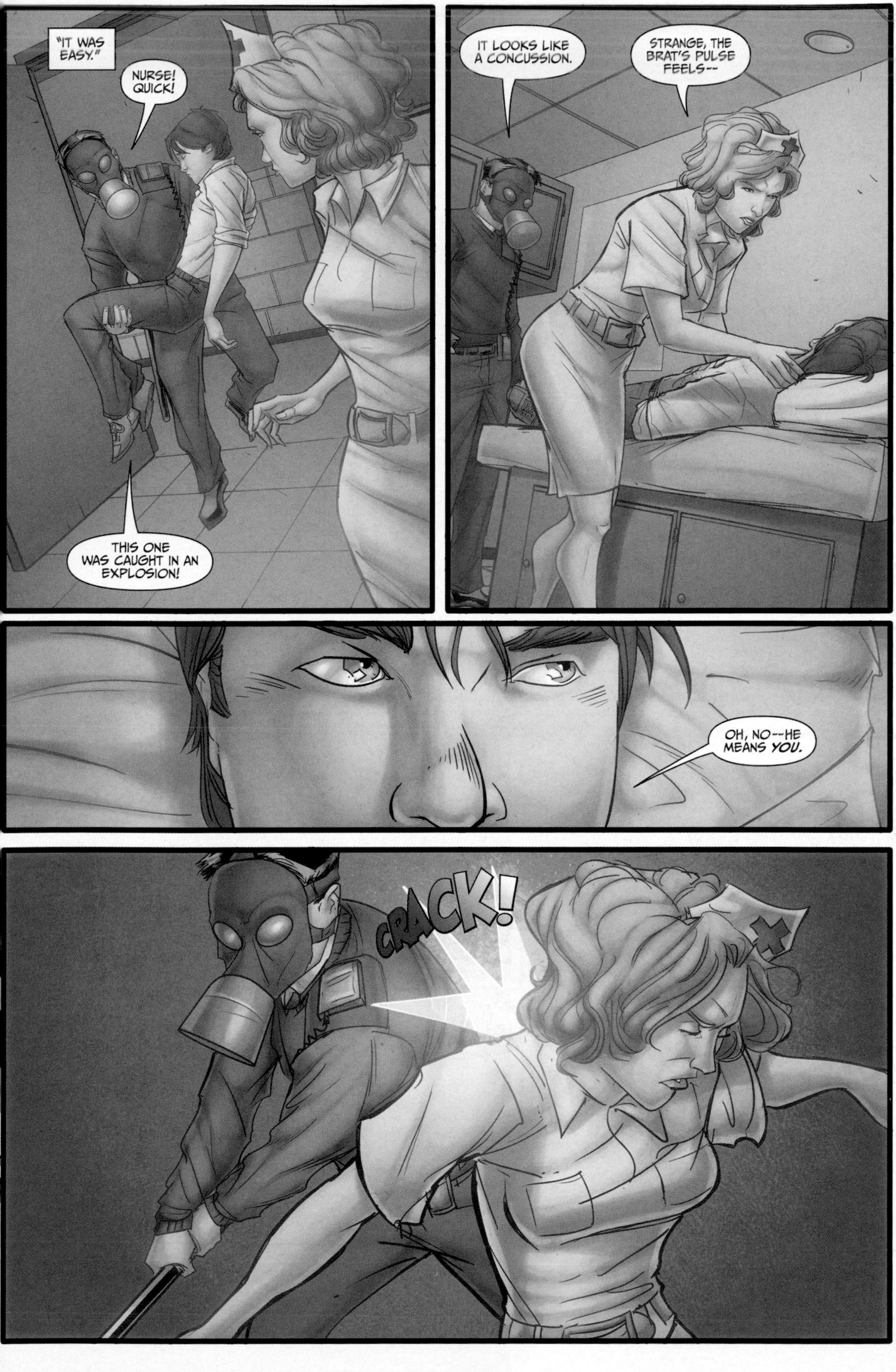
"IT WAS EASY."
NURSE! QUICK!
THIS ONE WAS CAUGHT IN AN EXPLOSION!
IT LOOKS LIKE A CONCUSSION.
STRANGE, THE BRAT'S PULSE FEELS--
OH, NO--HE MEANS *YOU*.
CRACK!

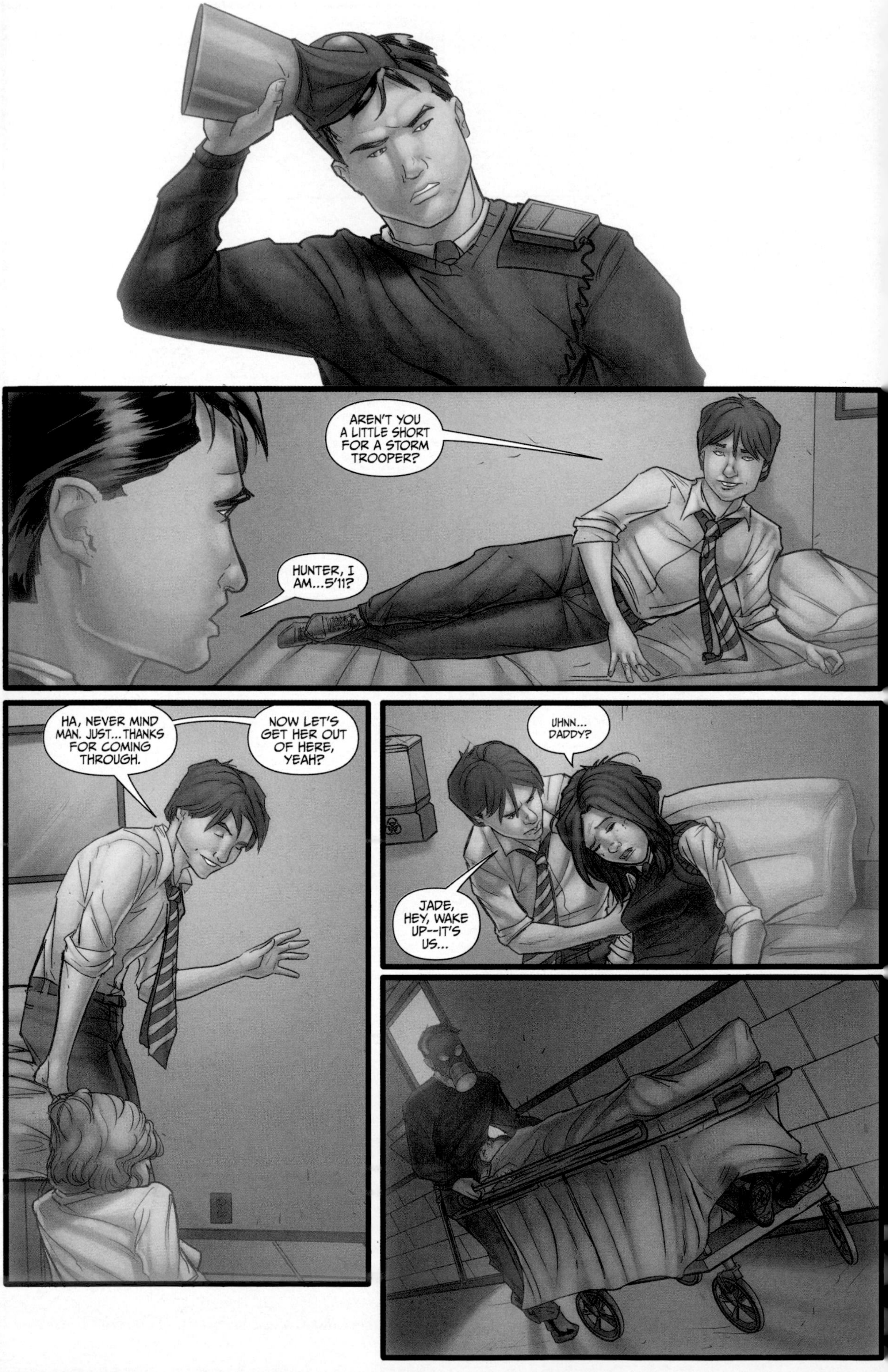
AREN'T YOU A LITTLE SHORT FOR A STORM TROOPER?
HUNTER, I AM...5'11?
HA, NEVER MIND MAN. JUST...THANKS FOR COMING THROUGH.
NOW LET'S GET HER OUT OF HERE, YEAH?
UHNN... DADDY?
JADE, HEY, WAKE UP--IT'S US...

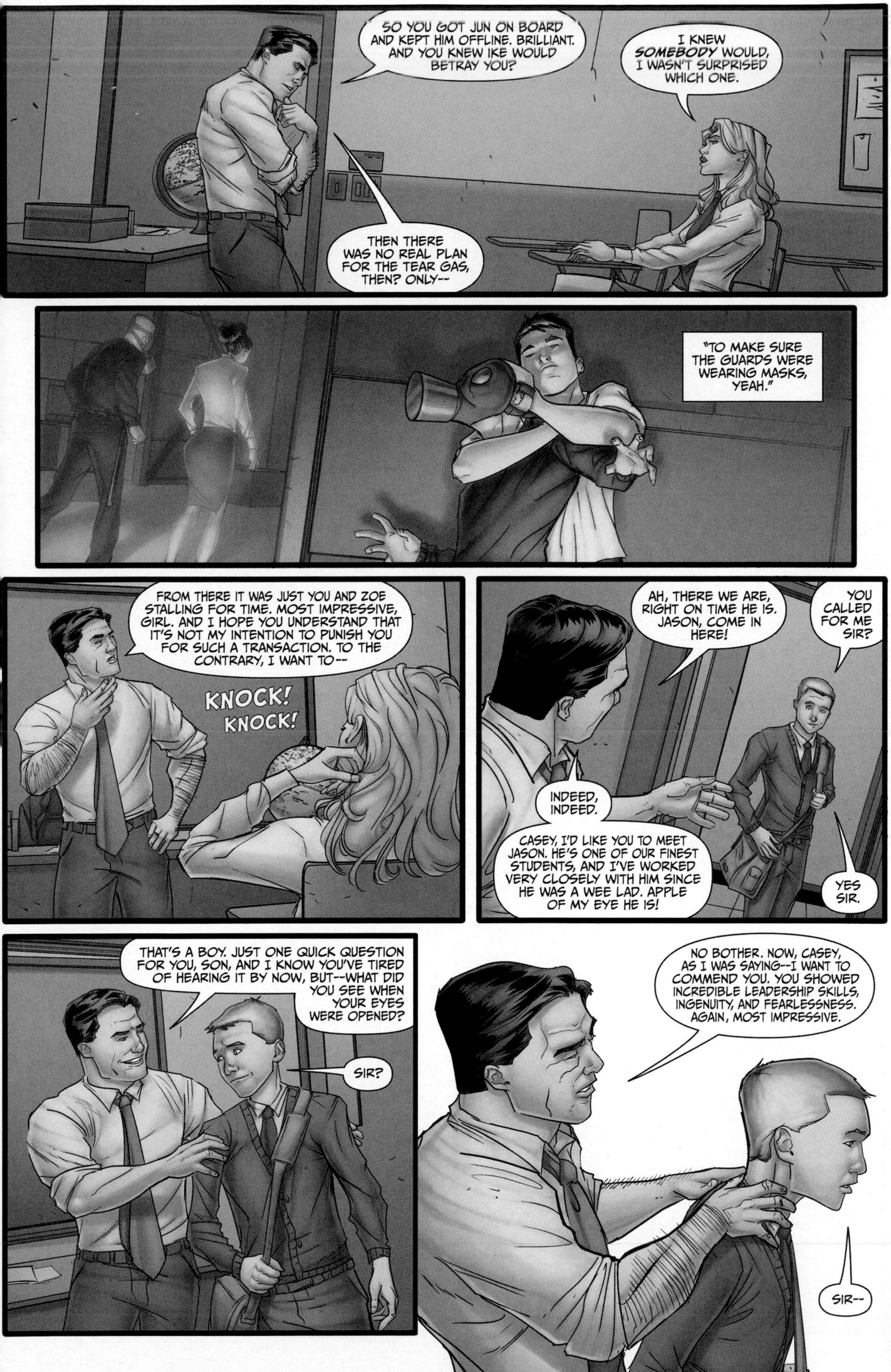
SO YOU GOT JUN ON BOARD AND KEPT HIM OFFLINE. BRILLIANT. AND YOU KNEW IKE WOULD BETRAY YOU?
I KNEW SOMEBODY WOULD, I WASN'T SURPRISED WHICH ONE.
THEN THERE WAS NO REAL PLAN FOR THE TEAR GAS, THEN? ONLY--
"TO MAKE SURE THE GUARDS WERE WEARING MASKS, YEAH."
FROM THERE IT WAS JUST YOU AND ZOE STALLING FOR TIME. MOST IMPRESSIVE, GIRL. AND I HOPE YOU UNDERSTAND THAT IT'S NOT MY INTENTION TO PUNISH YOU FOR SUCH A TRANSACTION. TO THE CONTRARY, I WANT TO--
KNOCK! KNOCK!
AH, THERE WE ARE, RIGHT ON TIME HE IS. JASON, COME IN HERE!
YOU CALLED FOR ME SIR?
INDEED, INDEED.
CASEY, I'D LIKE YOU TO MEET JASON. HE'S ONE OF OUR FINEST STUDENTS, AND I'VE WORKED VERY CLOSELY WITH HIM SINCE HE WAS A WEE LAD. APPLE OF MY EYE HE IS!
YES SIR.
THAT'S A BOY. JUST ONE QUICK QUESTION FOR YOU, SON, AND I KNOW YOU'VE TIRED OF HEARING IT BY NOW, BUT--WHAT DID YOU SEE WHEN YOUR EYES WERE OPENED?
SIR?
NO BOTHER. NOW, CASEY, AS I WAS SAYING--I WANT TO COMMEND YOU. YOU SHOWED INCREDIBLE LEADERSHIP SKILLS, INGENUITY, AND FEARLESSNESS. AGAIN, MOST IMPRESSIVE.
SIR--

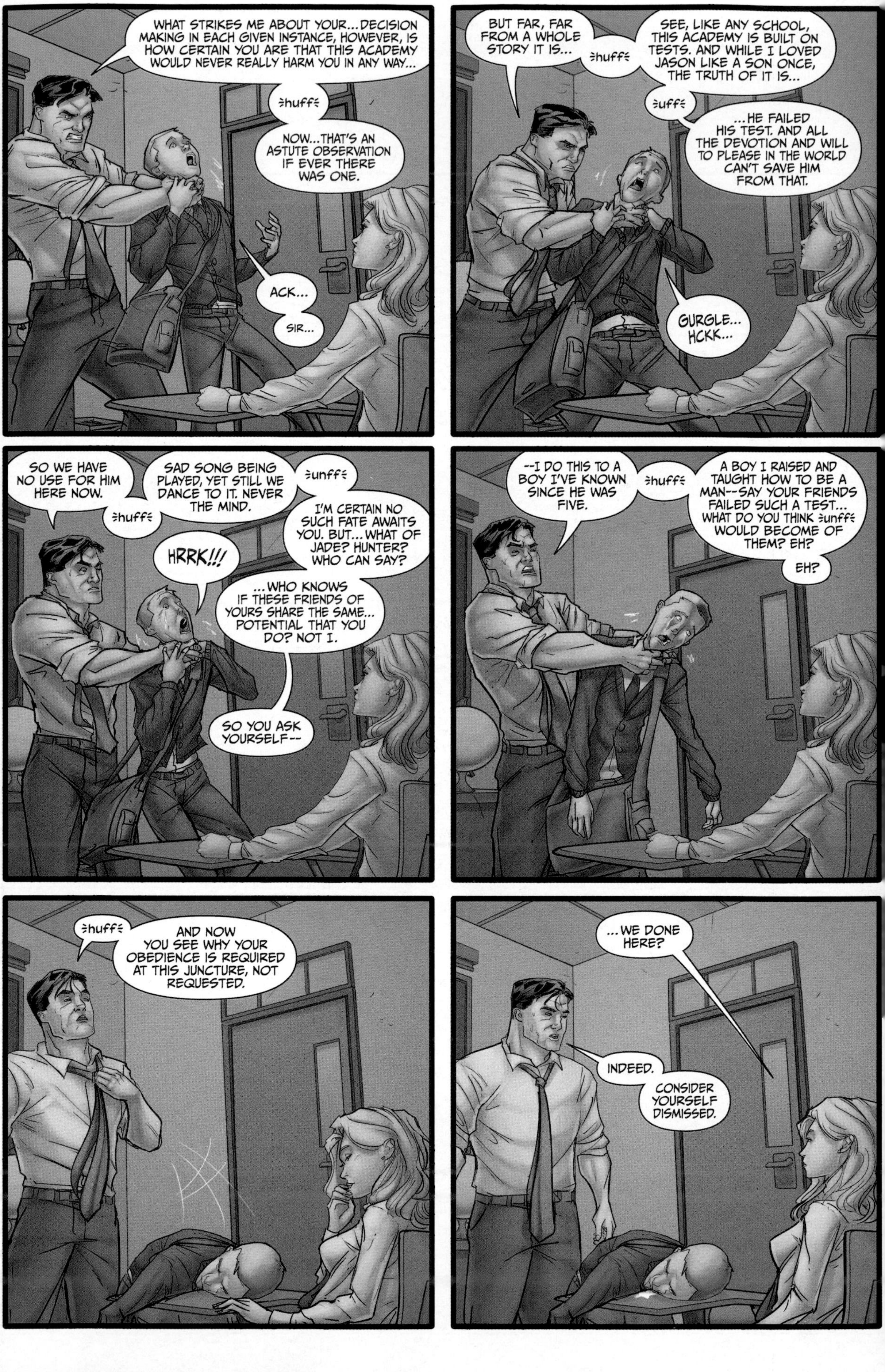
WHAT STRIKES ME ABOUT YOUR...DECISION MAKING IN EACH GIVEN INSTANCE, HOWEVER, IS HOW CERTAIN YOU ARE THAT THIS ACADEMY WOULD NEVER REALLY HARM YOU IN ANY WAY...
huff
NOW...THAT'S AN ASTUTE OBSERVATION IF EVER THERE WAS ONE.
ACK...
SIR...
BUT FAR, FAR FROM A WHOLE STORY IT IS...
huff
SEE, LIKE ANY SCHOOL, THIS ACADEMY IS BUILT ON TESTS. AND WHILE I LOVED JASON LIKE A SON ONCE, THE TRUTH OF IT IS...
uff
...HE FAILED HIS TEST. AND ALL THE DEVOTION AND WILL TO PLEASE IN THE WORLD CAN'T SAVE HIM FROM THAT.
GURGLE... HCKK...
SO WE HAVE NO USE FOR HIM HERE NOW.
huff
SAD SONG BEING PLAYED, YET STILL WE DANCE TO IT. NEVER THE MIND.
unff
I'M CERTAIN NO SUCH FATE AWAITS YOU. BUT...WHAT OF JADE? HUNTER? WHO CAN SAY?
HRRK!!!
...WHO KNOWS IF THESE FRIENDS OF YOURS SHARE THE SAME... POTENTIAL THAT YOU DO? NOT I.
SO YOU ASK YOURSELF--
--I DO THIS TO A BOY I'VE KNOWN SINCE HE WAS FIVE.
huff
A BOY I RAISED AND TAUGHT HOW TO BE A MAN--SAY YOUR FRIENDS FAILED SUCH A TEST... WHAT DO YOU THINK unff WOULD BECOME OF THEM? EH?
EH?
huff
AND NOW YOU SEE WHY YOUR OBEDIENCE IS REQUIRED AT THIS JUNCTURE, NOT REQUESTED.
...WE DONE HERE?
INDEED.
CONSIDER YOURSELF DISMISSED.

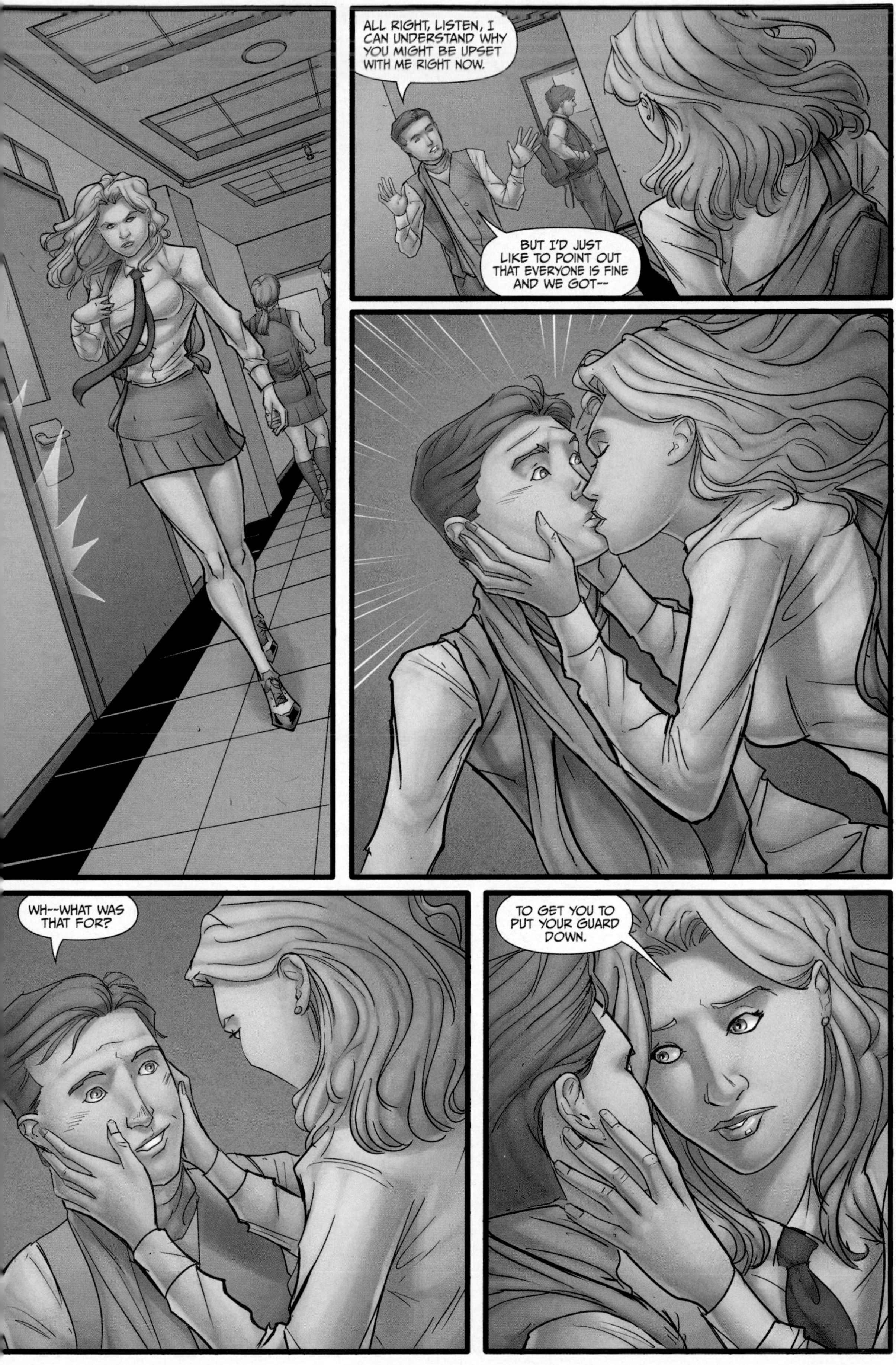
ALL RIGHT, LISTEN, I CAN UNDERSTAND WHY YOU MIGHT BE UPSET WITH ME RIGHT NOW.
BUT I'D JUST LIKE TO POINT OUT THAT EVERYONE IS FINE AND WE GOT--
WH--WHAT WAS THAT FOR?
TO GET YOU TO PUT YOUR GUARD DOWN.

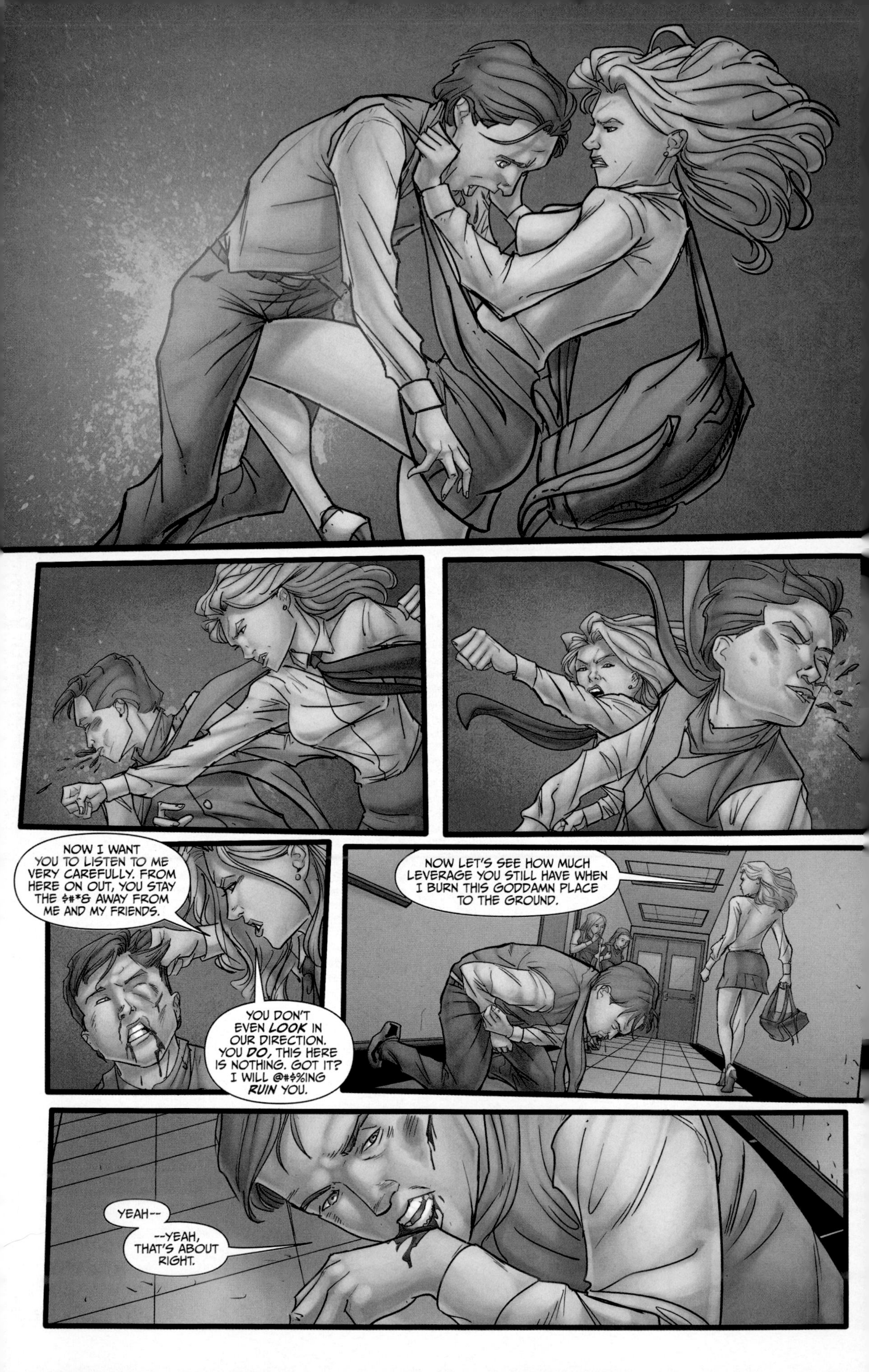
NOW I WANT YOU TO LISTEN TO ME VERY CAREFULLY. FROM HERE ON OUT, YOU STAY THE $#*& AWAY FROM ME AND MY FRIENDS.
YOU DON'T EVEN **LOOK** IN OUR DIRECTION. YOU **DO**, THIS HERE IS NOTHING. GOT IT? I WILL @#$%ING **RUIN** YOU.
NOW LET'S SEE HOW MUCH LEVERAGE YOU STILL HAVE WHEN I BURN THIS GODDAMN PLACE TO THE GROUND.
YEAH--
--YEAH, THAT'S ABOUT RIGHT.

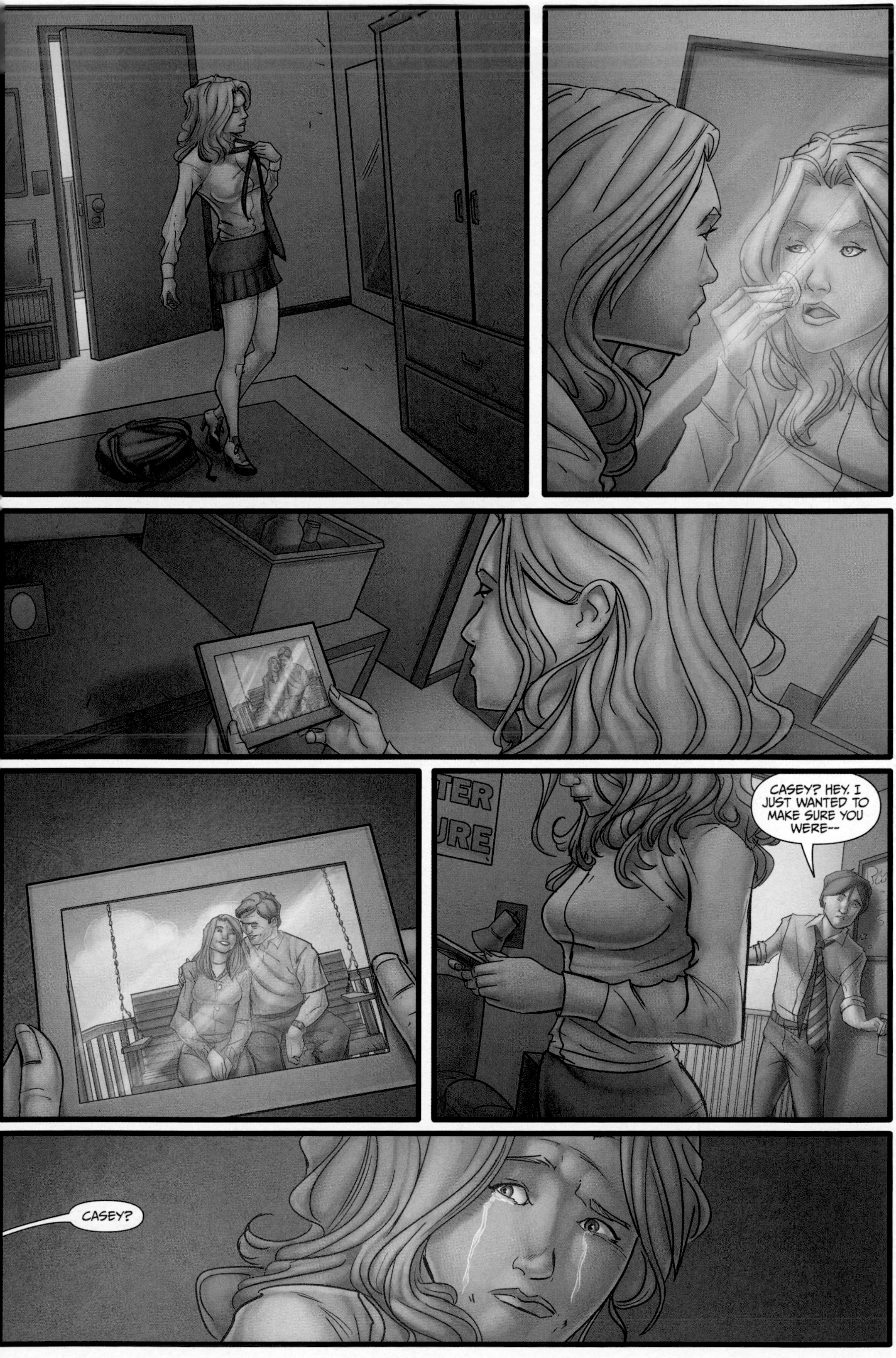
CASEY? HEY. I JUST WANTED TO MAKE SURE YOU WERE--
CASEY?

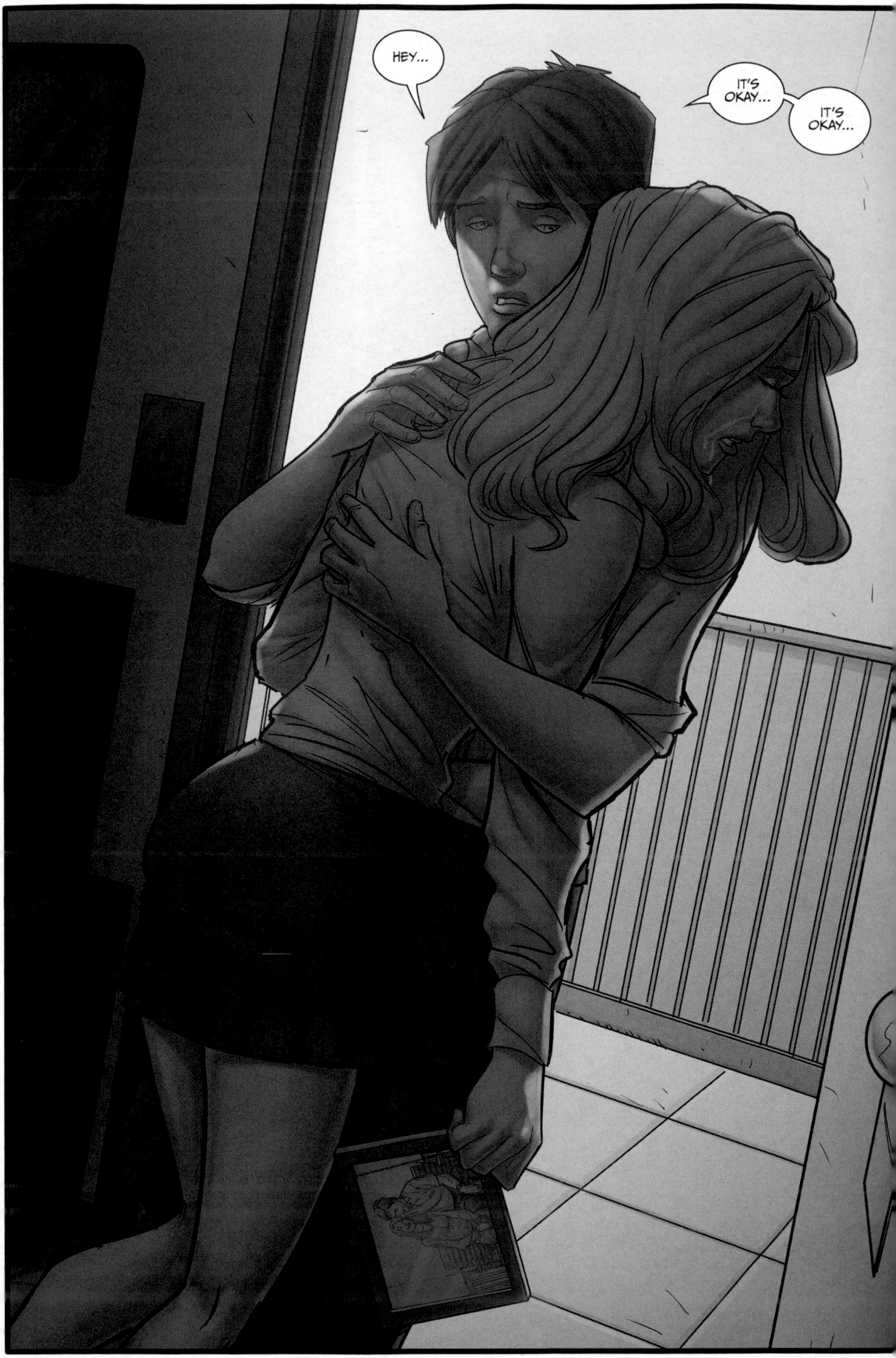
HEY...
IT'S OKAY...
IT'S OKAY...

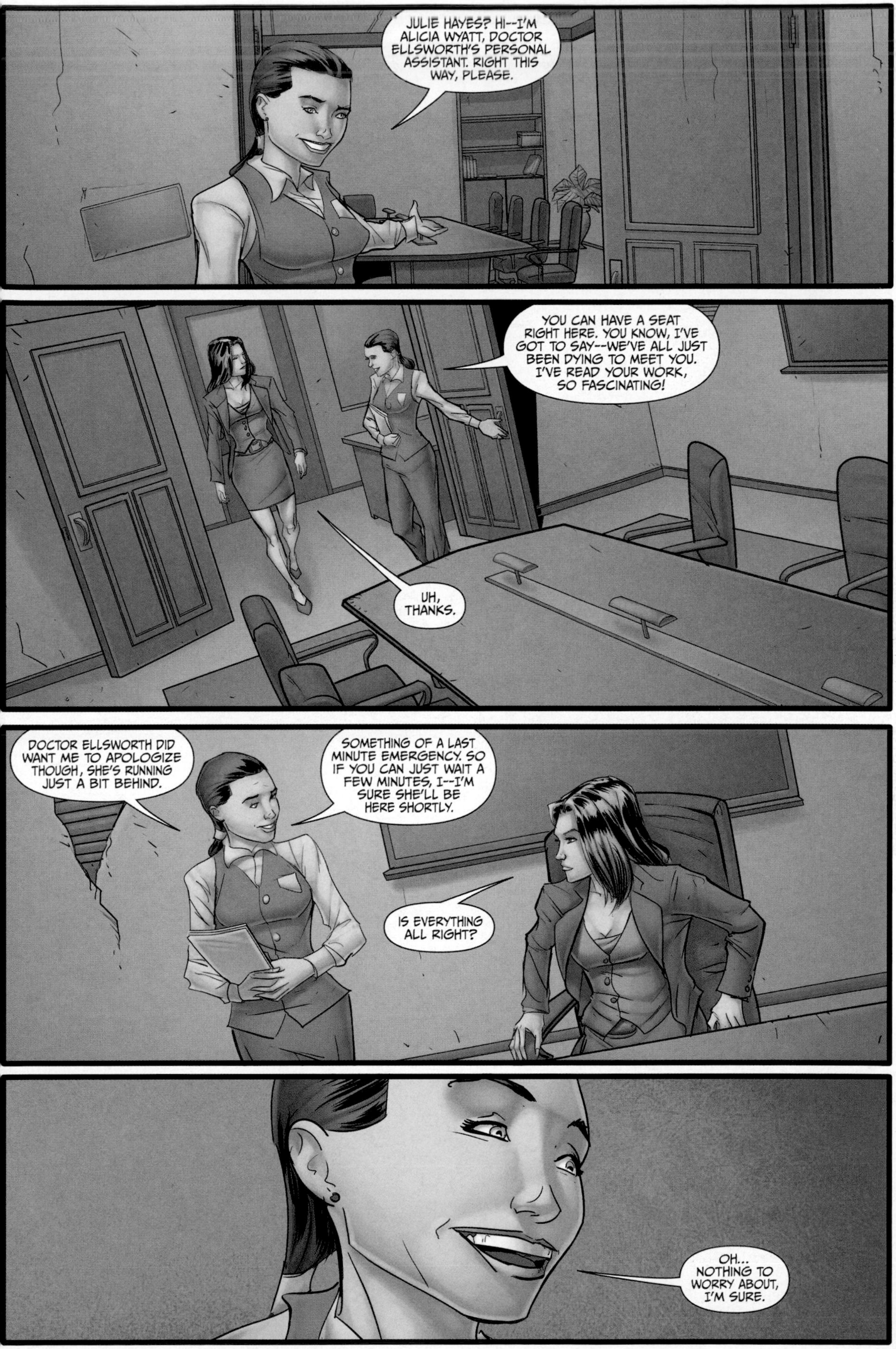
JULIE HAYES? HI--I'M ALICIA WYATT, DOCTOR ELLSWORTH'S PERSONAL ASSISTANT. RIGHT THIS WAY, PLEASE.
YOU CAN HAVE A SEAT RIGHT HERE. YOU KNOW, I'VE GOT TO SAY--WE'VE ALL JUST BEEN DYING TO MEET YOU. I'VE READ YOUR WORK, SO FASCINATING!
UH, THANKS.
DOCTOR ELLSWORTH DID WANT ME TO APOLOGIZE THOUGH, SHE'S RUNNING JUST A BIT BEHIND.
SOMETHING OF A LAST MINUTE EMERGENCY. SO IF YOU CAN JUST WAIT A FEW MINUTES, I--I'M SURE SHE'LL BE HERE SHORTLY.
IS EVERYTHING ALL RIGHT?
OH... NOTHING TO WORRY ABOUT, I'M SURE.

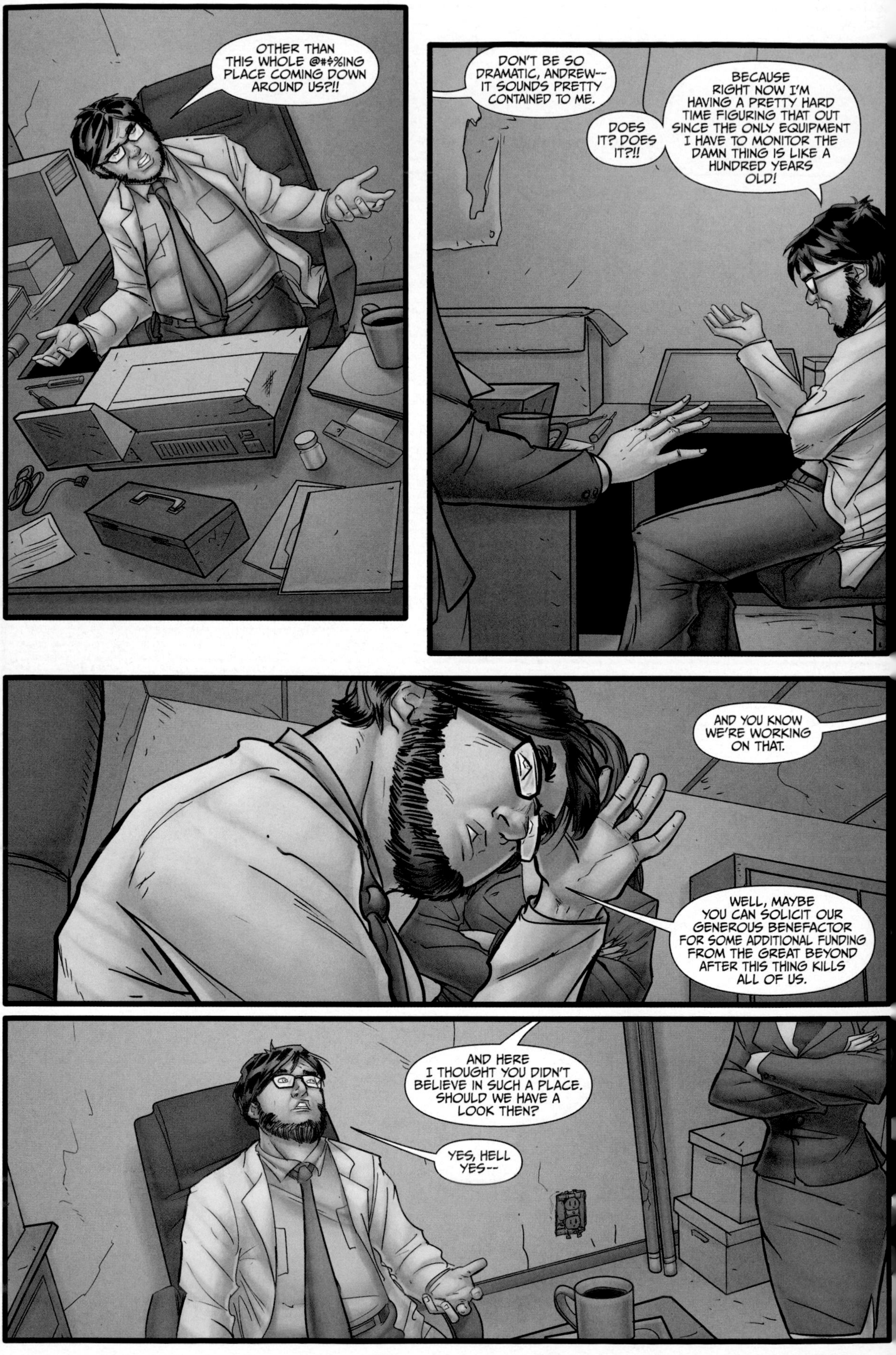
OTHER THAN THIS WHOLE @#$%ING PLACE COMING DOWN AROUND US?!!
DON'T BE SO DRAMATIC, ANDREW-- IT SOUNDS PRETTY CONTAINED TO ME.
DOES IT? DOES IT?!!
BECAUSE RIGHT NOW I'M HAVING A PRETTY HARD TIME FIGURING THAT OUT SINCE THE ONLY EQUIPMENT I HAVE TO MONITOR THE DAMN THING IS LIKE A HUNDRED YEARS OLD!
AND YOU KNOW WE'RE WORKING ON THAT.
WELL, MAYBE YOU CAN SOLICIT OUR GENEROUS BENEFACTOR FOR SOME ADDITIONAL FUNDING FROM THE GREAT BEYOND AFTER THIS THING KILLS ALL OF US.
AND HERE I THOUGHT YOU DIDN'T BELIEVE IN SUCH A PLACE. SHOULD WE HAVE A LOOK THEN?
YES, HELL YES--

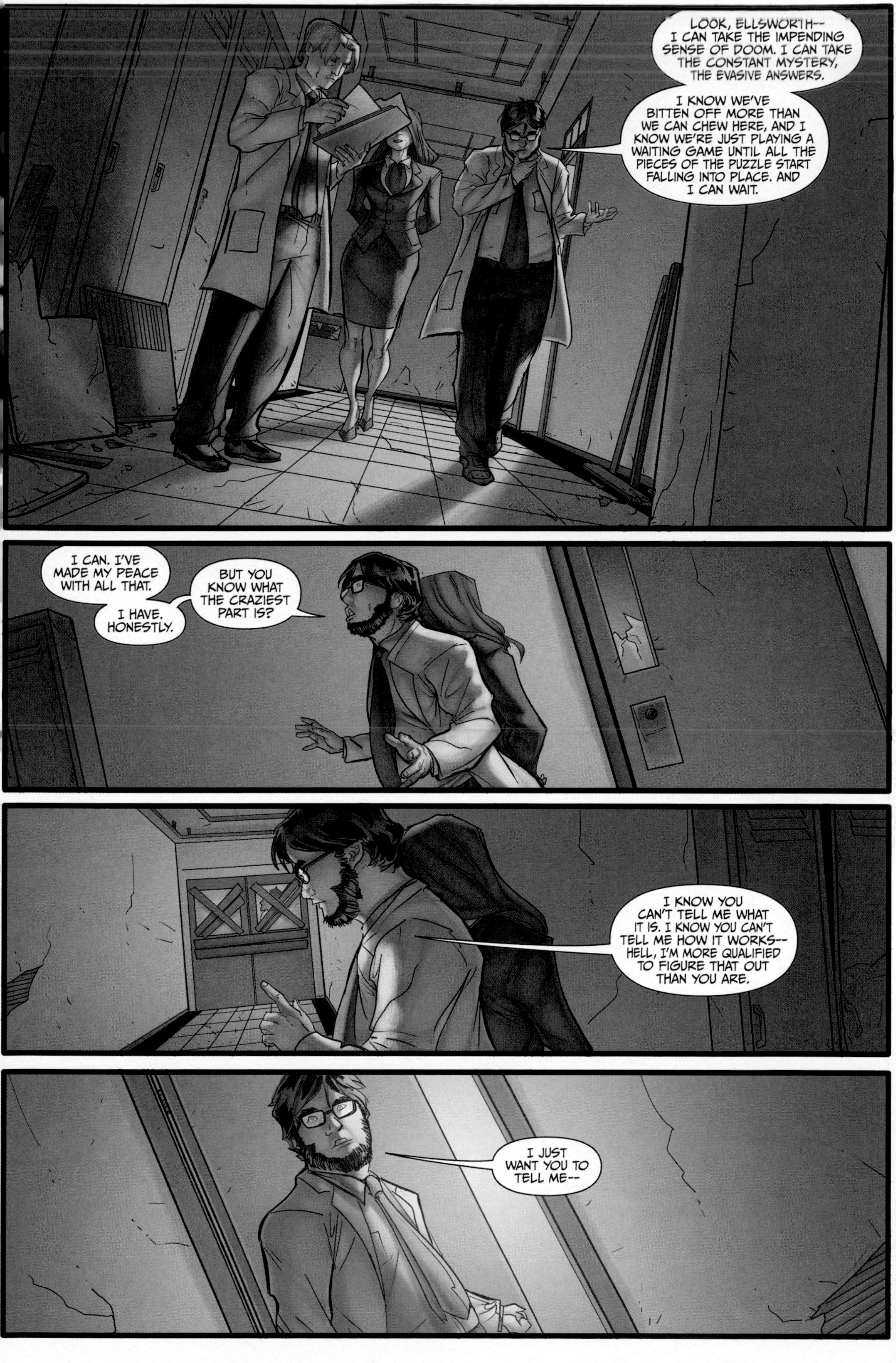
LOOK, ELLSWORTH-- I CAN TAKE THE IMPENDING SENSE OF DOOM. I CAN TAKE THE CONSTANT MYSTERY, THE EVASIVE ANSWERS.
I KNOW WE'VE BITTEN OFF MORE THAN WE CAN CHEW HERE, AND I KNOW WE'RE JUST PLAYING A WAITING GAME UNTIL ALL THE PIECES OF THE PUZZLE START FALLING INTO PLACE. AND I CAN WAIT.
I CAN. I'VE MADE MY PEACE WITH ALL THAT.
I HAVE. HONESTLY.
BUT YOU KNOW WHAT THE CRAZIEST PART IS?
I KNOW YOU CAN'T TELL ME WHAT IT IS. I KNOW YOU CAN'T TELL ME HOW IT WORKS-- HELL, I'M MORE QUALIFIED TO FIGURE THAT OUT THAN YOU ARE.
I JUST WANT YOU TO TELL ME--

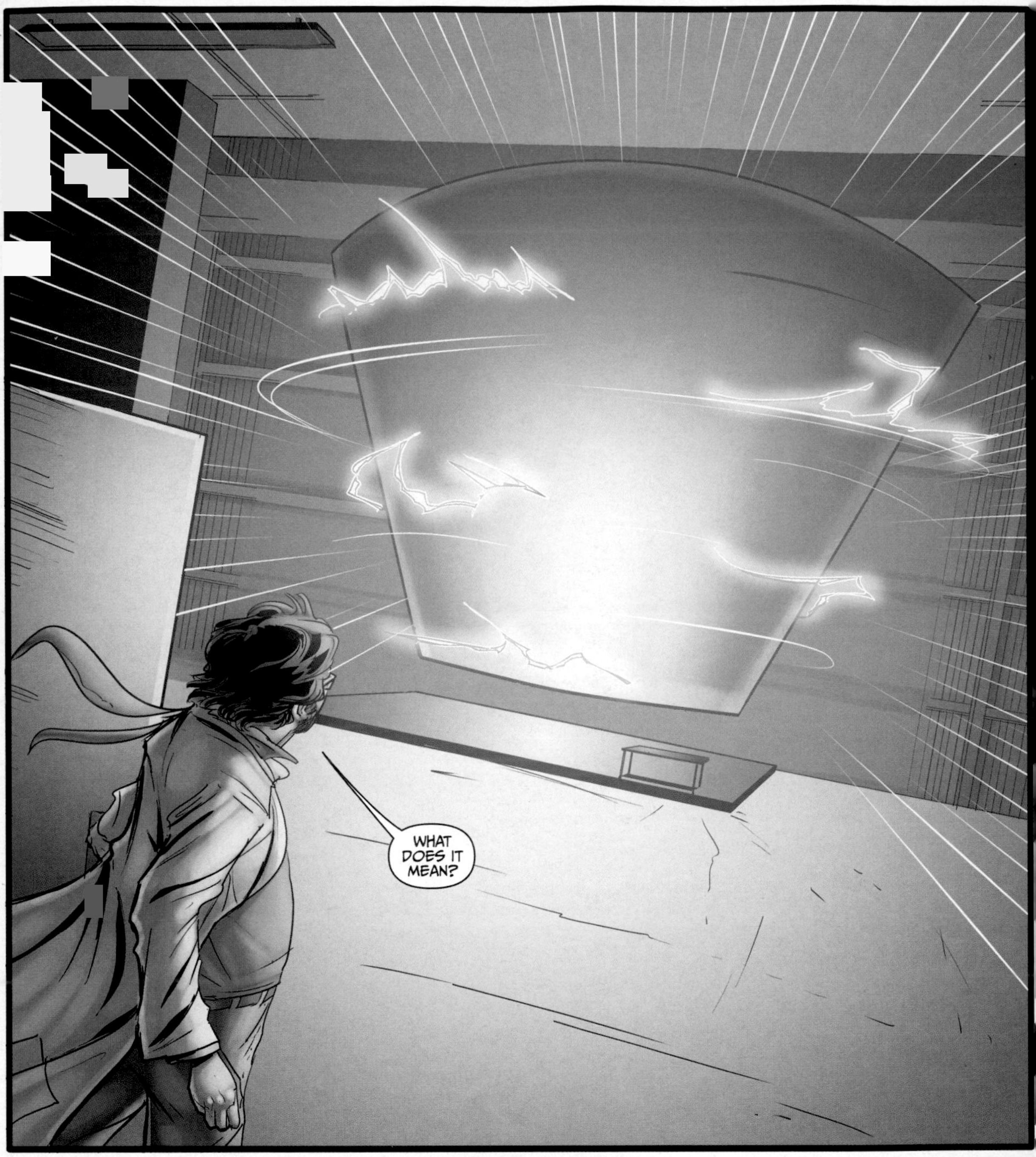
WHAT DOES IT MEAN?

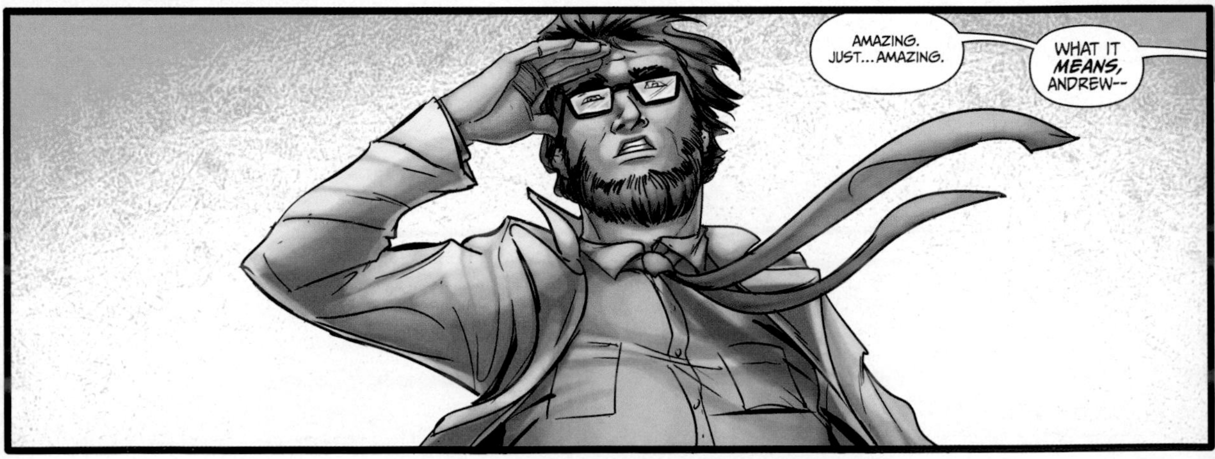
AMAZING. JUST...AMAZING.
WHAT IT MEANS, ANDREW--

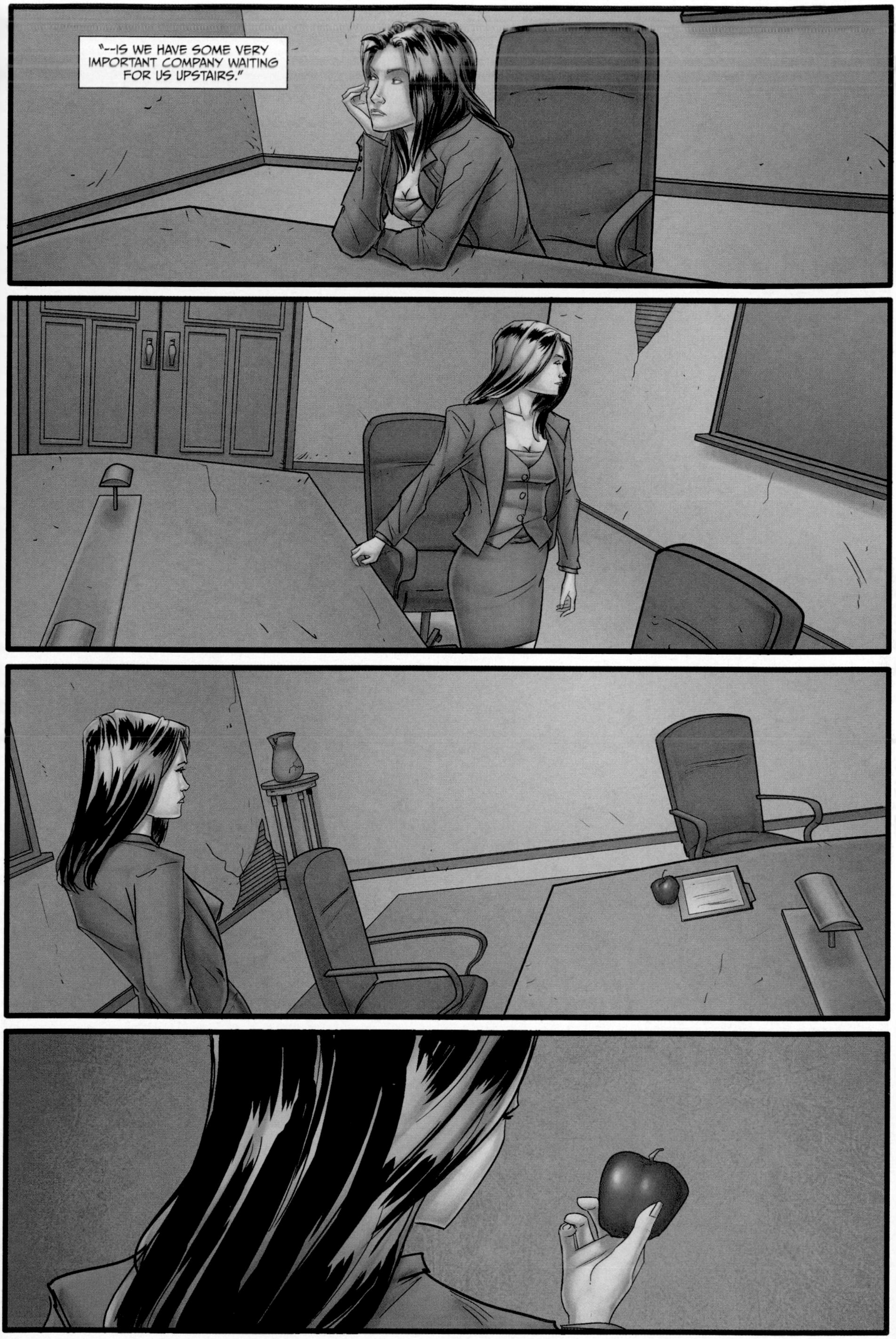
"--IS WE HAVE SOME VERY IMPORTANT COMPANY WAITING FOR US UPSTAIRS."

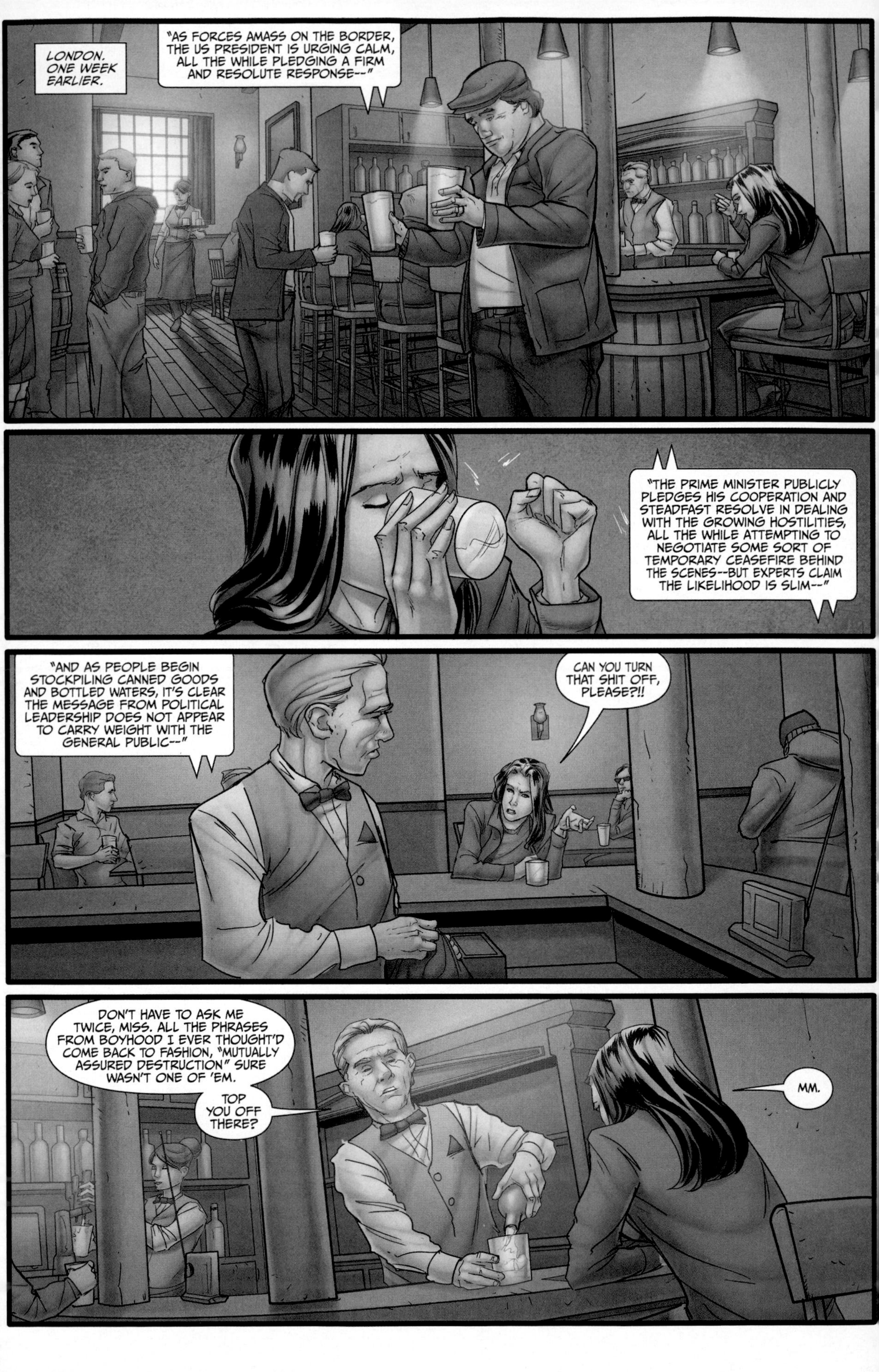
LONDON. ONE WEEK EARLIER.
"AS FORCES AMASS ON THE BORDER, THE US PRESIDENT IS URGING CALM, ALL THE WHILE PLEDGING A FIRM AND RESOLUTE RESPONSE--"
"THE PRIME MINISTER PUBLICLY PLEDGES HIS COOPERATION AND STEADFAST RESOLVE IN DEALING WITH THE GROWING HOSTILITIES, ALL THE WHILE ATTEMPTING TO NEGOTIATE SOME SORT OF TEMPORARY CEASEFIRE BEHIND THE SCENES--BUT EXPERTS CLAIM THE LIKELIHOOD IS SLIM--"
"AND AS PEOPLE BEGIN STOCKPILING CANNED GOODS AND BOTTLED WATERS, IT'S CLEAR THE MESSAGE FROM POLITICAL LEADERSHIP DOES NOT APPEAR TO CARRY WEIGHT WITH THE GENERAL PUBLIC--"
CAN YOU TURN THAT SHIT OFF, PLEASE?!!
DON'T HAVE TO ASK ME TWICE, MISS. ALL THE PHRASES FROM BOYHOOD I EVER THOUGHT'D COME BACK TO FASHION, "MUTUALLY ASSURED DESTRUCTION" SURE WASN'T ONE OF 'EM.
TOP YOU OFF THERE?
MM.

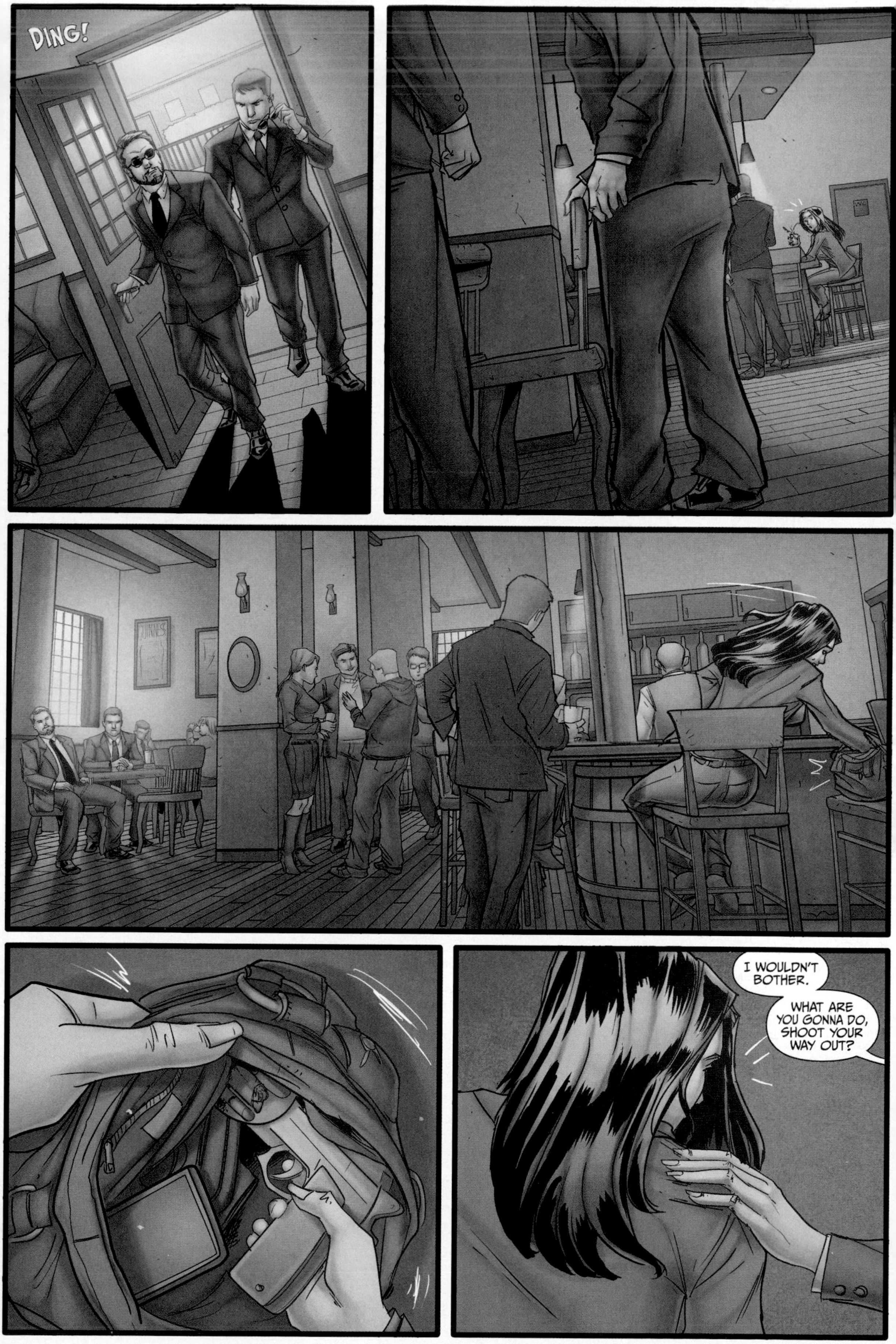
DING!
I WOULDN'T BOTHER.
WHAT ARE YOU GONNA DO, SHOOT YOUR WAY OUT?

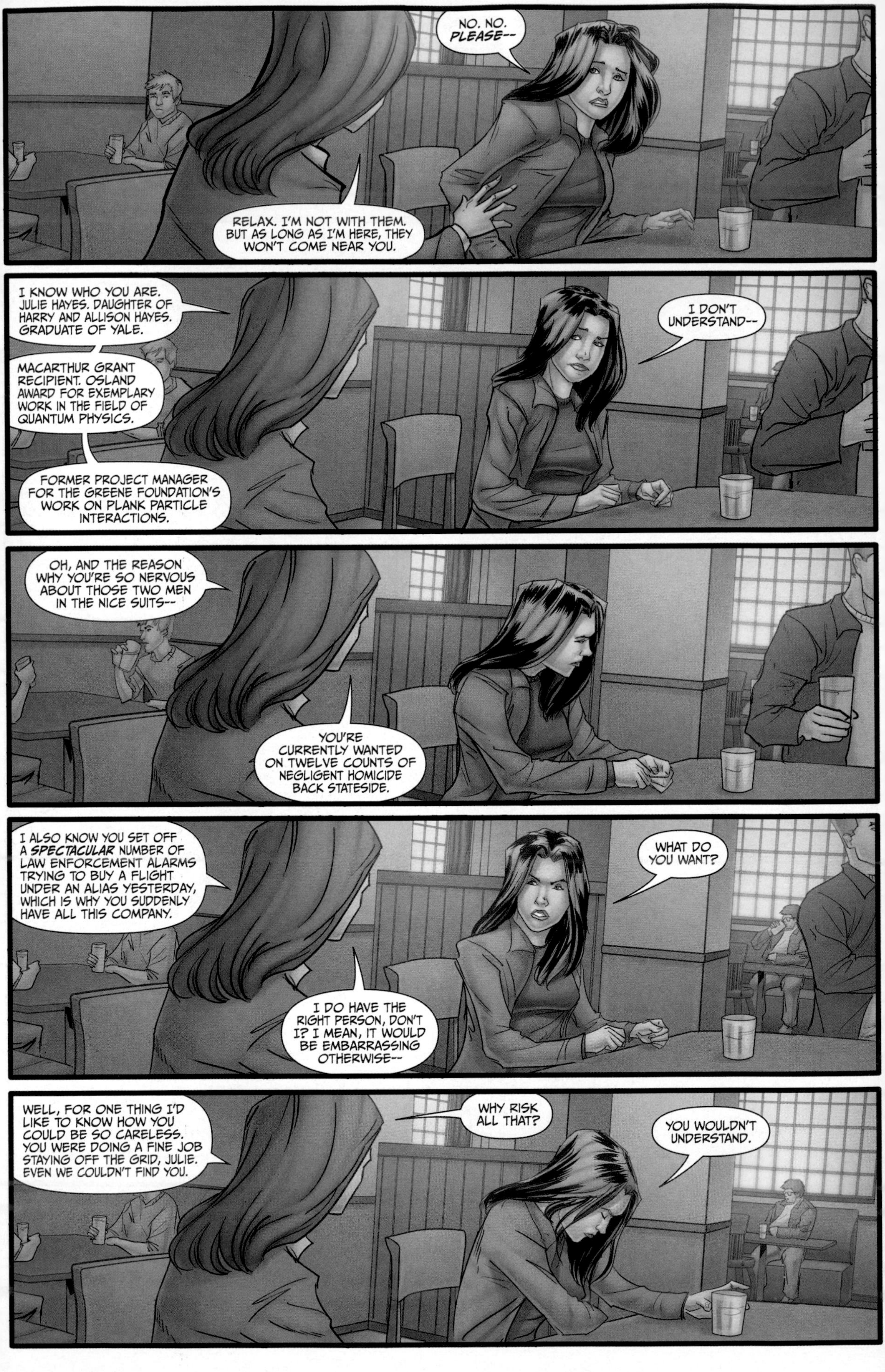
NO. NO. PLEASE--
RELAX. I'M NOT WITH THEM. BUT AS LONG AS I'M HERE, THEY WON'T COME NEAR YOU.
I KNOW WHO YOU ARE. JULIE HAYES. DAUGHTER OF HARRY AND ALLISON HAYES. GRADUATE OF YALE.
MACARTHUR GRANT RECIPIENT. OSLAND AWARD FOR EXEMPLARY WORK IN THE FIELD OF QUANTUM PHYSICS.
FORMER PROJECT MANAGER FOR THE GREENE FOUNDATION'S WORK ON PLANK PARTICLE INTERACTIONS.
I DON'T UNDERSTAND--
OH, AND THE REASON WHY YOU'RE SO NERVOUS ABOUT THOSE TWO MEN IN THE NICE SUITS--
YOU'RE CURRENTLY WANTED ON TWELVE COUNTS OF NEGLIGENT HOMICIDE BACK STATESIDE.
I ALSO KNOW YOU SET OFF A SPECTACULAR NUMBER OF LAW ENFORCEMENT ALARMS TRYING TO BUY A FLIGHT UNDER AN ALIAS YESTERDAY, WHICH IS WHY YOU SUDDENLY HAVE ALL THIS COMPANY.
I DO HAVE THE RIGHT PERSON, DON'T I? I MEAN, IT WOULD BE EMBARRASSING OTHERWISE--
WHAT DO YOU WANT?
WELL, FOR ONE THING I'D LIKE TO KNOW HOW YOU COULD BE SO CARELESS. YOU WERE DOING A FINE JOB STAYING OFF THE GRID, JULIE. EVEN WE COULDN'T FIND YOU.
WHY RISK ALL THAT?
YOU WOULDN'T UNDERSTAND.

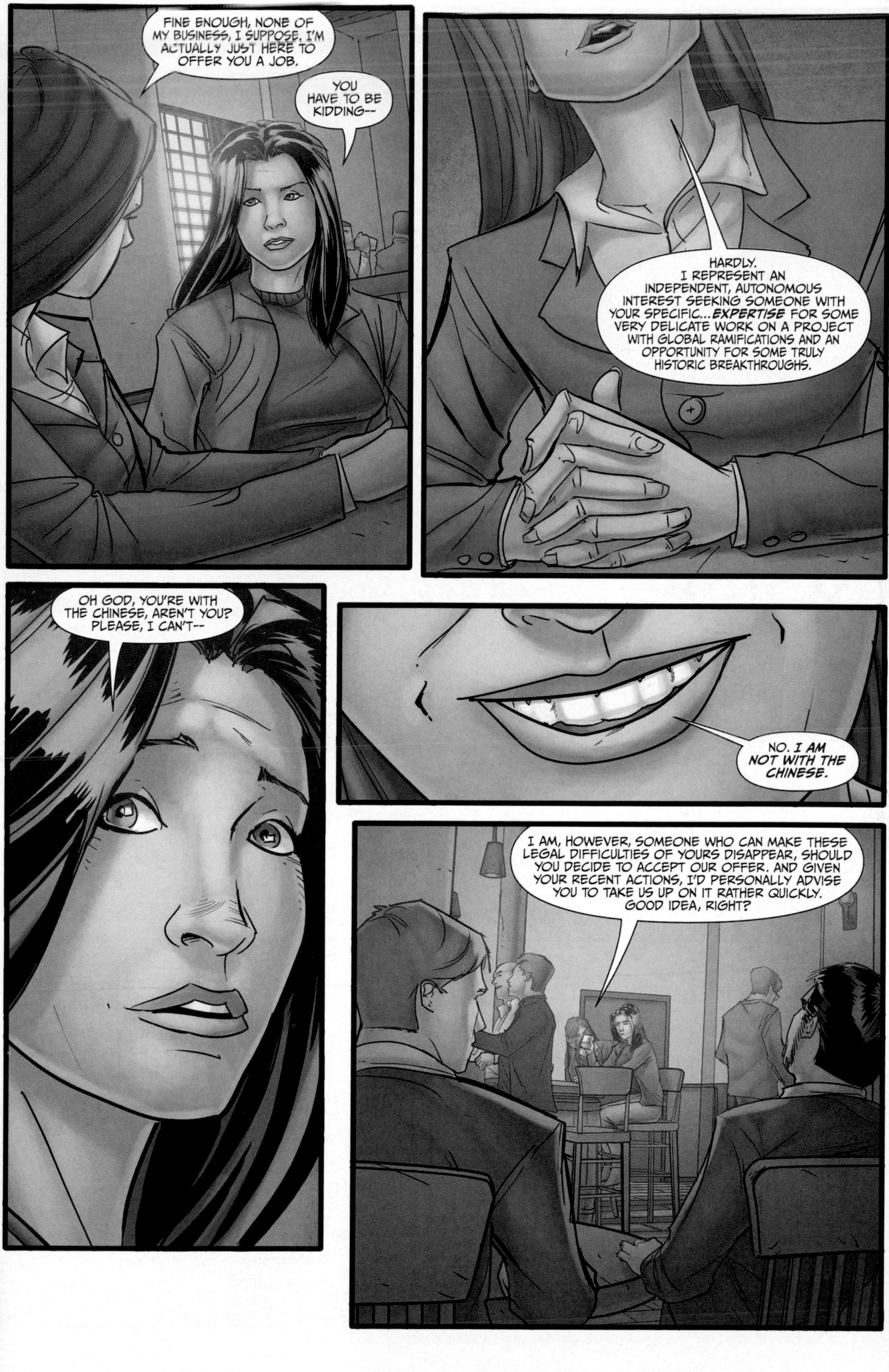
FINE ENOUGH, NONE OF MY BUSINESS, I SUPPOSE. I'M ACTUALLY JUST HERE TO OFFER YOU A JOB.
YOU HAVE TO BE KIDDING--
HARDLY. I REPRESENT AN INDEPENDENT, AUTONOMOUS INTEREST SEEKING SOMEONE WITH YOUR SPECIFIC...EXPERTISE FOR SOME VERY DELICATE WORK ON A PROJECT WITH GLOBAL RAMIFICATIONS AND AN OPPORTUNITY FOR SOME TRULY HISTORIC BREAKTHROUGHS.
OH GOD, YOU'RE WITH THE CHINESE, AREN'T YOU? PLEASE, I CAN'T--
NO. I AM NOT WITH THE CHINESE.
I AM, HOWEVER, SOMEONE WHO CAN MAKE THESE LEGAL DIFFICULTIES OF YOURS DISAPPEAR, SHOULD YOU DECIDE TO ACCEPT OUR OFFER. AND GIVEN YOUR RECENT ACTIONS, I'D PERSONALLY ADVISE YOU TO TAKE US UP ON IT RATHER QUICKLY. GOOD IDEA, RIGHT?

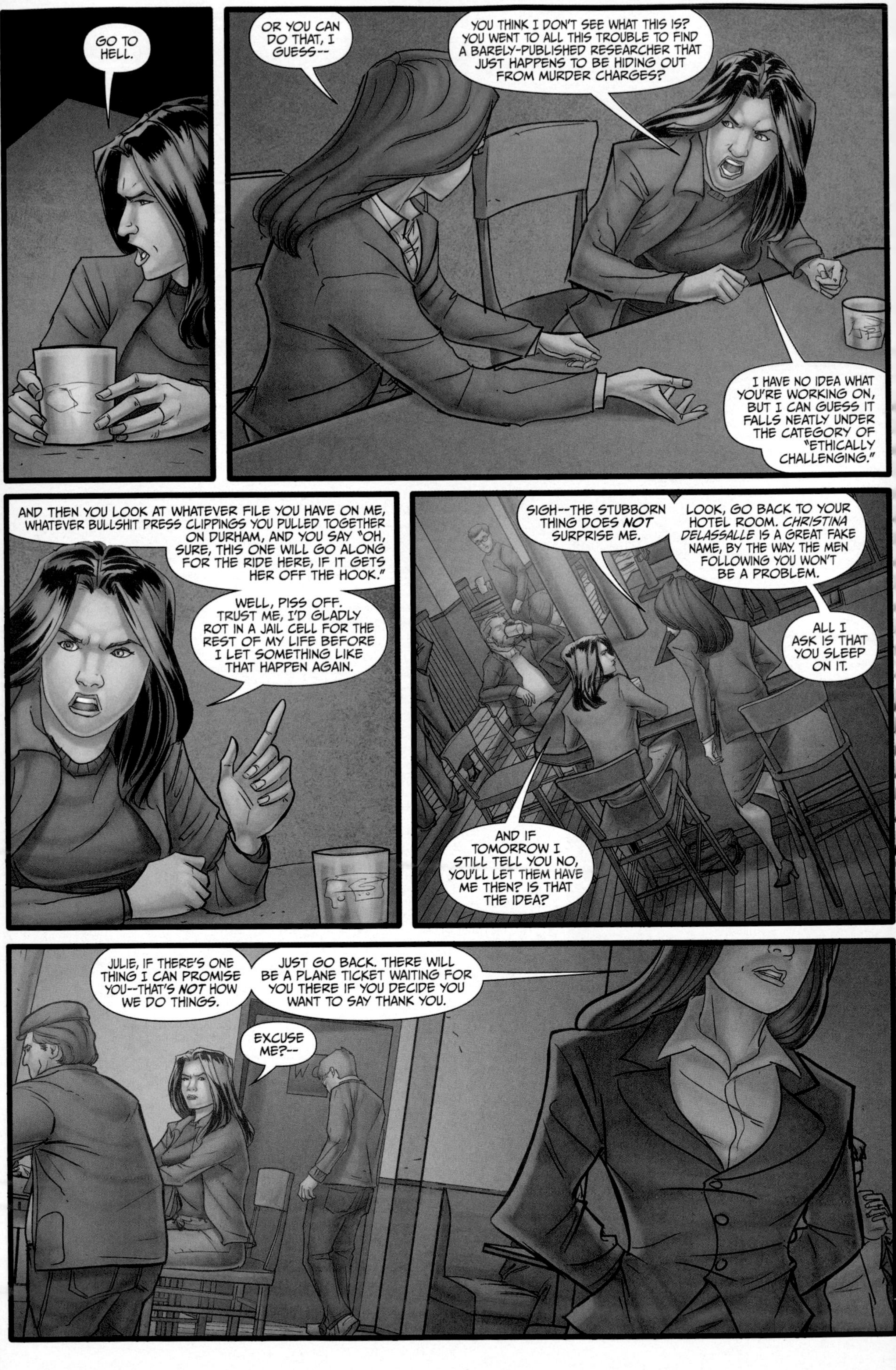
GO TO HELL.
OR YOU CAN DO THAT, I GUESS--
YOU THINK I DON'T SEE WHAT THIS IS? YOU WENT TO ALL THIS TROUBLE TO FIND A BARELY-PUBLISHED RESEARCHER THAT JUST HAPPENS TO BE HIDING OUT FROM MURDER CHARGES?
I HAVE NO IDEA WHAT YOU'RE WORKING ON, BUT I CAN GUESS IT FALLS NEATLY UNDER THE CATEGORY OF "ETHICALLY CHALLENGING."
AND THEN YOU LOOK AT WHATEVER FILE YOU HAVE ON ME, WHATEVER BULLSHIT PRESS CLIPPINGS YOU PULLED TOGETHER ON DURHAM, AND YOU SAY "OH, SURE, THIS ONE WILL GO ALONG FOR THE RIDE HERE, IF IT GETS HER OFF THE HOOK."
WELL, PISS OFF. TRUST ME, I'D GLADLY ROT IN A JAIL CELL FOR THE REST OF MY LIFE BEFORE I LET SOMETHING LIKE THAT HAPPEN AGAIN.
SIGH--THE STUBBORN THING DOES ***NOT*** SURPRISE ME.
LOOK, GO BACK TO YOUR HOTEL ROOM. *CHRISTINA DELASSALLE* IS A GREAT FAKE NAME, BY THE WAY. THE MEN FOLLOWING YOU WON'T BE A PROBLEM.
ALL I ASK IS THAT YOU SLEEP ON IT.
AND IF TOMORROW I STILL TELL YOU NO, YOU'LL LET THEM HAVE ME THEN? IS THAT THE IDEA?
JULIE, IF THERE'S ONE THING I CAN PROMISE YOU--THAT'S ***NOT*** HOW WE DO THINGS.
JUST GO BACK. THERE WILL BE A PLANE TICKET WAITING FOR YOU THERE IF YOU DECIDE YOU WANT TO SAY THANK YOU.
EXCUSE ME?--

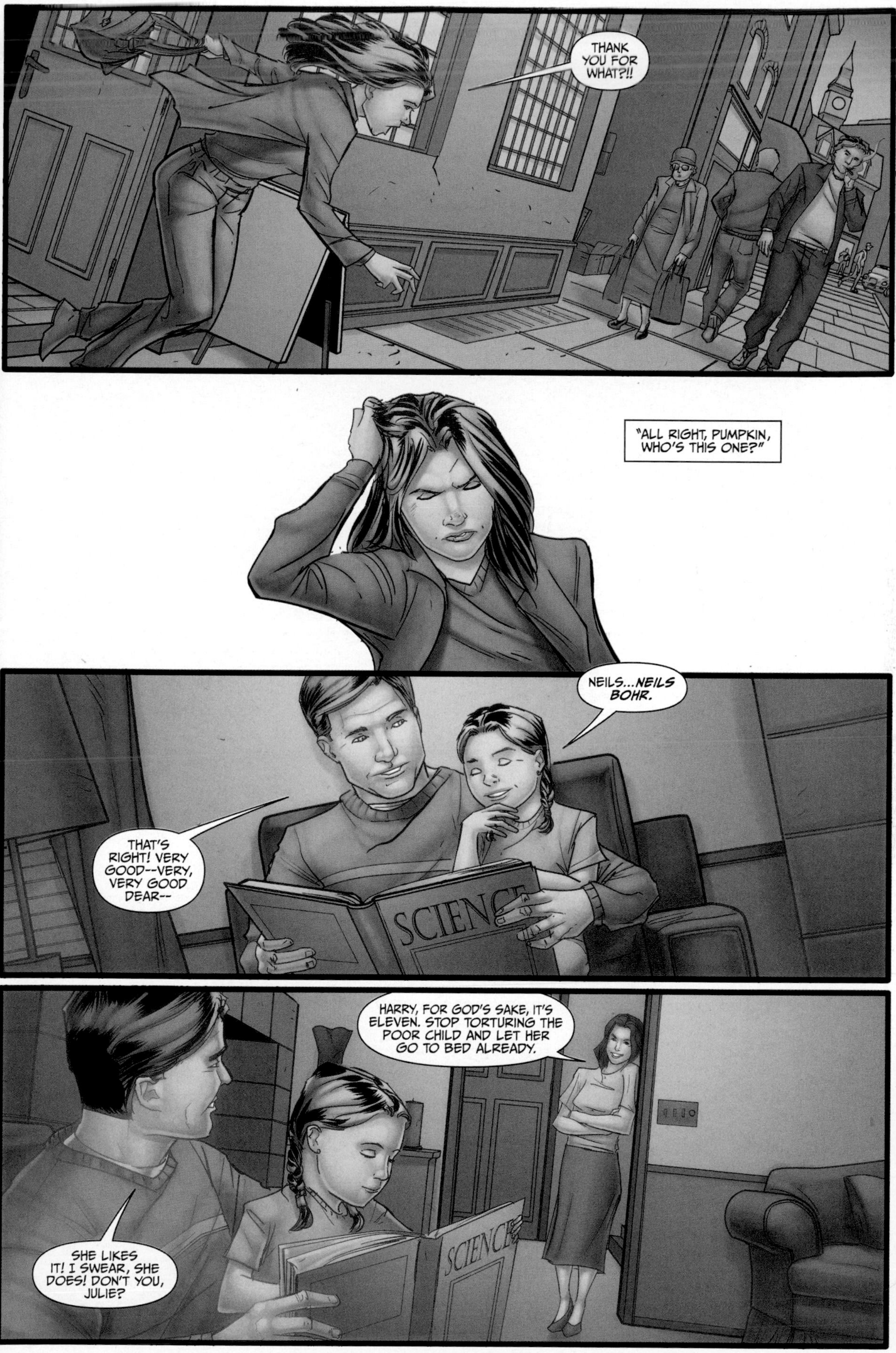
THANK YOU FOR WHAT?!!
"ALL RIGHT, PUMPKIN, WHO'S THIS ONE?"
NEILS...NEILS BOHR.
THAT'S RIGHT! VERY GOOD--VERY, VERY GOOD DEAR--
SCIENCE
HARRY, FOR GOD'S SAKE, IT'S ELEVEN. STOP TORTURING THE POOR CHILD AND LET HER GO TO BED ALREADY.
SHE LIKES IT! I SWEAR, SHE DOES! DON'T YOU, JULIE?
SCIENCE

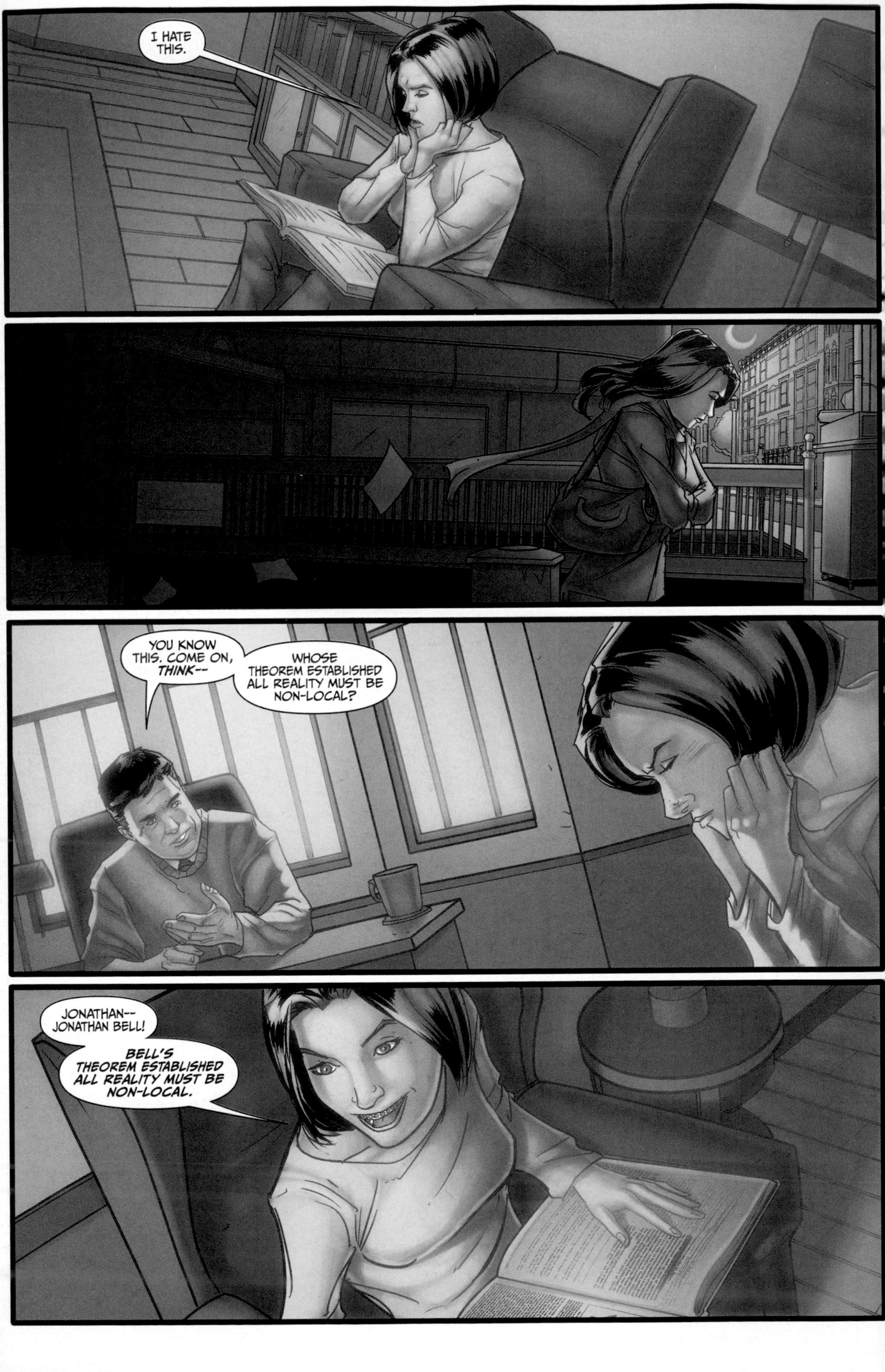
I HATE THIS.
YOU KNOW THIS. COME ON, THINK--
WHOSE THEOREM ESTABLISHED ALL REALITY MUST BE NON-LOCAL?
JONATHAN-- JONATHAN BELL!
BELL'S THEOREM ESTABLISHED ALL REALITY MUST BE NON-LOCAL.

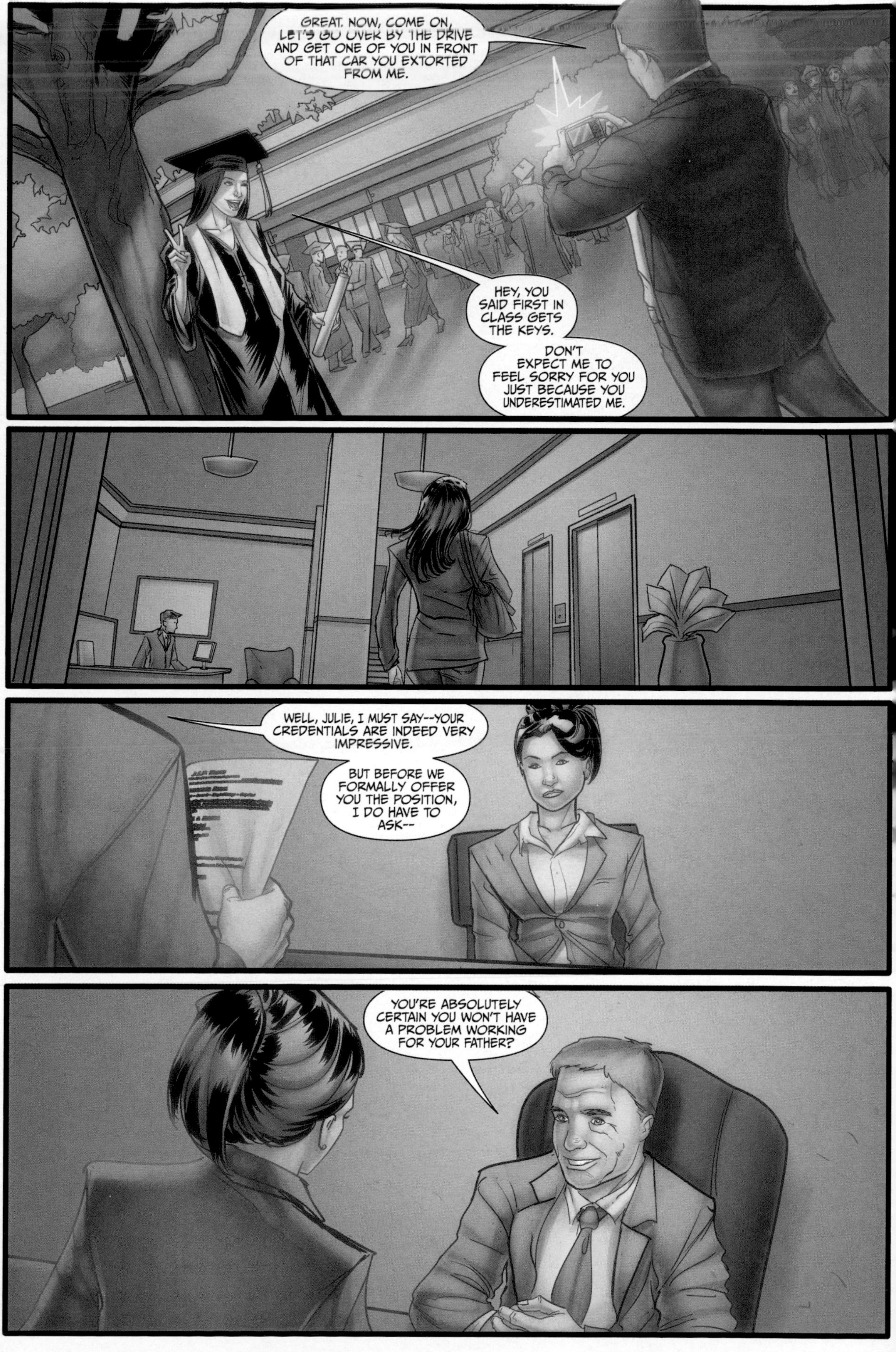
GREAT. NOW, COME ON, LET'S GO OVER BY THE DRIVE AND GET ONE OF YOU IN FRONT OF THAT CAR YOU EXTORTED FROM ME.
HEY, YOU SAID FIRST IN CLASS GETS THE KEYS.
DON'T EXPECT ME TO FEEL SORRY FOR YOU JUST BECAUSE YOU UNDERESTIMATED ME.
WELL, JULIE, I MUST SAY--YOUR CREDENTIALS ARE INDEED VERY IMPRESSIVE.
BUT BEFORE WE FORMALLY OFFER YOU THE POSITION, I DO HAVE TO ASK--
YOU'RE ABSOLUTELY CERTAIN YOU WON'T HAVE A PROBLEM WORKING FOR YOUR FATHER?

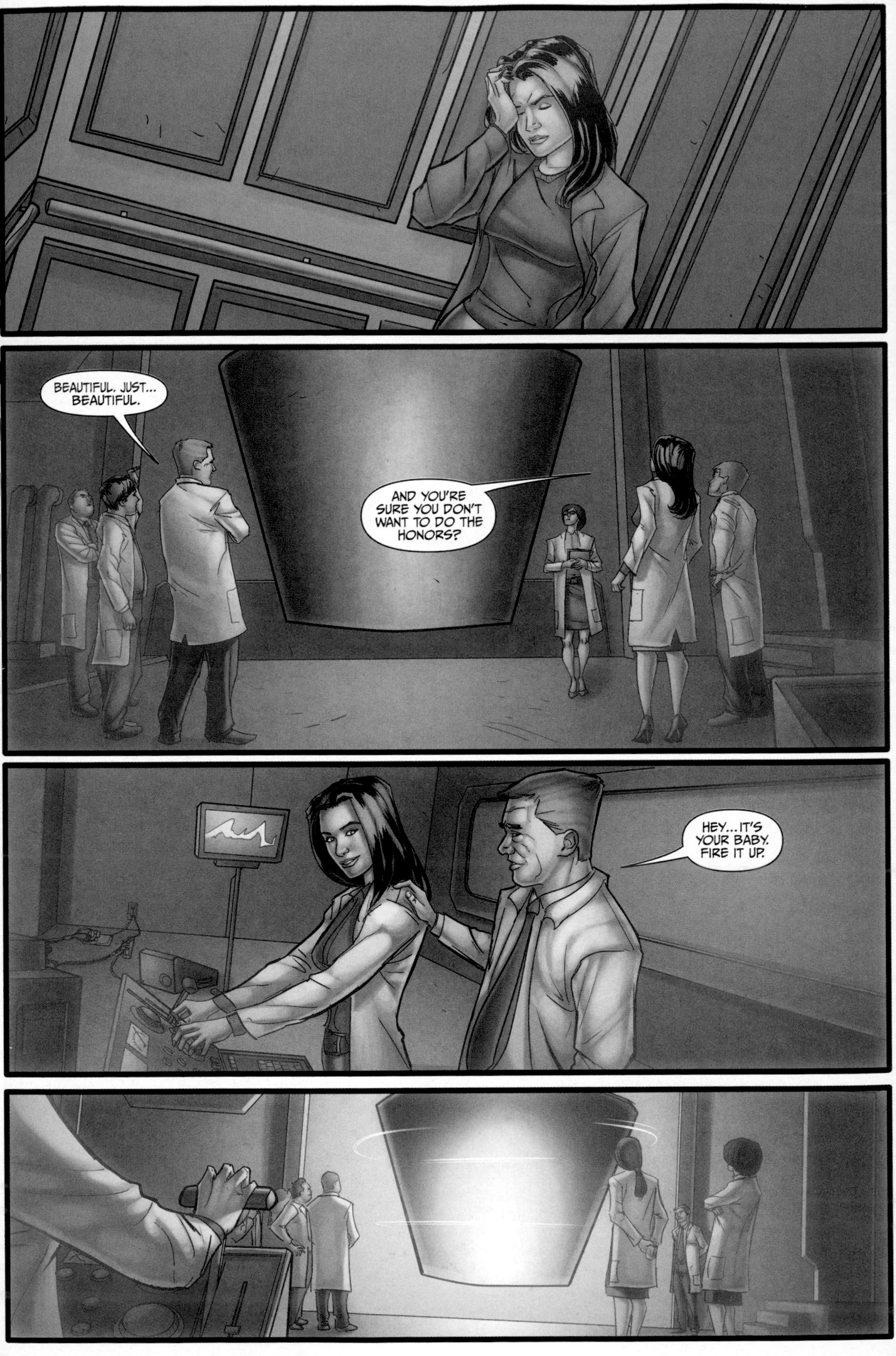
BEAUTIFUL. JUST... BEAUTIFUL.
AND YOU'RE SURE YOU DON'T WANT TO DO THE HONORS?
HEY...IT'S YOUR BABY. FIRE IT UP.

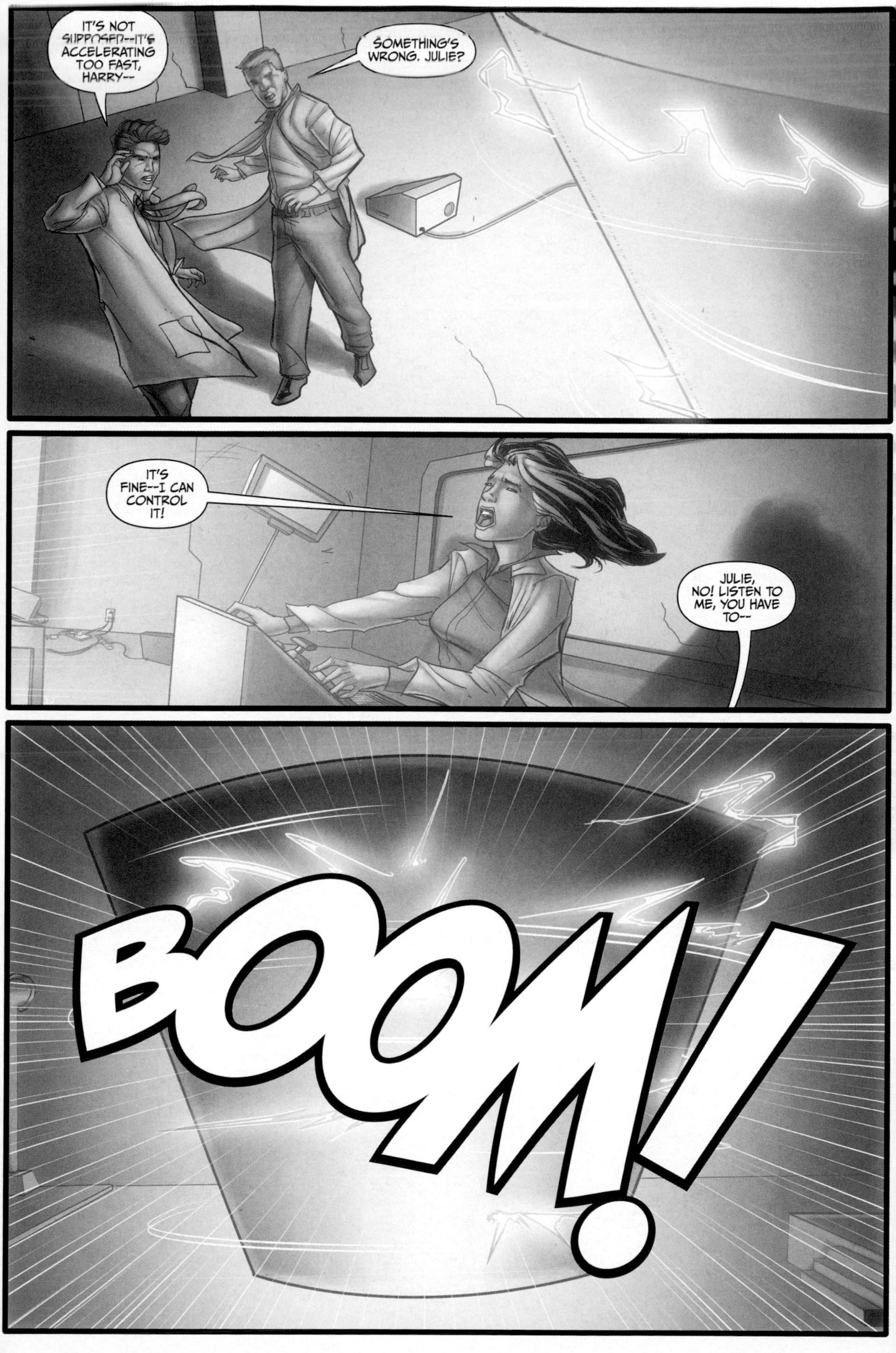
IT'S NOT SUPPOSED--IT'S ACCELERATING TOO FAST, HARRY--
SOMETHING'S WRONG. JULIE?
IT'S FINE--I CAN CONTROL IT!
JULIE, NO! LISTEN TO ME, YOU HAVE TO--
BOOM!

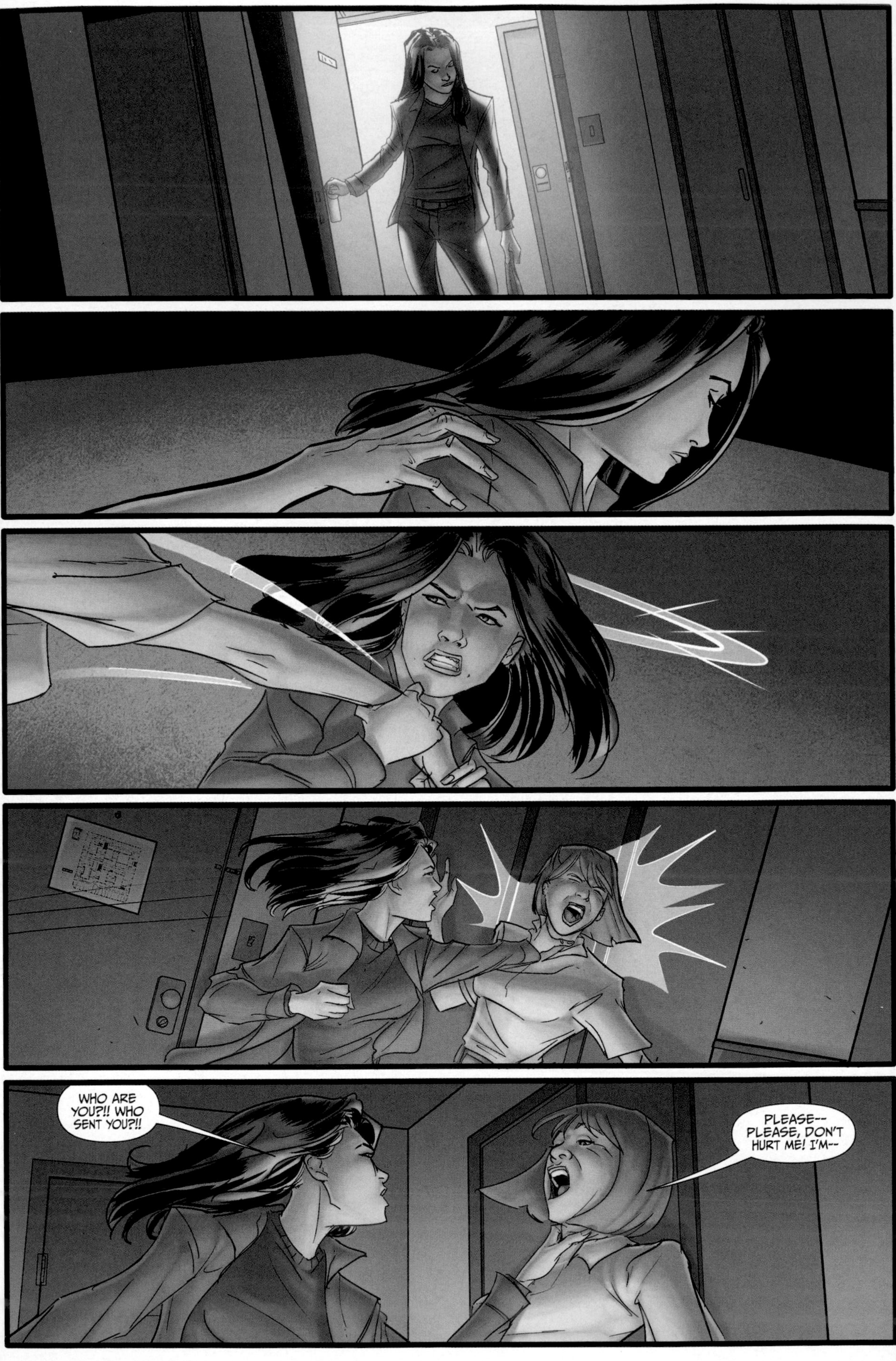
WHO ARE YOU?!! WHO SENT YOU?!!
PLEASE-- PLEASE, DON'T HURT ME! I'M--

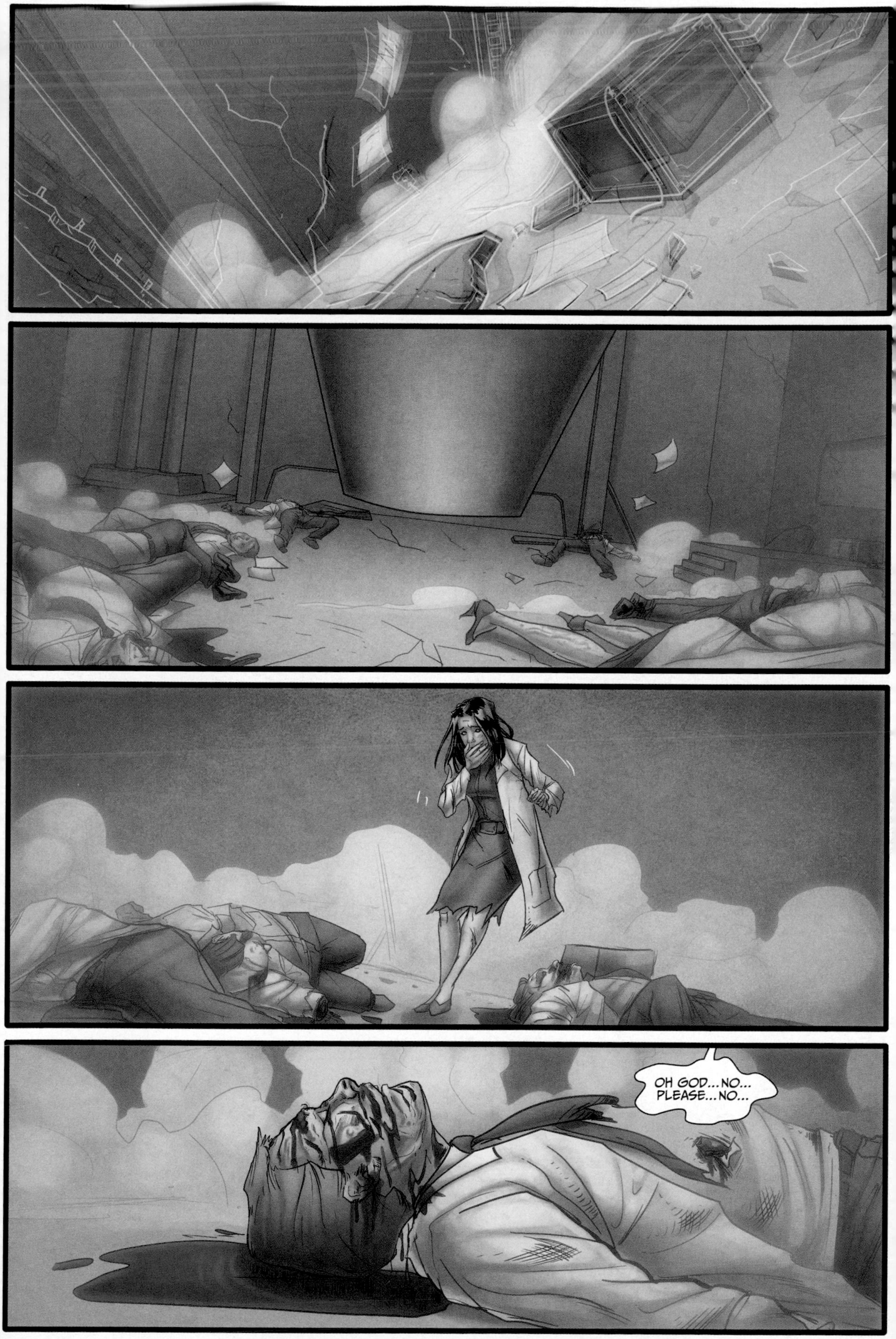
OH GOD... NO...
PLEASE... NO...

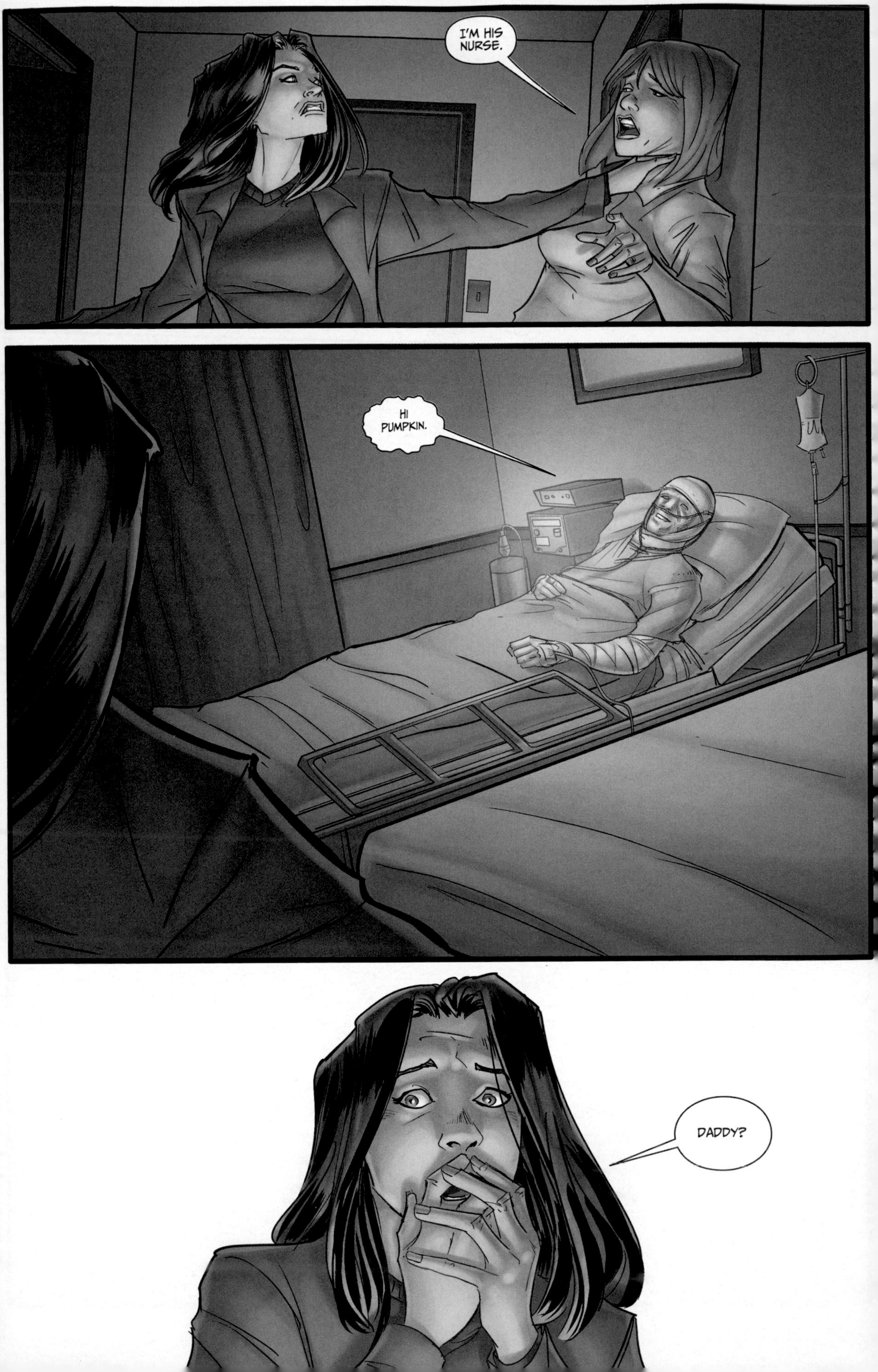
I'M HIS NURSE.
HI PUMPKIN.
DADDY?

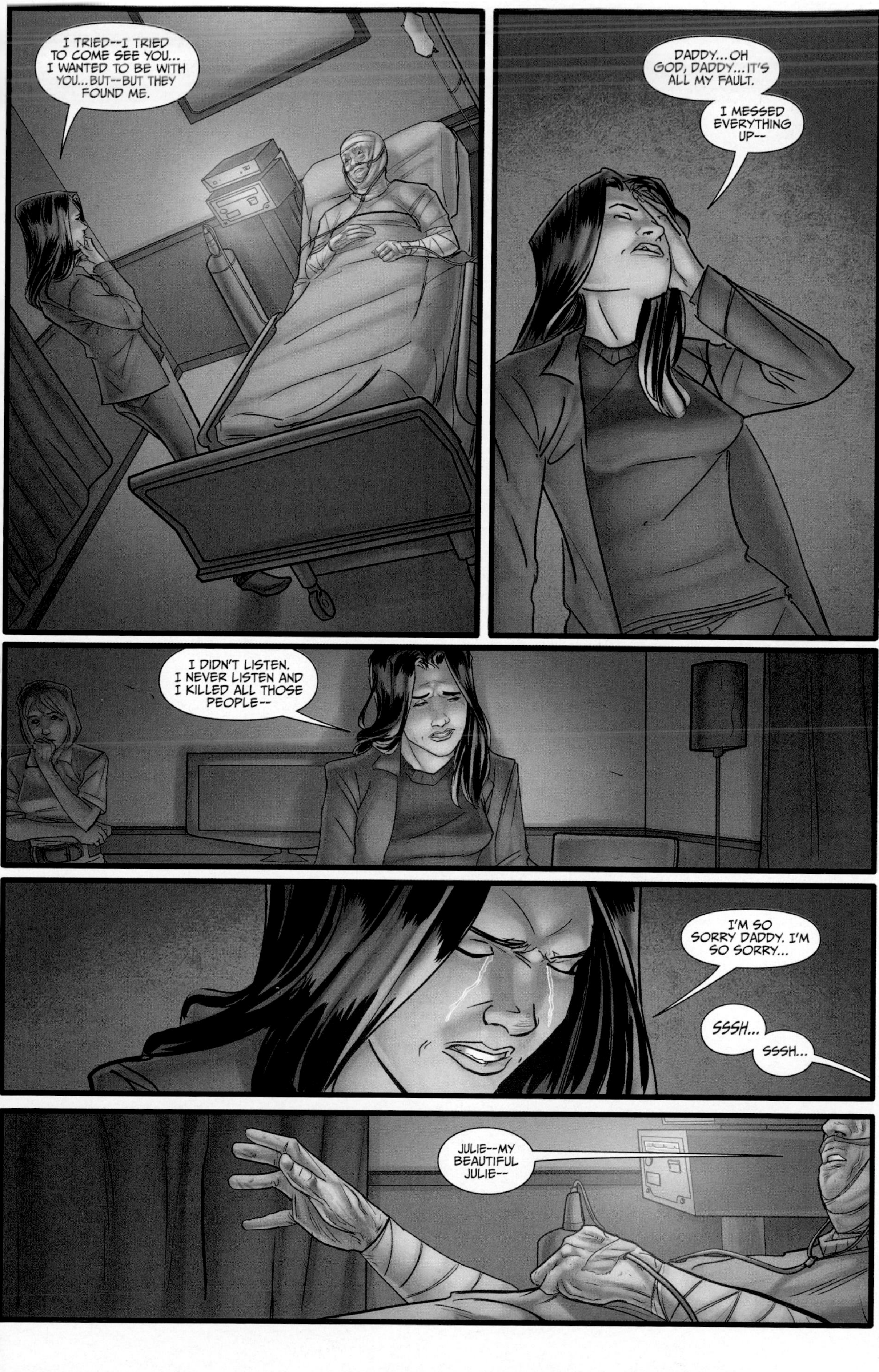
I TRIED--I TRIED TO COME SEE YOU... I WANTED TO BE WITH YOU...BUT--BUT THEY FOUND ME.
DADDY...OH GOD, DADDY...IT'S ALL MY FAULT.
I MESSED EVERYTHING UP--
I DIDN'T LISTEN. I NEVER LISTEN AND I KILLED ALL THOSE PEOPLE--
I'M SO SORRY DADDY. I'M SO SORRY...
SSSH...
SSSH...
JULIE--MY BEAUTIFUL JULIE--

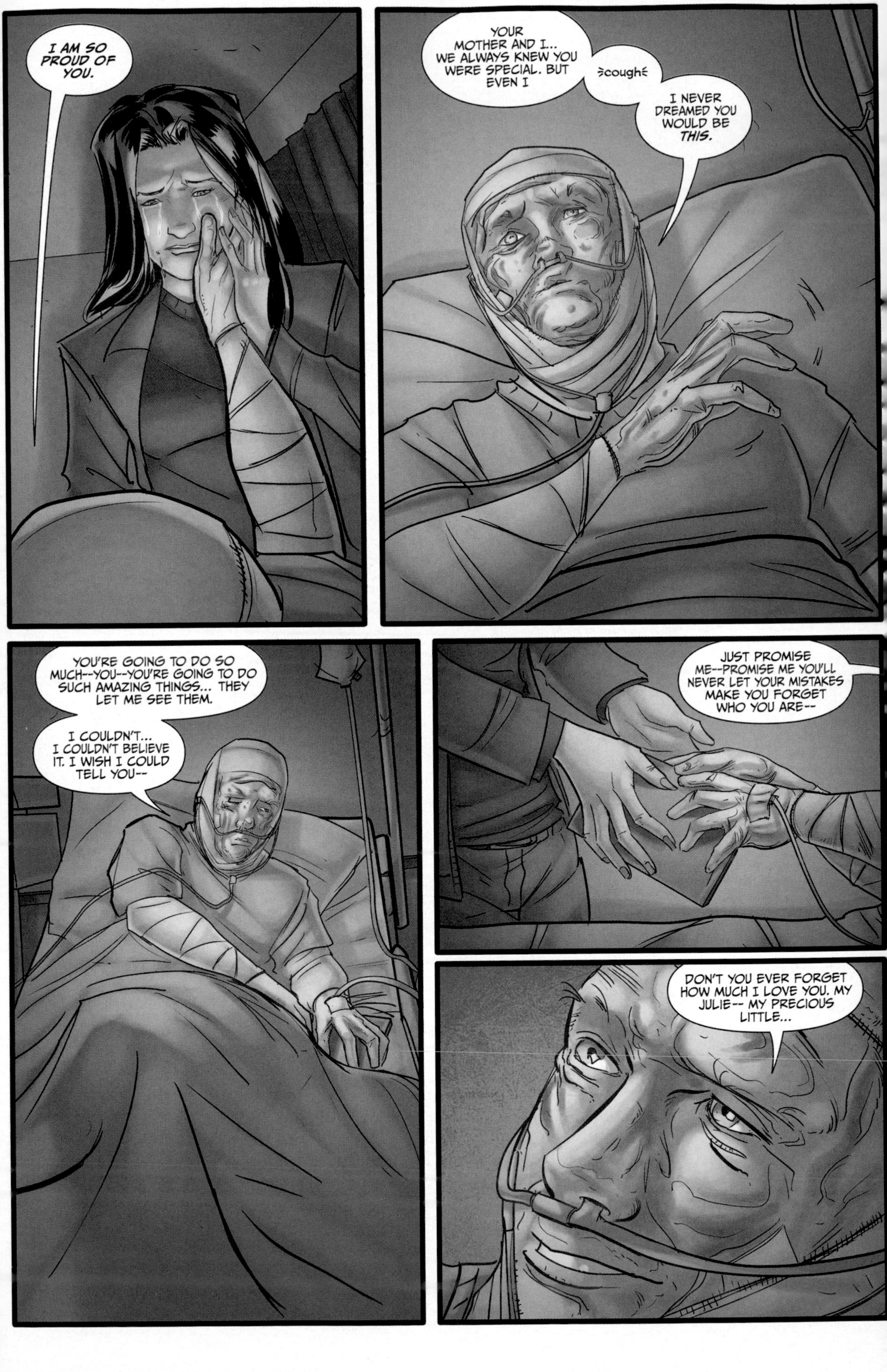
I AM SO PROUD OF YOU.
YOUR MOTHER AND I... WE ALWAYS KNEW YOU WERE SPECIAL. BUT EVEN I
cough
I NEVER DREAMED YOU WOULD BE *THIS.*
YOU'RE GOING TO DO SO MUCH--YOU--YOU'RE GOING TO DO SUCH AMAZING THINGS... THEY LET ME SEE THEM.
I COULDN'T... I COULDN'T BELIEVE IT. I WISH I COULD TELL YOU--
JUST PROMISE ME--PROMISE ME YOU'LL NEVER LET YOUR MISTAKES MAKE YOU FORGET WHO YOU ARE--
DON'T YOU EVER FORGET HOW MUCH I LOVE YOU. MY JULIE-- MY PRECIOUS LITTLE...

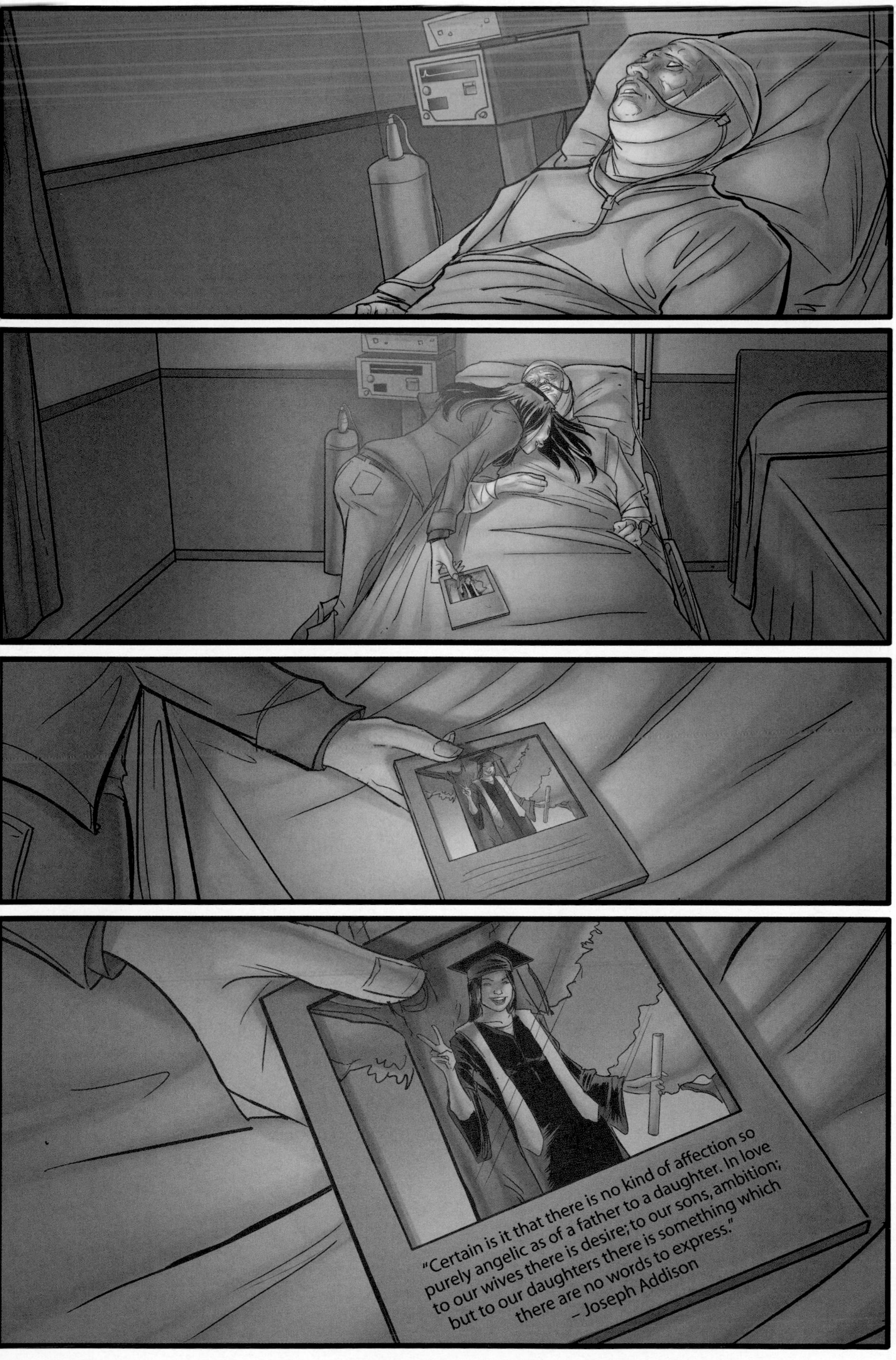
"Certain is it that there is no kind of affection so purely angelic as of a father to a daughter. In love to our wives there is desire; to our sons, ambition; but to our daughters there is something which there are no words to express."
– Joseph Addison

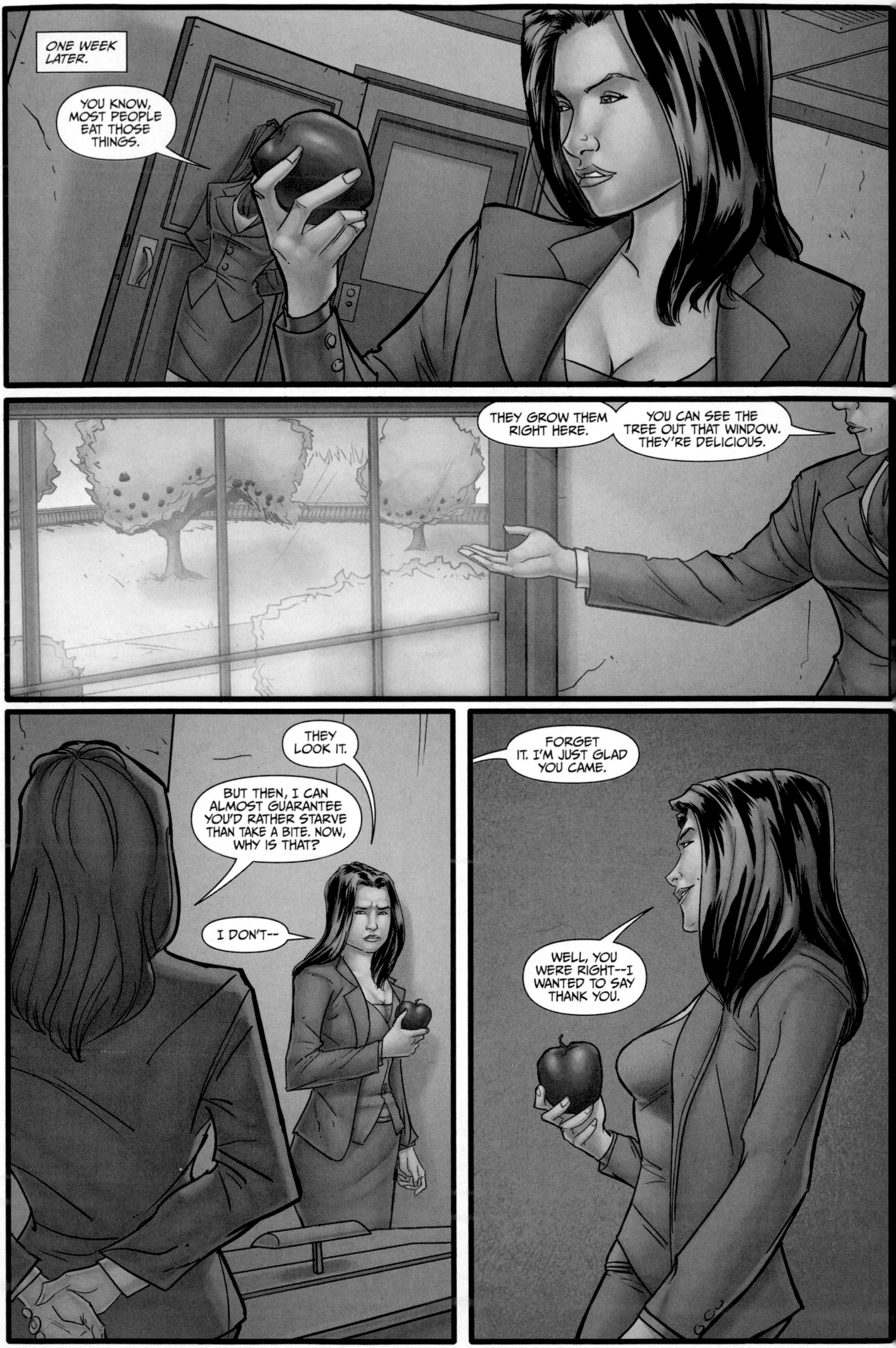
ONE WEEK LATER.
YOU KNOW, MOST PEOPLE EAT THOSE THINGS.
THEY GROW THEM RIGHT HERE.
YOU CAN SEE THE TREE OUT THAT WINDOW. THEY'RE DELICIOUS.
THEY LOOK IT.
BUT THEN, I CAN ALMOST GUARANTEE YOU'D RATHER STARVE THAN TAKE A BITE. NOW, WHY IS THAT?
I DON'T--
FORGET IT. I'M JUST GLAD YOU CAME.
WELL, YOU WERE RIGHT--I WANTED TO SAY THANK YOU.

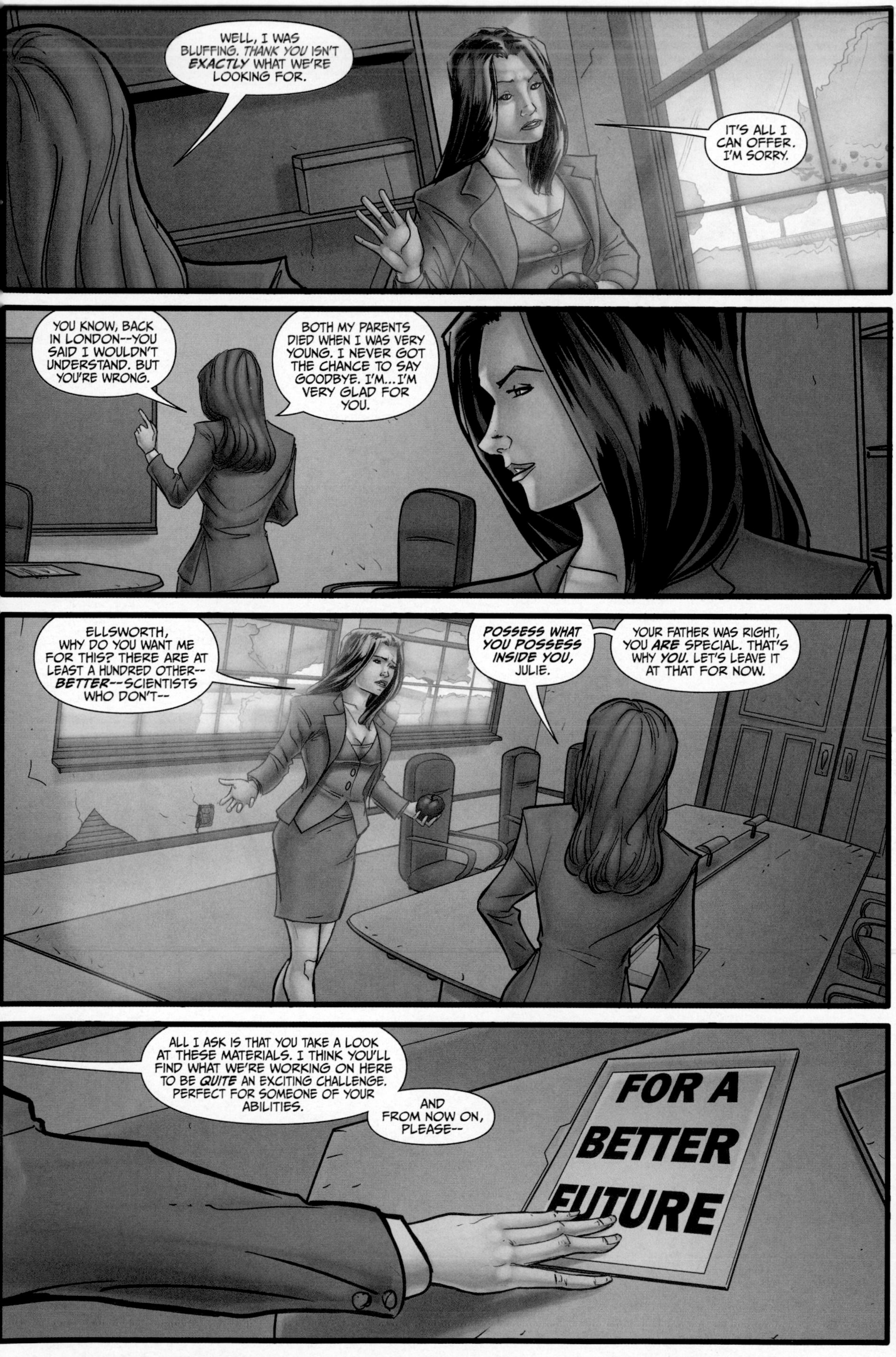
WELL, I WAS BLUFFING. THANK YOU ISN'T EXACTLY WHAT WE'RE LOOKING FOR.
IT'S ALL I CAN OFFER. I'M SORRY.
YOU KNOW, BACK IN LONDON--YOU SAID I WOULDN'T UNDERSTAND. BUT YOU'RE WRONG.
BOTH MY PARENTS DIED WHEN I WAS VERY YOUNG. I NEVER GOT THE CHANCE TO SAY GOODBYE. I'M...I'M VERY GLAD FOR YOU.
ELLSWORTH, WHY DO YOU WANT ME FOR THIS? THERE ARE AT LEAST A HUNDRED OTHER--BETTER--SCIENTISTS WHO DON'T--
POSSESS WHAT YOU POSSESS INSIDE YOU, JULIE.
YOUR FATHER WAS RIGHT, YOU ARE SPECIAL. THAT'S WHY YOU. LET'S LEAVE IT AT THAT FOR NOW.
ALL I ASK IS THAT YOU TAKE A LOOK AT THESE MATERIALS. I THINK YOU'LL FIND WHAT WE'RE WORKING ON HERE TO BE QUITE AN EXCITING CHALLENGE. PERFECT FOR SOMEONE OF YOUR ABILITIES.
AND FROM NOW ON, PLEASE--
FOR A BETTER FUTURE

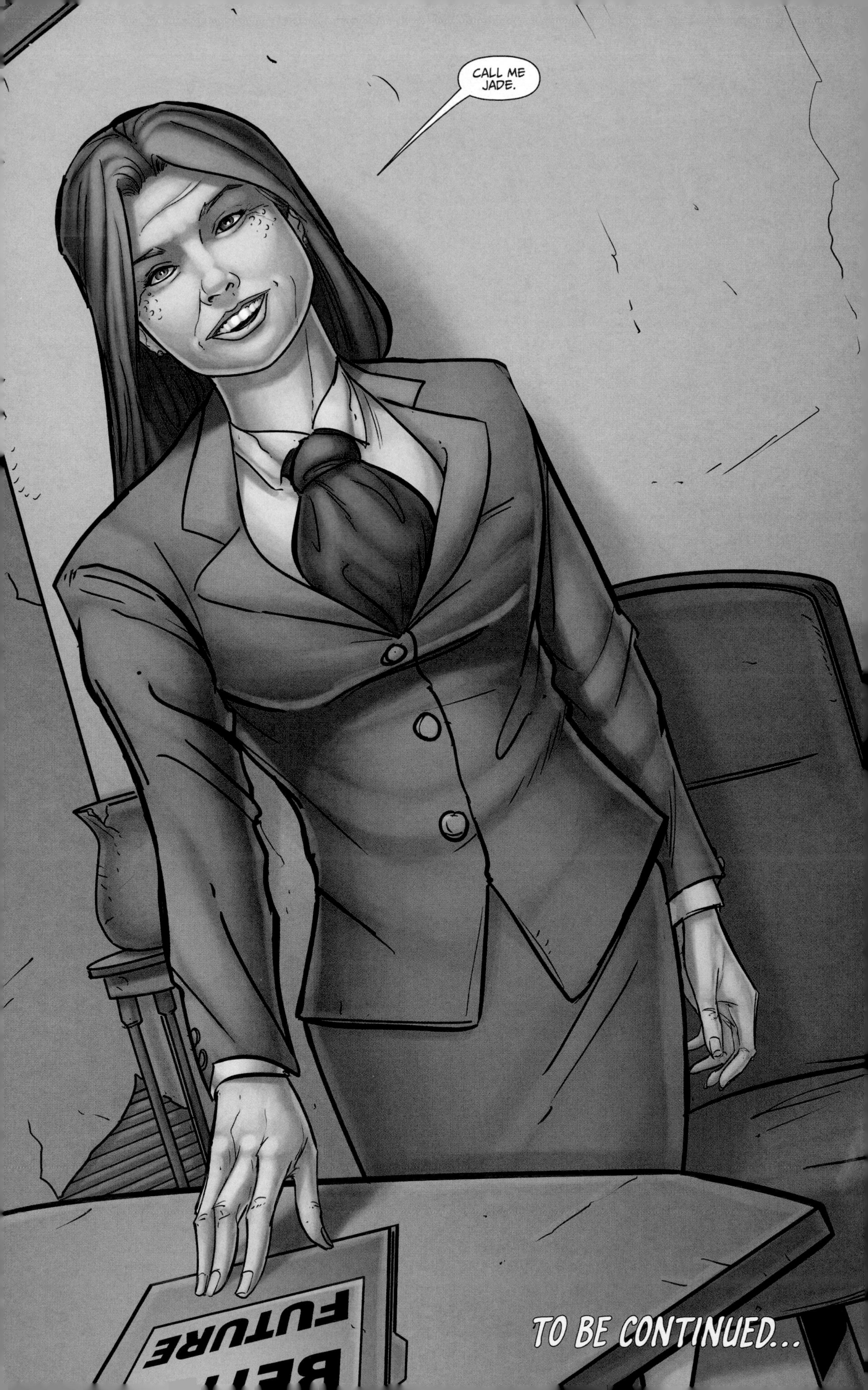
CALL ME JADE.
TO BE CONTINUED...

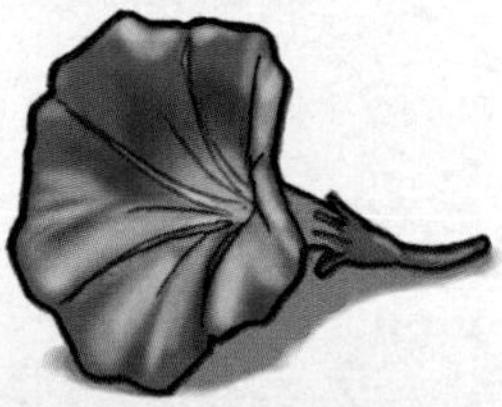

Other books by NICK SPENCER you will enjoy

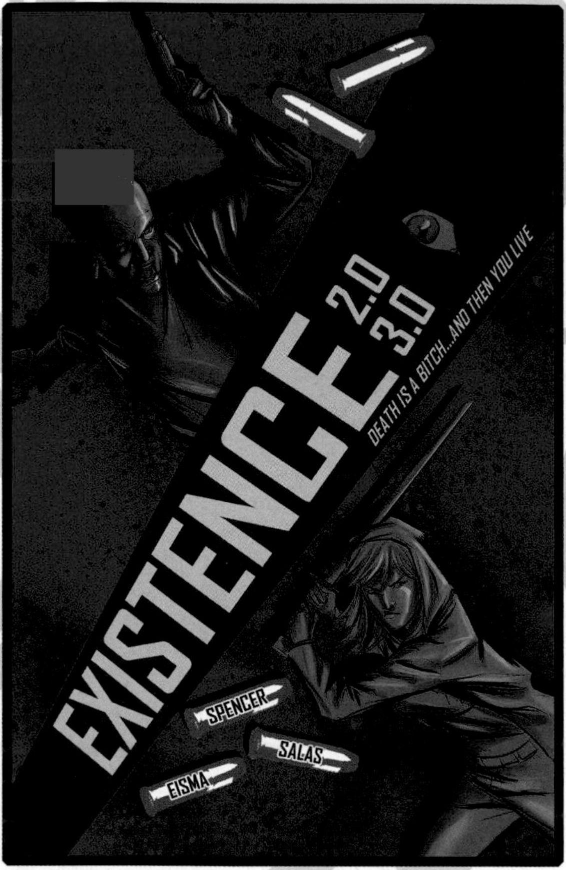
EXISTENCE 2.0 3.0
DEATH IS A BITCH...AND THEN YOU LIVE
SPENCER
SALAS
EISMA

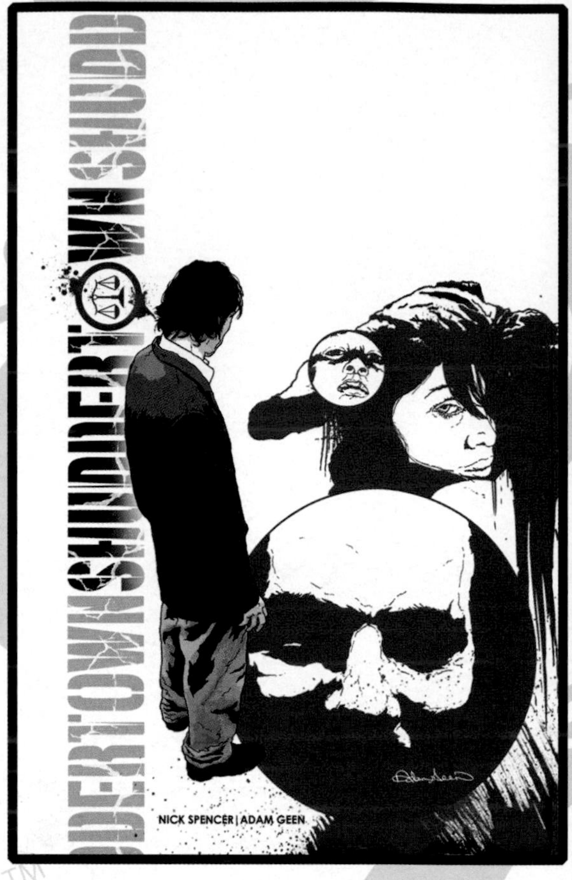
SHUDDERTOWN
NICK SPENCER | ADAM GEEN

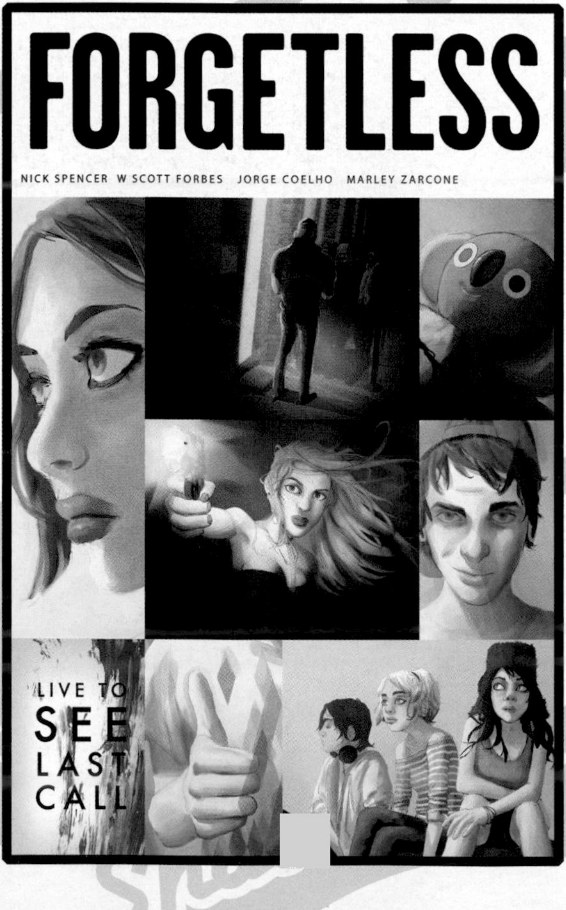
FORGETLESS
NICK SPENCER W SCOTT FORBES JORGE COELHO MARLEY ZARCONE
LIVE TO SEE LAST CALL

EXISTENCE 2.0/3.0
With RON SALAS and JOE EISMA
What happens when a scientist finds his consciousness transferred into the body of his murderer!
168 FC pages $14.99

FORGETLESS
With W. SCOTT FORBES, JORGE COELHO and MARLEY ZARCONE
Forgetless isn't the last great club in New York City because it never existed...did it?
128 FC pages $12.99

SHUDDERTOWN Hard Cover
With ADAM GEEN and MENTON J. MATTHEWS III
Homicide detective Isaac Hernandez investigates a string of murders in which all the forensic evidence points toward perpetrators who are already dead themselves.
128 FC pages $19.99

ONLY FROM
image® Shadowline™

more morning glories goodness

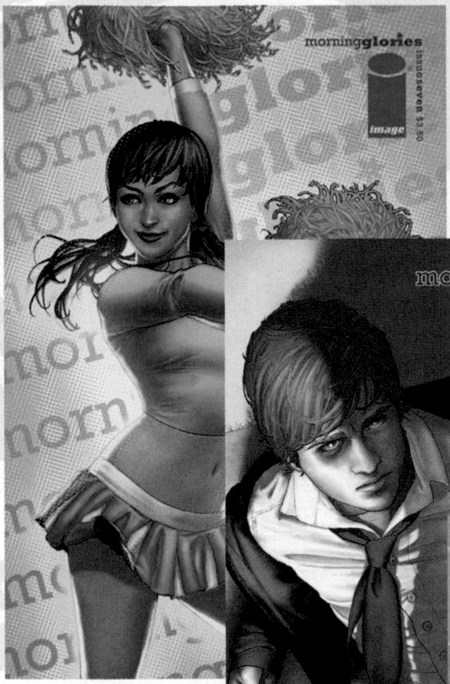
morningglories
issueseven $3.50
image

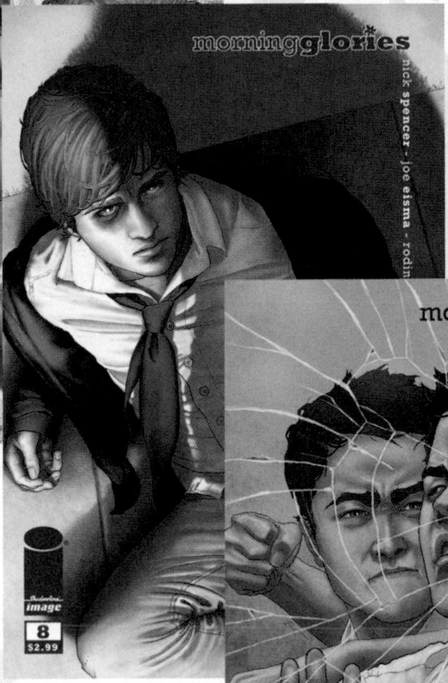
morningglories
nick spencer · joe eisma · rodin
image
8
$2.99

"Morning Glories is such a great book, with a cast of entertaining, well-defined characters and a promising central mystery surrounding the mysterious Academy where our teenaged protagonists attend. What's so special about these kids, who all have the same birthday? What's that weird ghosty thing that attacks rule-breakers, Prisoner-style? I don't know yet, but I can't wait to find out."

Jason Sachs, Comics Bulletin

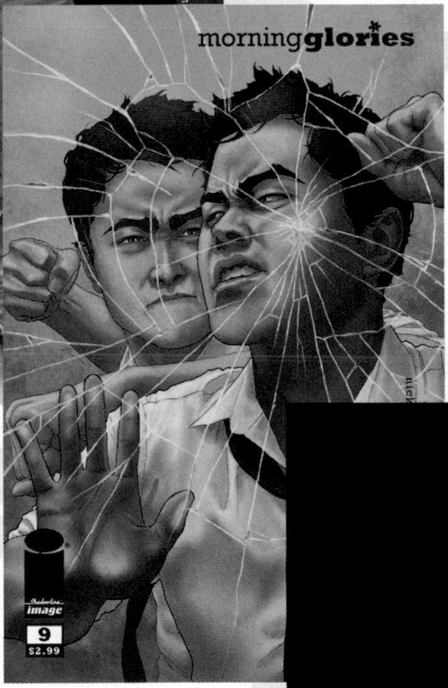
morningglories
image
9
$2.99

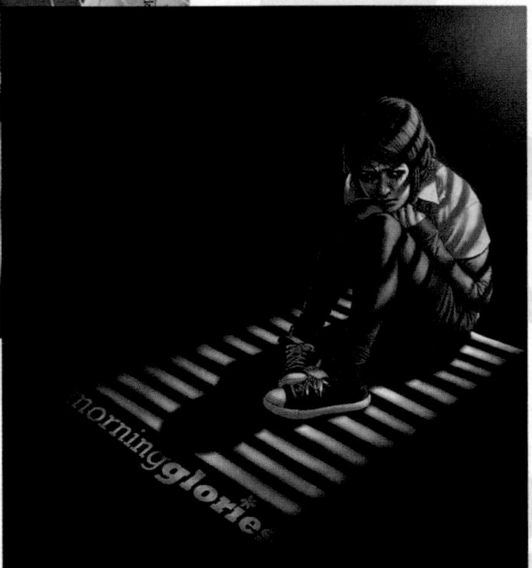
morningglories
10

"I didn't know what to expect with this book. I've seen previews, I've read reviews, I've checked out the internet buzz that preceded the release of this title, but I withheld judgment. When I opened the book, the first scene quickly grabbed me by the back of the head and pulled me in. This book is off the beaten path, a little bit horror, a little action adventure, a little teen drama, a whole lot of riveting story. I knew nothing of these characters coming in, but I'm hooked, like the titular flower around a garden trellis."

Doug Zawisza, CBR

every month from image® Shadowline™

A Book For Every Reader...

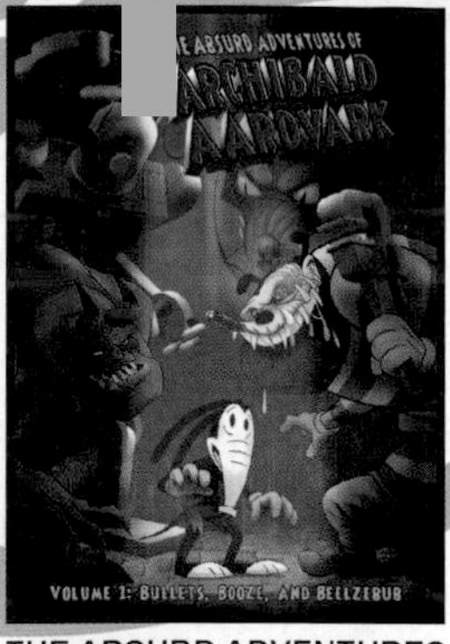
THE ABSURD ADVENTURES OF
ARCHIBALD AARDVARK
VOLUME 1: BULLETS, BOOZE, AND BEELZEBUB

THE ABSURD ADVENTURES OF ARCHIBALD AARDVARK

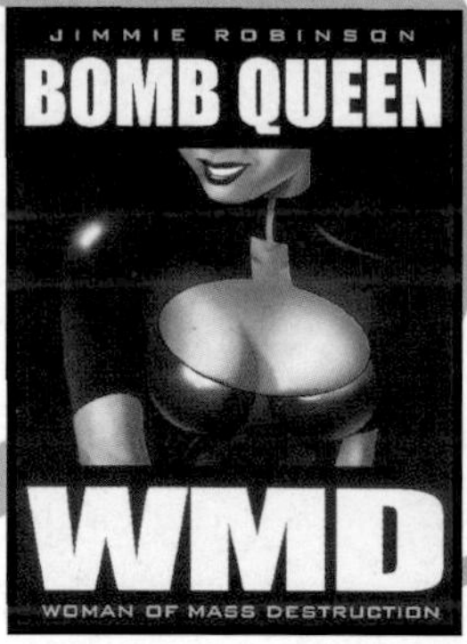
JIMMIE ROBINSON
BOMB QUEEN
WMD
WOMAN OF MASS DESTRUCTION

BOMB QUEEN: WOMAN OF MASS DESTRUCTION

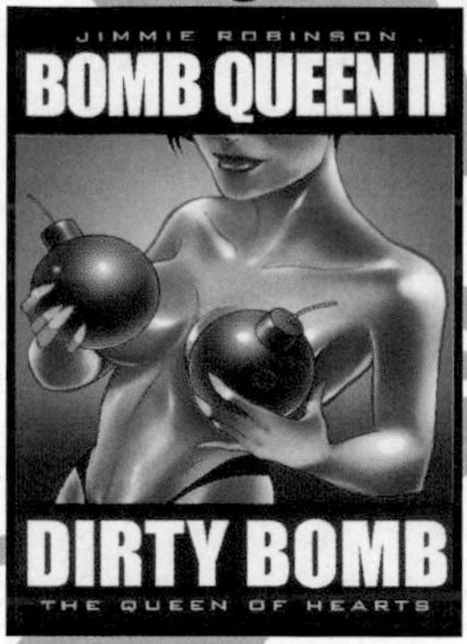
JIMMIE ROBINSON
BOMB QUEEN II
DIRTY BOMB
THE QUEEN OF HEARTS

BOMB QUEEN II: DIRTY BOMB

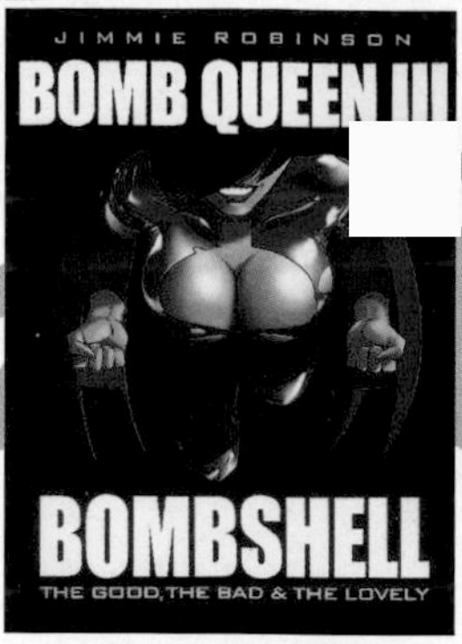
JIMMIE ROBINSON
BOMB QUEEN III
BOMBSHELL
THE GOOD, THE BAD & THE LOVELY

BOMB QUEEN III: BOMBSHELL

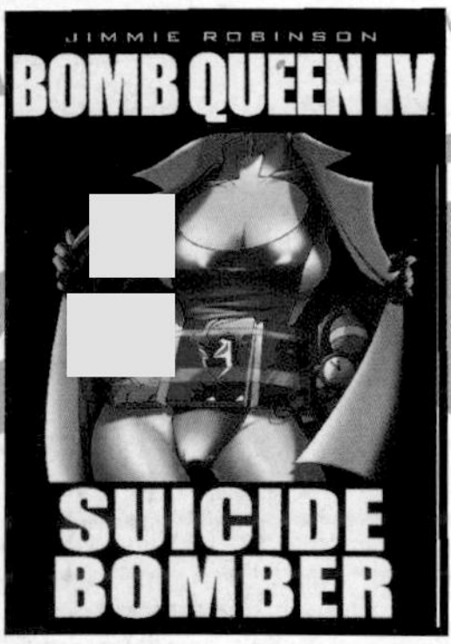
JIMMIE ROBINSON
BOMB QUEEN IV
SUICIDE
BOMBER

BOMB QUEEN IV: SUICIDE BOMBER

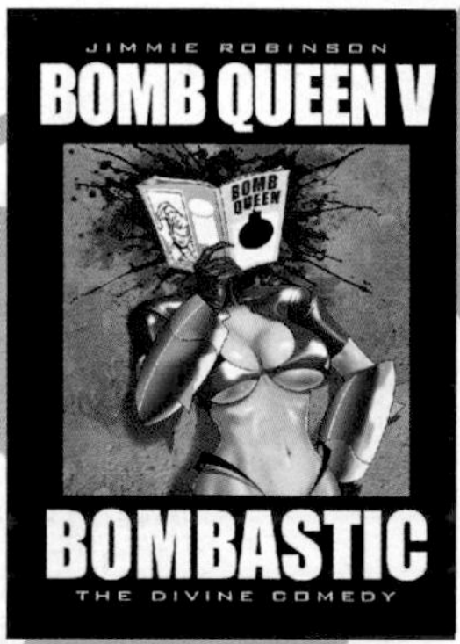
JIMMIE ROBINSON
BOMB QUEEN V
BOMBASTIC
THE DIVINE COMEDY

BOMB QUEEN V: BOMBASTIC

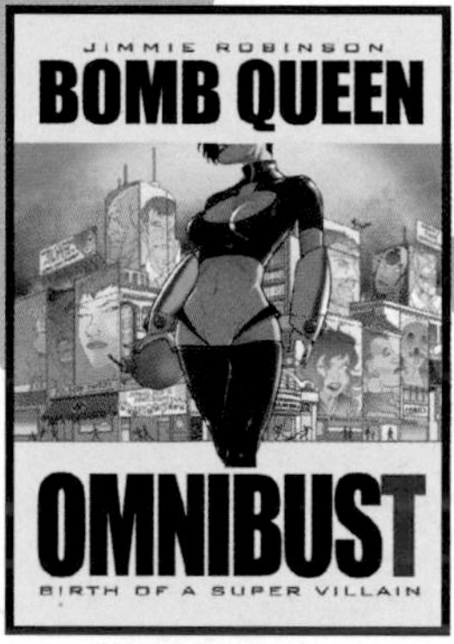
JIMMIE ROBINSON
BOMB QUEEN
OMNIBUST
BIRTH OF A SUPER VILLAIN

BOMB QUEEN OMINBUS(T)

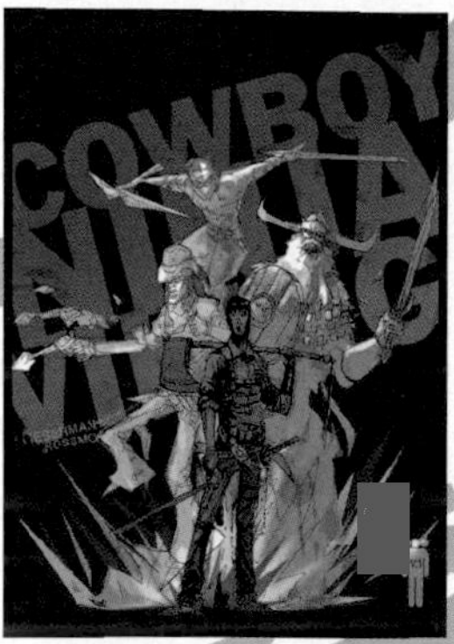
COWBOY
NINJA
VIKING

COWBOY NINJA VIKING VOLUME ONE

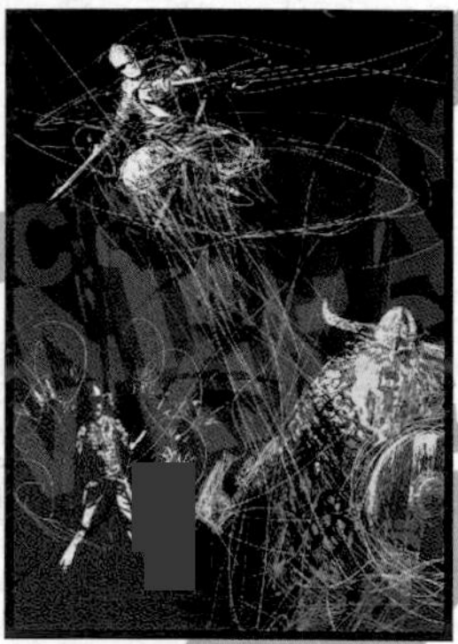

COWBOY NINJA VIKING VOLUME TWO

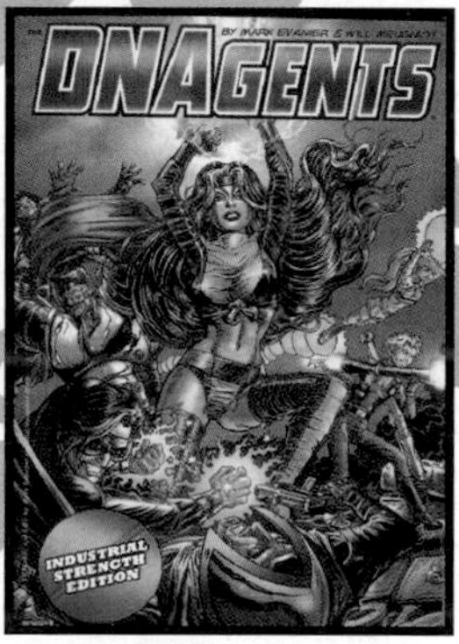
DNAGENTS
INDUSTRIAL STRENGTH EDITION

DNAgents: INDUSTRIAL STRENGTH EDITION

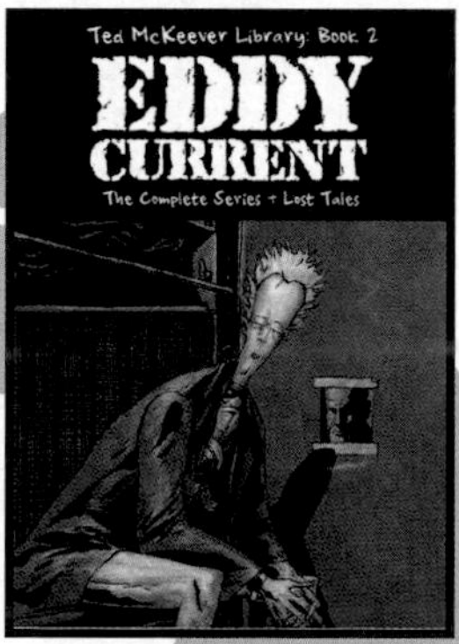
Ted McKeever Library: Book 2
EDDY
CURRENT
The Complete Series + Lost Tales

TED McKEEVER LIBRARY BOOK TWO: EDDY CURRENT

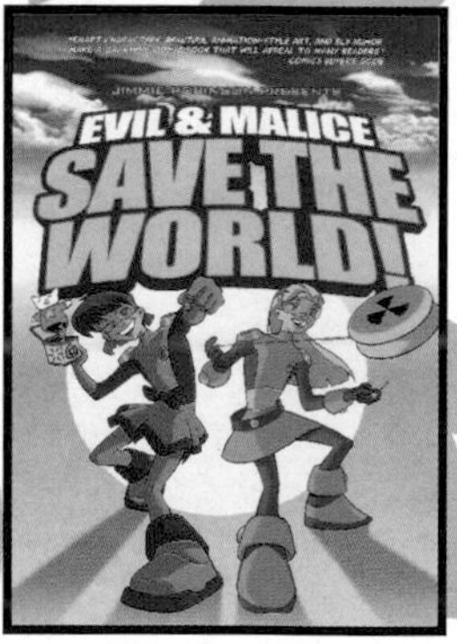
EVIL & MALICE
SAVE THE
WORLD!

EVIL & MALICE SAVE THE WORLD!

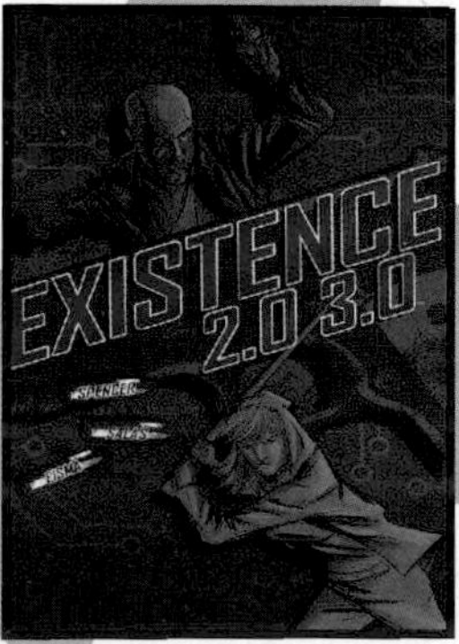
EXISTENCE
2.0 3.0

EXISTENCE 2.0/3.0

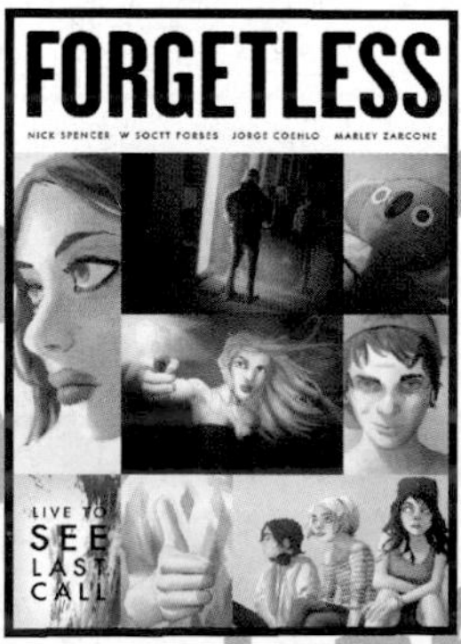
FORGETLESS
LIVE TO
SEE
LAST
CALL

FORGETLESS

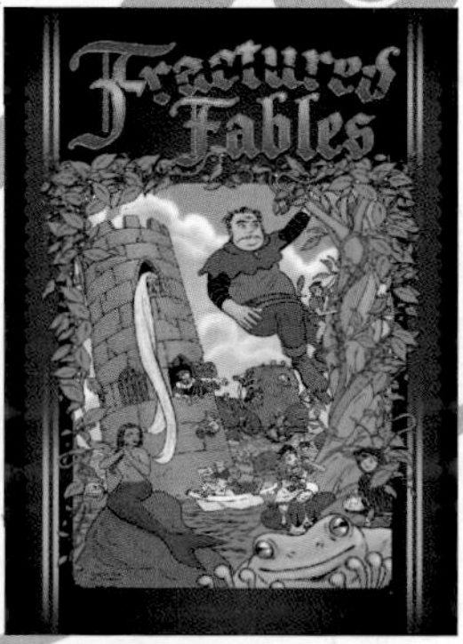
Fractured
Fables

FRACTURED FABLES

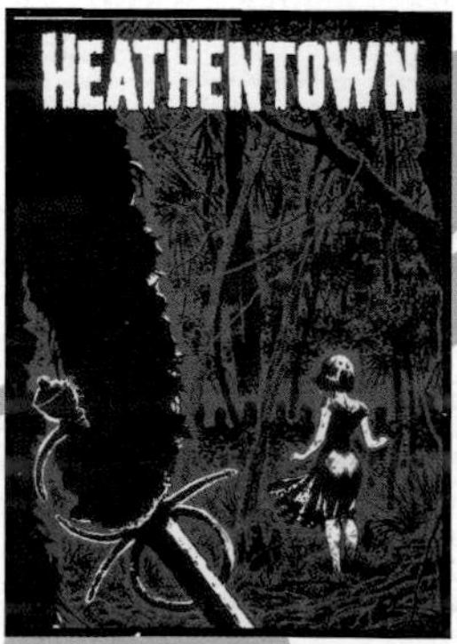
HEATHENTOWN

HEATHENTOWN

WWW.SHADOWLINECOMICS.COM

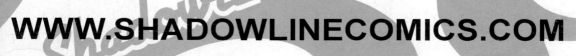